CLEAN BREAK

ALSO BY DAVID KLEIN

Stash

CLEAN BREAK

David Klein

Helen —

Thanks for your support. Hope you enjoy Clean Break

David Klein

BROADWAY BOOKS

New York

BROADWAY

This is a work of fiction. Names, characters, places, and incidents either are the product of the author's imagination or are used fictitiously. Any resemblance to actual persons, living or dead, events, or locales is entirely coincidental.

Published in the United States by Broadway Books, an imprint of the Crown Publishing Group, a division of Random House, Inc., New York.
www.crownpublishing.com

BROADWAY BOOKS and the Broadway Books colophon are registered trademarks of Random House, Inc.

Library of Congress Cataloging-in-Publication Data

Klein, David (David Matthew)
Clean break : a novel / David Klein.
p. cm.
1. Mothers and sons—Fiction. 2. Family violence—Fiction. 3. Interpersonal relations—Fiction. 4. Psychological fiction. I. Title.
PS3611.L4435C57 2012
813'.6—dc23

2011041589

ISBN 978-0-307-71683-5
eISBN 978-0-307-59025-1

Printed in the United States of America

10 9 8 7 6 5 4 3 2 1

First Edition

For Bob

Acknowledgments

While conducting research for this book, I relied on a number of people who gave generously of their time and expertise. On legal issues and family law: Peter Klein, John Walsh, Gerard Maney, Roger McDonough, David Kavanaugh, Louis Pozner. New York Police Department Real Time Crime Center: Gary Maio. Gambling: Jim Maney, The Noontime Winner's Circle. Child development and psychology: Amanda Nickerson. For editorial assistance during the writing process: Heather Lazare, Loretta Weingel-Fidel, and team Jaffe—Phyllis, Rosalind, and Harriet. Thank you all.

PART 1

Imaginary Friend

1

You can't ask your nine-year-old for advice on how to conjure up an imaginary friend, but it might be nice to have such a companion. A confidant for sharing private feelings. A soul mate for lonely nights. Spencer didn't seem worse for it, most of the time. In fact, since he'd taken Kathy as his friend, he had become a better listener and made eye contact when speaking with Celeste. He never complained of being bored. He performed better in school.

Celeste researched the subject and believed Spencer adopted an imaginary friend to help work through his father's absence. The therapist she'd taken him to agreed with this assessment, although other self-proclaimed experts on the Internet stated that age nine was too old for such make-believe, potentially indicating an inability to separate fantasy from reality.

How about age thirty-four? What would the experts say if Celeste adopted a pretend pal? She wouldn't mind a break from reality. She could use some comforting.

"Spencer," she called from the bottom of the stairs. "What are you doing up there?"

No response, although she could hear him talking.

She climbed the stairs and found him in the hallway sprawled across one of the stuffed plastic garbage bags, rocking back and forth as if on a raft in the water, his face buried in his book, reading aloud.

"Chet Baker's real name was Chesney," Spencer said, not looking up from the page. "He started playing trombone, but it was too big so he switched to trumpet, just like me."

"He was a talented trumpeter, just like you," Celeste said, kneeling next to her son. He turned to her with his round blue eyes that were so much like Adam's. Along with his straight, dark hair and angular jaw and sloped nose, Spencer was practically a clone of his father, other than the lush smile and full lips he'd gotten from Celeste.

"Now I need your talents to help carry those bags," Celeste said. "They have our sheets and towels."

"Okay, Mom." Spencer obediently closed his book and stood and lifted one of the bags, holding it from underneath with both arms. He negotiated the stairs and waddled out the front door, straining under the bag's bulk. Celeste lifted the other one and followed him down.

Stephen returned from loading the truck. "We've got room for a few more things," he said. "A small piece of furniture, if you want."

Her friends from around the corner—Emery and Stephen Weber—were helping, Emery having volunteered her husband, along with his pickup truck. Celeste's move didn't fit the usual protocol for Brookfield's Cider Mill neighborhood, where residents hired big moving companies that arrived with long, padded vans and muscular men who wrapped and carried every item. By contrast, Celeste, along with Emery and Stephen, managed to jam a bed and dresser each for her and Spencer, a love seat and chair, three lamps, plus their clothes, Celeste's computer and desk, basic kitchen equipment, and Spencer's games and books into two loads in the back of Stephen's truck on an autumn Saturday morning while neighborhood kids played in the street, fathers paused in their leaf-raking to watch, and mothers pushing strollers stared as they walked past.

Celeste was a few anxious moments away from abandoning her home of ten years. A two-and-a-half-story Craftsman built in 1910, with a wraparound front porch, plush lawn, and private backyard fenced by an evergreen hedge. Just forty-five minutes by train to Grand Central Station on the Hudson line, an easy commute for Adam when he still worked in Manhattan; and for Celeste, a safe, idyllic community with her closest friends on the same block and one of the top elementary schools in the state for her son to attend. The house had been too big for the three of them, but at one time she and Adam planned to have more children. They would raise a large family and grow old in this house, they would pay off the mortgage, their grandchildren would visit. If needed, they'd install a wheelchair ramp someday and one of them would lovingly care for the other.

She took a quick survey—what else to take? She hadn't made a dent in removing their possessions, not surprising considering she was moving out of a 3,000-square-foot home outfitted with the accoutrements of a decade of married life. Almost all of it she was leaving behind, even the cherished bedroom set, a wedding gift from Adam's parents. It was called the Antoinette Collection, crafted from black walnut and inlaid with cherry accents: the wide dresser and mirror for her, the tall dresser for Adam, the armoire to share, the two night tables, and the spectacular sleigh bed. She'd made love with her husband hundreds of times in that bed; now she didn't want to look at it.

"What do you think—anything else?" Stephen asked.

"Just a sec." She started up the stairs and lifted the photos hanging on the wall across from the banister. The one of the three of them hugging a snowman they'd made in the backyard, the snowman four balls high, as tall as Adam, Spencer standing in front, Celeste and Adam to either side, the self-timer capturing three happy faces—four if you count the arrangement of acorns forming the snowman's mouth. Next was the photo of her and Spencer on the beach in Florida three years ago when they'd visited Celeste's mom. She looked at herself in the picture and realized she'd changed since then: gained a few pounds, although not so many her clothes didn't fit, and she wore her hair longer now, all one length to her shoulders rather than the layered style and wispy bangs. And she'd started coloring her hair, adding red highlights to complement her natural auburn shade. At least her eyes were the same green, her teeth still white. The third photo she took from the wall was the one of Adam holding eight-month-old Spencer overhead in the palm of his hand, as if he were a quarterback about to throw a pass, their son squealing with delight. She'd been terrified seeing Spencer perched so high and had rushed the photo, causing a slight blur, but Adam had maintained firm and perfect balance, completely in control, with Spencer safe and secure—her husband could handle things back then.

She returned to the foyer, cradling the frames like books in her arms. "Just these, I guess," she said. "We'd better get going."

Emery reached out and held Celeste's arm. "It's hard right now, but you'll feel better. You'll see."

"I know I'm doing the right thing, but I still feel guilty with Adam not here and I can't tell him."

"You've given him a lot of chances. And if things change when he comes back, well, nothing's permanent. You can always get back together."

Emery was right, although she didn't know the full extent

of Adam's offenses. Celeste hadn't shared all the sordid details, even with her best friend, and Celeste couldn't contemplate the idea of getting back with Adam—she hadn't even left yet.

"I'd say this is the best wake-up call Adam could get," Stephen said. "What more motivation does he need if he finally realizes he's losing you?"

Yes, but would that be motivation enough for Adam to change? She honestly didn't know.

"I'm really going to miss you guys," Celeste said. Emery was a mother to three fine children, fulfilled in her own part-time career writing grants for the Trollope Women's Foundation, and married to a successful architect who adored her. Celeste and Emery raised their kids together, ran in the park, went for drinks on girls' night out. They shared recipes. They used the same pediatrician. But they weren't both moving out on their husbands, and Celeste understood that this difference could change their relationship.

As if reading her thoughts, Emery said, "We'll still see you all the time, even if we're not right around the corner anymore."

She found comfort in her friend's words, and hoped they were true. "I'll lock up here and then drive over and meet you," she said.

"We'll pick up our kids and get some bagels on the way," Emery said. "We can eat after we unload."

"Here, I'm paying." Celeste reached for her purse hanging on the newel post. "I should at least feed you for the work you're doing. I couldn't have done this without you."

"Oh, stop. After all you did for us after Maya was born?"

Before Celeste could get out her wallet, Stephen and Emery were in the truck, backing out of the driveway. Celeste started to wave, then put her hand down: This wasn't goodbye. She went back inside and called for Spencer. Again she got no answer. This time she found him in the bathroom, sitting on the toilet but not using it, his pants still on, reading in a voice at the high end of a whisper. He saw her and quieted.

"Are you ready? We're all packed—it's time to get going."

"Chet Baker went to prison. He had to go to prison because he was a drug addict."

"Let me see that." Celeste studied the page. This was supposed to be a children's book about American musicians; she'd found it in the middle readers section of the library and thought Spencer would enjoy the short biographies now that he was taking trumpet lessons. She scanned the Chet Baker profile. There was one paragraph about how his life as a musician and vocalist derailed when he started using drugs. He was arrested on a number of occasions and spent a year in prison in Italy prior to getting his life back together and reinvigorating his career.

"Did Dad go to prison because he was a gambling addict? Is that why he has to be gone for so long?"

"No, Dad isn't in prison," Celeste said. "He went to a rehabilitation center. Remember, I told you it was like a hospital where doctors will help him sort things out."

"What things?"

"His behavior . . . his mistakes," Celeste said. "It's kind of like when he used to see the counselor but this time he's staying at a special health center until he gets better." She'd answered the same questions repeatedly, which Celeste didn't mind and Spencer's therapist said was normal. The most important thing was to be patient and caring and respectful of his feelings.

"He's there so the doctors can help him understand what he did wrong and how to change."

Spencer pursed his lips into trumpet position while he digested this information. "Will he know where our new house is?"

"Sure he will," she said, then added, "Everything's going to be okay. I promise. You know that, right? You know you can completely trust me."

Spencer mumbled, to himself or his pal Kathy; Celeste couldn't make out the words.

"You ready?" She reached out to him. He closed his book and held her hand on the stairs and Celeste locked the door behind them, resisting a glance back once she'd turned away.

2

Celeste sat at her computer, doodling variations on a logo she'd been hired to design for a health and healing center in town. The ideas came slowly today, her concentration wandered. The center offered massage therapy, Rolfing, acupuncture, and a host of spa services. Her logo concepts made use of a sun with rays and an orange and yellow palette to foster a sense of healing warmth. Not the most original treatment, although the simplest designs were often the most successful. The project was a rush job and she had to work over the weekend, but at least the center was paying a premium due to the compressed time frame. The client had even thrown in a few massages as part of the deal. She could use one of those massages now. She knew Adam would be coming over today when he got back to town and she was apprehensive about their reunion—would he be astonished and angry that she'd moved out, or contrite and cured from his stay in rehab? She and Spencer had agreed to stay home and wait, and they'd both been distracted all morning, watching the clock, trying to keep busy.

Spencer sat cross-legged on the floor, playing both sides of a chessboard. Celeste had promised to take him ice-skating later. Saturday-afternoon outings were part of the new routine she'd cobbled together since their move to Amherst Street six weeks ago. The main requirement was the outings be inexpensive: apple picking, hiking in Bear Mountain State Park, walking the sculpture fields at Storm King Art Center. Also as part of her routine, two or three mornings a week after the school bus picked up Spencer, Celeste drove to Emery's and they ran together to the park and back, a three-mile loop, then went for coffee; their friendship hadn't suffered with Celeste moving to a different neighborhood. The rest of the time she tried to drum up work for her graphic design business by calling and e-mailing everyone she knew, but with the economy sputtering, she didn't get many projects. A brochure here, a Web site there, an ad or two, a restaurant menu. Enough to pay for Spencer's trumpet lessons and keep the lights on and refrigerator stocked. She was overdue to have her hair cut and highlighted. Her car needed new tires and an oil change. Spencer had outgrown his bike. She'd been offered work through an agency to design promotional posters for the New York State Lottery that would hang at OTB parlors, but she had turned down that project, for obvious reasons.

Their rented four-room bungalow, at the limit of her current financial means, was situated just within the Brookfield school district boundary on a side street crammed with older houses. No landscaping. No driveway. Parking spaces on the street were as precious as gemstones. A tavern occupied one corner and Sacred Heart Church the other end of the block. Cracks veined the front sidewalk. The loose railing on the stairs wobbled and rot had turned several porch floorboards into sponges. That got you as far as the front door. Inside, half the windows were painted shut; the others leaked cold air. They discovered that the lone toilet clogged easily, so they flushed early and often. Circuit breakers tripped at odd times. But Spencer liked his bedroom, which faced the rear and had a window that let him peer into other yards and houses. They didn't have to shout up the stairs or room to room to find each other. The woodwork and moldings were natural oak. Living in the house gave Celeste a sense of roughing it, as if she were a pioneer on the edge of a wilderness. She felt resourceful and independent and slept well at night. She didn't pine for Adam, and the decrepitude of her surroundings didn't bother her as much as she might have expected—the place reminded her of a flat she had rented in college, and she'd been happy there—although the dramatic change in her living conditions was obvious to anyone familiar with her house in Cider Mill. Case in point: When Adam's father paid her a visit last month, he spent the first moments openmouthed and speechless, looking around with bewilderment and dismay.

Joseph Vanek had called before stopping by. He'd come to check up on his daughter-in-law and grandson, Celeste knew, making sure they were okay, and she appreciated his gesture. Why else would a banker who worked in Manhattan come to Brookfield in the middle of the day? She took his coat and offered to make coffee. He raised his hand against the idea, as if consuming anything in this house was enough to grind his stomach.

"This is where you're going to live?" Joseph said. The Vaneks lived in Chappaqua, home to tall shade trees and historic single-family homes and country clubs.

"Spencer gets to stay in the same school, and that was the most important thing in choosing a new place," Celeste explained. "That, and finding somewhere I could afford."

"You didn't have to do this, Celeste," he said. Joseph Vanek had once been tall, like Adam, but age had stooped him a few inches and stolen hair from the crown of his head. Still, he was a handsome man, with crisp features and those Vanek blue eyes. He said, "I'm covering the expenses on the other house and now it's sitting vacant. Even if you and Adam decide to put the house on the market, the mortgage has to be paid until the sale closes. There was no reason to move."

You'd think he'd be tired of writing checks to make up for Adam's failures. Many times Adam had lied to him the past few years, asking for a loan, sheepishly admitting he and Celeste weren't careful money managers, they tended to overspend—yet promising to be better. Celeste resented Adam including her as careless with money; she knew how to live within her means.

"I think this is best for right now," she said. "It's something I needed to do."

"Do you think it's best for Spencer?"

She momentarily bristled that her father-in-law would presume she hadn't considered what's best for Spencer, but she decided his question was natural, without insinuation or malice.

"Spencer and I have talked this over. He understands. It's hard for him—for both of us—it wasn't an easy decision."

When Joseph spoke again his voice sounded sad and resigned. "You've had enough," he said. "You're not giving up the house, you're giving up on my son."

Celeste looked at the floor and didn't respond.

"I want to defend Adam because he's my son, but I have no ground to stand on and neither does he," Joseph said. "You've already put up with quite a bit from Adam. You've stuck by him through a lot."

More than you realize, Celeste thought.

"Eva is heartbroken, as you can imagine. But I want you to know we support you in every way. It will be up to Adam to win back your trust. I hope he's up to the task." He leaned forward in his chair. "Which brings me to the other reason for my visit."

She'd been expecting this.

"Adam comes home next weekend," Joseph said. "Eva and I are driving to Virginia on Friday to pick him up. Are you and Spencer planning to come along? We'd like you to."

"I don't think we can," Celeste said. "I . . ." She faltered.

"What should I tell Adam?"

"Maybe it's best if I tell him myself when he gets back."

Joseph considered her response. "Fair enough. I'll say that Eva and I wanted to come by ourselves, that we all thought the trip might be too much for Spencer."

Joseph stood and went to the front window, spent a few seconds looking out, then turned and scanned the room again. "Celeste, let me at least write you a check. I'm sure you could use a little extra cash right now."

She thanked him but declined his offer. She didn't feel right taking money from the parents of the husband she'd abandoned. Celeste had already borrowed money from her sister to pay in advance the first and last month's rent on her new place. Chantal, three years older, was a clinical psychologist with her own practice specializing in geriatrics and married to a thoracic surgeon. They lived in Burlington, Vermont. Their two kids attended private schools. They could afford to help her out, and didn't hesitate to do so. Celeste's mother, Barbara, a widow for twenty years, lived in Florida on a fixed income; she couldn't financially contribute, although she managed to contribute a bit of advice when Celeste told her she was moving: "You think it's easy to start over and meet another man?" she said.

"Mom, I'm not trying to meet another man. And nothing's permanent at this point."

"You better think twice about what you're doing."

She had thought about it. A hundred times, a thousand times. There was never a clear answer, only the compelling feeling that she had to change her situation.

She was experimenting with different shades of orange for the healing center logo when the front door handle rattled, as if someone were trying to get in. Then the bell rang.

The acid reflux singed her throat. Had she taken her Prevacid this morning? She had. Spencer crawled up on the love seat and peeked out the window. He turned back to Celeste, his face feverish, eyes wide and expectant. "It's Dad," he said.

Celeste joined her son at the window. The two of them peered like spies from behind the bunched curtain. Adam looked thinner than the last time she'd seen him. He'd recently gotten his hair cut; the skin on his neck was pale along the trim line. The rest of his face appeared tanned and healthy—he must have spent time outdoors in the Virginia sun. He carried a duffel bag slung over one shoulder, like a sailor about to board a ship, and he stood tall, his eyes alert and observant, as if he'd regained his confidence and control.

Celeste hadn't known what to expect from this moment: a wave of love or a wall of bitterness? She'd tried to prepare for both, but experienced neither. Rather, she felt a wary flutter, as if a stranger had appeared at the door.

"He found our new house," Spencer said.

Celeste drew in a breath, straightened her posture, and unlocked the door.

Adam immediately dropped his bag and hugged her, pinning

her arms to her sides. "I've missed you," he said, nuzzling his face in her neck.

"Adam, stop. Please." She tried to raise a hand to separate them. "Stop."

He let go and stepped back, confused.

"What . . . Celeste, I haven't seen you in months," he said. "You smell so good." He moved to touch her again.

"Wait." She leaned back, still in the doorway, Adam a step below her on the porch. After three months, she might have at least welcomed him in her arms, but the sudden physical contact caused her to tense and withdraw.

Spencer stood behind her. Adam looked past Celeste and into the living room.

"Spencer!" he said. "Hey, how's my buddy boy?" Adam came inside with his duffel. He dropped to one knee. "Come here, buddy, come on. Come give your dad a big hug."

Spencer stared at a point somewhere past his father's shoulder, then flicked his eyes to Celeste for instructions; he hadn't missed her reaction when Adam touched her.

"It's okay," Celeste said. "Say hello to Dad."

Spencer inched closer but stayed out of Adam's reach. He didn't know how to behave and Celeste put a hand on Adam's shoulder to show her son it was okay. Spencer let his dad hug him, and Adam bundled him against his chest. "Hey, hey, I'm still your dad," Adam said, his voice cracked with hurt. "I missed you so much. So much." He rubbed his face in Spencer's hair, then stood back from him at arm's length. "Look at you—you've grown taller. You're getting so big." He noticed the game board on the floor. "You've got a chess game going. You're playing Mom? You taught her how to play chess?"

"No," Spencer said.

Adam straightened from his squat.

"You can tell him who you're playing," Celeste said.

"My friend. Kathy."

Adam quickly scanned the room.

"You can't see her," Spencer said. "She's invisible."

"What? Oh, ha, ha." Adam's brief laugh sounded like a snort through his nose.

"Here," he said. "I brought you a present." Adam zipped open his duffel and lifted out a new basketball. He tossed the ball to Spencer, who fumbled the pass and let the ball roll into the corner.

"Remember, squeeze the pass with both hands," Adam said. "Grandpa said you're not on the team. I was surprised to hear that."

"Spencer decided he didn't want to play sports this season," Celeste said.

"I got you some pucks, too." He rummaged in the bag again and his hand came out holding two pucks with the Rangers logo imprinted on one side. He handed them to Spencer, who took one in each hand and let his arms drop without looking at the pucks.

"You're not on the hockey team, either," Adam said. A frown crossed his forehead and he sighed. "That's okay. You can skip one season. It's been a tough year for all of us. Hey, I know that more than anyone."

Adam took off his coat and draped it over the duffel. He wore a T-shirt that hugged his athletic frame. Celeste could see the e-s-t-e of her name below where his sleeve ended. A week before they'd gotten married, he'd had her name tattooed down his bicep, a gift to her she had mixed feelings about. She didn't particularly like tattoos, but the lifelong vow inherent in her fiancé's gesture was pretty special, and at least the letters weren't large or garish.

Adam said, "Spence, it's so great to see you. I thought about you every day when I was gone. Thinking about you—and Mom—getting better and looking forward to coming back home, that's what kept me going. Every day, that's what got me out of bed and working hard."

"I thought about you," Spencer said, his voice flat and empty as a fallow field.

"I'll bet you did. Hey—you haven't forgotten?" He changed to a broadcaster's banter. "Vanek breaks out of the zone, skates up the left side, crosses the blue line, cuts to the circle . . ."

Adam waited for Spencer's response. Spencer glanced at Celeste; she nodded.

"Drops it back to center," Spencer said.

"The one-timer . . ."

". . . He scores," Spencer added, but none of the exclamation, the energy and passion, that used to be part of the routine when they announced hockey plays together.

"Okay, buddy." Adam cupped his hand around the back of Spencer's neck. "I'm telling you, it's like heaven seeing you again. But how about you give Mom and me a few minutes to speak in private? You don't mind, do you? Then we'll take that new ball to the park and drain a few shots. It's not too cold out."

"Mom said we were going ice-skating."

"That's an even better idea, although I haven't been on skates in a while. I'll probably fall a few times."

Spencer left the basketball and pucks on the floor and retreated down the hall to his bedroom and shut the door.

"He can still hear us, sound carries in the house," Celeste said, and a few seconds later the progression of musical scales came from Spencer's room.

"What's that—a trumpet?" Adam asked. "He sounds pretty good."

"He started taking lessons at school this year. He's in the fourth-grade band."

"You didn't sign him up for basketball and hockey?"

"I gave him the choice and he didn't want to. I think his view of sports has been poisoned."

"But he loves sports—and he needs to keep up with the other players. He should be on a team, playing with other kids," Adam said. "And what's this invisible girlfriend he's playing chess with? He's almost ten years old, for Christ's sake."

"We've been to a therapist, and I've discussed the situation with Chantal, too. Spencer's perfectly normal for his age—it's just his way of working out some issues. I'm sure he'll give up Kathy when he's ready."

"That's what your sister said? What a surprise."

"You know, Spencer didn't start having an imaginary friend until you ruined our family," Celeste pointed out.

Adam winced. "You're right. I don't want to argue with you."

"And I'm sorry, I didn't need to say that." She didn't want to argue, either.

"I was hoping you and Spencer would be with my parents when they came to get me." He studied the room: the love seat, one armchair, a television sitting on a coffee table, Celeste's desk and computer. The cracked plaster walls and worn wooden floor. When he turned back to Celeste she saw tears gathering in the corners of his eyes.

"I can't believe you moved out while I was away," Adam said.

"I couldn't reach you to tell you."

"It was all part of the treatment, this isolation from the outside world," he said; then his voice perked up. "The great thing is it worked. I know I have to say one day at a time, or even ten minutes at a time—that's something new I learned—but, Celeste, I feel so much better. I feel like some demon has been exorcised from me. I really believe it's all behind me now." He stopped and waited for her to agree with him, and when she didn't say anything, he added, "Honey, you look so beautiful. I can't believe how much I missed your face."

Celeste had intended to stick to her wedding vows. She meant for better or worse, she meant in sickness or in health. She had always wanted a stable, traditional family. And she'd never questioned her decision to marry Adam, never doubted his integrity or goodness—until these past few years, when he began to change in ways that made her cringe. Dramatic mood shifts began to appear: one day the outgoing, confident, optimistic man she'd promised her life to, the attentive dad, the loving husband, the hardworking provider building a lucrative career; and the next day a dark, sullen, oppressive mope who wouldn't make eye contact and treated her and Spencer like two grifters out to cheat him. He became so much more interested in sports—watching, not playing. Adam had played college basketball and always liked sports. Fine. She admired his athleticism and strength. Celeste wasn't a serious athlete, although she liked to swim, hit the tennis ball, go for a run or hike. She cheered Spencer at his basketball and hockey games and as a team mom helped at the concession stand and arranged car pools to away games and coach's gifts for the end-of-season banquet. It was all fun. But she had little interest in sitting in front of the television for hours at a time and shouting at the screen. Or watching *SportsCenter* every night before bed instead of kissing.

The worst was the emergence of Adam's temper. He didn't yell, exactly; he seethed and simmered, his tension chaotic and visible, which Celeste found more frightening than shouting. When he got angry for no apparent reason he would lean forward and loom over her like a menacing shadow, clench and unclench his fists again and again. He'd grumble at Spencer over the littlest things: toys left out, a missed pass in hockey, a glass of juice spilled. He stopped talking to Celeste in any kind of confidence, he refused to share with her what was bothering him. At first she feared he had a brain tumor or some other illness; she suggested he see a doctor. Then she suspected an affair.

At the time, he was working in sales for Weir Microsystems—this was before he lost his job for booking revenue he hadn't earned and taking home undeserved commission checks—and he traveled often, and once after a three-day business trip to Miami he'd been scheduled to fly into LaGuardia. Usually he took a car service back up to Brookfield, but Celeste wanted to drive down with Spencer and surprise him at the airport because it was their wedding anniversary. She checked his flight status online and found out the flight from Miami was delayed two hours, which would put him into New York after nine o'clock, too late for Spencer to stay up on a school night. She canceled the plan to meet him. Then, twenty minutes before his plane from Miami was supposed to land, Adam walked in the house. Huh? He concocted a story about a change in his itinerary—he had spent only two nights in Miami, then flew to Atlanta for an appointment, then back to New York. Oh, come on. She accused him of having another woman and his eyes blazed with panic and he swore she was his only love, forever and always. There would never be another woman. *Never! Never!*—the spittle hanging in the corners of his lips as if he were some kind of rabid animal.

Okay, okay—she believed him; there wasn't another woman. Thank God for that. But why had he lied about his trip? What was his problem? She found out a week later when she tried to put a down payment on a new car to replace the Camry, and the dealer came back and said her Visa card was declined, and then her MasterCard, and then the AmEx. When she confronted Adam, he finally broke down and cried like an abandoned child. The trip to Miami she'd questioned him about had been a gambling jaunt to Las Vegas; he'd lost a staggering amount of money. In fact, he'd been juggling the home finances and managed to hide that he'd lost almost everything—income, savings, 401(k) accounts, credit lines—to a gambling habit she didn't know gripped him until the world crashed down. How she managed not to see the signs of trouble was a question that still gnawed at her. Had he been that stealthy? Or was she that oblivious? Probably a little of both: Adam hiding his habit, and Celeste avoiding stepping into the cracks in their life.

She tried to be sympathetic, she told him they could get him help, she encouraged him to go to counseling and Gamblers Anonymous. Naively, she expected the problem to go away quickly—because she didn't understand. The lure of an affair she could understand, with its illicit sexual desire, but she couldn't comprehend how anyone could ruin himself gambling. Where was the joy, the need, the satisfaction in that? What on earth was so compelling that you would lose all your money, your savings . . . to *gambling*? How could *gambling* take such total control of your life? She read about its addictive qualities, the stimulation of the brain's pleasure centers, the similarities to drugs and alcohol, and the high incidence of drug and alcohol abuse in gamblers. But why Adam? He didn't have an addictive personality. He never took drugs. He rarely drank. So why gamble? He had a good life, a wonderful son, a wife who loved him. Why wasn't that enough?

Each time he promised he was through, and then he wasn't. He attended Gamblers Anonymous meetings, and then he didn't. He stayed away from his bookie, and then called him. He went to a daytime rehab and counseling center in White Plains and quit gambling for two months, and then relapsed. Celeste gave him many chances, forgave him many times. During those periods of forgiveness—for a few weeks, or a few months—she felt enormous relief: Her husband had given up his destructive habit, her marriage wasn't ruined, the nightmare was over. She clung to fragile optimism. And then the cycle started again.

Because she didn't understand the power gambling could exert, every relapse of Adam's increased her frustration and bewilderment, moved her one step closer to thinking her marriage had been a lie, she'd committed to a man who had been deceiving her all along, a man she didn't know at all. It was almost impossible to believe this was her husband. One day, after yet another bet was laid and confession extracted and she was expected to grant forgiveness and show compassion, instead she lashed out at him, she lost her composure when she'd sworn to herself she wouldn't. She threw in his face the meanest words she could come up with—calling him weak and a cheat and a disgrace and a loser—and he coiled and jumped toward her as if jolted by electricity, his fists tight as grenades, a heartbeat from smashing her apart. His hand opened like a claw and he reached out and snatched her chin and jaw between his thumb and forefinger, squeezed for a second and let go, sending her stumbling back against a kitchen chair and she cried out in pain and fear.

After that incident, Celeste asked him to move out, but

her husband begged for another chance. She gave him one. She never thought she'd tolerate any kind of abuse from any man, yet she tolerated Adam because she still held out hope that her husband would get better. He didn't. He went back to gambling. And then on another occasion when she said he was ruining their lives, he grabbed and wrenched her arm. Again she told him to leave the house. This time he didn't plead with her; he simply refused. She probably should have sought help or called the police, but she didn't want Adam to get in trouble; she just wanted him to stop. Plus, she was ashamed to be married to a man who could behave this way, and if she told anyone the truth and Adam eventually purged the gambling and violence and they remained together, people would know her husband had struck her and she'd stayed with him despite that. Then one night at the dinner table when Adam told Spencer to stop holding his fork over his head and lowering the spaghetti into his mouth, Spencer responded by saying, "Watch this," and swallowed a long strand of spaghetti in small gulps and then pulled it back up from his throat, and Adam's hand shot out and smacked Spencer on the side of his head. The first sound came from Celeste: "Stop it!"—she screamed at Adam, and after a few seconds of stunned silence Spencer burst out crying, his ear and cheek reddened from his father's hand. Adam apologized, but couldn't take back the blow he'd delivered. Celeste warned him never to strike their son again—never—even though she herself had been spanked a few times as a kid. But this was different. This wasn't discipline, this was anger—this was uncontrolled brutality.

And that was the real, untold reason she moved from their home while Adam was in rehab. Not only the repeated relapses into gambling, the evasions, the financial ruin—but the ongoing threat of violence. She could no longer pretend that physical aggression wasn't a pattern in Adam's behavior. She couldn't live in the same house with a man who made her tremble. She would not be one of those trapped, battered women, a helpless victim waiting for her husband to come home and hit her or beat their son. She wouldn't live each day fearing for their safety. She wouldn't.

Spencer stopped playing his trumpet, but stayed in his room. Adam lowered his voice. "I have a job, thanks to my father. This company, GeoPol, they make software and do computer systems work for police departments. The job is only in production and shipping, but I swear I'll be promoted into sales in no time. My father knows somebody on their board and he said once I got my foot in the door . . . well, I'm going to have a regular paycheck again, it won't be a lot at first, it will be like our early days together and—"

Celeste interrupted him. "Adam, I'm not ready to take you back. I need to take some time and see how things go. I don't want to rush into anything."

"Rush? Like you didn't rush to move out? I come home after three months and find out my wife and son have left me. My home is empty. Do you know what that did to me? I was counting on you to be there for me."

"Please don't make me out to be the one at fault here."

"I'm just saying—that was a pretty devastating discovery the first minute I got out. And look at this place—it's a dump. You should have stayed in the house. My father was paying the mortgage. We can still move back there."

There was something about him, veiled behind his eyes. He wanted to be better, but he wasn't. She wanted to welcome him home, but she couldn't. The gambling, the violence—it was still in him somewhere, caged perhaps, but sniffing around the door. "I've been doing a lot of thinking," she said. "I don't know if I can live with you again. I don't know if I still love you."

"Don't say that, Celeste. I know I let you down, I know you're angry. But I'm healthy again. The counselors at Glendale were fantastic, they helped me understand my trigger points, they gave me techniques. It was pretty amazing what they can do. This one day—"

She cut him off again. "You can't just come back here and expect everything to be okay. You can't pretend nothing happened."

"I'm not pretending anything," Adam said, his voice dull now. "I know everything that happened. I was a part of it, I was the cause of it. But we're still a family, Celeste—you and Spencer and me. I want to go back to what we had."

"You were deceiving me for years. You're completely different from the person I thought you were."

"You know what I mean. Before that. Before I got caught up in . . . in the gambling. But that's over now. I told you I'm better."

"And grabbing me and pushing me," she said. "That's worse than the gambling. You made me afraid of you. You hurt me—and you hurt Spencer." She felt a thread of that fear now, not knowing how Adam would react.

His face flushed and he turned away. "One time I spanked Spencer, and I know it was a mistake. And what happened with you, Celeste, I swear to God, I'm sorry. Never again, I promise. That's something else they helped me with at Glendale."

"You can see Spencer if you ask me in advance. That's only fair."

She saw his fists clench and unclench, like two mean hearts pumping open and closed, and it made her own heart beat faster. Was he going to hit her now? The acid burned her throat, but she pressed on. "And from now on, you need to call before you come over. That's the best I can offer. I need to take a break for a while."

The muscles in his jaw flicked. "You just had a three-month break. Celeste, I—"

"Adam, please. You have to respect my decision. You have to give me time."

Silence eclipsed the house, the only sound Adam's quick, hard breaths. His fingers scratched the air at his sides and he looked around, as if searching for something he'd set down but couldn't remember where.

3

At the Y on Saturday morning he played pickup games to fifteen, call your own fouls, friendly but competitive. Adam's team won all three games he played, although he exchanged hot words and almost shoved one jarhead who cried foul every time Adam challenged him on defense. But losing his temper defeated the reason he came here to play, which was to relax and focus his energies on healthy activities he enjoyed.

He showered and dressed, and on his way out he passed the gym where the kids' basketball league was now in session. He stopped and sat at one end of the bleachers away from the parents screaming at their children. You could already spot the kids who would be gamers someday: their athletic grace, nose for the ball, their sense of the court and strategy. Spencer had played in this league last season. He was a decent athlete and understood the game, but he didn't demand the ball, he didn't have that drive you needed to really succeed. Still, the boy was only nine; he could play, and Adam loved having a son to bond with over sports.

At first, he'd been angry with Celeste for letting Spencer skip basketball and hockey this year. He blamed her for how much Spencer had changed since he and Celeste had been apart. Now on those Saturdays when Celeste let Adam see his son, instead of taking Spencer to his hockey or basketball games, or spending an afternoon bowling, or checking scores and standings in the paper and talking about favorite players, or wrestling on the floor, Adam played chess with Spencer at his parents' house. They did art projects, which used to be exclusively Celeste's domain. He took Spencer to the library. Sometimes Spencer would start whispering and Adam would say, *What? I can't hear you,* only to realize Spencer wasn't speaking to him. The boy got this distant look in his eyes, as if he'd been drugged or had some kind of disorder.

His pretend friend. Kathy.

Adam wanted to shout out the alarming fact that Spencer had given up everything he once shared with his dad and now lived in an imaginary, sedentary world; on the other hand, he wanted to slit his own wrists for causing the problem to begin with.

Sitting in the bleachers now, Adam closed his eyes and listened to the sounds, the squeaky sneakers, the calls for the pass, the coaches yelling instructions, and the parents just yelling. Then he heard a voice calling his name, a voice he didn't immediately attach to its owner because the context was wrong: Adam with his eyes closed, the sounds of children playing, thinking of Spencer, imagining living again with his son and Celeste, wondering how to win them back.

He heard his name a second time and opened his eyes to see Vincent Canto at the bottom of the bleachers displaying his familiar whitened smile, the wormy posture and caved-in chest. Adam's insides instantly hollowed out, replaced by a shaft of pain shooting from his skull to his stomach. Of all people to run into.

"Adam! Hey, AV." Canto liked calling Adam by his initials, his own construction, he was the only one to use it.

Adam forced a grin and a halfhearted wave in return.

"I haven't seen you in ages," Canto said. "Where've you been?"

Adam wished Canto wouldn't talk to him from down there. Other parents were turning their heads now, noticing him. Adam didn't want to engage with Canto, but he had to get up and step down from the bleachers to stop Canto from speaking so loudly.

Canto offered his hand. Adam gave him the fish grip and said nothing.

"You haven't forgotten your old pal Vince, have you? You're not using someone else?"

"No, I—"

"Hey, that's Kyle bringing up the ball right now," Canto said, turning his attention to the court. "Come on, KC! Make a play!"

Canto's son dribbled left, then back between his legs and got open for a ten-foot shot, which he buried.

"Didn't your boy play in this league last year?"

"Spencer," Adam said. "He's got other interests now." Last year, when Spencer's team and Kyle's team played each other, Adam and Vincent Canto placed a bet on the game. Gambling on a kids' basketball game, that was bad enough, but Adam had been an assistant coach on Spencer's team, which made the transgression even worse.

Canto owned a gentlemen's club called Mario's that served as a front for a gambling business where Adam had done most of his betting. He was a dangerous man, Adam knew, not only because of the gambling. There were rumors about Canto, that he once tortured someone over an unpaid debt, that he'd been involved in the murder of a jockey a few years ago. Vincent Canto was a man Adam should not be talking to now. Should not even be looking at. Adam was about to make an excuse and put distance between himself and Canto, when Canto said, "You played for Taconic State, right?"

"Yeah, two seasons, a long time ago."

"Come here a sec." Canto placed a hand on Adam's back and led him into the hall, away from the players and parents. "I think they might be ranked this year, definitely tournament material," Canto said.

"They were Division II in my day."

"Maybe you'd like to take a ride up there and check them out. I've got passes to their practices."

The alarm sounded in Adam's head. He could feel his counselors at Glendale looking over his shoulder, telling him to walk away, that's all he had to do. But Canto wasn't asking him to gamble. And Adam didn't recognize an urge he needed to suppress or an insidious seed trying to sprout—the therapy at Glendale was doing its job. This was simply an invitation to check out his old team.

Except not. Canto took a few more steps down the hallway, lowered his voice, and explained how he wanted Adam's help evaluating a player named Kevin Elevet, a senior forward for the Taconic Tigers. The evaluation didn't involve scouting Elevet's game—the book was already published on that. Thirty-nine-inch vertical leap, twelve-foot shooting range, excellent court awareness and speed; but also a me-first player, poor passer, inconsistent work ethic. And Vincent Canto knew more about Elevet than his game: growing up poor on the streets of Albany, arrested at age seventeen for assault, five years of high school and a summer to graduate, the scholarship to Taconic.

What Canto wanted help with was approaching Elevet to participate in Canto's new business venture, a game-fixing scheme.

"Stop right there. No way," Adam said. "I'm not involved in gambling anymore."

"This ain't gambling, my friend. I'm not asking you to place any bets, or even touch any money—except for the money I'll pay you. Simply talk to Kevin. A guy like you, a former Taconic player and alumnus, you've got instant cred with this kid. You introduce yourself, chat him up, mention a business proposal, ask permission for me to meet with him."

"I can't do it."

"All you're doing is making an introduction. It's nothing but a business deal."

Adam shook his head. No.

"There's a $3,000 consulting fee in it for you, payable if Elevet simply agrees to meet with me. All you have to do is get him to say yes to a meeting, and then you're done."

Jesus. Three grand.

No, he couldn't. But three grand. He would earn in a couple of hours almost as much as he did in a month in the production department at GeoPol. He could give that money to Celeste. Maybe then she'd appreciate him more. Maybe then she'd stop looking at him with resentment simmering in her eyes every time he picked up Spencer for the afternoon. Maybe then his wife and son could move out of that shitty house, that ugly neighborhood where she'd fled while he was in rehab, and they could find a new home as a family. They had put the Cider Mill house on the market and would use some of the proceeds to help Adam chip away at his pay downs, but there was a long way to go. By Adam's calculations, at the current rate he was repaying debts he'd be 164 years old by the time he was debt-free. Ha!

Adam had no way to get ahead, or get even; no way to provide for his family again. His father wouldn't give him money, not anymore; he'd only write checks to Celeste, although she had turned down his repeated offers. And while Adam voluntarily had his paycheck garnisheed for child support, his salary was embarrassingly low compared to what he once earned at Weir, and he hadn't been promoted into sales at GeoPol, as he told Celeste would happen; he hadn't even been granted an interview.

Three thousand dollars. It wouldn't be gambling money, it would be money he earned as a consultant to an athlete. Adam could present a compelling case to this kid Kevin Elevet, and it might be helpful for Kevin to leave college with a little spending money in his pocket if he wasn't turning pro. Which Kevin Elevet wasn't. Adam knew about basketball players like Kevin because Adam had been one himself. Not the black part—Adam's skin was white as winter. And not the impoverished part—Adam's parents had enough money to send him to college even if he hadn't gotten the scholarship, whereas Elevet grew up fatherless in Albany's drug-infested Arbor Hill. What Adam knew about Kevin, and what they shared, was the experience of transition. You could call it a period of maturation, or acceptance of reality, or simply the dream vanishing.

That period of slow, grudging recognition of the inevitable: You were not NBA material. You were not even European league material.

Adam recognized his own transition beginning senior year in high school. He starred for Haverton, captain of a team that lost to St. Joe's in the state finals his senior year. He had attended Haverton—over an hour from his home—because the school was a perennial basketball powerhouse, a secure stepping-stone to Division I. But Adam ran out of stepping-stones when not one Division I school recruited him. How could he have been overlooked? Okay, maybe he lacked expert dribbling skills, maybe he was a streaky scorer. Maybe he'd been goaded into a fight on the court once or twice.

He did get a ride to Taconic State, though, back when they were a Division II program, and he played twenty minutes a game his freshman year and averaged seven points, but sophomore year his playing time decreased because a freshman from Philadelphia, four inches taller and a better athlete in every way, forced Adam to the bench. He raged at the conspiracy against him—the fast-break game the coach wanted to play didn't fit well with Adam's pick-and-roll skills, the nagging sprained thumb affected his shot. He simmered on the bench, on a Division II team, a lonely outpost NBA scouts didn't visit.

This is how he handled the transition: self-pity, moping, cutting classes more than usual. Punching out a teammate in the locker room after practice one day. Dabbled in dope and drinking, though he'd never leaned that way, and never felt better for abusing substances. He couldn't say his future looked bleak—it looked blank. All along he'd dreamed of an NBA career, and now he couldn't construct that picture, as if many pieces of a jigsaw puzzle he'd worked so hard to assemble were missing. The missing pieces weren't still in the box; they hadn't fallen to the floor. They simply didn't exist. All that effort and you have these gaping holes in what would have been a perfect scene.

Then in his psychology class he learned about Dr. Kübler-Ross and the five stages of grief, and Adam realized he'd passed through four of them—denial, anger, bargaining, depression—with only acceptance to go before his NBA dream could die peacefully. And he finally did accept his fate. He couldn't change who he was, no matter how hard he worked or wished.

The dream died. The excitement vanished.

A new dream took its place. He found excitement again when, just for fun, he placed his first bets on NFL games with a guy in the dorm who ran a weekly pool. He had a knack for picking winners. When football season ended, he bet NBA games and Division I college games on the point spread, and hockey games straight up. He became as much a fanatic as the Giants fan who took off his shirt in December and painted his fat belly blue and red and drank himself blind at the stadium. As amped up as the UConn students decked out in blue and white and banging inflatable noisemakers and screaming the lining of their lungs raw when the opposing team took foul shots. The difference being that Adam was in the game again. Part of the action. He won and he lost, just like when he was playing. The adrenaline gushed through him. He passed hundred-dollar bills back and forth and they felt like velvet in his hands. He learned more about the thrill of victory and the agony of defeat as a gambler than he ever had as an athlete.

He didn't consider himself a problem gambler—never thought about it and would have scoffed at anyone who suggested it—and his habit pretty much disappeared when he started dating Celeste two years after graduating college. He was introduced to her at a meeting with Weir Microsystems' advertising agency. Celeste Stafford was the art director on a marketing campaign the agency was pitching, Adam the sales associate asked to join the meeting and give his opinion. His opinion was that Celeste was smart, beautiful, and poised. She had a serious, thoughtful, understated glow that mesmerized him. Wide-set eyes that somehow were both green and brown at the same time. Thick, coppery hair. An almost boyish figure, narrow in the shoulders and hips, with just enough curves to churn his imagination.

When he first asked her out, she turned him down because she was seeing someone else. But he persisted and called her every week, and eventually she said yes. And then yes again. And then they were in a relationship. He discovered they were opposites, and it was true what they said about opposites attracting. He was a jock, she liked art. He strolled through museums with her and she went to Knicks and Rangers games with him. He ate anything: fast food, takeout, fancy fare from top-end restaurants—as long as it came ready to consume. She had a quirky stomach and acid reflux; she took cooking classes and prepared complete meals with fresh ingredients. She cooked for him, he took her out to eat. He was a night owl, she was an early bird. Antigua and the Bahamas for him, Yosemite and San Francisco for her. They made fun of each other for their different tastes, in a tender way. She had this stunning smile she doled out like a gift to charity, and he spent all his time trying to be deserving of it.

Where they intersected was on a practical, traditional level. They both had career ambitions. He saw himself becoming a senior vice president of sales; she had abandoned fine art for commercial art and a steady income. They engaged in lots of pillow talk about wanting to settle down and raise a family . . . someday. Maybe with each other. It could happen. They met after work for drinks and discussed their day. They reserved Saturday night for each other. He wrote her love letters. They bantered about names they'd give their kids. Some weekends they visited Chappaqua. His parents loved her. Celeste helped Adam's mother in the kitchen. She listened patiently to his father's stories about the vagaries and evils of Wall Street. Adam courted her for six months, proposed to her, and she was three months pregnant on their wedding day.

After Spencer was born, Celeste got depressed about going back to work when her maternity leave ended. Adam said he'd be honored to support their little family. A baby needed his mother, and Celeste was an amazing mother. She wouldn't let her baby cry himself to sleep just because she happened to be tired of waking up four times a night. She comforted Spencer when he needed soothing, she carried him in a sling. She breast-fed him even though her nipples were live nerves and Adam couldn't so much as breathe on them. She dressed their baby in nice clothes and fed him good food and read him acclaimed books and bought educational toys and chose the safest car seat and the best preschool. Of course, all that stuff had to be paid for. Not that money was the most pressing issue. It meant something, it mattered—but it wasn't everything. Yes, they'd just bought this huge house and faced a mountainous mortgage, but they had the rest of their lives to pay for it and his parents provided a safety net. Fortunately, Adam reached his quota every quarter and earned his year-end bonuses. So it wasn't the need for money that drove Adam back to gambling. Gamblers weren't really in it for the money.

What happened was his emotional state peaked and began

to decline. Meeting and marrying your true love, becoming a father, stepping up as a husband and provider—the whirlwind of change and responsibility gave him purpose for almost four years, filled every empty corner in him, cooled his competitive nature, and satisfied every craving. He asked about having a second child, but Celeste had changed her mind, even though they had both talked about a big family. She'd been sick all through her pregnancy, she'd had an emergency C-section with Spencer, she suffered now from endometriosis. She couldn't go through the ordeal again; even her OB-GYN was dubious. She didn't want to adopt. Okay, so they would be a happy family of three.

But as sure as the sun sets, the excitement fades, and when it did, the horizon appeared strikingly flat and uniform to Adam. He'd already made all the big decisions in his life: who to marry, where to live, what career to pursue. Yes, each one turned out to be a winner. But now what? Where would the thrill come from? What in his life would be dynamic? As soon as he asked himself these questions, his period of remission ended. When he started gambling again it was like he started cheating on his wife, because of course he hid his habit from her, and that made him feel guilty and mean, which wasn't fair because he really did love Celeste. He adored her. It's just that the urge had ideas of its own.

For a few years he managed his habit. But soon the losses piled up like a train wreck while the distance between wins lengthened. That compulsive, driven nature, which made him a competitive athlete and gave him the confidence to pursue Celeste and commit to a house beyond his means and dream big dreams, now took control of him and he gambled beyond reason, not thinking through his bets half the time, the anger mounting along with the losses.

When Celeste found out the first time and the extent of his debt was exposed, he felt foolish and humbled and promised to stop. Same with the second and third time. He realized he needed help. He agreed to counseling and attended GA meetings. He'd quit for a week or a month and then the itch got him. By the fifth or sixth time Celeste confronted him, Adam was tired of her nagging. One night she said he was a loser and she had this defiant stare in her eyes like she hated him and the next instant his hand shot out and grabbed and squeezed her pretty little jaw and the only reason he didn't smack her . . . well, he didn't that time, but during another argument when she wanted him to move out he gave her a shove, and then there was the time he almost broke her arm. After that, he applied to the Glendale Wellness Center.

Adam waited for Kevin Elevet outside the athletic building at Taconic State. He sat on a concrete bench that fronted a stone urn. The leafless branches of a tree grown too big for the urn cast spindly shadows over him—these same trees were saplings when Adam attended Taconic. He imagined the tree roots inside there, cramped and tangled and pinching each other, about the way his own nerves felt right now. He hadn't gambled in almost five months and would not be gambling today. He'd spent three months at Glendale, he'd been to dozens of GA meetings since his return. He couldn't let that repair job go to waste. He shouldn't be involved with Vincent Canto but he told himself he was here simply to earn money and help dig his family out of their hole, to win back Celeste.

He spotted Elevet walking out with a teammate, each of them shouldering athletic bags. Adam called out to him. Kevin fisted his mate and peeled off toward Adam, as if he were expecting him and wanted a private conversation.

"Kevin, let me introduce myself. I'm Adam Vanek." He shook hands with Kevin, a business gesture, none of this slapping or pounding.

"You an agent?"

Adam smiled. "I once stood in your shoes, Kevin. I played for Taconic when you were just a kid."

Kevin remained silent. Adam started walking across the plaza and Kevin fell in alongside him. Elevet had four inches on Adam, but the kid was skinny as a comb. He may be quick and agile, but his kind of frame will get you blown around like snowflakes against the big men.

"You think you got a shot at the NBA?" Adam asked.

"I don't know," Kevin admitted. "I could get a free agent tryout."

"Maybe you could," Adam agreed. "There's always someone who beats the odds." He regretted his use of the word *odds*, more for his sake than Kevin's. "No agents met with me, either. No NBA scouts hung around practice or came to games to watch me. I gotta tell you, it was a hard reality to face. Because growing up I had the NBA dream."

"Who the fuck are you?" Kevin challenged him.

Adam laid out the numbers: thirty NBA teams, about 360 active players on rosters. Two rounds of the draft each year. That's sixty players drafted each year from a candidate pool consisting of over three hundred Division I college teams, say about forty-five hundred players, plus foreign players, plus those superhuman kids coming right out of high school like LeBron and Carmelo. What percentage of Division I college players do you think ever play a single minute in the NBA, Kevin? Less than 2 percent is the answer.

Kevin Elevet didn't drop his head or slow his pace or slouch, which meant everything Adam explained wasn't entirely out of the blue or a shock to him.

The last thing you want to do, Adam said, was to get out of school penniless and without prospects. What are you going to do? Go back to Albany and hang around on the streets until trouble comes knocking on your door? Wouldn't you like some cash in your pocket to help you get launched, to give you an opportunity to explore different options? Maybe to take some extra courses to graduate or treat yourself and your family to a few of those things you've always wanted and thought might be coming your way if you'd made the NBA. I'll bet you dreamed of buying your mom a few presents, didn't you, Kevin?

You work just as hard at your game as the guy getting drafted in the first round, don't you? You deserve something for your effort.

"Yeah, like what?"

"I know this guy who would like to talk to you. I'm here to open a door to an opportunity and I want your permission to make an introduction."

"Who with?"

"A businessman who wants to make an investment in you. Who thinks you have some potential for earning money playing ball. Right now. This season. And to help others earn, too."

"How much money?"

"Good money." Adam reached into his pocket and retrieved the business card Vincent Canto had given him. He offered it to Kevin.

"Vincent Canto, give him a call. It'll be worth your time," Adam said, then glanced at his watch and said, "Oh," as if he'd forgotten the time and was late for another appointment.

"Kevin, I gotta run. Good luck this year—and don't forget to call Mr. Canto."

4

Adam asked Celeste and Spencer to come to his parents' house for Christmas, but Celeste opted to spend Christmas and New Year's in Vermont with her sister and Howard. She and Chantal normally took turns visiting each other over the holidays and this would have been Chantal's year to come to Brookfield, but a switch this Christmas made sense given Celeste's living arrangements.

As sisters they had always been close, even though Chantal was three years older. Chantal was a self-described late bloomer, didn't need a bra until she was almost fifteen. She and Celeste got their first periods within a month of each other and became interested in boys around the same time, but didn't compete. They wore the same size and lent each other clothes. Their mother had given them what she believed were alluring, exotic names. She thought a pretty name would make them appear prettier and therefore help them find good husbands. Their mother's strategy insulted the girls, who, yes, wanted good husbands but desired more out of life than a man, and the naming convention produced mixed results. Celeste had married first, and for a while appeared to have found a husband and marriage worthy of envy. Chantal married Howard two years later and endured several rough years when Howard was hardly ever home during his surgical residency, but he and

Chantal settled into a satisfying relationship, especially after the twins were born.

Chantal and Howard lived in a restored farmhouse on twenty acres just outside the Burlington city limits. The day after Christmas, Spencer cross-country skied with his younger cousins and they all rode in an actual horse-drawn sleigh that belonged to one of Howard's colleagues. They went ice-skating on the frozen pond in the back. One night after the kids and even Howard had gone to bed, Celeste stayed up with Chantal drinking wine in front of the fire. They got a little drunk and Chantal floated the idea that Celeste and Spencer should move to Burlington. Celeste was open to the possibility, but wasn't ready to make the decision. She had to see what happened with her and Adam. She wasn't about to take him back, yet wasn't able to accept that her marriage had failed, and therefore she drifted along in limbo. She didn't want to reunite with Adam only to realize it was a mistake, and she didn't want to pursue a permanent split unless she was absolutely sure she couldn't love him again.

The part of her that wished to save her marriage also wanted to believe Adam had put his destructive habits permanently behind him. He'd been on his best behavior recently, and she'd been granting him more time with Spencer. He always returned Spencer home from an outing when he said he would. He provided regular child support from his paycheck. He showed no signs of losing his temper and, although disappointed, didn't argue when Celeste said she was going to Vermont for the holidays. She didn't see any evidence that he'd started gambling again, although she wondered about the thousand dollars in cash he'd given her last month. He said he earned the money advising players on the Taconic State basketball team about planning for their future. He explained to her that the athletic department had started a program to help the players because many of them left school unprepared and ended up in trouble of one kind or another. Adam knew the athletic director from his own playing days and this consulting role was a good fit. He could relate to the players. Adam sounded so earnest, so eager to please her, that she started thinking he really had pulled himself together. Sure, being in limbo was safe, but lonely, too; Celeste hadn't been held in forever, and was tempted to fall into his arms again. But she didn't. The money from Adam bothered her, although she managed to spend a good portion of it right away. She finally got her hair cut and colored and new tires for the car. She treated Emery to a nice dinner out one night, because her friend had been picking up most of the tabs. And she bought the bike Spencer wanted, which she was storing in the basement under a tarp behind the furnace until his birthday.

A week after her trip to Vermont, Celeste sat with Spencer on a Friday evening in the Apollo Diner across from the entrance to the Brookfield Technology Park. Elderly couples occupied a few of the perimeter booths. A lone man perched on a counter stool. Every clink of silverware against a plate or cup carried across the room. You could hear the squeaky shoes the waitress wore and faint music in the background. Business was slow; on a Friday after work, everyone headed home or out to the bars.

The plan was for Adam to pick up Spencer at the diner and take him for a sleepover at his parents' house, then Adam would drop him back home by ten o'clock tomorrow morning, which was Spencer's birthday. Instead of a party, Celeste was taking him and three friends to the Pottery Place to paint and glaze pottery figures, an activity Spencer had chosen.

After placing their orders and while waiting for their food, she and Spencer played Hangman on the back of Celeste's paper placemat. Spencer went first. His word had seven letters and Celeste knew what it was before they started because he'd used the same word the last two times they played. She guessed the *e* and the *i*, then misfired on a number of letters and Spencer had almost finished his hanging man when Celeste went on a run and got the *b* and the *y* and guessed *bicycle*. This was Spencer's way of reminding her what he wanted for his birthday tomorrow. On Celeste's turn, Spencer got the *o* and the *i*—she'd taught him to start with vowels. Then he got the *s* and the *m* and guessed *optometrist*, because he'd had his eyes checked recently. He was very close, but her word was *optimistic*, which they should both try to be, because one way or another, things have a way of working out for the better.

The waitress brought their plates. The Greek salad tasted good, although the cook had added the onions that Celeste had asked to be left out. They were diced and mixed in, so she went ahead and ate the salad knowing she might have regrets later. Onions, among many other foods, aggravated her acid reflux.

"So is Kathy going on the sleepover with you?" she said.

Spencer took a bite of his grilled cheese and eyed her guardedly, as if she'd asked a trick question. He shrugged but didn't answer.

"Don't forget to brush your teeth before bed," she reminded him. "And if you change your mind at any time, even in the middle of the night, you can call me and I'll come bring you home." She tried to give her son the option of backing out without totally undermining Adam.

"What are you going to do?" he asked her. "Tonight, when I'm at Grandma and Grandpa's?"

How many boys would notice anything beyond their own universe and have the sensitivity to ask their mother how she planned to spend a solo overnight?

"I'm going out, actually," she said. "With Emery and some other friends." She was taking advantage of her freedom for a girls' night out Emery had arranged—five of them were going. Cocktails at the Point, followed by dinner at McLellans. True, a lot of the talk would be domestic dialogue about husbands and kids and schools, and there would be tiptoeing around the fact that Celeste was the only one of the five not in a stable marriage, but Emery was sensitive enough to steer the conversation away from the petty complaints about husbands that would sound ridiculous compared to Celeste's situation.

"You could come with me," Spencer suggested, as if she hadn't just told him her plans. "We could all have a sleepover for my birthday."

She reached out and held his hand. "January 7," she said. "The day you were born. It was the best day of my life, my son coming into the world. It snowed that day, a big storm, and I nursed you and watched the snow out the window and thought how beautiful the world is."

"You and Dad are never getting back together, are you?" Spencer said.

A surge of emotion caught in the back of her throat. Celeste had explained a number of times that no decisions had been made yet, and although uncertainty was difficult to live with, there was no uncertainty about Spencer living with her and Celeste loving him completely, loving him always, and they would get through this period together. The key was to be *optimistic*—her Hangman word. Celeste's explanation was always accompanied by dry, set eyes and elicited a simple nod of understanding from Spencer. Her reaction now must be related to his birthday, or the sleepover: She'd never spent an entire night away from her son. Not once had she and Adam gone away and left Spencer in the care of his parents or a sitter. They'd done everything together as a family.

"I don't know what's going to happen," she said, the same answer she'd given her sister, but this time she added the line about how Mommy and Daddy both loved him and that wasn't going to change, even if they never lived together as a family again.

"You understand that, don't you?" she said.

"Yeah, I guess so."

The waitress cleared their plates and served Celeste's tea and Spencer's ice cream, with a maraschino cherry on top. Spencer plucked it off and placed it on his napkin, where the wet, red blob soaked through the thin paper. He spooned the remaining red syrup from the top of the ice cream, adding that to the napkin as well.

"Since when don't you like the cherries?" Celeste asked.

"You told me they were full of chemical dye and no cherry has that color in the real world."

"Once in a while won't hurt you." She picked up the cherry and ate it, the extent of her dessert. She opened her purse and got out money for the check. It was a few minutes past seven o'clock, the agreed-upon meeting time. Then seven-fifteen came and went without Adam showing. She poured more hot water into her teacup. Then seven-thirty. She called Adam's cell phone number. His voice mail picked up and she left a message saying they were waiting at the Apollo and wondering where he was. Yesterday, he'd told her he'd be working late because he'd fallen behind during the week and had to catch up before he left, but could definitely meet them at seven, which Celeste knew meant seven-fifteen.

"When's Dad going to be here?"

"Maybe there was a mixup," Celeste said. "I thought we agreed on seven o'clock. Come on, let's go see where he is."

They put on their coats and on the way out she gave Spencer a quarter for the gum-ball machine in the entryway and he barked a triumphant *Yes!* when he got a green one, his favorite color.

The Brookfield Technology Park was a sprawling, half-completed campus of tech companies, science laboratories, and small corporate offices, with more on the way as the buildings went up and companies moved in. The campus was being built from back to front, so the first companies to move in occupied the farthest reaches of the park, with the newer construction taking place near the entrance. To reach the GeoPol building, Celeste had to drive along roadways lined with orange construction cones and giant concrete drainage pipes still to be installed. There were two roundabouts in the park and the temporary signage was hard to read at night. She took a wrong turn off one of the roundabouts and had to backtrack and try again.

It was well past business hours and only a few cars remained when she pulled into the GeoPol parking lot. She spotted Adam's car under an overhead light and parked next to it.

"Honey, why don't you wait while I go see where your father is."

She preferred to face Adam alone and hear what he had to say about being so late before she made any decision about releasing Spencer to him for the night.

"Lock the door when I get out," she said.

"Can I sit in the driver's seat?"

"Sure."

"What about the light?"

"If you want to."

Celeste got out and Spencer climbed from the back into the driver's seat and switched on the overhead courtesy light. She waited for him to lock the door—probably an unnecessary caution, but an easy one to take—and then she turned and faced the building. She'd never been inside. It was a long, low structure of gray brick and black glass. There was a main entrance at one end and a loading dock and back door at the other.

Celeste crossed the parking lot to the front entrance. The glass doors were locked. Just inside she could see a reception area with armchairs along one wall. There was an electronic card reader mounted to the outside wall next to the door and a phone above it. She picked up the receiver and then replaced it; she didn't know Adam's desk extension. She got her own phone out and tried his cell number again. Voice mail. She cupped her hands to the side of her face and pressed against the glass for a better view, but there wasn't much to see: hallways extending from either side of the reception desk, closed doors, a few lights in the distance.

She walked around the building to the rear entrance. There was an overhead garage door and another glass door protected by a card reader. She tried the door. Locked. She peered through the glass. Inside she could see a large room filled with steel shelving and stacked with boxes.

Okay, she'd made an effort, she'd done a lot for Adam to make this sleepover happen. She helped Spencer get ready, showed up at the appointed meeting place, and even tried to track down Adam when he was late. And for her reward she gets to go back to Spencer and tell him that his father forgot or didn't care about his son's birthday.

But Adam had never been late picking up Spencer. He would never forget Spencer's birthday sleepover. There had to be a reason.

Unsure what else to do, she was about to leave when someone appeared and pushed open the door. Celeste stepped back to keep the door from hitting her.

"Oh, excuse me." A tall, skinny, twentysomething in a puffy down coat stepped clear of Celeste and held the door for her. "Are you waiting for someone?" he asked.

"Um—yes." She took hold of the open door. "Do you know if Adam Vanek is here?"

"Adam? Yeah, he's back there. Hope you brought his chill pills." He shook his head and kept walking, into the lot to a car a few rows behind Celeste's.

She saw her own car and Spencer inside illuminated by the dome light, two hands on the wheel, inching it left and right to steer whatever road he traveled, his lips moving in conversation.

She turned back to the entrance. *Chill pills.* That didn't sound good. She swallowed back an acidy taste: the onions from her salad. She hesitated, holding the door, unsure whether to close it and go home or step inside and find Adam.

5

At four o'clock, Adam began duplicating the master DVD to make copies of GeoPol's crime-analysis software. While the duplicator ran, he stuffed the cover art into the plastic cases and prepped the FedEx envelopes. Drudge work, menial labor, but at least he received a twice-monthly paycheck, a big chunk of which went to Celeste and the rest to his parents, who gave him a spending allowance.

At five o'clock, with the packages ready for the FedEx pickup and his workday finished, Adam made a bag of microwave popcorn and settled on the couch in the employee lounge to watch Taconic State take on Siena College in a Division I game. The game would be over before seven and he'd have plenty of time to meet Celeste and Spencer for the handoff. Adam's mother had baked a cake and Adam had gotten Spencer a computerized chess set. This would be the first time he and Spencer slept under the same roof in more than six months. If only Celeste would be a part of the celebration, too.

After he'd been paid by Vincent Canto for setting up the meeting with Taconic's Kevin Elevet, Adam said he didn't want to know more about the game-fixing scheme, he just wanted his money and wanted out. Canto respected his request. But in the end Adam couldn't contain his curiosity and he looked up the point spread and results for Taconic's first game; they were favored by seven points and won by four. In the second game, they were favored by eight and won by five. Anyone who took the points and bet against Taconic earned money.

Taconic had a history of scheduling easier opponents outside the MAAC conference early in the season, until they hit their stride and tested their mettle against higher-ranked teams. If Adam was going to get in, the best time would be early. But that would mean gambling, and Adam was a compulsive gambler who no longer gambled. No sports betting, no casinos, no online poker, no lottery tickets. Hell, he couldn't play a game of bingo at the town hall, he couldn't buy a raffle ticket for a school fund-raiser. And he hadn't done any of those things since returning from the Glendale Wellness Center.

He had gained a ton of insight at Glendale, such as how gambling is considered a disease, as much a disorder of the brain as any other neurological or psychiatric illness. And that gambling increases dopamine levels, which increase feelings of pleasure, making you physically crave more. But aside from all the technical and conceptual knowledge, what Adam benefited from most was the practical technique of waiting ten minutes whenever the urge to gamble—or do anything self-destructive—took hold of him. Put off the decision for ten minutes, that's all there was to it.

The problem was he had given Celeste $1,000 and put another thousand dollars on his AmEx account, but that left a thousand in his pocket from the three grand Canto had paid him. One thousand dollars at a time when he should never be holding more than a $20 bill. That's something else he learned at Glendale: *Don't carry cash.* But he held on to that thousand dollars for a month, ten $100 bills, sitting like a fuse in his pocket, waiting for an accidental spark. The voice gnawed at him: He could get in with Canto and double his thousand, and double it again. He'd done all the tricky work of approaching Kevin Elevet in the first place. Sure, he got paid, but what about future dividends?

On the morning he woke up with the urge hurting him the most, he employed the ten-minute strategy he learned at Glendale: put off the decision to gamble for ten minutes. For ten minutes he would do something else, like, like . . . shower for work. That took ten minutes. Now what? Wait ten more minutes before he made the decision to gamble. Fill those ten minutes with . . . get dressed. Now what? Wait ten more minutes before he decided to gamble. Fill those ten minutes with . . . drive to work. Now what? Wait ten more minutes before he decided to gamble. Fill those ten minutes with . . . boot up his computer and see what orders needed to be filled.

Now what? Ten minutes.

Now what? Adam reached that decision point fifty-seven times over the course of the day, and fifty-seven times he found a way to occupy himself for ten more minutes without deciding to gamble. But rather than the urge passing, it became stronger, more insistent. Tugging at him like a demanding child. The money in his pocket began to itch his leg, right through the fabric of his pants. He scratched his thigh, again and again, so that by the time he dropped his pants to examine the raised red flesh of his leg, he didn't know if he'd contracted an actual rash or had clawed himself raw.

He'd lasted ten minutes and ten minutes and ten minutes and what difference did it make? It never worked, because there would always be the next ten minutes and he was forced to make the same decision over and over, and that in itself was like placing a bet because every ten minutes there was an equal chance of waiting another ten minutes or doing what he'd set out to do. It was like calling heads or tails. No matter how many times you flipped, no matter how many times you came up with heads, the next flip was just as likely to be a head as it was a tail. There was no getting out in front. Eventually, it flipped the other way. The wrong way. They said the urge eventually passes. When? In another thirty years? Think of those poor souls at GA who'd been attending meetings for fifteen or twenty years and still battled the disease.

To stop his leg from itching he drove to Mario's on the far south end of Delaware Avenue where Canto spent evenings socializing and conducting business, a nightclub Adam had visited hundreds of times to place a wager, collect a win, or pay a debt. Canto's bodyguard, Wally, escorted Adam to Vincent's office down a hallway. "You been watching the scores?" Canto said. "As close to a sure thing as you can get. Elevet's playing his part perfectly—and he's still having good games. The kid's a natural at making a fucked-up play or two that makes the difference in the points. The other team covers the spread and Taconic still takes the game. Everybody wins."

"He's pretty reliable?" Adam asked.

Vincent Canto got up from his desk and put an arm around Adam's shoulder, as if they were old friends. "I knew you'd be back," he said. "You deserve to make some serious money. After all, you helped us launch this venture."

Then Canto said something that eased Adam's conscience, wiped away the guilt. "Betting is for schmucks. What we've got going here is a business venture. We're getting all the kinks worked out with Taconic, and then I see this spreading to dozens of teams, millions of dollars. And the early investors are the ones who are going to earn a big payday. You did a great job warming up Elevet. I want you in that same role for other players."

Adam invested his entire grand on the next Taconic game and won. Put two grand on the following game and won again. He forgot the difference between an investment and a bet, and put the four thousand on the NFL that weekend and lost most of it. He realized his mistake—only the Taconic deal delivered a guaranteed return, the other bets were for losers—and to get ahead he put $25,000 on tonight's Siena game; he had to convince Canto to front him an investment of that magnitude.

Adam had the employee lounge to himself. He turned up the volume on the television during the pregame warm-ups.

Kevin Elevet leaped high for a dunk and grabbed the rim on the way down, which normally wasn't a problem—you always saw NBA players swinging like monkeys from the rim after a dunk. But there must have been a stress flaw in the construction of the backboard that weakened the composite over time, because when Elevet grabbed the rim, it pulled out from the backboard and Elevet fell hard to the floor. The tempered glass shattered and the backboard rained down on him in a million little pieces.

Stunned, Elevet stood up slowly and shook himself free of the glass nuggets. He favored his right leg for a few steps, but then started to laugh and slap with his teammates once he realized what a spectacle he'd just caused—at least until the camera showed the coach right up in Elevet's grill, yelling at his player for showboating during warm-ups.

The two sides retreated to their locker rooms while a repair crew took forty-five minutes to clean up the mess and install a new backboard and rim. When the game finally got underway almost an hour late, the first half played out as Adam had expected. Elevet knocked in ten points and the Taconic Tigers jumped out to an early lead. But it wasn't just Elevet. The team had recruited well and its starting five all were solid. Their lead varied between six and thirteen points, just right for a team favored by nine. Adam had bet against Taconic, of course, knowing they would not win by nine. They would win by five, or three, or even lose, depending on how Elevet played his part.

At halftime, Adam was sweating, and could smell his own pits. He wished he had a fresh shirt to change into. He'd drunk two sodas and the sugar and caffeine pulsed in his veins. He rinsed his face in the men's room and returned for the second half. Elevet missed an easy jumper and a few minutes later clanked two free throws off the rim.

Adam was afraid Elevet was overdoing it. The announcers made excuses for him, bantered back and forth about whether Elevet had in fact been slightly injured when the backboard shattered pregame. Taconic's coach appeared to have a different view. He sat Elevet on the bench and sent in a skinny white sophomore named Sullivan.

Suddenly, Siena went up by three, then five—the Sullivan kid was overmatched and giving up four inches to the Siena forward he guarded. Elevet had to go back in for Taconic. Now he could play hard to erase the deficit, and did. On one trip down the court, he got free underneath for a dunk; the next time he took it to the basket and scored while getting fouled. Then Elevet collided with a Siena player and went down. He had to be helped off the court, favoring the same leg he'd tweaked when the backboard shattered. Sullivan entered the game again and the Siena forward he was guarding posted up twice and hit two baskets and the Siena home crowd roared, sensing a potential upset. It didn't matter to Adam if Siena won outright, although he did feel nostalgia for his old team.

But Sullivan, the backup for Taconic, came to life. He grabbed a rebound and raced the length of the court for a basket, then stole the inbounds pass and sank a quick jumper. Over the last two minutes of the game, Adam watched in disbelief as Sullivan, a player who rarely got off the bench, tallied nine points for Taconic, with the final blow a heave-ho shot he threw up just before the buzzer that swished through and gave Taconic a ten-point victory. Anyone who had bet on Siena and taken the nine points just went bust.

Adam blinked a few times and watched the replay, trying to reverse what he'd just witnessed. You don't shoot a long three-pointer when you're up by seven in the last seconds of the game; you dribble the ball and run out the clock. You don't shoot. You don't score. You don't—

The tension in him snapped, a firework exploded in his brain. He'd just lost $25,000! He began to repeat over and over, as if reciting his "Ten minutes" mantra, when in fact he was hyperventilating: *Fuck, Fuck, Fuck, Fuck* . . . until someone walked by the lounge and looked in on him and asked if he was all right.

Adam couldn't focus his eyes. He let out a hard breath and grunted, then resumed his litany of cursing. The person who'd stopped for him quickly headed for the exit.

Adam spun and head-butted a dent the size of a dinner plate into the plasterboard wall of the lounge. Two quick fists followed, a combination that opened two more holes in the wall and shredded the skin on his knuckles. His knees buckled—a delayed response to the head collision—but he kept his balance. Blood rushed through his body, drummed in his ears. Stabs of hot pain struck his neck and head. He finally dropped to one knee.

Then he heard another voice in the hallway.

"Adam? Are you here?"

The ruin of his life toppled upon him, like a building torn apart by an earthquake, a deep and uncontrollable and inevitable force of nature.

"Adam?"

"I'm here!" he called, not meaning to speak, but words escaping him. "Here!" As if he were buried and panicking and reaching out for any semblance of rescue.

6

Celeste recognized his expression; it was embedded in her memory. The shell-shocked eyes. The mouth a crumpled line. His jaw a slump of despair. The same face Adam wore when he confessed to her last time, and the time before that, and the time before that.

Adam had already taken to one knee, preparing to beg forgiveness. The television flickered behind him, talking heads blabbering away in front of a basketball court. Broken pieces of plasterboard lay scattered on the floor.

She should have the right words, she'd been through this before—the accusations, the desperate denials, the subsequent confession and pleading—yet she didn't know what to say. *Aha! Caught you!* Or, *I knew it!* Or, better yet, she should berate herself for having hoped for a different outcome from Adam.

"Celeste." Voice faltering. "Let me explain . . ." Adam rose to his feet. His mouth moved before the words came out, a sound track out of synch with an actor, each word punctuated by a rapid breath. "Please. There was. A mistake."

He stepped closer. She stepped back into the hallway. His physical presence loomed over her. She stared at his raw, red knuckles, the ripped skin. Fists closing and opening, fingers curled and splayed. Fear began to churn inside her: She knew what those hands could do.

Turn around and leave. Get out of here.

Adam cleared his throat. "I—I . . . Something went wrong in the game. He got hurt. Kevin got hurt."

He wasn't making sense. "I'm leaving," she said. She turned for the door but he was quick, stepping around and blocking her passage.

He began to babble. "We have this business, one of the players for Taconic is working for us, it isn't gambling, it's a business, but he got hurt and . . ."

Now she was fighting tears. Do not. Do not cry in front of Adam. Not over this. Not again.

"I did it for you," he said. "To give you a better life, to get us out of this mess."

"Oh, please! What—you thought you'd win a bet and come back to me with money? Is that how you got the money you gave me last time? You were lying then, too. Don't you get it? I don't care about the money. What was the point of the rehab center? Didn't you learn anything?"

"Celeste, please believe me. This was—"

"It's your son's birthday, for God's sake! He's out there in the car wondering why his father didn't come to pick him up. Destroy your life if you want to, but not his, not ours. Not anymore. I won't let you hurt us more than you already have."

Her breaths were short and shallow in time with her chattering pulse. Do not. Do not cry in front of Adam.

"No, you don't understand—"

"I thought you were getting better," she said. "I was stupid enough to think you were."

"I'm trying, I am. I'm not a bad person. I'm a sick person, I'm trying to get healthy."

"I'm done with you, Adam. I'm seeing a lawyer and getting a divorce. That's what I should have done from the beginning."

Adam was shaking his head back and forth. "No, Celeste. You can't."

"I'm done," she repeated. She slid past him and pushed

open the door. He followed and grabbed her coat from behind and horse-collared her. She yelled out and braced her legs, but he yanked her back. She struck her knee on the steel frame of the door and pain shot up her leg. He spun her around and pinned her against the open door, pressing her against the glass.

She looked into his burning eyes. "Leave me alone!" She tried to shake loose. His grip held. He twisted her collar in his fist.

"You have to listen to me—"

"Stop. You're choking me—let go." She struggled but was no match for his strength.

Another wrench of his wrist and her collar constricted. Her windpipe pressed against the back of her throat, cutting off air. She grabbed at his hands, his wrists thick and hard as baseball bats.

"Listen to me, you have to listen!" Adam shouted, a spray of spit hitting her face.

Adam, please. It's me, Celeste. We have a son. We loved each other once. Not that she said those words, she couldn't speak with Adam tightening her collar against her throat. A switch had flipped in him that he could not turn off and she could not reach, and a violent, uncontrollable current flowed through him and into her and he pressed harder and her head felt like it was swelling, her eyes bulging, focus blurring. No air. No breath. Tighter.

Oh my God he's strangling me he's going to kill me. Adam please stop.

Then a voice from outside: "Hey! Hey, what's going on! Let go of her!"

Nothing for a few beats, then Adam's grip relented. Celeste coughed and gulped the air. She sucked in deep, panting breaths.

A man approached them from the parking lot. "Are you okay?" he called.

Her neck throbbed and her throat stung when she tried to swallow. She looked out the door, beyond the man who had called out, and located Spencer in the car. He sat there as she'd left him behind the wheel, facing away from them, paying no attention to what was happening in the doorway to the building.

The man stopped several paces from the door, beyond arm's reach. He stood with his legs spread, arms angled, as if ready to run in any direction, toward them to help or away to escape.

No one moved. Adam still held her collar, the fabric sagging now. His hot breath blew in her face. The pupils of his eyes had become dark, lifeless points.

"Please, sir, step away from her."

"This isn't your business," Adam said. But he let go of Celeste's coat and moved to face this guy, who took a step back in response and held one hand out in front of him, as if telling Adam to slow down or stop.

"Are either of you with the boy in that car?" he said.

"He's my son," Celeste said.

"He's my son, too!" Adam shouted. He took one more stride toward the guy; they stood a few feet apart. "I told you this is none of your business. Get the fuck out of here!"

"Please, stay calm. I work here. My name is Jake." He looked from one to the other. "Which one of you works here?"

When Adam didn't answer, Celeste did. "Adam does," she said.

"I thought you looked familiar," Jake said to Adam. "Now, please . . . let's be calm and reasonable. Whatever your trouble is, this isn't the place for it."

Adam said, his voice settled now: "Everything's fine. It's a personal matter and we just had a misunderstanding."

Jake addressed Celeste. "Is that right? Are you okay?"

She considered her options. Her throat ached and she was embarrassed at having a witness to this ugly scene, but it could have gotten a lot worse if this Jake hadn't shown up. She was being given an out and decided to take it.

"I just want to leave," Celeste said. "My son is waiting."

"Do you want me to call the police?" Jake said, speaking to her eyes, ignoring Adam. She saw concern in his expression, but also something else: fear or uncertainty. Of Adam. Or this situation. He didn't want to be here any more than she did, probably regretted getting involved.

She wanted this to be over. "No, I just want to go home."

"I'll walk you to your car," Jake offered.

"*Fuck you*, you will," Adam said. "You want to look at someone, you look at me."

"Please, I'm only trying to help," Jake said.

"You don't need to walk me," Celeste said. She slipped away from Adam and past Jake, trying to thank him with a glance, meeting his eyes to telegraph her gratitude, then making her way across the lot to the car. She turned around once to see if either of them was following her, but Adam had already gone back into the building, and the one named Jake stood on the walkway watching her.

She hadn't gotten out her keys to unlock the door, so she knocked on the window and Spencer jerked his head up, startled, then let her in. He moved over to the passenger seat.

"Sit in back, it's safer," Celeste said, digging in her purse for her keys.

"I'm ten years old tomorrow."

"I said in back!"

Spencer scrambled over the parking brake into the rear seat.

"I'm sorry, honey, I shouldn't have yelled at you."

"Mom, are you crying?"

"Buckle your seat belt, okay?"

"Where's Dad?"

"There isn't going to be any sleepover." She started the car and began to drive. She couldn't swallow and couldn't turn her neck without pain. She felt battered, violated. Completely defeated. Her phone rang in her purse and she ignored the sound. She found her son's eyes in the rearview mirror.

Spencer looked away from her and out his window. "He's doing it again," he said.

7

Sara answered her hotel room door dressed in jeans and a red sweater, tennis shoes on her feet, her hair free from its usual clip or ponytail. Her casual style was in contrast to her workday appearance, when she erred on the conservative side and wore a dark suit or blouse and pants. Nothing form-fitting. Nothing that could be interpreted as sexy or that accentuated her ethnicity.

Jake entered the room, his gait slow and stiff. He glanced at her roller suitcase sitting on the center of the bed, noticed the $5 bill and the room keycard on the counter by the sink.

"You packed already?"

"I wasn't sure if you were coming," she said.

He tried to kiss her, but she turned her head and his lips landed on the side of her face. "What's the matter? The contract is signed, we're a team—GeoPol and the NYPD. It's time to celebrate."

There was something wrong with her posture; she appeared shorter and sunken, shoulders curved downward, as if someone had delivered bad news.

"I'm not sure I want to celebrate my part in this," she said. "I . . . What happened to you?" She noticed the rip in Jake's pants. A flap of limp, torn fabric, a bloodstain showing through. Another tear in his jacket near the elbow.

"Jake, you're hurt. What happened?"

"I fell in the parking lot at work."

"Fell," she repeated. "How bad is it?"

He removed his jacket and inched up his shirtsleeve, peeling the material back from his wound. He spread the rip in his pants to make the hole wider. The elbow was worse than the knee, raw and sticky, the flesh stripped and the abrasion studded with gravel specks.

Sara wet a washcloth to clean his wounds. Jake told her about the couple by the back door at GeoPol. What had first gotten his attention was a car parked a few rows away from his with its inside light on and a boy sitting behind the wheel. The child appeared to be talking to someone, but Jake didn't see anyone else in the car. He wasn't sure if he should approach. He didn't want to frighten the child, but why was this kid on his own behind the wheel of a parked car? Where were his parents? Before he could decide what to do, he heard the shipping door open and slam against the outside wall. Two people were locked in a struggle.

The man had pinned the woman against the door and it looked like his hands were around her throat. Jake called out for him to step back. He hurried toward them and called again.

After a few tense minutes, he managed to talk the guy down. The woman mentioned his name—Adam; he worked at Geo-Pol, although Jake didn't know him. He warned Jake to mind his own business, but Jake stood his ground and waited while the woman walked to her car and Adam went back inside the building. Jake remained outside the door for a moment, collecting his composure, waiting for the adrenaline to drain, his pulse to settle. He experienced a sense of triumph and power, the way he imagined a soldier must feel after acting heroically in combat, or a cop after a gunfight—self-assured and courageous, but also queasy and shaky, knowing things could have gone the other way.

He started back across the lot. The door opened again and Adam bolted out at a full run, angling away from Jake, in his car before Jake reached his. He started his engine and gunned toward Jake, tires yelping, and Jake dove to the side to avoid getting struck. He landed on the asphalt with arms outstretched to protect his face and head; his elbow skidded along the blacktop, knee slapped and dragged behind, his clothing ripped and skin burned.

"These are nasty scrapes," Sara said. They sat facing each other in two chairs, his leg up on her lap. She dabbed at his knee with the washcloth.

"I might have misread the situation," Jake said. "Maybe they were just having the kind of lovers' argument people have every day and I butted in."

"Not if he was physically harming her—that's not the everyday spat."

He made the decision to get involved before he was close enough to read the woman's expression. As he approached, he noticed she was slight in stature compared to the man who had hold of her. He was a big, broad-shouldered type. And very upset. When Jake did get a look at the woman, she was terrified and trembling, her face pale and eyes wet and glassy.

Jake couldn't say he rescued her; he wasn't 100 percent sure the guy was choking her. But he did intervene and enable her to get away.

"You should talk to the police," Sara said. "Identify the employee and have him picked up."

"I am talking to the police."

"The Brookfield Police," she added. She finished with Jake's knee and rinsed the washcloth in the sink, came back to clean his elbow.

"I asked her if she wanted me to call the police—she said no."

"What about him?"

"I'm pretty sure he didn't want me to, either."

"I meant are you just going to let him get away with this? He attacked her."

"If I call the police, then I have to go back to the office and look through personnel files to find out who this Adam is and where he lives. I'll have to give a statement. It will take hours. I want to be with you tonight."

He examined the wounds Sara had cleaned. He'd left a lot of skin on the pavement.

"You can file a complaint tomorrow," she said. "He tried to run you down—that's a felony assault."

The more Jake thought about it, if anything, he panicked and dove. The approaching car had been on a different trajectory and would not have hit him. That guy Adam might not have even noticed him and was simply driving fast through the lot, maybe a little too close to Jake.

"I'm pretty sure the whole thing is over," Jake said. At least it was over for him. He'd played the Good Samaritan and now was done.

"The domestic assault needs to be reported," Sara said.

"Shouldn't she be the one to call it in if she wants to press charges?"

Sara answered by reciting statistics, counting off the fingers of her right hand: "More than half of all violent crime goes unreported or undiscovered. Of the violent crimes that *are* reported, less than half are cleared. Seventy-five percent of domestic assaults by intimates are never reported by the victim because the victim is afraid."

"We're not analyzing crime stats here."

"Don't add to those numbers, Jake," Sara said. "Choking is a violent crime. So is assault with a motor vehicle. There should be an official record of this incident, that's the business we're in: reporting, tracking, analyzing, and solving crime. But it all starts with the reporting. We can't reduce crime rates if we don't know about the crime."

"And this one incident is going to make a difference."

"You of all people shouldn't be saying this. What if everyone took that attitude?"

He wished she would drop the subject. "Please, can we let it go? I don't need to be any more involved."

Sara's face tightened and the corners of her mouth curled down. A vein pulsed on her temple.

"What did I say?" Jake asked.

She spoke without looking at him. "You don't want to be involved any further," she said. "Not to any point of inconvenience."

"I stepped in and broke up the argument. I've got this to show for it." He held up his elbow, which had begun to throb with a dull, drumming pain.

"Keep your distance. Show you care, but not too much. That's you, Jake."

"Sara, why are you saying this? Tell me what happened. I came over here to celebrate the contract with you and now you're attacking me."

"I should have seen this coming," she said. "I did, actually, I just didn't want to do anything about it." She stared at him, her expression narrow and hard.

They'd met three months ago on the second day of the Law-Tech conference in Washington. Jake had flown the shuttle from LaGuardia to give a keynote presentation at lunch. He spoke about trends in crime analysis and made a veiled pitch for GeoPol's crime-mapping software and database-integration capabilities. After his presentation, he visited the trade show floor. He walked past vendors exhibiting products for video surveillance, alarm management, GPS tracking, citizen crime reporting, computer-aided dispatch, and dozens of others. He approached the GeoPol booth, situated in a high-traffic location near the coffee stands and main door to the exhibition hall.

The marketing staff working the booth had trouble keeping up with the number of visitors. Jake stayed to help out for a few minutes. Greeted prospects. Gave the company pitch. A woman stood off to one side of the exhibit, watching a screen that displayed a self-running presentation highlighting GeoPol's software. She wore her black hair tied into a ponytail ending at her shoulder blades. Her skin was the color of wet sand and flawless except for a mole the size of a pencil eraser in the center of her left cheek. Her eyes were dark, her face constructed from a series of angles. She stood straight with her hands clasped behind her back, holding the handles of her tote bag.

Jake approached and read her name and organization imprinted on the badge hanging from the lanyard around her neck: the New York Police Department.

"Hi—Sara Montez? Hi, I'm Jake Atwood."

"Nice to meet you. I heard your presentation at lunch, so I thought I'd stop by and see what GeoPol has."

"The NYPD is looking for crime-analysis software? Aren't you pioneers in that area?"

"We've been using crime maps for years," she said. "But we like to stay on top of the market and see what's new out there. These conferences are good for that."

"And for collecting goodies." He gestured to her bag, which was full of candies and stress balls and pens and water bottles and other branded giveaways from vendors.

She shrugged and smiled guiltily, like a kid caught with her hand in the cookie jar. "I like free stuff."

She told him she was part of a team in the CompStat Division that used computer statistics and analytics to help reduce crime rates. She was currently engaged in a search for a vendor to integrate new databases into their crime-analysis and statistical applications. Their goal was to access crime data from outlying communities and suburbs because an increasing amount of crime taking place in the city had connections to adjacent towns. Some of the headquarters for organized crime, even terrorist cells, were now being set up outside the city within commuting distance. Or striking distance, in the case of terrorists.

The NYPD was soliciting bids from Oracle, Unisys, IBM—the usual behemoths. "It's a big project," Sara said. "We need a company with a dedicated team and expert technical resources."

"GeoPol has a talented technical team. We've completed projects for dozens of law enforcement agencies."

"Why haven't I heard of GeoPol before?"

"You're hearing about us now. You said that's why you come to these conferences—to stay on top of the market. We've grown 50 percent in the past year."

She studied him a moment before responding, her eyes quickly scanning up and down his length. "You must be a well-kept secret."

He felt a shift inside him, a stirring of possibility. Other than shaking hands, he hadn't touched another person in months, an exceptionally long drought. Things had gotten to the point where his radar beeped every time he got near an attractive woman. That radar sounded now, prompting him to take a chance and invite Sara for a drink.

At Lola's on Capitol Hill, Jake stayed away from business talk and asked Sara about herself. She'd worked for the NYPD for almost twenty years, she said. Two years ago, as part of a regular rotation to keep detectives from burning out, she moved from homicide to investigative systems and into the CompStat division.

"Isn't that a little dull compared to homicide?"

"I liked homicide, but I was fried. I was angry," she said. It wasn't so much seeing the victims that bothered her—she'd become immune to that. By the time she arrived on scene she wasn't dealing with a person, simply a collection of evidence and clues, the person gone, the remains an empty shell. The investigation held her interest, though, assembling the pieces, hunting the killer, but the majority of homicides were not complicated. Ninety percent of the time you knew who committed the crime right from the start, and it was just a matter of gathering evidence, locating the suspect, and making the arrest. A small business owner siphoning money discovered facedown in a dark alley? Have a visit with his partner. A drug dealer with a hole in his head? Check the rival gang rolls. A woman in bed with her throat sliced? Let's chat with her boyfriend. A baby dumped in a trash bin? Find the mom. Half the time the killers wanted to confess, especially the one-offs, those who never would have committed such a crime except for suffering an insane moment of stupidity or misplaced passion.

There were exceptions, of course, the other 10 percent of cases, whose investigations led into complicated mazes or down dark, dead-end tunnels, the complexity of the crime more often a product of chance and circumstance than any brilliant criminal maneuvering. These cases required diligence. The unsolved files came from this group and there were never enough resources to conduct lengthy investigations, unless the victim was well-known or well-connected. All homicide detectives had their names attached to a certain number of unsolved files, even Sara. One case in particular still haunted her because she knew who committed the crime but evidence had been mishandled and she wasn't able to close the case before transferring to CompStat.

Sara Montez was sick of being around killers. What upset her more than seeing the victims was seeing the suspect when she made an arrest. A victim met a fate we all eventually meet, although often in a painful, violent way, and she would do her best to avenge that death and deliver justice. But killers made decisions. Not all of us had to become murderers, and those of us who chose to were the lowest form of humanity. There were hundreds of types of crimes and the one that every culture deemed the worst was murder. Well, maybe cannibalism, but murder usually preceded it.

The emotional toll of Sara's profession both disturbed and fascinated Jake. While she spoke, her left hand was on the table, halfway to him, palm down, her fingers undulating up and down as if lifted and settled by a gentle, intermittent breeze. He watched her moving fingers; they were short and slender, and he sensed she was inviting him to touch her and at one point he moved his hand toward hers, then a few minutes later he covered her hand. Her fingers became still, as if his touch had calmed her. She looked down at what he was doing, then they exchanged a look and she gave him a tiny smile.

Later, he walked her back to her hotel. Outside her room, he stood behind her while she searched her purse for the key-card, but her hands, which he had soothed earlier, now trembled. He put his arms around her waist and she turned and then they were kissing. He'd hoped from the moment he saw her in GeoPol's booth that they'd end up like this. He stroked his hand along her spine, slipped his fingers inside her waist-band. She made a sound while locked onto his lips.

Someone passed them in the hallway and said, "Hi, detective."

Jake slid his glance in that direction and watched the back of a man heading toward the elevators. Sara kept her eyes closed and pressed into him. She hadn't heard or didn't care.

He missed his flight that evening. They spent the night together, getting out of bed only to use the bathroom or answer the room service call. The next morning she drove him back from DC to LaGuardia in her unmarked Crown Victoria and left him in the short-term lot next to his Audi. Before he got out of the car, she said, "I'm married."

No wedding ring—it had been one of the first things he'd

checked. He'd wondered if she might be hiding something from him, but figured detectives just make you feel that way: They knew stuff you didn't, they had information they wouldn't divulge. Jake had worked with other detectives and experienced the same feeling, although he hadn't slept with any of them.

"I'm just saying, that's all," Sara said. "Because you should know."

"You're telling me now?"

"I understand if you don't want to see me again."

Over the next month he met her for afternoons in New York at a hotel. He toured the NYPD's real-time crime center. She came to Brookfield to visit GeoPol's offices and booked a room at the Hilton Garden Inn. They became close but not too close. They knew each other's sexual preferences but not family histories. Jake knew about the birthmark on her right breast that looked a lot like the mole on her cheek. Sara knew he lived alone in a sublet house on a tributary of the Hudson River but didn't know the frequency with which he had hopped relationships and jobs. He knew her husband was a criminal justice professor at Pace University and had married his favorite student eighteen years ago. Jake wouldn't have called theirs an intense, torrid affair and it wasn't love and he wouldn't have fought to keep her, knowing she belonged to another man, but their relationship was sexual and satisfying without excessive demands, and he enjoyed Sara's company and analytical mind.

One night when they were in bed in her hotel room in Brookfield—she wouldn't go to his house, had never seen it—they were holding hands after making love and she asked if he was sleeping with her only in hopes of getting the NYPD contract for database integration.

"What if I said yes?"

She let go of his hand. "I'd say you were dumb to admit it, and I was naive to allow it. But I wouldn't blame you for being opportunistic."

"The answer is absolutely not," Jake said.

"But GeoPol is submitting a bid, aren't you? The deadline is the end of the month. I guess we'll find out after that why you're seeing me."

"Because you provide me with comfort in a dark world where I'm alone and growing older."

She started to laugh at his response, then stopped and blushed when she understood he was not jesting. She sat up and her normally inscrutable face wore an expression of alarm. "I can't leave my husband for you."

"I know. I'm not asking you to."

"But if you did ask, I'd have to say no. I love Connie, and I shouldn't be here with you."

Then, instead of coming to her senses and rising from the bed and breaking off their affair, she snuggled close and whispered in his ear. It was a dollar amount: the NYPD's budget for the project. This was a government contract and would automatically be awarded to the lowest bidder who could meet the project requirements. The next day, she e-mailed him a copy of an internal document outlining project budgets, approval processes, preferred systems architecture, and security protocols.

Sara tossed the soiled washcloths in the sink, then washed and dried her hands and slipped her coat off its hanger in the closet.

"I don't know what I expected," she said. "I'm wrong for cheating on my husband, wrong for giving you classified information about the contract. I'm risking my marriage, my job—everything—and you don't want to be *too involved.*"

He remained in the chair, stunned by her ambush. "Sara, we're talking about an unrelated incident. This argument I broke up—this couple at GeoPol—I don't see how that has anything to do with us."

"Now that GeoPol has the contract, you're ready to let me go."

"I'm not letting you go. I came here to spend the night with you. I thought we'd be opening champagne."

"How long were you going to wait? Were we going to have a talk tonight? See each other a few more times until the project goes live? Or was your plan to wait for me to break it off? That's it, isn't it? String it along. You were going to wait for me to end it."

He didn't know how to handle her, what she expected or wanted. "I thought you were okay with what we have. You said you didn't want more."

"And what about you, Jake. What do you want?"

"I'm happy we can see each other when we do. I don't expect anything else."

"Happy," she said. "I get winked at by Jake Atwood and the next thing you know I'm staking my entire career on him and his little company."

"Sara, come on. Winked at? We slept together before you mentioned anything about pricing or system requirements. And you brought up the subject first, not me."

She laughed, and he hoped her dark mood had passed, that she'd been joking or teasing him in some cruel, ironic way all along. But it hadn't been that kind of laugh.

"You're not expected back until tomorrow, right?" he said.

"Let's get some dinner and then we'll come back. Or we'll order in. You'll feel better."

Sara took a moment to consider his offer. There was that vein in her temple again. Then she put her coat on. "I know you don't love me," she said. "You've never once said that to me. You never talk about the future, what comes next for us."

There was no next—Sara had made that clear from the beginning.

"Have you ever been in love with someone?" she said. "Have you ever cared that much for anyone where you could even *use* the word *love*?"

Now she was throwing darts and, frankly, hitting the mark. He held his hands up in surrender.

"I need to get back to the city," she said.

He didn't want her to leave. Not like this. But he recognized a breakup when he was in the midst of one. "Sara, please don't be this way. I don't want you to go."

She dropped her overnight roller to the floor. She paused and kissed him, getting half mouth, half chin.

"I'm sorry. It's just . . . I'm done, that's all."

8

Sara couldn't find a spot on the street. She drove the extra blocks to the Tenth Precinct, where she parked in one of the spaces reserved for police vehicles. She lifted her suitcase from the trunk, extended the handle, and started walking. By the time she reached the corner of Eighth Avenue, the cold night had penetrated to her core. She hunched her shoulders against the chill. At the bodega she bought a cup of coffee and two scratch-offs. She pocketed the tickets, carried the steaming cup in one hand, pulled the roller with the other—both hands occupied with her purse slung over one shoulder, the tourist with her luggage. Easy target. Couldn't help thinking that way, twenty years on the force will ingrain every nuance in you, but the likelihood was low in this neighborhood, even at this hour. The city was safer today by an order of magnitude than it had been ten years ago.

Her roller veered off the sidewalk onto a patch of frozen dirt at the base of a tree. She yanked the suitcase back in line. The closer she got to home, the more her pace slowed to a wandering stroll; maybe she wasn't the vulnerable tourist, instead the Hispanic bag lady scouting for bottles and cans.

She slowed at the corner of Twenty-first, trying to remember why she'd been in a hurry to get home. Earlier that evening she had imploded with Jake, suffering what any doctor would call a panic attack. Or a panic question: What on earth had she done to her life and why? Eighteen years of faithful marriage and twenty years of honest police work—thirty-eight combined years of integrity tossed aside for a love affair. And why? Because she thought she'd never be made love to again. Because she wanted to feel desired. Because a sultry phrase kept passing through her head, like a banner pulled by a plane: *Se dice que tiene un amante—They say she has a lover.* And what she got was a few simmering months of passion, suspense, and pretense that boiled down to a handful of stolen hours spent with each other. She enjoyed the sex, volunteered the secrets, and disregarded the consequences. She dressed in her suits and brushed her hair; sat in meetings and evaluated proposals and chose a vendor; lived with a husband who held no clue or key to the heart of the woman sleeping six inches from him in bed. She rendezvoused with Jake every chance she could, and each time was more intense and poignant than the previous one because each time was the last time. She promised herself she'd end the affair. Easy to say when physically sated after making love and crushed by guilt. Then she'd find herself back in his arms at the next opportunity.

It was Jake's comment about not wanting to get too involved that unhinged her. He was referring to the altercation he'd witnessed and defused, but his words contained a coded message for Sara: He didn't want to be too involved with her, either. And why should he? A single, professional guy biding his time with a convenient lady friend until the next one came along. She suspected serial monogamy was his modus operandi, not a crime although *serial* in front of any word almost always indicated deviance. *Serial killer. Serial rapist.* She was flattered Jake had picked her and she slipped neatly into the role of the friend with benefits: not just the sexual kind, the kind that advanced your career. And although it's true she wouldn't leave her husband, still she wanted to be asked so she would have to turn Jake down. *Serial nitwit.*

She covered the last block to her building with greater fortitude. Bumped the roller up the stone stairs and keyed herself through the outer door, advanced down the dim hallway to the rear unit. She found Connie in the second bedroom that served as his home office. He was slumped in his chair, head down and chin on his chest, and for a second she thought he was dead, just as she'd pictured him a thousand times since his heart attack last year: She would come home and discover him collapsed at his desk, or on the floor in the bathroom, or she'd wake up in the morning to a dead man sharing her sheets.

Connie was by no means overweight, although his metabolism had slowed enough that even five days a week at the gym couldn't prevent the creep to a new waist size. He ate a balanced diet, never spread butter, rarely ordered dessert. And still every molecule of fat stuck like cement to his arteries and one day he became dizzy and ill in front of his class and within moments fire consumed his chest and shoulders.

Even before the heart attack they lived different schedules. She worked days, he mostly taught evening classes; sometimes they met at restaurants for dinner but rarely kept up the ruse of a date by going home and making love or even making out on the couch. Her husband had simply drained of desire for her. And after the heart attack—well, forget it. His doctor told Connie his sexual performance could be hindered, ha-ha, and wrote him another prescription to add to his cornucopia of meds, and the few times they went that route it was like operating a sex toy attached to a man overcome not with desire but mortal fear.

They had first met at Pace, where he was a professor and she a student taking night courses during her early years on the force. She was twenty-four and he was thirteen years her senior, but now he looked twenty years older than her, mostly because she had skin as rich as caramel while his had dried like newspaper in a warm oven. No one believed she was forty-two; everyone believed he was fifty-five—or older. No kids. They'd tried for children and when nothing happened after three years they consulted a reproductive endocrinologist. Initial testing turned up no obvious clues and the next phase called for fertility-drug injections, masturbating into plastic cups, and in-vitro fertilization attempts. They endured the regimen for a year before deciding nature would take its course. Connie promised her their lives would be happy and fulfilling whether or not they had children. But since you could travel only one road at a time, Sara couldn't compare the no-children versus children life path, although most of the time she longed for the road not taken. She stared with pinched heart at babies and children. She once had a conversation with a female colleague of Connie's at a faculty holiday party who said there was nothing stronger than the love between a parent and her child; she proclaimed she would willingly, even eagerly, give up her life for her child. Imagine having that feeling—Sara craved it.

She stepped closer to Connie and realized he wasn't dead. She heard him breathing, saw his chest rise and fall. The clamp inside her loosened. He woke when she whispered his name, opening his eyes but showing no surprise.

"You're here." He sat up straighter. "I thought you were coming in tomorrow."

"We finished up. I wanted to get home for the weekend." She waited for his reaction and got none. "I wanted to see you," she added.

"Contract signed?"

"Sealed and delivered." She wondered if he missed her at all, if he noticed when she was gone. She examined the wreckage of paperwork across his desk. "Student papers?" she asked.

He taught an Intro to Criminal Justice course this semester and grumbled about classroom time taking away from his research. CJ 101? That's adjunct work. But the school was facing budget cuts and the tenured professors were asked to do more.

"Survey results," he said. "I didn't tell you about this before because I didn't want your opinion or experience to skew my approach. Do you remember that retired police captain, Ernest Powers, who came to see me last fall?"

"CO at Queens 105th, wasn't he?"

"I've been working with him the past few months. We put together a survey of retired police commanders with firsthand experience working within CompStat. I guess mandating the use of computer statistics for crime fighting is a subject cops feel strongly about. Got 153 responses—that's 40 percent, an almost unheard-of rate for any kind of survey. That alone tells you a lot."

"So far you haven't told me anything." She didn't like where this was heading.

What about this: More than half of the officers surveyed stated they were under such intense pressure to produce crime reductions that they manipulated crime statistics. When dealing with the seven major index crimes measured by CompStat, commanders or aides at crime scenes often persuaded victims not to file complaints or urged them to change their stories in ways that resulted in the downgrading of major offenses to lesser crimes. Grand-larceny felony to petit-larceny misdemeanor, for instance. Reclassifying burglary as criminal trespass.

"There was a lot of incentive to cook the books," Connie said. "These commanders sat in CompStat meetings every week and were grilled before their peers and superiors. Careers and promotions were on the line. So what do they do—start fudging the stats to make the crime rates appear lower. It's all right here."

He stopped speaking and looked at his wife. Sara remained silent. She thought of Jake, who had chosen not to report a crime, another device to help lower the crime rate, although that hadn't been his motivation.

"So you've seen it?" Connie said. "When you were in the Tenth? I've been wanting to ask you and now I can."

"It's kind of hard to downgrade a homicide to a lesser

crime," Sara said. "Bludgeoning your neighbor to death can't be classified as disturbing the peace."

"But what about the others? The city can't be as safe as the stats say."

"Even if you account for a little fudging, CompStat has been a huge success. The only reason some cops complain is they don't want to be held accountable."

"The *Times* would love this. The *Daily News* even more. Citizens have a right to know."

"You said this was for your textbook."

"It is, but leaking news like this would build prepublication excitement."

"Don't you think it might be a little uncomfortable for me if my husband the academic criminologist claims the NYPD manipulates stats to make the crime rate appear lower than it is?"

"This doesn't have anything to do with you," Connie said. "You're in systems now."

"IT oversees CompStat," Sara said. "You know how cops are. I can't risk it, everyone will think I helped you."

For all his brilliance and respected body of research and publications, Professor Conrad Fulton, PhD, could show a startling lack of common sense. You can't be the author of a research study slamming your wife's profession and her colleagues, even if it is the kind of news the public would devour or is slated to be a chapter in your new textbook.

"What am I supposed to do with this?" he said. "It's all relevant data. I have an ethical obligation to report my findings."

"Connie, I'm ten months away from retirement. If this gets out while I'm still on the force, there's going to be trouble for me." How about if word gets out she acted unethically in awarding a vendor contract? That might hurt a bit, too.

Connie hung his head like a scolded boy. Sara got out the lottery tickets she'd bought earlier, gave one to Connie. "Here, a present. If we win, let's go to Florida over your spring break."

She used her fingernail to scratch off the silver coating on hers. Loser. "Anything?" she asked.

He used the rounded end of a paper clip, then tossed the ticket aside.

"Let's go anyway," she said. "I've got vacation time coming."

"I'm counting on that week to work on the book. But you could go—if you want to get away."

She had a fleeting thought of meeting Jake on Marco Island, spending a week with him on the beach and by the pool and rubbing lotion on each other. Oh, wait, she'd ended that relationship earlier tonight.

"I want to go with you," she said.

Connie sighed, as if tired of repeatedly explaining the same concept to a dense student, which made Sara feel demeaned and inconsequential to him. She said, "Once you're dead you won't be able to spend time with me. It'll be too late."

He shot her a look, startled. "Why did you say that? I'm not going anywhere, I'm not dying," Connie said. "I don't have any greater chance of having a heart attack than anyone in the general population. My counts are all excellent. Everything is fine."

"Then kiss me, or something," she said. "Hold me. Show me."

But he didn't move. He stayed in his chair and stared at her, confusion filling his eyes, as if a stranger had commanded him in a foreign language. Then he shook his head and returned to his papers.

9

Jake paddled fifty yards from his dock around the bend to where the Vloman Creek flowed under the railroad bridge. The kayak glided through steel shadows and emerged from beneath the trusses and the Hudson River opened before him, its corrugated surface glinting in the moonlight. Above him the brightest stars shone and he picked out Orion's belt and followed the Big Dipper up to the North Star and thus exhausted his knowledge of astronomy.

He paddled toward the middle of the river, navigating by a cluster of lights a mile across on the far bank. The tide from the Atlantic flowed upstream at this hour and confronted the downstream current of the estuary. The water chopped and whirled. Sweat welled up beneath his waterproof outerwear. Every time he sank the left blade his skinned elbow whined, but the pinches became part of the stroking rhythm, tolerable enough, although it would be more tolerable to be in bed with Sara right now and expending his energy on her.

Use of the kayak and a canoe were included with the house he sublet from a banker who'd been transferred to Malaysia but retained his property for his eventual return to the States. The stained cedar house had a front porch and sloping, grassy yard that faced the Vloman and a private dock of poured concrete, now chipping at the edges and exposing the iron rebar, but still serviceable. Two bedrooms: a master and a spare. A gourmet kitchen he mostly avoided. A garage big enough for the boats and his car.

Rentals he was good at; temporary living arrangements defined him. GeoPol was his fourth career move in ten years, each job better pay, more power, working up the chain to become a COO or CEO someday. He competed with colleagues for promotions and against other companies for market share. Back and forth across the country. Seattle. Charlotte. San Francisco. New York. He owned an MBA from Northeastern University and a knack for developing business. He analyzed merger and acquisition opportunities; he uncovered customer needs in organizations and opened the door to large enterprise sales. He used the word *synergies* without laughing at himself. He spoke with poise and cadence, was an articulate and interesting presenter, always showed up prepared. He had vision, which allowed him to look at every company he worked for as if from thirty thousand feet in the air, see the entire landscape of the industry, the connections, the potential. By any measure, he was a professional success.

His personal life was a different story. Outside of a Rolodex of business contacts and a string of failed relationships, he was mostly alone in the world—a difficult concept to grasp on a planet of seven billion people. He'd been the only child of elderly parents who looked like other kids' grandparents and he was terrified from an early age that he would become an orphan. And sure enough, he did. His father died when Jake was in fifth grade, his mom during his third year of college. He skipped his graduation ceremonies because who was going to come and congratulate him? His father's brother from Montreal—or was it Quebec? With degree in hand and ambition as his motivation, he set out on his own to forge a career. He never remained in one city long enough to establish roots or permanent friendships and he lamented the lack of any foundation in his life. Here he was pushing forty and still flying solo. Jake had expected to be married by now with a family of his own, a partner to love, children to raise. Wasn't that every orphan's dream? But he'd begun to question if that dream would ever materialize. You couldn't control who you met or were attracted to. This one lived in Houston and that one didn't click and the next one was married. He experienced spells of crushing loneliness when he felt like giving up, yet women were drawn to him: They liked his eyes, his banter, his self-assurance, his availability. He was a good listener. He was attentive in bed. But he picked the wrong women and the wrong women picked him. Onward to the next relationship, and for three weeks or three months he'd wonder if those initial stirrings were the opening of his soul, the seeds of real and lasting love finally taking root; then one day he'd wake up next to a stranger and look for the door. Or she would. The concepts of love and commitment were as elusive as a desert mirage: You're dying of thirst, and there's a blurry oasis in the distance that vanishes as you approach. He feared there might be something inherently wrong with him, a design flaw in his character that made him crave a permanent and loving relationship but unable to recognize or afraid to nurture one. Of course, it didn't help to date a married woman.

He felt awful about what happened with Sara. He hadn't begun the affair in hopes of getting an inside track to business with the NYPD, yet he didn't ignore confidential information when she whispered in his ear. Favoritism and collusion and sometimes romantic liaisons were staples of business negotiations. Sara said early on she wouldn't leave her husband, but had she been waiting for Jake to prove his love and ask her anyway? He wasn't lying when he told her—too dramatically—that she provided him with comfort in a dark world. He understood this was not the same as love, but still, she'd left him too soon and now he was alone again. He should consider this a lesson learned and a chance to take a break from misguided relationships and straighten out his priorities and perhaps his character.

Jake reached the middle of the river, paddled hard upstream for fifteen minutes, then returned at a leisurely pace. His elbow throbbed and sweat trickled down his skin. He angled back toward the mouth of the Vloman, guided by the red lights dotting each end of the train trestle.

Now he had something else on his mind. He kept replaying the assault he'd broken up at GeoPol. Adam and . . . he'd never found out the woman's name. He had met her eyes for an instant and saw shame and disbelief and fear all reflected back at him. He wanted to reassure her, but couldn't with Adam cocked and pointed at him like a human weapon.

He hadn't taken Sara's advice to call the police. The woman said not to and that was Jake's preference as well. Once the police were involved, the incident became part of the department's database and public record. He didn't want his name associated with a complaint or felony, even if he was the witness and not the perp. As long as he worked for GeoPol, it would be a question he'd answer over and over again for customers, because he knew cops always dug up background on anyone they worked with.

But Jake had to do something about the incident. You can't bully people that way and not face consequences. He was an executive of the company and responsible to the organization and its employees. What Adam did he could do again—and possibly worse next time, perhaps harming others. The question was: How should Jake respond? His first impulse was to have Adam fired, but that was too retributive, too vengeful. For all Jake knew, the guy might be perfectly reasonable when he cooled down. Perhaps the woman had provoked him. Perhaps he hadn't been choking her and it just looked that way to Jake.

He should at least hear Adam's side of the story before making any decision.

On Monday when he got to the office, Jake scanned the list of employees and found out the only Adam employed by GeoPol was Adam Vanek, who worked in the production department, a place Jake rarely visited because his work was performed in the executive offices up front, on conference calls, and in meetings at the technology command centers of police departments.

He walked to the far end of the building. The GeoPol production room consisted of three rows of floor-to-ceiling racks loaded with boxes of supplies for packaging and shipping product and maintaining the building. A DVD duplicating machine sat on a table in front of the department's one office, which had a window looking out to the warehouse area. Jake saw Adam sitting behind the desk, his attention on his computer screen.

He knocked on the open door. Adam looked up and stood quickly. He met Jake's eyes and his glance dropped away.

"Adam, hi. I'm Jake Atwood, I'm the VP of business development. We sort of met the other night."

Jake offered his hand and Adam shook, his grip firm, meeting his eyes now.

"Yeah, things got a little out of hand," Adam said. "I have to apologize for that."

"As you can imagine, I'm concerned this incident took place at GeoPol, but I'm also concerned it took place at all. The woman you were with . . ."

"She's my wife." Adam rocked slightly on the balls of his feet. Jake found the movement discomfiting. It appeared that Adam was repeatedly leaning toward him, then backing away.

"Is she okay?" Jake asked.

"I discovered something very important," Adam said. "No matter what your wife says, no matter how mad she is or how much she insults you or goads you on—don't touch her. Don't raise a hand to a woman."

"Or anyone, I would think," Jake said. "Things like that can't happen at GeoPol."

"No. I mean, I know. It will never happen again, not from me."

Jake wanted to know what the argument was about, or how Adam's wife might have played the role of instigator. But he shouldn't ask personal questions. With all the workplace rules these days, he had to be careful to keep the conversation strictly professional.

"There are counseling services available through human resources, if you feel like you want to talk to someone."

Adam stopped rocking on his feet. "Yeah, that's a good idea. Maybe I should look into that. I . . . I really don't know what got into me. We had this argument, she wasn't listening to my side. But you're right, it was my fault. You can't believe how sorry I am. I never should have grabbed her like that. No excuses."

"I could have called the police," Jake said. "It looked like you were choking her."

"I appreciate that you didn't. It was enough you came along," he said. "We needed someone to separate us. Not that anything more would have happened, but . . . sometimes all it takes is a reasonable person to open your eyes."

Jake noticed a customer order on Adam's computer screen.

"So how long have you worked at GeoPol? The company's growing so fast, I don't know everyone anymore."

"Me? About four months."

"You like working in production?"

"It's okay. But sales is where I belong—I used to sell for Weir Microsystems—and I was hoping to get an interview in sales here. I guess that will never happen now."

Jake could believe Adam had worked in sales. When he was calm, he had a handsome, likable face with balanced and well-defined features, and a talent for telling you what you wanted to hear. *My fault. No excuses. Won't happen again.*

"This situation, it's pretty serious," Jake said.

"I know. But I learn from my mistakes. And, like I said, I learned a lesson from this one."

Jake was about to let the situation die. It bothered him that Adam had assaulted a woman—his wife, no less—and that the attack took place on company property. And that Adam had threatened him as well. But the entire chain of events took place in the intense heat of a wild moment, and at this point, Adam appeared genuinely contrite. There wasn't much else for Jake to do, other than report the situation to Carly Pearson in human resources, although that would lead to an investigation, possible suspension, or even termination for Adam.

He decided to give Adam the benefit of the doubt. Let the matter drop. Keep human resources out of it.

"Mr. Atwood?"

"Jake. Jake's fine."

"When I was driving out I noticed you fell in the parking lot. I should have stopped but, well, I wasn't thinking clearly. Did you get hurt?"

Jake hesitated. The corners of Adam's mouth turned up slightly—was that the hint of a smirk? Something in his tone.

Was Jake being taunted? Had Adam actually driven toward him to scare him—or had Jake overreacted and taken a dive?

"No, I'm fine. Thanks for asking." His elbow began to throb.

Later that morning, Carly Pearson dropped by Jake's office, a file folder in her hands. She'd worked as head of human resources for GeoPol since the days when the company consisted of five employees in a start-up incubator out of RPI.

"I'm looking into an incident that took place here Friday night," Carly said. "Someone damaged the employee lounge—there are three big holes in the wall. I'm talking to everyone who was here after hours. The security system recorded that you swiped your card at seven o'clock to enter the building."

After meeting with the NYPD team, Jake had walked Sara to her car so she could return to her hotel and change and then he came back to his office for another hour to catch up on e-mails and phone calls he'd missed that day while finalizing the contract.

"The timing sounds about right," he said.

"I have another employee who left around eight and claimed there was someone swearing at the television in the employee lounge."

"Adam Vanek?"

"You saw it, too?" Carly tapped the file folder in her hand on the edge of Jake's desk.

"Not the part in the lounge," Jake said. He explained about witnessing the altercation between Adam and his wife by the back door, and how he'd intervened.

"I went and talked to Adam about it this morning," he said.

"You did? Usual protocol would be for HR to handle something like this."

"I didn't mean to encroach, I just wanted to hear what he had to say. He seemed pretty embarrassed, and sorry about what happened." Although Jake wondered again if Adam had been digging at him at the end of their conversation with his comment about Jake falling in the parking lot.

"Do you know if anyone else witnessed the fight?"

"I'd call it more an assault than a fight," Jake said. "Their son was waiting out in the car. But I don't know if he was paying attention."

Carly sighed. "How's that for modeling good behavior for children?" She had two kids of her own, in high school.

"What happens now?"

"Damage to the building, physical assault on company property," Carly said. "This is a firing offense. We're going to have to terminate Adam Vanek's employment."

Jake remembered that his own first impulse was to have Adam fired, but he'd decided to let the matter go.

"I feel sorry for his wife," Carly said. "Adam's paycheck was being garnisheed for child support. It's unlikely he'll continue making payments once the money is no longer automatically deducted from his paycheck."

"Yeah, that's a shame," Jake said. He indicated the folder in Carly's hand. "Is that Adam Vanek's personnel file? Do you mind if I take a look at it?"

"Go ahead." She placed the folder on his desk. "Can you send it back before the end of the day?"

Jake flipped through the pages of the file. Adam Joseph Vanek. Employed by GeoPol for four months, position of production associate. Previous employer Weir Microsystems, as an account executive, just as Adam had told him. But it was odd. He went from a sales position at a prestigious tech company like Weir to production associate at GeoPol, with a six-month gap between jobs. What happened in that period of time? Before Weir, stints at MicroWatch and Datatech. Graduated from Taconic State College in 1998, BS in business. Originally from Chappaqua, just down the road, land of the privileged.

He scanned a few more pages in the file until he came to what he was looking for. Emergency contact: Celeste Vanek. Different address and phone number, here in Brookfield. Hmm. They must be separated. Or divorced—although Adam had said Celeste was his wife.

Pretty name. *Celeste*. *Celestial*. A name that meant heaven.

An unexpected feeling washed over him: He shouldn't have let her just drive off that night, he should have done more for her. He had no idea what.

10

Celeste hadn't known about the bruise until Spencer pointed it out when they got home that night. "Mommy, there's a mark on your neck." She looked in the mirror: Sure enough, a red streak crossed her throat, like the tail of a comet. She tried to downplay the incident. She said Dad had been angry and *grabbed* her, even though he shouldn't have. She didn't use words like *attack* or *choke*. She tried to be honest, while still protecting Spencer. The presence of the bruise scared him; her son had never witnessed Adam physically assaulting her—Spencer only knew about the one time he'd been struck at the dinner table.

Then she made the mistake of double-checking the lock on the front door, even though she knew she'd turned it. "Is Dad coming here?" Spencer said. "Is he going to hit me, too?"

She gathered him in her arms. "No, no, honey. Everything is going to be fine. Don't worry." Spencer asked her to rest in his bed and after he fell asleep Celeste lay there replaying the incident over and over in her mind, besieged by the violence in Adam, impossibly wishing for a different result. Eventually she fell asleep, too, and didn't wake until morning.

The next day, Spencer's birthday, he didn't want to go to the Pottery Place with his friends. Celeste had to call the other moms to cancel. Then she phoned Emery, who had left three messages last night wondering where Celeste was, why she hadn't met them at the Point for drinks. By the third message, Emery sounded worried. When Celeste called back, she apologized and told Emery the sleepover for Spencer got canceled because she had a big argument with Adam and had been so upset she forgot about their plans to go out and wouldn't have had a babysitter at the last minute anyway. "What can I do to help?" Emery said. Celeste was about to decline her friend's offer, but then invited the Webers over to have birthday cake that afternoon; it would be too lonely just her and Spencer trying to celebrate.

Moments after she got off the phone with Emery, her phone chimed again and Adam's name came up on the caller ID. She was tempted to ignore him, but he would just keep trying. As soon as she answered, the apologies flew out of him. "I'm sorry, Celeste. Believe me, I'm sorry, I completely messed up. I wanted to check on you last night, but I knew you'd be too angry. Are you okay?"

"No, I'm not okay. You hurt me, you were choking me. I have a bruise on my neck."

"I wish more than anything I could take it back. I'll make it up to you, I swear. You know how much I love you."

"That's your way of showing you love me?" She wasn't letting him off the hook this time.

"I need to apologize to Spencer, too. I ruined his birthday. The cot is still set up in my room and I kept looking at it last night and it was empty. I want to come over and give Spencer his present, and my parents have something for him, too. I had to tell them Spencer had a stomachache and that's why we didn't have the sleepover."

"Why didn't you tell them what really happened?" she said. "Maybe I should."

"Celeste, please."

She hated the whiny sound of his voice right now, a tone you would never match to Adam's physical appearance.

"I meant what I said—I'm getting a divorce. I'm talking to a lawyer and you'll be hearing from me." She disconnected the call. She felt a tiny measure of payback simply for hanging up on Adam, but the victory lasted only a few short seconds. Ultimately, she was admitting defeat: She'd chosen the wrong man, her marriage was over.

She gave Spencer the present that she'd hidden in the basement—the bike he'd wanted with the shock absorber on the front fork for riding over bumps, and Spencer kissed her about ten times to say thank you and took a few turns around the block and bounced up and down the curb in front of the house until he got too cold. Then the two of them baked his birthday cake: chocolate, from a box mix with an extra egg thrown in and cream to make the recipe richer, a trick she'd learned from one of her cookbooks.

Emery and Stephen arrived with their three girls—Lindsey, Grace, and Maya—and after singing happy birthday and eating cake the kids went into Spencer's room to play, even taking little Maya along. Celeste told Emery and Stephen what happened the night before.

She showed them her neck.

Emery's mouth opened, but no words came out. A look of disbelief passed over her face.

"That fuckhead, just when I was starting to feel sorry for him," Stephen said.

"You were not," Emery said, her tone harsh and corrective.

"I meant I was missing him," Stephen said. "We used to be friends. We used to all hang out together."

"No, it's okay," Celeste said. "I know what you mean. I was starting to feel bad for him, too. Not bad, but . . . he'd been doing everything right and I thought he was getting himself back together, I didn't think he was gambling. I was so wrong."

"He was actually choking you? Did you fight back?" Emery asked.

"I tried, but he's too strong. I'm lucky someone came by and made Adam let go of me."

"Thank God that happened," Emery said.

Yes, what if Jake had not intervened? Celeste had never been so scared in her life. So physically brutalized. Honestly, Adam could have strangled her if Jake hadn't shown up. A complete stranger—and he'd risked his own safety to step in and save her. For the first time, she wondered what happened to Jake after she'd left. She'd only been thinking of herself and hadn't considered that Adam might have come back out to deal with Jake.

"I can't believe Adam did that to you," Emery said. "What kind of man would ever strike a woman?"

And then Celeste admitted to her friends what she'd never

told anyone before: Adam had grabbed her on other occasions, he'd pushed her a few times. She'd kept that information to herself because she'd been too ashamed to divulge it and had kept hoping for a turnaround from her husband. But now, this last assault—this was the tipping point, and in finally confiding to her friends Celeste felt a great weight of secrecy lift from her.

For an instant, Emery looked as if Celeste had betrayed her, then she quickly recovered and said, "Oh, Celeste. You could have told us—we're completely here for you. We'll do anything to help you and protect you."

"I know. Thank you. I told Adam I'm seeing a lawyer and getting a divorce. I'm done with him."

Emery put a hand on her shoulder. "I'm so sorry."

"I should have done it sooner. I never should have put up with him for so long."

"Really, anything we can do, just let us know," Emery said.

When the Webers got up to leave, Celeste stepped outside with them to wave good-bye. She noticed a wrapped box and two envelopes tucked under one of the porch chairs and brought them inside. The box and one envelope were addressed to Spencer. He unwrapped the box to find a computerized chess set; the envelope contained a hundred-dollar check made out to Spencer from Adam's parents. The other envelope had her name written on the front.

She waited until after Spencer had gone to bed that night before opening her envelope and reading the letter. She expected another outpouring of remorse, but the letter contained only one sentence in Adam's slanted, sharp handwriting: *This is my way of saying I'm thinking of you when we're not together.*

Really. Did he think this sentimental ploy could still work on her?

When they were first dating, Adam wrote to her almost every day, sometimes twice a day, even though they lived only twenty minutes from each other and both had cell phones and were seeing each other at least three or four nights a week. But getting a real letter delivered by the post office was old-fashioned and strummed Celeste's heartstrings: She believed in courtship and romance. Every one of Adam's letters started with that same sentence—*This is my way of saying I'm thinking of you when we're not together.* Sometimes that was the extent of his message, other times he told her where he was at that moment—in the office, at the coffee shop, waiting for a customer, at the gym—and how he wished she were there, too. He'd recall a conversation they had. He'd tell her about a dream he'd had in which she appeared. He'd write on lined paper, send art cards or postcards. Once he mailed her a cocktail napkin with a note. She rushed home from the agency every day to check the mail; sometimes she skipped going out with friends after work because she wanted to get home to find out what Adam had written to her one or two days ago, even though she'd spoken to him several times since then.

He even used a note to ask her out the first time. She was working at the Kellen Agency in the city and served as art director on the pitch to land an advertising campaign for Weir Microsystems. Her manager invited her to the client presentation because Celeste had a knack for explaining why her design concepts would be effective. She made others comfortable by listening closely and repeating back what she'd heard. She always responded positively to the ideas of others. Plus, it never hurt to have a young, attractive woman on your team when you were trying to impress a potential client—she knew that much about business.

On the other side of the table at Weir sat the vice president of marketing and his minions; they also had invited one of their account managers to provide feedback on the presentation, knowing that salespeople were on the front lines and closest to the customers. Throughout the meeting, Adam didn't say a word, yet Celeste noticed that he nodded at all the right times, particularly when she spoke about the principles behind her designs. He reminded Celeste of an attentive student. He kept his eyes on her. He sat tall in his chair. He looked great in his suit and patterned tie.

After the presentation, the Weir marketing VP asked Adam for his thoughts.

Finally, Adam spoke. "I've seen campaign pitches from other agencies," he said. "And the thing is, most of them I could take or leave. But there is something in these ads that . . . it's Celeste—right?"

She answered with a smile.

"There's something in Celeste's work that excites me more than anything I've seen," he continued. "There's nothing fancy or tricky or loud about these ideas—they simply get to the point: that choosing Weir Microsystems is choosing a winner. We have to make clear to our prospects that going with Weir is every bit as safe a bet as going with IBM—only less expensive and with greater individual customer service."

"So your interpretation of the message is that customers should feel confident when purchasing from Weir?" Celeste said.

"Exactly. You nailed it," Adam said.

The discussion moved on to timetables and budgets, and

at one point Adam slipped his business card across the table to her. On the back, he'd written, *I don't want to wait until the meeting ends to ask you out.* She immediately looked up at him. He met her eyes for a flirty instant and then turned his attention to the VP now speaking.

Although she was tempted, she declined his invitation; she was seeing someone else at the time, an artist named Julian who lived on the Lower East Side. He was moody, talented, and broke, a painter of large canvases packed with people, often crowd scenes, with one or two figures distorted and highlighted. He displayed his work in tiny galleries no one visited and was depressed over his lack of success. He smoked cigarettes, which annoyed her. He would get drunk and make love with overwrought passion and then wouldn't touch her for a week. He was beautiful and remote and she was somewhat obsessed with him. At the time, she still thought of herself as an artist, too, and tried to accept that tumultuous relationships were part of the package of artistic sensibility. But she also knew her own work was less than inspiring, and she didn't embrace the starving artist lifestyle. She had a practical side of her and when she grew weary of being poor she had taken the job at the Kellen Agency, which Julian derided her for. She admitted to him that she wanted to get married and raise a family one day, she wanted to cook for her husband and children, she wanted a nice home. He said, How depressing.

Soon she broke up with him and the next time Adam asked her out, she said yes. He was interested in her job as a graphic designer. He didn't think marriage and family were ridiculous relics of the past. He treated her with respect. He started sending her love letters and she started falling in love.

Thinking about that period of her life made her both

nostalgic and angry. She had abandoned the idea of being an artist, understanding that she didn't have the talent or temperament for it, and instead got a good start on a rewarding career; she shed a gloomy boyfriend and met a charming, romantic man; she could see a life she'd always wanted coming into focus. But now? Those days seemed so impossibly far away and gone forever, they might have been lived by someone else. Which meant she was a different person now, with a new life ahead of her, a prospect that was both exhilarating and terrifying.

Tuesday morning, Celeste chose a gray pencil-cut skirt hemmed an inch above the knee and a black turtleneck sweater. She brushed on mascara, applied a pale lipstick, and added a barrette to her hair. She wore shoes with a one-inch heel. She wanted to look professional and respectful, especially given the distraught and battered impression she must have made on Friday night.

"I have a meeting and can drop you off at school on my way," she told Spencer. "You don't need to take the bus."

"I could walk," Spencer said. "It's only half a mile."

"By yourself?"

"Lots of kids do it. I don't like the bus, it's noisy and hot. The driver has all these rules—he won't let us open the windows."

"I'll drive you today," Celeste said. "We'll talk about walking another time."

Celeste finished by patting foundation on her neck, just above the collar of her sweater, where the edge of the bruise showed. After the first day, the red streak across her throat had morphed into a purple shadow. She tried massaging apple cider vinegar on the mark and using her toothbrush to rub out the blood clots—two remedies she read about on the Internet. Neither had worked very well. Therefore, the turtleneck.

She dropped Spencer at school, then drove to GeoPol. This time she used the main entrance. Although she didn't actually have a meeting scheduled, she had a mission, one she felt compelled to fulfill to convey her gratitude.

A receptionist greeted her in the lobby. "Welcome to GeoPol. May I help you?" She was about Celeste's age, with a bright, wide face and a telephone headset that flattened the top of her hair.

"Hi, I'd like to speak to Jake. Is he here?" Celeste asked.

"Do you mean Jake Atwood?"

Celeste didn't know his last name. If necessary, she planned to described him as best as she could remember: dark hair and gray, deep-set eyes. She'd hardly had a chance to study his features that night. A few inches taller than her. Courageous under fire. Able to handle stressful situations.

"Yes, Jake Atwood," she said.

"Is he expecting you?"

"No. My name's Celeste Vanek."

The receptionist typed on her keyboard. "Oh, he is here. I thought he was in Charlotte. Let me check if he's available." She picked up the phone and said, "Celeste Vanek is here to see you." She listened for a few seconds, then turned to Celeste. "Could you sign the guest register, please? Mr. Atwood will be right out."

She signed her name and sat in one of the upholstered chairs along the wall of the lobby. While waiting, she perused the rack containing marketing literature about GeoPol's customers. She skimmed stories praising the company's crime-mapping software, which aided police departments in tracking and fighting crime. There were write-ups from Milwaukee, Memphis, Albany, Scranton, Buffalo, and one from the U.S. Citizenship and Immigration Services. The literature was printed in four colors on a pale, uncoated paper stock. Each one included a picture of a computer monitor with a map on its screen.

A door opened to the left of the reception desk and Jake appeared, approximately fitting the description she'd been prepared to give of him. He looked at her without surprise and she wondered if he recognized her. "Celeste?"

"That's me." She gave a quick, modest wave of her hand, then stood and smiled, sensing the receptionist observing her.

"Sorry to keep you waiting," he said. "We haven't formally met. I'm Jake Atwood." He returned her smile—no teeth, nothing dazzling, but a welcoming expression. He offered his hand and she shook. His palm was soft and dry. He wore tailored pants and a black V-neck sweater with a T-shirt underneath, prototype business casual, but his clothes were well-made and fit perfectly.

"Can I offer you something to drink? A coffee? Tea?"

"No, thank you. I don't want to take up much of your time."

"No, no, I'm glad you stopped by. We can sit in here," Jake said. He led her across the lobby to a small conference room with a frosted glass window. He closed the door and pulled out a chair for her. He took her coat and draped it over a chair and sat adjacent to her at the head. The room was empty except for a speakerphone in the middle of the table with wires extending down through a round hole in the tabletop. On the wall across from her hung a map showing the entire Hudson River estuary and its tributaries.

"You must be wondering why I'm here," she said, then

stopped. She hadn't rehearsed what she'd wanted to say, and sitting in this conference room now she felt as if she'd come to an interview unprepared, even though she'd simply come to say thank you.

Jake's eyes held hers, encouraging her to continue. He looked like someone about to hear good news he'd been waiting and hoping for.

"You helped me out of a difficult situation the other night, and I didn't have a chance to thank you. So that's why I'm here." She hesitated, then added the obvious: "So thank you."

Jake relaxed in his chair. "I was actually thinking I should have done more. I wanted to. I wasn't sure what happened after you left, if you were all right."

"And I didn't know if you were all right. I didn't know if Adam came back out or what happened."

"Nothing happened," Jake said. "Everything was fine."

"Well, I really appreciate what you did for me," Celeste said. "Adam was very upset. He made a mistake taking it out on me."

"It looked like he was choking you."

He hadn't asked her a question, therefore no response was required. But her heart bumped and that sense of shame washed over her, as if getting attacked by her husband had been her fault, and needing rescue a sign of her own weakness. At the same time, she felt reassured now in Jake's presence: He'd come to her aid under the worst circumstances.

"I considered calling the police afterward," Jake said. "I probably should have."

"No. I thought about it, too. It's just . . . it's a mess," she said. "This is embarrassing. Adam's got some problems he's working out, and getting the police involved would only make things worse for him."

"I spoke with Adam yesterday when I came into work. He seemed pretty sorry for what had happened, so it's unfortunate he lost his job."

"What do you mean?"

Jake made a noise, almost a groan. "I'm sorry, you must not have heard yet," he said. "I guess I'm the bearer of bad news. There was an investigation about damage to the building and what happened with you. GeoPol has pretty clear guidelines on workplace behavior. Adam was let go yesterday."

"You fired him?" There goes her child support.

He must have sensed her thoughts. "It was an HR decision," he said. "I know his wages were being garnisheed. Will you be okay? I mean, now that you won't be getting that child support?"

She waved off his question. "We'll be fine," she said, realizing she sounded defensive. "I work, too, from home—I have my own business as a graphic designer. Brochures and Web sites and logos, all kinds of projects. But . . ." She trailed off. But what? Now she would need more work, that's what. She had been getting $600 twice a month from Adam's paycheck, which did a lot to help make ends meet. She'd just have to keep calling around and finding more clients.

"So you're a graphic designer. What do you think of our marketing material?" Jake said.

He motioned to the brochure on the table. Celeste hadn't realized she'd carried one of the case studies into the room.

"It's nice," Celeste said. Then added, "Maybe a little hard to read with all that text crammed in, and photos of computers don't add much of a human element—" Shut up. At least say something positive now. "The paper is good quality. And your logo is really sharp."

The logo appeared in two typefaces and colors, the *Geo* in a green, rounded sans serif; the *Pol* in a black, traditional serif.

"And I like the company name: GeoPol," she said.

"It's a shortened combination of the words *Geography* and *Police*. But you probably already know that from Adam."

"I didn't know much about his job. We're separated . . . and getting divorced. We don't have a lot of contact with each other." She'd just told this man she didn't know about her separation and divorce; it wasn't Celeste's nature to reveal personal details to strangers. Maybe by speaking the words out loud she'd get used to the idea of her marriage ending. Yesterday she'd called an attorney—her sister had given her the name of a woman she went to college with—and Celeste had set up a meeting for later in the week.

"By the way, how's your son? That's him I saw sitting in the car, wasn't it?"

"His name's Spencer. He's doing okay. I mean as okay as you can when your father is like that. He's been through a lot, but he's a pretty resilient kid."

"I have to tell you, I was walking through the parking lot and I saw this boy sitting in the car with the light on. It was strange, the way the light from the parking lot and the dome light in the car came together it was like some kind of glowing halo around him."

"I do think of him as an angel."

"I thought he was talking to someone."

"Yes. Spencer was having a conversation with himself . . . well, he has an imaginary friend. He was talking to her." Yet another personal disclosure.

Jake's eyes widened and face brightened. Had she said something amusing?

"I was an only child and had a make-believe friend," Jake

said. "His name was Armando the Great. He was great because he was super smart and could solve any problem in the world."

"I could use a friend like that now."

"Yes, couldn't we all."

Celeste felt a tug inside her, almost as if she and Jake had moved an inch or two closer to each other. "So how old were you when you gave up your imaginary friend?" she said.

"Who said anything about giving him up?"

She smiled and waited.

"Okay, about your son's age, I guess. Seven or eight is he?"

"Spencer's ten, he just had a birthday."

"Sorry, I'm not good with kids' ages—and I didn't get a good look at him. But I hope when he's an adult he has as good memories of his friend as I do of Armando the Great. Because—" He glanced over his shoulder as if to make sure no one was eavesdropping. "—Because I still think about Armando sometimes when I have a big problem to solve."

She knew he was kidding, of course, and had made that comment to put her at ease. It worked. For the first time since the incident with Adam, she felt relaxed; the tension in her uncoiled, the acid stopped burning her stomach.

Jake started to say something, hesitated, began again. "I wanted to contact you to see if you were okay. I wasn't sure what the right thing to do is in these situations. And I wasn't sure about your husband."

"I know what you mean," Celeste said. "This is all new for me, too, and pretty chaotic." Then she thought of what Jake had just said. "But how could you contact me? You didn't know my name or who I am."

"You're listed in Adam's personnel file as his emergency contact."

"Oh, that. Every time I have contact with Adam it's like an

emergency." She meant to sound lighthearted, in keeping with Jake's comment about Armando the Great, and Jake did smile at her remark, but then his face turned serious. His eyebrows narrowed and lines etched his forehead.

"Can I ask—why did he attack you like that?"

After what Jake had done for her, she decided he had a right to know. He didn't seem like the voyeur type, asking only because he wanted to feast on the lurid details. And she'd already shown a willingness to open up to him.

"Adam has a big problem with gambling. For a while he seemed to be getting past it, but that's not the case now. And it's not just gambling, it's . . . well, you saw what he did to me. I think he lost a bunch of money on a basketball game that night. He freaked out and that's when—" She stopped.

"Sorry," he said. "I didn't mean to pry. This must be hard for you to talk about."

"No, I don't mind telling you. It actually helps to talk about it. That night wasn't the first time Adam has turned violent, although it's never been anything as bad as that. He's never tried to choke me before."

"I should have called the police."

"No, it's okay. Really." She felt hot suddenly. "I should get going. I've taken up enough of your time, and I just wanted to say thank you."

"Knowing you're okay makes my day a lot better. I mean that." He reached for his wallet and handed her a business card. She glanced at it: *Vice President, Business Development.*

"We don't know each other very well, but if you need any help—anything, you can call me," Jake said. "I'm sure you have plenty of people you can count on, but I'll throw myself into the mix anyway. I really hate what happened to you. There's no excuse for it."

"That's nice of you," she said, choosing a neutral response. She put his card in her purse and lifted her coat from the back of the chair. "You've already done a lot. You put yourself at risk."

"I was just a helpful bystander. You, on the other hand—you seem to have a challenge on your hands."

"Maybe you can get Armando the Great to help me," she said. "Do you ever lend him out?"

"For you, definitely. Call anytime."

When she stood he touched a hand on her back to guide her out the door.

PART 2

No Strings Attached

11

Igneous. Sedimentary. Metamorphic. The three kinds of rocks. We learned that today in school. I can tell you all about rocks now.

"What?" Josh Hogan said.

Spencer usually sat next to his friend Peter Beller on the bus, but Peter was absent today. Sometimes he sat next to Rachel Albright, but she was sitting with Maria O'Connor and the only seat Spencer could find was halfway down the bus, next to Josh, who was not his friend.

"What'd you say?"

"Nothing."

"Quit mumbling."

Igneous rocks are formed by magma cooling. Granite is an example of an igneous rock. Granite is often used as a building material. Obsidian is an igneous rock.

"Vanek's talking to himself," Josh said.

Two kids seated in the row in front of him turned around. Jon Rellis and Sam Marino. "What's he saying?"

"Hey, Spence, you okay?"

Had he said something out loud? He rubbed the steam off the window and looked out. The air on the bus was hot and wet. Three more stops, then his block.

Sedimentary rocks are formed by layers of the earth's material. Shale and limestone are sedimentary rocks.

"Are you a wacko?" Josh said. "I don't want to be sitting next to a wacko."

"He was talking to himself again."

"I bet you were," Sam said, leaning over the back of his seat. "Wanna bet, huh? Wanna bet?"

"No."

"Who are you talking to? Are you talkin' to me? Are you talkin' to me?"

The bus stopped. Three kids got off. It didn't get any quieter. Thirty kids talking. Heat turned up. No taking off your coat, the bus driver said it was against the rules. No opening windows. Two more stops.

Metamorphic. That's the third kind of rock. Metamorphic rocks are rocks that have changed due to heat and pressure. Marble and slate. Those are two examples of metamorphic rock. Morph *means change.*

"No, look. He's talking to himself."

"Spencer. Hey, Spence," Jon said.

Someone punched his arm. He looked up. Kids all around, forming a posse, staring at him. "What?"

"You're talking to yourself."

"No, I wasn't. I was talking to—"

"Wanna bet, wanna bet? I heard your dad likes to bet. I heard he lost all his money betting."

"Leave him alone."

"Yeah, leave him alone, you might lose a bet."

He wished Peter was here today. The teacher announced that Peter had the flu. He could be out all week. He wished Rachel had saved him a seat.

His other two friends rode a different bus, the one that went to Cider Mill. He wished he still lived there, but Mommy said that's never going to happen again.

Never going to happen again. Dad will never get better.

"Hey, who were you talking to?" Another punch, this time on his shoulder.

"Cut it out."

"In your seats back there," the bus driver shouted. "Face forward."

Everyone settled, until the bus started moving again. Then Josh elbowed him in the ribs. Then Sam Marino swung around from the seat in front. "Wanna bet, wanna bet?"

"Shut up."

"Bet you can't make me? How much you wanna bet? Maybe your daddy wants to bet me?"

Spencer punched him in the face. There wasn't much room to swing, but he squeezed his fist tight and landed his knuckles on Marino's mouth, splitting the lip against the teeth. Right away his mouth began to bleed and Sam cried out and dove over the seat into Spencer's lap, trying to wrestle and punch but mostly squirming on top of him while Spencer swung again. Josh, in the next seat, stood and yelled, "Fight! Fight!"

The bus came to a halt. The driver marched down the aisle.

12

Adam arrived ten minutes late to the Winner's Circle meeting in the basement room below Holy Trinity Church. The room was outfitted with a long conference table and a row of high casement windows looking out on the lower branches of evergreen shrubs. Adam tossed his dollar bill in the wicker donation basket, took a folding chair from a stack leaning against the wall, and found a spot next to Betty, who was a fixture at every meeting Adam attended. She possessed the physical presence of a half-inflated inner tube and next to her on the floor stood her oxygen tank on wheels with two transparent hoses snaking up underneath her sweater, across her cheeks, coming together in a double-nostril insert. The tank hissed like a bicycle pump every time Betty drew a breath.

She smiled and nodded at Adam, whispered, "How you doin'?"

Not good.

Adam counted fourteen people at the table, a big crowd today. The New York Mega Millions drawing had been yesterday and the pot up to $172 million, an irresistible siren call for a number of gamblers here today, who may have gone a month or two, or even six months, without placing a bet, but had succumbed to the frenzy of last-minute lottery ticket buying, the wild hope, the anxious thrill.

Someone has to win—it could be you.

Hey, you never know.

You can't win it if you're not in it.

Perfectly tuned New York State Lottery marketing slogans, developed and tested against focus groups, designed to capture every spare dollar in any chump's pocket.

Now the gamblers were back at GA, every one of them a loser. Plus the NFL playoffs had started and the Super Bowl was coming up. March Madness to follow. Might as well have Eve offering the apple.

Adam recognized the guy across the table who was speaking. His name was Carl. Today's topic, written on a chalkboard, was the dream world of the gambler. Carl was saying he once believed he had a surefire system that would lead to riches and enable him to buy a new car and a mink coat for his girlfriend and they would have a yacht and sail the Caribbean.

Yup, that qualified as a gambler's dream world.

Carl knew his dreams were just around the corner, just another bet or two away, and that's why he kept it up until he lost everything: his girlfriend, his friends, his home. He lost his job after he'd been caught embezzling money from the hardware store he managed. He borrowed from friends and family and never paid back a cent. He stole from his kids' accounts and his ex-wife had him arrested. That's when he came to Gamblers Anonymous. It hasn't always been easy, in fact it's never been easy, and over the years he's fallen down several times only to get himself back up again.

"It's easy to quit gambling," Carl said. "I've done it a hundred times."

Chuckles around the table. They all knew the tired joke.

But the urge has abated for Carl. He hasn't bet since March 27, 2005, that's almost six years ago. Yet he still came to meetings because he felt safe here, among those who understood.

The room murmured in affirmation. Thank you, Carl. Good to hear from you.

Adam hadn't gambled since the Taconic game or even felt the urge, although he did experience a dull desire to kill himself, the way you might consider shooting a crippled dog to end its misery. This was the black hole the counselors at Glendale talked about. The dark pit that pulls you down and swallows you up and will finish you off until YOU decide you've had enough. YOU ADMIT YOU ARE POWERLESS.

Yes, you are powerless all right, except when it comes to bashing your wife. You're real good at crushing someone you outweigh by eighty pounds.

Besides Betty there was one other woman at the meeting. She wasn't a gambler but attended every meeting to demonstrate her commitment and support for her husband. If Celeste had shown such loyalty to Adam, he wouldn't be here today. He wouldn't have needed to gamble again if Celeste had stood by his side. There never would have been that incident at GeoPol.

Stop it, you pathetic piece of crap. Don't blame your problems on Celeste. She's given you more chances than you deserve—and look what you did to her in return. There is one person and one person only responsible for his situation. That was the first lesson to learn for any compulsive gambler.

Betty launched into a wheezy story about how she once dreamed of hitting the lottery and having money to send her daughter to college and buy her parents a nice retirement home in Florida. And for herself—well, she didn't want much. Maybe a house by the river or on a lake. Or better doctors. Real specialists, from the big cities. With her mention of doctors, she transitioned to her emphysema, and said quitting smoking had been easier than quitting gambling. With smoking, she stopped and that was it. With gambling, she kept going back. Because of the dream. There was no dream with cigarettes. She'd lasted seven months without placing a bet but bought a ticket yesterday for the Mega Millions; now she was back at day one.

When Betty finished, the others turned to Adam sitting next to her.

He knew the drill: *Hi, I'm Adam, I'm a compulsive gambler, my last bet was January 6.*

He stopped and was about to pass and let the next person speak because his dreams had never included hitting the lottery, which most people were talking about today. Adam never played the lottery. Come on—the odds of winning the jackpot were something like 175 million to one. The probability of winning even $150 was about fifteen thousand to one. Adam preferred sports betting, where the odds were much more in his favor—and completely stacked his way on the point-shaving scheme. Until they weren't.

He decided to speak up after all.

"My dream was believing if I won a big bet I could get out of financial problems and win my family back and then I would stop," Adam said. "I thought I had a can't-lose system. I didn't even think I was gambling. I told myself it was a business investment."

A few sage grins around the room.

"What an idiot I was—I couldn't stop myself. When I lost, I got angry. Not just angry—furious. I did some things I shouldn't have. I lost control, I hurt my wife. And now I have to live with that. I can't take it back."

He fought the thickness gathering in his throat, the pooling in his eyes.

"I lost my job—again. Everything. I know winning a bet will not help me achieve my goals, it will never work that way. And my wife, she wants to divorce me, she won't see me or let me see our son. My family has given up on me." The present he'd left for Spencer, the love note for Celeste: nothing. No response.

The others nodded respectfully, but their eyes stayed down, staring at their hands or the table.

The wife of the gambler spoke up. Her voice was both sage and shrill. "Your family has to protect themselves. That's their first priority. They have to do what's necessary to make sure they're safe. It's one of the fallouts of being a gambler."

Adam began to sweat. The radiator beneath the window was spewing heat, the pipes below clanking.

She said, "I've been through it myself when Peter acted the same way." She took her husband's hand. "He hit me. He pushed me around. It took a long time for me to trust him again. He had to earn that trust."

Shut up, you bitch. Rub it in, why don't you.

"I have to work at it every day," Peter added, nodding like a bobblehead doll. "It's not easy. You can't expect the people you love to just forgive you. You have to show you deserve forgiveness. I had to earn it over and over again."

"And you need to do the same," the woman said to Adam.

"Shut the fuck up!" Adam shouted. "You think I don't know that?" He pushed back from the table and toppled his chair and stormed out of the room, took the stairs two at a time up from the basement, blasted through the doors and out into the cold.

Light angled from the south and he turned and squinted into the bright sun. He gulped at the cold air and exhaled great puffs of steam. He started to walk and passed in front of the church and continued down the sidewalk and began to calm down. Wow, he'd totally lost it in there. Not good.

The passenger door of a black Mercedes idling along the curb opened and Vincent Canto got out. He stepped up on the sidewalk directly into Adam's path. Adam stopped and met Canto's eyes, waited for what was coming next.

"Hey, AV, I wasn't sure I'd see you here," Canto said. "Now that you've moved, I don't know where you live. And it seems like your phone isn't working, you never answer."

"That game was a push, right? No one loses or wins," Adam said. "We agreed if Elevet got hurt and couldn't play, all bets were off."

"Whoa there, pal, we didn't agree to anything like that.

The line is the line, and we all ended up on the wrong side of it this time."

"We set up for a push," Adam said, his voice cracking like a teenager's.

"Twenty-five grand," Canto said. "You heard me whistle when you wanted to bet that big. I told you to go slow, I told you to ease in."

"You guaranteed this would work, that's what you kept telling me. It was an investment, we were building a business. You said it wasn't gambling."

"Who knew the kid would get hurt and Snow White would turn superstar? You think you're the only one upset?"

Adam looked back at Canto's car, still idling at the curb. Behind the wheel sat Canto's favorite goon, Wally, a former NFL lineman with a mashed knee and a neck wider than his head.

Canto stepped closer to Adam, inflated his concave chest like a blowfish trying to appear menacing. He glanced back at the church. "Let's take a walk."

Canto started down the block, Adam fell in beside him.

"I figured you for someone who might show up here," Canto said. "Did you know I do some of my best business outside these meetings? I get 'em going in, I get 'em coming out. I'm like the hunter who sets up his tree stand right along the deer trail. Just wait for them to come by. You ever go hunting, AV?"

"I can get the money, Vince."

"What I like is bow hunting," Canto said. "Guns are too easy, you just blast them from far away. With a bow, you've got to be up close—fifteen, twenty yards—get a good, straight shot and slice 'em through the vitals, wait for them to bleed out. That's gotta hurt, don't you think? Even an animal like a deer, it's going to feel pain."

"I said I can get the money."

"Twenty-five Gs," Canto said. "I'll give you one more week grace period, but only because we worked together on this—and that's private information, understand? I don't want anyone knowing I'm giving you extra time."

"One week? Vincent, come on, you have to work with me a little."

They reached the corner and Canto pivoted and started walking back. "AV, AV," he said. "I'd hate to see anyone get hurt. I don't like doing business that way. It wouldn't be good for either of us."

"I did all the work on Elevet for you."

"I thought I already paid you for that," Canto said. "Listen, pal, my business is all about reputation and respect, and if I let you slide, then word might get around that Vincent Canto doesn't mind if debts don't get paid. I can't operate that way."

They were back at Canto's car now. Adam could see Wally's face behind the wheel, his expression somewhere between bored and amused.

"Find me soon, because you don't want me to come searching for you again," Canto said. "Next time I'll be hunting."

He got back in his car and Wally eased away from the curb, slow as a hearse.

13

Celeste was on the phone with her sister, telling Chantal what happened with Spencer on the bus. "According to the driver,

Spencer was provoked, but they think the whole situation may have started because Spencer was talking to himself."

When Celeste had questioned Spencer, he admitted he was talking to Kathy. She could understand how he might forget and begin speaking to her out loud in front of others, but Celeste had told him before it would be like drawing a target on his back.

"And some kids were teasing him about making bets," Celeste said. "I think that's what angered him the most. They must have heard Adam has a gambling problem."

"Up until this incident on the bus, had he played with his friend in front of others?" Chantal asked. "Has he talked about her—or to her—when kids were around?"

"Not that I know of."

"My specialty is geriatrics, not children. So I'm no expert." Her sister always qualified her advice this way, but still, she was a clinical psychologist, and in Celeste's experience, Chantal's opinion was usually insightful. "If I had to venture a theory, I'd say what Spencer did was a reaction to Adam attacking you. I don't think he made a conscious decision to speak out loud, but I'd also say he doesn't want to keep his imaginary friend a secret. Which might mean he doesn't want anything hidden from him. Maybe he's afraid you aren't telling him everything, that information is being withheld, and that's adding to his anxiety."

"He knows what Adam did to me, he knows we're getting divorced. But I'm also trying to protect him and keep a positive outlook."

"Kids are much more perceptive than we give them credit for," Chantal said. "Children who are seriously ill, they almost always know it—and almost always know when their parents are trying to keep the truth from them."

"I'm being honest with him. And everything's going to be okay for Spencer, I'll make sure of that."

"I know you will," Chantal said. "I think what Spencer did on the bus is understandable if he was being taunted."

"But he hit someone," Celeste said. "Spencer's never been aggressive before." What if Adam's rage had been genetically passed down to Spencer and was only now beginning to emerge? It's possible. Look how Adam had suppressed his violent tendencies all those years.

"He has to be able to defend himself," Chantal said. "Sometimes it's the only way. It doesn't mean he's a violent kid. It doesn't mean he's like Adam." Emery had told Celeste basically the same thing: Spencer defending himself was not a sign of aggressive or violent behavior. He was just standing up to bullies.

Celeste's call waiting beeped. She looked at her display and saw the name GeoPol. The only person she knew from GeoPol now was Jake.

"Sis, I got another call coming in I need to take," Celeste said. "Thanks for your advice. I'll talk to you later."

"Moving to Burlington must be sounding a lot better these days, right?"

"I'm definitely thinking about it," Celeste said.

She switched to her other call. It wasn't Jake, and she felt a vague disappointment until a woman named Margo Roberts introduced herself as the marketing director at GeoPol and said she was looking for a freelancer to help with several design projects. She'd gotten Celeste's name from Jake Atwood. She described the work: a new design template for their case studies and two trade show graphics for their roll-up banners. If Celeste was interested, Margo would e-mail her the specifications and Celeste could submit a proposal.

"You'll need to respond right away because we're ready to start on these projects," Margo said. "We already had lined up an agency to work on them."

"Can I ask what happened with the agency?" Celeste said.

"They're still around, but we had a last-minute change in strategy, and we like to have a stable of freelancers available."

"I'm very interested. If you send me the information I'll get right back to you."

By the time she hung up the phone and turned on her computer, there was an e-mail waiting from Margo Roberts, outlining the project, attaching samples of other marketing pieces, setting the following Tuesday as the due date, and asking Celeste to submit a cost estimate.

Next Tuesday. That would give her six days, including the weekend, to come up with a winning concept. She could do it.

She found Jake's card and called his cell phone number. "I just had a call from Margo Roberts, offering me a freelance assignment," Celeste said.

"Good, I was hoping that would work out. I looked you up on the Web and saw some of your portfolio. Looks to me like you're pretty talented. Margo agreed with me."

Celeste had a simple Web site highlighting samples of her design work.

"You know this is well above and beyond the call of duty," Celeste said. "It's getting a bit one-sided, you've done so much for me."

"I told you I wanted to help you out—and this was easy for me to do."

"Can I at least do something in return? Maybe take you to lunch to say thank you?" She asked the question in innocence, almost automatically, but immediately afterward experienced a taut few seconds while waiting for Jake's answer.

"You don't have to do that," Jake said.

He was turning down her invitation. The important thing was she offered. Then Jake said, "But I think it's a great idea. When is your project due?"

"Margo said next Tuesday. I'm coming in to present my ideas."

"Let me check." There was a brief pause. "How about I meet you and we'll go out after your meeting with Margo?"

Celeste worked on the project during the day when Spencer was at school and got up early both Saturday and Sunday mornings to work before Spencer woke, and she put in another hour at night after he'd gone to bed. She didn't know anything about crime mapping, although good design principles could be applied to any content, and she enjoyed the long hours and concentration of energy. She felt productive and useful, her creative side stimulated.

She produced color printouts showing her concept for a new case study design—a light and airy page with lots of white space and a color scheme to complement the GeoPol logo. She added stock photos of police officers and vehicles, and created a faint watermark of the company logo behind the copy area. She also created two versions of roll-up banners for GeoPol's trade show booth. The one she liked better blended a map showing crime hot spots with the outline of a police badge so that the map appeared in the shape of a shield. Margo hadn't asked her to write copy, but she'd put in the headline *Crime Stops Here*.

On Tuesday, she packed up her portfolio, drove to GeoPol, and asked the receptionist for Margo Roberts. The receptionist showed her to the same conference room where she had met Jake last week. Celeste took off her coat, chose a chair, and waited. She was pleased with her work and hoped Margo would be impressed. Still, she was anxious; she needed the money, and wanted this project to lead to more assignments.

She was also nervous about her lunch date afterward with Jake. *Nervous* might not be the right word—and *date* definitely wasn't the right word—but their lunch would be a social occasion, not a business meeting, and Celeste hadn't been out socially with another man since before she met Adam eleven years ago. She didn't know what to expect, she wasn't sure she'd remember how to act. Legally, she was still married to Adam, and it was way too early to start dating (wrong word again) or even thinking about it, given her current situation. But no matter, she was going out to lunch with Jake, nervous or not, and deserved to have a good time after all the chaos recently.

The conference room door opened and a woman stepped in. She was tall and every part of her—from her smile to her hips—was wide but well-proportioned. She offered her hand to Celeste. "Hi, we haven't met in person. I'm Margo Roberts."

Forty-five minutes later, Celeste stepped out of the conference room, radiating enough positive energy to perform a levitation. Margo *loved* her design concepts. She didn't ask for any changes, just the artwork files. And she promised to call Celeste when she had another project available, and from the way Margo spoke, GeoPol was a marketing machine and plenty of projects could be coming her way. Celeste felt better and more confident than she had in months.

And now for lunch with Jake. A glass of wine was definitely in order. Jake had told her to ask the receptionist to call him when she finished with Margo. Celeste approached the front desk but before she could say anything the receptionist said, "You're Celeste Vanek, right? Jake asked me to give you a message: He can't make your meeting today, he had to see a client at the last minute. He said he'd call you."

The half-life of her positive energy spent itself. Her soaring spirit sank. But she recovered quickly, thanked the receptionist, and left the building. At least she'd done well with the design project. And Jake? He would either call her to reschedule or not. She wouldn't dwell on it. She'd have that glass of wine another time.

14

The Real Time Crime Center occupied a windowless room on the eighth floor of One Police Plaza in lower Manhattan. A theater-sized screen fronted by a half-dozen rows of computer workstations filled the space. The images on the screen changed and changed again. The room churned with activity. A dozen investigative analysts sat at their desks, talking on headsets and typing into keyboards, taking data inputs from cops in the field, conducting queries of databases, feeding information back to officers at crime scenes and traffic stops.

Sara led Jake and Ray Mellini to an open workstation in the last row. Ray was GeoPol's chief technology officer, responsible for the technical implementation of the NYPD project. He was in many ways Jake's opposite: paunchy, pale, and emotional to Jake's neat and trim reserve. Thinning blond waves of hair versus a straight dark groom. They weren't friends but as colleagues they worked well and complemented each other's skills.

Ray had spent long hours responding to the technical specifications of the NYPD proposal request, and there had been a lot of them: customizing maps with precinct and jurisdiction boundaries for outlying communities, shading boundaries to show trends in crime. Hooking up live data feeds. Integrating with the NYPD CompStat workflow to produce crime reports and statistics. Encryption and compression of data over the wide area network.

Now that the contract was signed, the heavy lifting belonged to Ray, with Jake on standby to make any financial decisions. Like if the scope of the project changed and price had to be renegotiated. Or if internal budgets needed reassignment in the event that Ray required more technical resources. The NYPD deal was the biggest in GeoPol's history, the most complicated integration of databases, the technical requirements beyond anything the company had performed in the past. They absolutely had to hit a home run.

But now this. Sara claimed there was an issue with the system and had insisted Jake and Ray get down to the city. Jake asked if they could discuss the matter by conference call. No. Could it wait until tomorrow? No. Partly he didn't want to see Sara, but mostly he'd been looking forward to meeting Celeste and regretted canceling without time to explain himself in person. He felt a responsibility to her now, and remembered an old saying that if you saved someone's life you were forever responsible for that person. Seemed a little backward—the debt remittance should flow in the other direction—and while Jake didn't believe he'd actually saved her life, he was concerned for her. Celeste seemed like a good person who'd been dealt a bad hand. He appreciated that she'd come to thank him, and he had enjoyed their brief time together. He would have sat across from her all day in that conference room if she hadn't gotten up to leave.

But GeoPol had to do NYPD's bidding and now the three of them huddled in front of a workstation near the back of the room, Sara and Ray in the two chairs in front of the monitor, Jake standing behind them. For the moment, their attention was not on their own monitor but on the large screen up front that showed the details of a robbery investigation. A number of separate windows projected onto the screen. One displayed a profile photograph of what appeared to be a Neanderthal-era man with an extended, apelike face. There was also a close-up photo of the man's neck with the words *Carpe Diem* tattooed into the skin, a file photo of a nine-millimeter handgun, and a map showing Neanderthal's known addresses and acquaintances.

"*Carpe Diem*?" Jake said. "That's a statement tattoo."

"I can't tell you how many cases we solve using the tattoo database," Sara said. "That mark must have been described by the robbery victim. The analyst conducts a query to generate a list of known felons, suspects, and anyone else in the database with that identifying characteristic." Sara called to an analyst sitting two rows ahead. "Hey, Baker, how many hits on that tattoo?"

"*Carpe Diem*? Just one," Baker said, without turning around.

"You display a mark like that while committing a crime, you might as well turn yourself in," Sara said. "*Seize the Day* becomes *Seize the Perp*. The analyst sends back the known addresses for the suspect and a patrol will track him down before he finishes counting his take."

Sara turned her attention to the computer and keyboard in front of her. Its screen was not integrated with the projection up front.

"I'll start by showing you what's working," Sara said. She

clicked the mouse and a map appeared of New York City and a fifty-mile radius beyond. She zoomed in on Manhattan: Central Park and points north. A mass of symbols began to appear, each representing a crime, each symbol colored by type: sexual offenses, hate crimes, extortion, drugs, gambling, assaults, larcenies, murders. Red squares, black crosses, green triangles, yellow circles, blue diamonds. A sprinkling of colorful confetti on the streets of the city.

A halo encircled some of the symbols. "Pick a crime, any crime," Sara said. "One with a halo—those have data associated with Brookfield."

Jake pointed to a haloed green triangle at the intersection of Ninety-fifth and Tenth.

"Grand larceny," Sara said.

She clicked the symbol and a new window popped up with a photo of the suspect, demographic information, and arrest details. The photo looked to be of a middle-aged, multiethnic man who'd been pulled out of bed—eyes half-closed, hair mussed, T-shirt collar askew—posed against a height scale and holding a plaque with a number. Name of Duane DePerro.

"That's like me on a bad morning," Ray said.

"Now we're going to see the link map, and here's where the Brookfield data comes in." Sara clicked again and the map zoomed out. A line extended from the green triangle to a point in Brookfield. She clicked on that point.

"This is live data from the Brookfield PD that you're feeding us," Sara said. "Look here, our perp DePerro has a connection to a gentleman named William F. Foster, residing at 100 Beard Avenue, Brookfield, New York."

Jake leaned over Sara's shoulder to get a better view of the screen. In doing so, he caught the familiar scent of the rosewater she wore and a memory surfaced of kissing her neck.

"Why is this information relevant?" Sara asked, then answered her own question. "An analyst now might look for a pattern of grand larcenies in the Brookfield area similar in nature to the larcenies committed by Mr. DePerro. We might determine that DePerro isn't acting alone but is part of a larger, organized crime ring operating across the entire metro region. I'd say William F. Foster is a good candidate for surveillance or a leverage name in dealing with Mr. DePerro."

Sara looked up from the screen at Jake and Ray. She said, "You never would have known this if the database from the Brookfield PD hadn't been integrated into the system, and it would be hard to see the connection so quickly without the mapping component. Well done, gentlemen."

"That's all Ray's work," Jake said. "Didn't I tell you he could make this system sing?"

"So I don't understand the problem," Ray said. "You said there was a technical issue, but it appears the system is working as advertised and we should start sending data from other police departments."

"That was the good news portion of the demonstration," Sara said. "Foster's address was accurately placed and his information retrieved. But let's see what happens when we try to map all Brookfield crime."

She opened a spreadsheet of incidents by type and location. "There were 2,160 incidents reported last year, about average for a community the size of Brookfield," she said. "Let's see them on a map."

She clicked a few times and the software chugged for a moment. A message displayed on-screen:

938 records matched
1222 records unmatched

"That's a 43 percent hit rate," Sara said. "Which means 57 percent of the addresses did not get matched to a longitude/latitude and don't show up on the map. It's not good enough to analyze patterns and connections."

Ray scanned the list of unmatched address records. "Garbage in, garbage out," Ray said. "Look at this. The addresses are incomplete, misspelled, elements in the wrong columns—you know how cops type up incidents."

"Better software would have the logic to recognize the mistakes and still match the addresses," Sara said.

"Why not let the system generate a list of address candidates," Ray suggested. "The user can choose from the list when an address isn't exactly matched. Go through the entire database once and you're done."

"Are you kidding? Twelve hundred unmatched addresses?" Sara said. "That's like a week of manpower we don't have in the budget. And what about every other database we're going to feed in? We'd have to do the same thing."

Jake had been quiet up until now. "You're right," he said. "The system should do a better job matching addresses. It's our responsibility and we'll take care of it."

Ray stiffened and was about to say something. Jake beat him to it. "Ray, can't we provide monthly updates to the address dictionary in the software? That would improve the matching."

"The contract is for twice-yearly updates," Ray said. "Not monthly refreshes."

"We'll amend the scope of work but keep the cost the same," Jake said, to both Sara and Ray. "We'll provide monthly updates if that's what it takes to get the match rates you need."

Sara didn't respond to Jake's offer. She appeared mesmerized by the screen of unmatched names and addresses from the Brookfield database.

"Sara?"

"What—sorry." She acted like he'd awakened her from a dream.

"You okay?"

"Yes. I just saw a name there I recognized."

At that moment, Sara's supervisor, Leonard Falcone, appeared in his office doorway at the end of the room. He looked over at Jake and Ray dismissively, then directed his stare to Sara. "When you have a minute, Montez," Falcone said. He closed the door behind him.

"Thanks for taking care of this," Sara said. "We want to start analyzing data from other jurisdictions next week, so let me know when the address dictionary has been updated."

"I'll call the office right now and get the ball rolling," Ray said. "Excuse me." He walked to the other side of the room, put one hand against his ear to block out background noise. Jake was left alone with Sara—other than the gang of investigative analysts sitting at their computers.

"He doesn't seem too happy," Sara said.

"Whenever there's a glitch, Ray's first reaction is defensive and negative. He's just wired that way. But then he dives in and solves the problem. Don't worry, Sara, we'll make this work."

"I've got a lot riding on this. Like my entire reputation."

Jake turned to make sure Ray was still on the phone and the other analysts in the room outside of earshot. He took the chair Ray had vacated, leaned closer to Sara, and spoke in a low voice. "I've been meaning to talk to you. I want to apologize if I misled you in any way."

Sara shook her head. "We don't need to discuss this. You don't owe me any explanations."

"No, I want to say something."

"Okay then, I do, too. I shouldn't have made that comment

about your never having loved anyone. I was out of line, I didn't mean it. And that stuff about your not asking me to leave my husband—can we forget about that?"

Jake hesitated, then blurted out his words. "I knew if we started seeing each other, then GeoPol would be in better position to get the contract." There, he'd come clean.

She hardly looked surprised by his admission. "Well, I guess your strategy worked."

"But it wasn't the reason I wanted to be with you," Jake said. "It was just something that was there."

"I don't have any regrets. We're colleagues now, but with a connection no one else has to know about. To be honest, I'm happier now than I've been in a long time."

"I hear that a lot from women after we break up."

She laughed a little. "How's your elbow?"

"What?" He cupped his elbow in his hand, then straightened and bent his arm. Ten days had passed since the incident in the parking lot. "Oh, pretty much healed. My knee, too."

"Did you end up calling the police?"

"No, the guy—Adam Vanek—he lost his job because the assault took place on company property," Jake said. "He also damaged the employee lounge by punching out the walls."

"If he only got fired, then he got off easy. He should have been arrested."

"Celeste didn't want him arrested, she wasn't going to press charges."

"Celeste?"

"The woman he attacked. His wife."

"You talked to her?"

"She came back to GeoPol to thank me for helping her out. She told me her husband is a compulsive gambler and he'd just lost a bet and took it out on her. She's had a rough time."

"You did help her out, Jake. You put yourself in a risky situation when a lot of other people would have looked the other way and kept walking."

Ray finished his call and came back. "I've got the team working on updating the address dictionary now. Give us a few days and we'll have a refresh."

"You guys are the best," Sara said.

Although Sara had insisted on the meeting with GeoPol, she hadn't looked forward to it. First, there was the technical issue to solve. Then, she didn't know how she'd react seeing Jake. Would she yearn for his attention? Would her knees weaken with desire—or remorse? No, neither. She ended up feeling strangely dispassionate, unable to reconcile that the man who stood behind her at the workstation used to reach around from behind her and kiss her neck and caress her breasts. Sara had never maintained a relationship with a former lover. Heck, she'd never had a former lover: Conrad had been her first real boyfriend.

But if she was going to have an affair, why not with a man like Jake? He was intelligent and attractive and had charmed her. He was discreet, he left no real mess to clean up. She had gotten away with her little liaison and somehow her relationship with Jake had created the faintest of sparks between her and Connie again, as if her husband had unconsciously perceived a threat and knew he needed to act.

Just this morning she'd sensed a change in Connie. She'd gotten out of the shower, as she had every other morning, wrapped a towel around herself, started combing her hair. Connie was already dressed and ready to leave for the university. He saw her standing in their bedroom and he approached her and kissed her. It wasn't a big kiss, or a romantic kiss, but he actually met her lips and delivered an impression. She could not remember the last time he'd kissed her good-bye.

He kissed her a second time and turned to leave.

She took a few seconds to find her voice. "Connie?" she called him back before he could get out the door. She pictured herself dropping the towel and Connie rushing her like a starving man, but the image dissolved as quickly as it formed. It didn't seem possible.

Instead she said, "What did you decide about the survey data of cops fudging crime stats?"

He looked disappointed by her question—maybe he, too, had imagined his wife dropping the bath towel. "I'm holding onto the information for now."

"Not calling the newspaper reporters?"

He sighed and turned out his hands, as if to show her they were empty. "I get so caught up in the research that sometimes I lose focus on the bigger picture."

"Which is?"

"It's you, Sara. And me. I was thinking . . . well, I'm due a sabbatical and could take the fall semester, right when you retire. We could take a trip. If you want to."

Had she heard him correctly? The corners of her mouth stretched and returned to place, a quick, involuntary gesture. "What about your book?" she said.

"I can get most of it done before that, and then bring it with me. You know, work a little in the mornings before the day gets going."

Why hadn't he done this five years ago? Or last year before his heart attack, when life still seemed ahead of them. Or six months ago, before she betrayed him.

"Think about it, we'll talk later," he said. His eyes ran up and down her, then settled on the spot where her towel tucked into itself just above her breasts. She was about to reach for him when he walked out the door.

After escorting Jake and Ray to the elevators, Sara returned to the computer and found the name she had recognized on the list of unmatched names and addresses. Vincent Canto. Address: Mario's, in Brookfield, New York. No street name or number. Of course it wouldn't match to a map location. This Canto had to be the same guy. In 2006, the year she worked out of a precinct in Queens, she arrested a Vincent Canto for the murder of a jockey who had just won the Belmont Stakes and was found later that night with the straps of a bridle tightened around his neck in the trailer housing the winning horse. Roberto Peña, that was the jockey. Smooth Operator was the name of the winning horse. Might have been Canto's name as well. Sara arrested him based on the testimony of a stable hand who claimed he heard a struggle and witnessed Canto exiting the trailer. The stable hand picked Canto out of a lineup, but later recanted, and soon after disappeared. The horse bridle used in the attack also disappeared from the evidence lab. The stable hand supposedly had gone back to the Dominican Republic, but there were no airline records corroborating that story. Canto got to him, she was sure, and with no other evidence or witnesses, Canto walked and the case dried up and Canto disappeared into the fabric of the thirty million people who lived within two hours of midtown Manhattan. Until now, when he resurfaced due to the work of GeoPol. She was about to query the system for more information when Falcone called her name again.

"Montez. I thought I asked to see you."

"Coming." She'd forgotten. She left the workstation and made her way to Falcone's office.

Leonard Falcone was six years younger than Sara and wore his hair shorn close to his bumpy skull. He had twice been awarded the department's medal of valor for his involvement in gun battles before he developed a case of nerves and transferred to the IT division. He was the only other cop besides her who had rotated from the street to working information systems, although he'd never moved back out and had climbed the ranks in IT over the last ten years. Having both worked the street, Sara believed they had a kinship, but there was no confusion about who was in charge, and he let her know that now when he closed his office door, turned on her, and said, "Those two monkeys from GeoPol giving you the runaround?"

"I'm not sure what you mean."

"I heard about problems with GeoPol's address matching. What's their excuse?"

That was quick. Who was the mole? Had to be one of the database administrators. She repeated what Ray had said: When cops key in reports, there are going to be a lot of clerical errors on data entry, making it hard for the software to match addresses accurately.

Falcone said nothing, as if she'd yet to answer his question or even utter a word.

"GeoPol is aware of the issue and promised a monthly update to the address dictionary, which will solve the problem," Sara said. "They're already working on it."

"You know, if anything goes wrong, the first question asked will be why we awarded such an important contract to a smaller company like GeoPol when Oracle and IBM submitted bids."

"Because their bid was the lowest," Sara reminded him. "And their proposal met all our technical requirements."

"I've had calls from both Oracle and IBM asking why their bids were turned down."

"We don't owe the losing vendors explanations. They miss out on business every day. You said yourself for every ten proposals a company submits, they get maybe two or three contracts."

"This one is different," Falcone said. "Everyone wants to do business with the NYPD. Everyone knows how much we spend. Even the big names realize the value of being associated with us—and we've given this contract to a little-known company."

"I'm confident GeoPol can do the job," Sara said. "They've done everything right so far and they're going to solve the address-matching problem."

Falcone stared at her and she held his eyes. She said a silent prayer for Jake to come through.

15

His old room had been preserved like a shrine. Two shelves were crammed with his trophies and plaques from basketball, football, and baseball. On one wall, framed photographs of every team he'd played on, from Little League through college. On another wall, his signed poster of Larry Bird. A bin of balls still sat in one corner of the room: basketballs, footballs, soccer balls, tennis balls, baseballs, golf balls—every ball you could think of; Adam hadn't even played half the sports, but he loved balls, holding them, tossing them, kicking them, squeezing them. A quilt stitched in a football-field pattern covered his bed. When he was a high school sophomore, his father removed the bed's footboard so his feet could hang over the end of the mattress.

Adam was afraid he was one of those guys who had peaked during high school, and the next fifty or sixty years would be nothing but a slow slide off the throne, marked by disappointments and fuckups—if he lived that long. In high school he'd been Mr. Varsity; tons of friends, girlfriends, vice-president on the student council, grades good enough that he didn't fall into the dumb-jock group but was considered one of the elite, one of the chosen. An alpha male. A ruler.

He'd grown up a king, the oldest of Joseph and Eva Vanek's three children. His sister, Cori, was an accountant living in Philadelphia with a husband and three kids; his little brother, Ben, was single and lived in some experimental urban community in Arizona. Ben was the one his parents had worried about, without interests or friends, the one caught smoking pot in high school, who switched his major three times in college; now he was an urban planner with expertise in environmental impact and had found his brethren out West. Adam's father still commuted to JP Morgan on Wall Street and his mother taught writing classes at Westchester Community College now that the children were grown and gone.

Except Adam. He was back, although he wished he wasn't. He missed the Glendale Wellness Center. He had forged a tight bond with the others in his group therapy, eight guys, all of them demented gamblers like himself. The days had been soothing at Glendale, sitting in a circle in those comfortable chairs and talking about the sickness, rallying each other, examining your behavior and believing you could make a change. Taking walks in the long meadow behind the building, stopping by the fountain, watching the carp swim around the pond. It was obvious that when you got back home you would be healthy again, you would maintain control. It was easy to say you would employ your *wait ten minutes* strategy when you got out, you wouldn't carry cash, you would call one of the counselors if you needed support. But then you do get out and discover you're back in the world you left, only worse. You forget to bring with you all the confidence and skills you gained at Glendale. There's your bookie and his game-fixing scheme, there's the Lotto machines and there's a sporting contest somewhere every day and most of all there's your wife who abandoned you and your son who's afraid of you and you can't contain or control your own damn weakness and rage and you want to hurt somebody, you really do, you want someone to suffer. Mostly you want to hurt yourself, but you end up hurting your wife.

Adam brooded on his bed until his mother called him down for dinner. He helped her set the table, putting out plates and pouring three glasses of water from the pitcher. His father emerged from his study in his wool cardigan and cords and took his place at the head. He didn't look at his son and Adam could almost see the anger shimmering off his head like heat waves off the hood of a car.

Uh-oh. How was Adam going to ask him now?

His mother put the brisket and potatoes on the table. They passed the serving bowls silently, filling their plates, and just as Adam was about to take his first bite, his father spoke. "I had a call from Bernie Cornwall today. I had gotten in touch with him to ask what was going on at GeoPol, why the company was trimming its workforce. He was actually surprised to hear that news. As far as he knew, the company had just gotten a big contract with the NYPD."

Adam's appetite vanished—poof!—and brisket was one of his favorites.

"Bernie should know, right?" his father said. "He's on the company's board of directors. I would have thought his name would be enough to protect you from any layoffs."

"They always get rid of the newer employees first," Adam said. Stupid. His father already knew what happened, or he wouldn't be bringing up the subject.

"What's this about?" said Eva.

"Your son can tell you."

"The brisket's good, Mom." He forced down a few forkfuls of meat and carrots.

"Adam wasn't laid off—he was fired for fighting on company premises. Even Bernie couldn't help turn that one around."

The meat lodged halfway to his stomach.

"Fighting? Fighting who? Did you get hurt?" His mother set down her fork. Her forehead contracted into its wrinkle of disbelief, an expression Adam had seen too often directed at him. He hated hurting his mother, especially given what she'd endured with the cancer.

"It was just an argument, it got a little out of hand," Adam said.

"How do you expect to get back on the right track when you act this way?" his father said. "You think you're some kind of child, not accountable for your behavior?"

"I'll find another job. I've already started looking."

"You act like a kid . . . fighting. Do you need anger management treatment as well?" His father raised his glass and hid his disgust behind a long drink of water.

"What did Celeste have to say? Does she know the real reason you lost your job?"

Adam groaned inside. "She knows."

"And that's going to help you reconcile with her?"

"I haven't seen her much," Adam said. Except from afar.

He would drive past the house, he'd watch Spencer walk to school. One afternoon he spotted Celeste on her porch talking with her neighbors and he circled the block again but she'd gone back inside. He was stalking his own family—and his heart contracted in pain every time he caught a glimpse of them.

"I thought you were spending time with Spencer on a regular basis," his mother said.

"I was, but—" But I lost $25,000, blew off my son's birthday, and almost strangled my wife. "Celeste won't let me see him," Adam said.

"That doesn't seem like Celeste," his mother said. "She's been fair to you about seeing Spencer. Has that changed?"

"She won't let me see him at all now, and she won't talk to me, either. She has an attorney and said she's divorcing me."

"Because of the fight at your job?" his mother said.

"I told you it wasn't a fight. It was a misunderstanding."

"One that got you fired," his father said, lips barely moving.

"Even if you don't have your job, you should still be allowed to see Spencer," his mother said. "And so should we. I haven't seen him since before his birthday."

"If Celeste has an attorney, you need one, too," his father said. "I know just the one. His name is Howard Jasper."

"Dad, I don't want lawyers involved. Celeste and I need to work this out on our own."

"Not if she's serious about getting a divorce. You'll need an attorney if that's the case."

"Doesn't she know you're better now?" his mother said. "That all the gambling is in the past? Can't she see that? Can't she forgive your mistakes?"

Adam pushed his plate away and put his elbows on the table. He buried his fists in his eyes. He made a moaning sound in his throat, and when he looked up, his parents were both staring back at him, anxious and waiting.

He finally said it, barely above a whisper: "I need money." He didn't say how much. He couldn't get those words out yet.

His father cleared his throat. "If it's for Celeste, I can write a check directly to her. Our offer to help her still holds, of course."

Adam noticed the gravy beginning to congeal in the serving bowl of brisket. He started to speak and stopped. How could he admit it? He couldn't. But he was backed into a corner. There was no other way out.

"What is it?" his mother said.

No one moved. Adam forced himself to meet his father's eyes. "I need $25,000." He grimaced when he said the words. His father's gaze turned flinty.

His mother said, "Twenty-five—"

His father raised his voice. "And next time you'll need $50,000!"

"Oh, no. No, Adam. When did you start again?" his mother said.

His father gaveled the table, his fist striking a single blow to the tablecloth. "Enough!"

The man should have been a judge. In fact, he was a judge—over his family. Countless nights at the dinner table his father would hear the issues and the arguments, then pound his pronouncement with his fist. Ben's not getting his homework done? Pound! No TV during the week. Cori came home two hours past her curfew? Pound! Grounded for two weeks. Adam overheard yelling at his girlfriend? Over what? Her spaghetti straps. Adam didn't like the thin straps on her top, thought she looked slutty. Pound! You don't yell at a girl. If you can't get along, break it off.

To his father's credit, he never yelled at Adam's mother. In fact, he only raised his voice when holding court at the dinner table. The rest of the time he was a mild banker and steady husband, father, and provider. Never made mistakes of his own, never a stupid decision—it was one of the things Adam couldn't stand about him.

"I will not give you the money," his father said. "It's pretty clear to us where that money will go and I will not be an enabler of your gambling."

"You don't understand. It's not to place a bet, it's to pay off a debt. If I don't pay him . . . I have to pay, I have no choice." He started to shake, his jaw trembling as if he were out in the cold without a coat.

"Joseph, we need to do something," his mother said.

"Is this the reason why Celeste won't see you, or let you see Spencer?" his father said.

"She found out."

"She found out," his father echoed, as if mumbling a curse. "So three months at Glendale and all the counseling didn't help? The Gamblers Anonymous meetings don't help? What else can be done for you? Tell us, Adam. Tell us how to help you. Tell us what you need."

"Nothing. There's nothing you can do." Then he tried again. "You can lend me the money."

"Where is your willpower? Where is your spine? Are you even a Vanek!"

"I don't know." The tears came now, his throat and nose clogging with mucus. "I don't know," he repeated.

"Who do you owe this money to? Who is this?"

Adam blew his nose into his napkin, waited a few seconds to compose himself. "It's someone I placed a bet with."

"For $25,000! Are you out of your mind?"

Adam stared at his plate. It would be easier to forget this and let Canto come after him.

"What's his name?" his father asked.

"Dad, I can't—"

"His name!"

"You don't want to get involved. This guy means business."

His father nodded, as if he understood perfectly. "He means business, does he? Fine, I can conduct business," he said. "You give this person my card and tell him to come see me at my office. If he wants his money, he can meet me and I will pay him."

"Dad, you can't just—"

"That's how it is. I can't trust you enough to give you the money. You can tell him that."

Court adjourned. Joseph Vanek pushed his chair back from the table, got up and went down the hall and into his study. He closed the door.

His mother rose from the table and began to stack the dinner plates, keeping her eyes away from her son.

16

Celeste was entering the restaurant with Jake when someone called out her name. "Celeste, hey!"

Brea Mendelsson, in her fur-collared coat, and another woman were just leaving. Jake stepped back and held the door for Celeste going in, the other two coming out. The four of them huddled in the open doorway.

"How are you?" Celeste said.

"In a hurry, I'm afraid. I've got an advertiser's meeting in five minutes." Brea turned to the woman accompanying her. "This is my newest sales rep, Melissa Jones. Melissa, this is my good friend, Celeste Vanek."

The younger woman smiled at Celeste and said hello. She and Brea glanced at Jake and waited. "Oh, this is Jake," Celeste said. "Jake—Brea and Melissa."

"Nice to meet you, ladies," Jake said. He shook hands with Brea, then Melissa.

"Well," Brea said, a cryptic, crooked smile appearing on her lips. "See you Sunday?"

"We'll be there," Celeste said.

"You're bringing your famous chili, aren't you?"

"I wouldn't show up without it."

"Okay, bye then." Then to Jake, her eyes lingering, studying him: "Nice to meet you."

Everyone moved and the doorway cleared. The hostess showed Jake and Celeste to a table near the back. Jake held out a chair for Celeste, then sat across from her. She said, "Brea runs the advertising department for *Westchester Home*, one of those glossy monthly magazines."

"She gave me this strange look, like she was sizing me up."

"I'm sure she was. She wants to know who I'm out with, since you're not Adam. Brea's okay, she just likes a gossipy story. I've done some work laying out ads for them, but I think they've cut back because circulation is down."

"Then it's good that you've gotten more projects from Margo."

"I'm working on a direct mail piece and we're talking about a new brochure. The work is interesting and I feel like I'm getting caught up financially, which is a huge relief."

Jake scanned the menu. "What's this about a famous chili?"

"I take the same thing every year to my friends' Super Bowl party. It's a silly ritual that everyone asks me if I'm going to bring my famous chili next year. *Celeste's Famous Chili.* It's nothing special, really, just a tradition. I can practically make it with my eyes closed." It was a simple dish, but popular, and one Spencer loved—and he ate like a fussy debutante. Whenever she tried a new recipe he left most of the food on his plate. They say some foods you have to introduce up to thirteen times to your kids before they accept eating them. Thirteen times she's going to make wild mushroom risotto or Mexican tortilla soup? Forget it. She rotated chili, spaghetti, steamed clams, mac and cheese, and a few other regulars, occasionally trying to sneak in something new.

"I'll bet you never order chili in a restaurant," Jake said.

"Definitely not."

"Because it could never be as good as yours." This was their first private joke. They'd been to lunch four times in the past three weeks and each time Celeste perused the menu and eliminated any dish she thought she could make better herself. She ended up choosing from only a few selections, dishes with ingredients that were hard to find or took too long to prepare. It wasn't lost on her that when eating in a restaurant she was as picky as Spencer, in her own way.

Other than their lunches, she and Jake had walked in Riverfront Park and driven to Beacon to visit the Dia Art Foundation after Celeste told Jake she'd majored in art and used to be a painter. The outing had been rushed; she needed to meet Spencer after school and it was a long stretch for Jake to be out of the office. Getting together for lunch was easier.

Celeste hadn't made a new friend since Spencer started kindergarten five years ago. None of her current friends were male. None of the married people she knew had friends of the opposite sex; the single people she knew didn't, either: They dated or were in relationships but never just friends. It was sort of sad how quickly you can establish a routine and stay on the same path in life, the big decisions already made—who to marry, what to do, where to live, your friends chosen and established, your tastes and style defined—unless something big knocks you out of orbit, such as what happened with Adam, and then you have all kinds of opportunities to have new experiences, meet new people. Like Jake Atwood.

Jake wasn't like any man she'd ever known. For one thing, he opened up to her as if confiding in his sister or best friend. She discovered this the first time they went out. Jake had phoned her the evening he'd canceled their first lunch due to his New York meeting and asked if they could reschedule for the next day. Calling at night, after business hours, reinforced to Celeste that their getting together was a social, not a business, occasion, yet she reminded Jake she was taking him out to say thanks for the referral to Margo Roberts.

During that first lunch she had asked him if he had any children. "You talked a lot about Spencer when I came to see you," she said. "It's usually other parents who ask about children."

"No, no kids. Not yet," he said.

"So you're hoping to someday?"

He explained he had given her his standard answer to a question he was asked many times. He'd learned that in business settings, either before or after meetings with clients and partners, the easiest transition from work conversation to safe social chat was the subject of children. Most people Jake worked with—single, married, or divorced—had kids. You asked: *How was your weekend?* The answers: I took my kids skiing, I went to my daughter's play. Or a client made a comment about a new cell phone and the discussion morphed into someone's teenager who can't stop texting, lives on Facebook, always begs for the latest electronic gadget, is glued to video games. Conversation about kids was neutral territory in the business setting. So whenever anyone asked if he had children, Jake said, "No, not yet," tacking on *not yet* to let others know that having kids was likely part of his future. It made people more comfortable. The single guy nearing forty, the fatherless guy at that age—he could be a creep, he could be gay. You don't want to be the social outlier in the chummy world of corporate deals.

Her next question: "Have you ever been married?" Celeste could ask him personal questions because Jake already knew an awful lot about her—*awful* being the operative word. Attacked by her husband. Separated, on her way to divorce. Raising a son with an imaginary friend. True, most of it was information she volunteered to Jake, yet now she wanted a little quid pro quo.

"No, not married—not yet."

"The boilerplate answer you give to people at work?"

"I always wanted to be married, and thought I would have been by now. Although maybe I need to rethink that position. Some of these marriages—" and he turned his hand toward her.

He wasn't insulting her, simply pointing out the obvious. "So you haven't met the right person?"

"I've been accused of being incapable of love and commitment."

"Haven't we all," Celeste said. "But I don't think that's true of anyone."

"My last relationship was with a married woman I slept with to help land a business deal for my company."

"Okay, so obviously she wasn't the right person," Celeste said. Although she hadn't expected such an intimate admission from Jake, it didn't faze her much; it sounded a lot like sleeping up the corporate ladder. When she worked at the Kellen Agency she knew a designer with a similar career strategy and it worked pretty well, helping her get promoted to director level. But the fact that Jake was telling her this, and on the first time they were out together—was he sending a warning signal of some type?

"Was that the only reason you were in the relationship?" Celeste asked.

"No, but it can be hard to know where affection ends and personal gain begins."

"Getting affection *is* personal gain," she said. "I think you're being hard on yourself. We all make mistakes. We all get attached to the wrong people and sometimes you discover it quickly and other times it takes years. I can personally attest to that."

So Jake told her another story, she supposed to illustrate his point. Back when he worked in San Francisco, his company brought in a consultant, a PhD in industrial psychology who was an expert in neurolinguistic programming, NLP it was called. The consultant's name was Elisabeth Manet. She led exercises with the executive team on mirroring, a technique in which you subtly mimicked another person's physical gestures and language choices to help build an unconscious affinity in them toward you. Interesting concept, maybe a little hokey. Jake started dating Elisabeth. She was intelligent and attractive and neither of them were anchored in the world. They both worked and traveled but saw each other whenever they had free time. They revised schedules, they once met for an overnight at O'Hare Airport, they snuck away for five days to Hawaii. Four months into their relationship Jake thought he might be falling in love. Then one night Elisabeth told him something she'd never told anyone else: As a child—ten years old, eleven years old—she was sexually abused by her neighbor. She gave Jake details. The things this man did to her, he couldn't help picturing the little girl and this awful experience. Yet Elisabeth spoke evenly, matter-of-factly to him. She trusted Jake; she wanted him to know. She appeared to have put the tragedy behind her, but it turned out the trauma had been repressed and now began to surface. Telling Jake had caused an eruption of emotional pain in her. She began to have these fits, like seizures. One night she started shaking and couldn't stop; she began thrashing around. She pleaded with Jake to do something, to help her. He had no idea what to do. He thought she was physically ill and ended up taking her to the emergency room, where he spent most of the night with her. She was sedated, tested, found physically fit, sent home. Over the ensuing weeks, there were more episodes of shaking, including another time when he had to drive her to the emergency room in the middle of the night, which made him an exhausted wreck at an important presentation the next day. He was getting annoyed at her erratic behavior and fits.

Elisabeth was sent for a psych consult; she began to see a psychiatrist. She was diagnosed with post-traumatic stress disorder: PTSD.

Why now? Jake asked her. Why is this surfacing after all these years? Because of him. He was the first person she could open up to, the first person she could reveal her long-suppressed feelings to. She believed they were somehow destined to meet and be together, that a greater power had sent Jake to help her vanquish her demons. No way. No one had sent him anywhere to do anything. That was just plain wrong. He said he needed a break from her and quickly ended the relationship. She begged him not to abandon her at her most vulnerable time. She said she would kill herself. He stopped answering his phone. She showed up at his apartment, she pounded on his door. Many times she did this. He finally escaped when a headhunter recruited him and he changed jobs and moved to Seattle.

Celeste listened without interrupting his story. This one dried her mouth a little more. When he finished, they both reached for their water glasses. "So she wasn't the right person for you, either," she said, careful not to pass judgment.

His forehead sweated and he dabbed himself with his napkin. She tried again. "We all do things that seem cruel because they're in our best interest but not in someone else's," she said.

"Why do I doubt that you've ever done anything cruel?"

"I left Adam when he was in rehab. I abandoned him when he couldn't do anything to stop me, when he needed me the most."

"He was abusive. You did it to protect yourself."

"Yes, but mostly I did it because I stopped loving him." Otherwise, she would have stayed, she would have put up with him longer.

Jake looked away. She wondered if he regretted telling her that story—or if she regretted hearing it. She'd come nowhere close to witnessing this side of Jake; he'd been only honorable, kind, and generous with her. It was hard to imagine Jake behaving so coldly toward anyone.

"Why did you tell me about her—Elisabeth?"

He nodded, as if he expected her question. "I don't want to mislead you in any way. If we're going to be friends, I thought you should know who you're dealing with."

"I thought I was dealing with a man who prevented me from getting hurt in a violent attack, who helped me get work, who is taking me out to lunch."

"I'm also that guy. Except the lunch part—you said you were taking me."

"Right. I knew that." They both smiled, more relaxed now that their conversation had lightened. When the check came, she expected him to insist on paying. He didn't. Okay, he was letting her thank him this way.

On their way out, she asked Jake what happened to her—that woman Elisabeth.

"I don't know," he said. "Up until now, I haven't thought about her in a long time."

That was their first lunch. Their conversation stayed with her for days afterward.

Today's discussion about chili was more chatty and less intense, and a lot more leisurely. Celeste ordered a salad with beets and roasted hazelnuts, something she could have prepared herself but Spencer wouldn't go near a beet if it was the only food left on earth. Jake chose the Caesar topped with grilled calamari.

"I used to take classes at the Culinary Institute in Hyde Park," she said. "Someday I'll cook a meal for you and you'll be very impressed."

"Just the idea that anyone would cook for me is impressive," Jake said. "You'll make your famous chili?"

"No, I'll make you something really yummy—the chili is just for the Super Bowl party. What are you doing for the big game?"

"Who's playing?"

"Hmm, I'm not sure."

He shrugged. "I'll probably be working. I have a plane to catch early Monday to Seattle. I have meetings with Microsoft on Monday about licensing their Web-mapping technology. Then a stop in Eugene, Oregon, to meet with their police department."

"What's it like working with the police?"

"I don't have a lot of interaction with street cops, but the administrators are a pretty forthright bunch," Jake said. "Although I always get this sense I'm around authority, and I end up thinking I'm a part of it, too. I'm some kind of peacekeeper, an arbiter and upholder of law and order."

"You were certainly that way when you stopped Adam."

The busboy filled their water glasses and left. "Have you seen Adam?"

Celeste shook her head. "He's keeping his distance. But I'm surprised he hasn't called again to see Spencer."

"Would you let him?"

"I told him to stay away, but he is Spencer's father. Although after what happened, he's just too unpredictable, he has no control. I don't trust him around Spencer. I don't think he deserves any rights at all. Is that too vindictive?"

"What kind of custody agreement do you have?"

"None, yet," Celeste said. "It will be part of the divorce settlement, but I expect to get full custody." Although the legal pursuit wasn't going as quickly or smoothly as Celeste had hoped. Her attorney, Iris Mair, had rushed through their initial meeting, telling Celeste her case was straightforward. But then Adam retained his own attorney and now the supposedly simple no-fault divorce had bogged down, thanks to the frustrating tactics employed by Howard Jasper. He kept asking for tax returns, bank statements, receipts, investments, each one requiring a call from Iris Mair to Celeste, only to have Celeste say she didn't have any of those documents; everything had been jointly held and Adam had handled all the finances—yet another reminder she should not have been so cavalier about money matters. So Celeste had nothing to hand over. Still, Howard Jasper filed a motion in court compelling Celeste and Iris Mair to comply with discovery demands. Also, although Iris had told Celeste she would likely be granted full custody of Spencer, Adam's lawyer filed for joint custody, so that would need to be hammered out as well. All delay tactics, Iris told her; he's hoping you'll have a change of heart. But the only way Celeste's heart was changing was to turn harder against Adam.

When their lunches were served, Jake said, "Tell me about your friends who are having the party."

"Stephen and Emery? They lived around the corner from us in Cider Mill. Emery and I have been close for years. Stephen is an architect, Emery works part-time as a grant writer. They have three girls, two around Spencer's age and one who's just a year old . . . let's see, what else can I tell you?"

"What do they know about what happened with you and Adam?"

"Now they know the whole sorry story, I'm afraid, from when I first found out about Adam's gambling to the night he attacked me."

Over the last few weeks, since Celeste had told her friends about Adam's violence, Emery had been calling almost every day, asking what she could do to help, getting together with Celeste more often for running and coffee and just making sure Celeste knew she had support.

"I think it's hard for them," Celeste said. "They knew Adam when he was just . . . well—when we were all friends and no one knew about his problems."

"Will Adam be at the party?"

"Emery and I already talked about it. She's not inviting him this year."

"So you got custody of the friends, at least."

"Stephen and Adam were friends, but not as close as Emery and I are. They mostly hung out together when the wives were involved."

Jake put down his fork and wiped his mouth. "Isn't the Super Bowl the biggest gambling day of the year?"

"Not for me, it isn't," Celeste said. "The party isn't about the game as much as it is a reason to get together in the middle of winter. It's the same group of families, all the kids come. Half the people don't pay attention to the game."

"What about you?"

"I mostly hang out in the kitchen with the other moms and help with the food."

Jake leaned across the table and stared with a directness that required an effort from Celeste to maintain eye contact. What had she just said? Or did she have food caught in her teeth?

"Celeste is a really beautiful name. It suits you."

She laughed, to buy a few seconds of time. "Oh—thank you," she said. She felt a blush rise. "My mother gave me a name she thought would help me seem prettier. My sister, too. Her name is Chantal."

"She didn't need to do that."

Celeste realized she was holding her breath. "Thank you," she said again.

"I'm really glad I met you," Jake said. "I wish it could have been under better circumstances, but you can't always pick the circumstances—maybe you never can." He moved even closer and for a second she thought he might try to kiss her. She quickly wet her lips. She wasn't sure if she was ready. Up to this point, Jake had not made any suggestive or flirtatious remarks to her. He made no move on her; he never touched her. He never complimented her about her appearance. Not that she wanted those things, not now, not yet. She had enough to deal with in her life. And she'd heard lots of times how pretty her name was. Nothing new there.

But Jake didn't kiss her. Instead, he said, "I want to see more of you. And not just for lunch."

17

Packers versus Steelers was the Super Bowl pairing, according to the hand-drawn sign taped on the Webers' front door. Spencer held the door for his mother because Celeste needed both hands to carry the pot.

"Rejoice! Rejoice! Celeste's here with her famous chili," someone shouted from inside. That had to be Bruce DeHaven, Nancy's husband, who usually started drinking early and finished late. Sure enough, there he was, holding up a beer in a toast to Celeste.

"Hi, Bruce," Celeste said.

Spencer immediately disappeared downstairs, where the kids played video games and wrestled on the carpet and emptied the toy chest. Celeste made her way toward the kitchen, passing the DeHavens, the Longs, the Persicos. Half a dozen others were staked out in the family room in front of the sixty-inch plasma, even though kickoff was more than an hour away.

Emery cleared a burner on the stove and Celeste set down her pot. "What can I help with?" Celeste said, kissing her friend.

"The coleslaw and salad are made, the cornbread is in the

oven, the water for the pasta is on," Emery said. "Should I put a flame under the chili?"

"It just needs to warm up," Celeste said.

Jenna Long appeared and waved the hat in front of Celeste. "Donation time," Jenna said. "Ten dollars for you and ten for Spencer."

Emery made a face and Jenna quickly corrected herself. "I'm sorry, that was stupid of me. You don't have to."

With Celeste and Spencer coming alone this year and the word spread far and wide, everyone knew Adam had been to a gambling rehab center and he and Celeste were separated now.

"No, it's okay," Celeste said. "I've got my purse right here. I want to play."

The deal was everyone contributed $10 to the hat and then wrote their name on squares in a grid. Numbers were drawn after all the squares were taken, each square getting assigned two numbers on the grid, from the vertical and horizontal axes. If the last digits of the score at the end of any quarter of the game matched your numbers, you got a portion of the collected cash as a prize.

Celeste found a twenty in her purse and dropped it into the hat. Jenna produced the grid. "You get two boxes each," she said. Celeste signed her name in two squares, Spencer's in another two. Jenna checked her list of names and continued on, searching for whomever hadn't paid yet, the grid almost full.

Celeste huddled at the stove with Emery. "You'd think she'd have a little more sense," Emery said.

"I don't mind. I'm not the one with the problem, and I don't want people treating me differently, like I'm fragile or something."

"No, you're not fragile," Emery said. "You're one of the strongest women I know, dealing with everything you have. In fact, you look great today." Emery took a step back and studied Celeste's face. "Did you do something different? Get your hair cut?"

"Weeks ago. I've seen you since then."

"Well, you still look fabulous."

"Thanks." Celeste did feel good today. She felt healthy; she felt hopeful. She was happy to be around her friends, many of whom she hadn't seen in a while, and she made the rounds to say hello to everyone inside, then slid open the door and stepped out onto the deck. The air was cold and the sky growing dark; the sun had already set and the deck lights were on, including the string of Christmas lights still wrapped around the railing. A few snow flurries kited past. Stephen huddled with Paul Mendelsson near the grill. An aluminum baking dish mounded with sausages sat on a tray table.

Stephen opened the lid and set the sausages one by one onto the heated racks. He saw her and stopped his task and hugged her, one hand still holding a raw sausage. Paul one-arm-hugged her as well, his other hand occupied with a beer.

"Hey, you made it," Stephen said. "Wow, you look great, Celeste."

"What's going on? Did Emery put you up to telling me that?"

"It's true," Paul said. "You've got a glow about you. Is that from already drinking too much or can I get you a beer?"

"That's what I came out here for."

"Not to help me with the cooking?" Stephen said.

Paul reached into the cooler and opened Celeste a beer. She took a sip and said, "Do you need help?"

Emery often commented that her husband's cooking skills began and ended with his pouring the kids a bowl of cereal; he was a novice in front of his own grill and rarely used it. At past Super Bowl parties, Adam had handled barbecue duties. He would tie one of Emery's patterned aprons around his waist and cook dozens of Italian sausages, standing in the cold, in the snow, in the rain. Didn't matter to him. He played the role of the man and his grill, a master of the domain, proud to make a guest appearance in front of his friends' barbecue.

"You can tell me when they need turning," Stephen said, putting the last sausages on.

"After they brown up, I think you should lower the heat and close the lid," Celeste said. "It will keep the flames down and help the sausages cook through."

"Roger that. Lower heat, close lid."

Brea Mendelsson and Emery came out. Paul opened them each a beer. Five of them stood around the grill, drinking, the long barbecue fork poised like a wand in Stephen's hand.

"We're cooking by committee today," Stephen said. "Whoever offers the best advice can become Adam's permanent replacement."

"At the grill, anyway," Celeste said. The others smiled or chuckled.

"Don't stab the sausages with the fork," Brea said. "The juices will run out. That's my best advice."

Stephen offered her the fork, but she declined.

Paul opened another beer for himself. "You ready, Celeste?"

"No, I'm good." She held up her bottle to show it was still half full.

"Who was that I saw you with at World Bistro?" Brea asked Celeste. Her voice suggested an interesting revelation, and the others quieted and paid attention.

"A new client," she said neutrally, not entirely the truth. Jake had gotten her the first project, but Celeste's only work contact at GeoPol since then had been with Margo Roberts. "He's a friend of mine, too," she added. No reason to hide it.

"That's what it looked like to me," Brea said.

"So that's why you're looking so good," Stephen said. "You've got a new romance going."

Emery gave her an elbow. "Are you keeping something from us?"

"No, I told you about him. Jake—he's the one who separated Adam and me that night when—" She stopped.

"You're seeing him?"

"No, I just said—I'm doing some work for his company. We've had lunch a few times. He's a nice guy, that's all."

"Okay, hon, we're not prying." But her eyes said Celeste should have revealed all, and much sooner, that if Celeste were going to confide the painful facts about Adam's destructive behavior, then exciting news about a potential new love interest must be shared as well—although at this point Celeste would hardly call Jake a new love interest.

"Except we are prying—a little," Brea said.

"You could have brought him along," Emery said. "We'd love to meet him."

In fact, she had considered inviting Jake, and wondered if the reason he asked whether Adam would be here today was because he hoped Celeste would invite him instead. But if Jake came, that would mean introducing him to Spencer and she'd already ruled out that scenario for now. She didn't want to confuse Spencer—he had enough to process without another complication. So no babysitters for an evening out with Jake. No get-together plans on the weekends. Celeste tried not to think about where her spending time with Jake might lead. She couldn't see that far ahead, and Jake had issues of his own.

For Celeste, managing each day, working or looking for work, getting through her divorce with Adam, being a good mother to Spencer—that's where she devoted her energy.

"I say good for you," Stephen said. "You should get back out there—"

"We're just *friends*. There's nothing to report." Except he thinks I'm beautiful—or at least my name is.

"Okay, okay." Stephen opened the grill cover and whooshing flames shot up from the fat drippings. He hadn't turned down the gas dial. Several of the sausages were on fire.

"Take them off, they're burning," Emery said.

"They haven't been on long enough to be cooked through," Celeste said.

"What should I do?" Stephen said.

"Pour your beer to put out the flames?" Paul suggested.

"Take them off." They turned to the sound of the voice. It was Adam, sliding the deck door closed behind him.

Everyone looked from Adam to Celeste and then quickly scattered their glances in other directions. No one spoke. The previous banter about Celeste's new friend lingered in the air.

Adam stepped up and began removing the sausages from the grill, grabbing them with his fingers, disregarding the flames, dropping them back into the aluminum pan. Celeste watched his hands perform the work. How could he not be getting burned?

Once the sausages were removed from the heat, the flames died down, and Adam turned to Emery. "How are you?" he said, leaning to kiss her cheek, Emery turning rigid at his touch. Then he awkwardly man-hugged Stephen, keeping his greasy hands away, and stood back and smiled at the Mendelssons. He hadn't looked at Celeste yet, but she was waiting, and he turned to her.

"Hi," he said, and immediately returned his attention to the sausages in the pan. "If you put these back on a lower heat, they'll cook through and be fine. The ones that got a little black you can scrape off the casing."

"It's all yours," Stephen said, untying his apron and handing it to Adam. The Mendelssons quietly made for the door to go back inside, leaving Emery and Stephen standing on the deck with Adam and Celeste. The *fearsome foursome* was how Adam used to refer to them, back when they'd go out as two couples for drinks and dinner.

Celeste looked at the bare maple in the backyard, its branches veining the gray sky. The first tendrils of a headache crept in.

"You made it over," Stephen said. "I didn't realize . . ." He didn't finish what he was going to say.

"It's been a while since we've seen you," Emery said.

"Well, yes. It's been a difficult period."

"I know. I'm sorry to hear that," Emery said, then turned to her husband. "It's freezing out here. Now that Adam's here, he can grill, you can help me inside."

Celeste wanted to tell Emery not to go inside and leave her here with Adam, but it was too late. Stephen slid the door closed behind them. Alone on the deck with Adam now, Celeste found her voice. "I didn't expect to see you here."

He fingered the sausages. "My parents went to the movies, they asked me to come but they didn't really want me . . . I hated knowing everyone was here and . . ." He stalled. He squinted, his face framed in pain. He turned away from her, lowered the burners, and started putting the meat back on the grill. "I wanted to be with my friends, the people I know. I wanted to be with my family."

She crossed her arms and held herself against the cold.

She'd been standing outside for too long. "Did you see Spencer when you came in?"

"First thing, I went downstairs, he's busy playing. He gave me a hug—I miss him so much. And I miss you. Everyone here is looking at me like I'm some kind of leper."

"It's an uncomfortable situation—what do you expect? People don't know what to say. Maybe that's why you weren't invited."

"We were never invited, we just came every year knowing this was the day of the party. I thought these people were my friends, too."

Celeste looked away. "It's different now, you know it is."

He opened the grill top, expertly rolled the sausages with his fingers to turn them. The flames stayed under control.

"Why is your lawyer trying to delay our divorce?" Celeste said.

"I didn't hire him, my father did. He said I have to protect my rights. But Celeste, we don't need to do this, I swear—"

She cut him off. "No. I told you I want out, Adam, and I mean it. I'm not going to discuss this here. I'm going back inside."

"Celeste, wait."

"I want you to stay away from me—and from Spencer." She left Adam standing on the deck. Once inside, no one spoke to her, but she felt the eyes like ants crawling on her, the questions like little bites. *What happened? Did they have an argument? Did you hear he had hit her? Are they getting back together?*

She helped Emery put out plates and silverware. "I'm sorry," Celeste said. "I didn't know Adam would just show up like this."

Emery waved the comment off. "I thought you two had something to talk about, or I wouldn't have stranded you. Do you want me to ask him to leave? I will if you want me to."

Celeste could see Emery had no desire to ask Adam to leave and risk an ugly scene. Neither did Stephen, who stood with his back to Celeste at the sink filling a pitcher with water, watching Adam out the kitchen window. They would talk to Adam if Celeste asked them to, although she couldn't put this burden on her friends.

"You don't need to do anything," Celeste said. Maybe she should be the one to leave; part of her wanted to, but she recognized the desire as an existential wish—if she could just disappear, vanish into the air and not have to deal with Adam anymore.

She stirred the chili simmering in its pot.

A moment later Adam came inside, the sausages piled high on a platter, giving off steam and a rich, meaty scent. He set the platter down on the counter next to the plates. Celeste braced herself for what was coming next. She saw Stephen take a breath, then lower his voice as he spoke to Adam. "Look, Adam, hey, I don't know if this is such a great idea. Maybe next week you and I can . . ." His words trailed away. Celeste took over. "Adam, I know this is hard for you," she said. "It's hard for all of us. But—"

He cut her off. "—But you don't want me here—none of you do," he said, loud enough for everyone to hear. The room became still as a photograph. "You can all relax now," he called out. "I'm leaving." Without a look at Celeste he walked through the house and out the front door.

18

Celeste told Spencer she was having dinner with a friend. She expected him to ask who, but he was too excited about seeing Kristin again, the kind of babysitter who actually paid attention to kids, or at least to Spencer; the two of them would chat, play games, make popcorn, watch movies—almost like buddies hanging out together. They hadn't seen each other in months.

"Hi, Mrs. Vanek," Kristin said, coming in with her phone and keys in hand. A high school senior now, she'd transformed into a woman from the skinny girl who had started babysitting for Celeste and Adam four years ago.

Spencer immediately mobbed her. "Do you have a phone? Does it text? I have a phone now, my mom got me one because I walk home from school instead of taking the bus. Can I text you?" He ran into his room and came back with his phone. "What's your number?"

Celeste interrupted to give instructions: in bed by nine o'clock, lights out by nine-thirty, Celeste's phone number if Kristin needed anything. She kissed Spencer and let him know she wouldn't be back until after he was asleep.

Her plan was to drive to the supermarket and then go to Jake's and make dinner for the two of them; she'd been a little boastful with him about her cooking skills and the time had come to demonstrate for him. But when she got in her car, she turned the key and nothing happened. She tried again: a click, a moan, followed by dead silence. Spencer must have left the overhead light on again and drained the battery. This wasn't the first time this had happened; the battery barely held a charge now and needed replacement. She had no jumper cables and her membership in AAA had lapsed months ago.

Sitting in the car, she called Jake to tell him she was stuck. "Maybe we should reschedule."

"I'm still at the office," Jake said. "I can pick you up. We'll go to the supermarket together, then the auto parts store to get you a new battery if you want. And I'll drive you home later tonight."

Exactly the response she'd hoped for. "I'll be ready," she said, and ended the call. Then she realized if Jake was picking her up, he'd come to the door and Spencer would be there. She could avoid the situation by waiting out front, or in her car, although it was freezing tonight and she hadn't worn her warmest coat or any gloves.

Okay, enough—why not introduce Spencer to Jake? It's true Spencer might think any male friend of Celeste's was taking the place of his father and so she'd have to be careful in her explanation. Her priority was to protect her son and help him avoid conflicting or confusing feelings, but she also wanted to be honest and open with Spencer and foster a trusting relationship. Besides, if Spencer could handle the topic of his father's destructive behavior and his parents' impending divorce, he could manage meeting Celeste's friend for two minutes, especially in light of their conversation the other day when Spencer came home from school and said, "I have two questions for you."

He opened his backpack and handed her a sheet of paper. "First, can I be in the science fair?"

"Let's see." Celeste read the entry form and said, "It says here that you should pose a question related to science and answer it."

"Mrs. Moore gave an example, she said *Why is the sky blue?* But we're not supposed to use that one."

"Well, there's lots of others. Do you have any ideas?"

"I want to do rocks," Spencer said. "*How are rocks formed?* Is that a good question?"

"I think that's an excellent question."

Spencer took the form back, wrote his name at the top, and started filling in the blanks. Celeste poured milk and cocoa powder into a pan, and lit the burner on the stove to make Spencer a cup of hot chocolate. Then Spencer asked his second question: "Are you ever going to get married again?"

Whoa—where did that come from? But the answer was easy. "Well, I don't know," she said. "It depends on whether I meet someone I want to marry. If I do, it won't be for a long time."

"But if you do get married again, Dad will still be my dad, right?"

"Yes, always," Celeste said. "That will never change."

"Dad told me at the party he wanted to do things with me, but you won't let him see me."

"Do you want to see him?"

Spencer made a chewing motion with his mouth. "The next person you marry will become my stepfather, right?"

"Honey, you're jumping ahead way too far." She poured the hot chocolate and set the cup in front of Spencer.

"Peter Beller has a stepfather," Spencer said, referring to his friend from school.

Ah, so that's where this originated. "That's right, he does. There are a lot of families like that. Where maybe a child has both a father and stepfather, or a mother and stepmother. Or just a mother or just a father. Or even two mothers or two fathers."

"Will I like him?"

"Like who?"

"The person you want to marry."

Again, she told Spencer about getting way ahead of himself, but also assured her son she wouldn't marry anyone he didn't like.

"Dad doesn't like me anymore—if he did, he wouldn't be a gambler," Spencer said. "He only said he wants to see me because he's supposed to. I don't know if I like him."

Sad to hear, despite all Adam had done. "He's not in control of his life right now," Celeste said. "But your father loves you, I can assure you of that. And your own feelings might change back and forth for a while. It can be hard to like someone who does something wrong to you. Forgiveness takes time. Do you know what I mean by that?"

Spencer nodded. "You can only forgive them a little at a time because there's so much."

"That's right. You understand."

"Kathy told me that. She said sometimes there's too much to forgive and you can't do it all."

"Your friend Kathy is very wise, isn't she?"

"So am I," Spencer said.

"Yes, so are you."

Celeste went back inside and told Kristin and Spencer her car wouldn't start and her friend, Jake, was going to pick her up. She waited for Spencer's reaction. He didn't say a word. Instead, he went to the front window and stared, as if starting a vigil. Celeste stood behind him, ready to explain that men and women are often friends, just like Spencer and Kathy are friends, or Spencer and Allison, the girl he sits next to in school.

He didn't have any questions.

Jake took longer to arrive than she expected, but Spencer stayed at the window the entire time while Celeste caught up with Kristin, who said she was getting ready for the track season and trying to decide between Colgate, St. Lawrence, and Geneseo for college in the fall.

"He's here, he's here!" Spencer called out.

Celeste let Jake in. Coming directly from work, he had on dress slacks and a wool coat, while Celeste was in jeans. She'd worn a favorite top—a fitted green scoop neck that brought out the color in her eyes and complemented the red in her hair. The top had a vertical line of fabric-topped snaps. She'd added a gold braided necklace and earrings.

Jake held a plastic bag in one hand. Celeste introduced him to Spencer, but Spencer stared at his socks and wouldn't look at Jake.

"I've been looking forward to meeting you," Jake said. "Your mom tells me so many great things about you."

At least Spencer put out his hand for a shake.

"And this is Kristin," Celeste said, introducing her babysitter.

"Hi, how are you?" Jake said. He turned back to Spencer. "Your mom said you like rocks."

"Yeah." Looking at Celeste and not Jake. She resisted reminding Spencer about the importance of eye contact, which he'd been so much better at recently. They could have that conversation later, in private.

Celeste decided to help. "For the school science fair, Spencer's doing an exhibit on how the different types of rocks are formed," she said. "Do you want to tell Mr. Atwood about it?"

"Jake. You can call me Jake—if that's okay with your mom."

Spencer remained silent, shifting his eyes back and forth, everywhere except on Jake.

Jake said, "I can't remember, aren't there four different types of rocks?"

Spencer sighed, as if he'd explained this concept a hundred times, or perhaps his mother's friend wasn't very smart. But he also perked up and looked at Jake now. "Three," he said. "Igneous, sedimentary, and metamorphic."

"That's right, I'd forgotten. Sedimentary rocks are the ones made from layers?"

"Yes, and igneous rocks form from cooling magma, and metamorphic rocks have changed from pressure."

"You know a lot about rocks," said Jake. "What about crystals—do you like crystals?"

"I like them."

"Good. Because I brought something for you." He reached in the bag and handed Spencer a box containing a grow-your-own-crystals kit. The cover showed a collection of colorful crystals sitting in clear plastic pans and two kids—a boy and a girl—with bright eyes and brilliant smiles.

"Cool," Spencer said. "Thank you." He held the box in both hands. "Mom, can we do this tonight?"

"I'll leave that up to you and Kristin. I'm saying good-night."

"I'm glad I got a chance to meet you," Jake said. "You take care."

Jake put out his hand, but Spencer wouldn't shake a second time. Celeste didn't intervene. She knew it could have gone either way—Spencer opening up and acting like a chatterbox or closing up like a clam. He had ended up somewhere in between, closer to the clam but pried partially open by Jake's clever statement about the four types of rocks and his gift.

She kissed Spencer again and told Kristin she wouldn't be too late.

In the supermarket, Jake carried the basket while Celeste read from her list and selected food items. Shrimp from the seafood counter, salad fixings in the produce section, French bread in the bakery aisle. She was making New Orleans–style barbecued shrimp she'd learned at a weekend cooking class with Emery at the Culinary Institute.

Each aisle in the market presented a new discovery about Jake's minimalist pantry. Did Jake have lemons at home? No. Garlic? No. Bay leaves? Are you serious. Butter? Maybe. Black pepper? Yes. Beer? Definitely.

"Do you have an oven at least?" Celeste said. "And maybe plates and silverware?"

He pretended to be insulted. "I think you'll find the kitchen acceptable."

After the supermarket, Jake drove past the auto parts store but it was closed, so he continued on to his house, turned down the sloped driveway, and parked in front of the garage. Before going inside he walked Celeste down to the creek to show her the property. They stood on the concrete dock. Near the creek's banks a thin window of ice had formed on the surface. Water gurgled beneath it. Bare trees lined the opposite side twenty yards across and you could see the lights of another house farther in through the trees.

"I put the kayak in here and paddle beneath the train trestle into the Hudson," he said. "Come on, I'll show you."

They returned up the path to the driveway and onto the road that continued another fifty yards, crossed the train tracks, and dead-ended at a public boat launch. They stood along the banks of the Hudson River now, the water black slate under a clear, moonless sky. The air carried a metallic scent. Green and red lights blinked on buoys marking the shipping lane in the river. Silver stars pricked the sky straight above and the horizon to the south soaked up the yellowy glow of millions of lights shining in and around New York City.

"It's so beautiful," Celeste said. "I've lived in Brookfield for ten years but have never been on the Hudson in a boat or even swimming."

"We'll take out the canoe on a calm day when the weather gets warmer. Spencer can come, too."

"He'd love that." A breeze swept across the water. Celeste shivered. She wasn't dressed warm enough.

They went back and carried the grocery bags from his car and Jake gave her the inside tour. The kitchen, except for the near-empty pantry and refrigerator, was loaded. Granite countertops, center island with stools, double sink, copper pots, forged knives set in a wooden block. The living room featured a bluestone fireplace, and a fat leather couch and matching recliner chair huddled around a glass-topped coffee table with a globe sitting on it. There were two bedrooms situated off a hallway, with a bathroom across the hall and a master bath off Jake's bedroom.

Jake opened a bottle of Bordeaux and poured them each a glass.

"I can't believe you have this amazing kitchen but you don't cook," Celeste said.

"I didn't put it in. Didn't I tell you—I'm just subletting. The owner of the house is in Malaysia. He was transferred by his bank for a temporary assignment."

"Oh." No, he hadn't told her, although he had talked to her about the number of times he'd moved to take new jobs, which Celeste attributed to the life of a single professional pursuing a career. And he'd confided in her about his high failure rate at relationships, which she interpreted as Jake not having met the right person yet. Now, all of a sudden, his transient lifestyle and inability to sustain a relationship appeared more habitual, a pattern, perhaps a character trait. But she shouldn't be surprised: That was Jake. He'd admitted as much to her from the beginning.

"Can we go out in the canoe tonight?" she asked. "It's clear. We can see the stars."

"The canoe is no good on choppy nights. You get out there and the wind blows and you just bounce around. You've got no control."

"Okay, it was just an idea."

"Is something wrong?" Jake said.

She shrugged. Nothing specific was the matter. She'd been the one to suggest cooking dinner, but now that she was here, alone with Jake, she kind of wondered what she was doing, what she expected or wanted. The last few times they'd been together she'd felt herself drawing closer to him, relaxing, experiencing the first tremors of desire, even though the practical side of her whispered that this was no time to get involved with another man—or the man to get involved with. But she also believed this was no time to suppress her feelings or deny herself anything or anyone. She needed enjoyment and pleasure, she needed to sustain the glow Emery and Stephen had recognized in her by telling her how great she looked.

"So where do you keep your cutting board?" she said.

Jake found a board in a lower cabinet. From the wooden block, Celeste chose a chef's knife with a blade honed to a fine edge. She arranged her ingredients and peeled and chopped the garlic. She gave Jake the dirty job of preparing the shrimp, showing him how to snip the underside with a scissors and peel off the outer shell.

"You were great with Spencer, you know—you did all the right things," Celeste said. "Asking about rocks. And it was nice of you to bring him a gift, you didn't have to do that. You know more about kids than you think you do."

"To tell the truth, I was a little nervous."

"You didn't know ten-year-olds could do that to you."

"Or twenty-nine-year-olds," Jake said.

"Ha, ha. You know I'm thirty-four. And I know I don't make you nervous."

Jake didn't respond to her comment; maybe she did beguile him a bit. He said, "I don't even know any other kids. How lame is that?" There wasn't one child in the world who was a part of his life, he told her. Every time he saw photos of children on the desks of his colleagues he felt a stab of envy, and every time the feeling surprised him.

"Spencer is the most important person in the world to me—I would do anything for him. I would give up my life for him. I suppose most parents feel that way, though."

"At 'Take Your Child to Work Day,' I see all these kids around the office and for me it's like we've been invaded by little aliens. I don't know how to act around them. But Spencer—there's something about him that reminds me of me when I was a kid."

"You mean because of the imaginary friends?"

"That's part of it," Jake said. "I was the type of kid who was never the first to speak, I always thought things through. I held back and observed a lot. I get a sense Spencer might be like that."

"Nothing gets past him, if that's what you're saying. He notices everything." She finished with the garlic and started slicing pats of butter to melt for the sauce.

"So what happens when the owner of the house returns?"

"If I'm still at GeoPol, I find a new place to live. For now, I have the use of this great house and access to the river."

"There's nothing keeping you in Brookfield? I mean other than your job."

"That's just the way it's been for me. I moved for college, then for career. You won't see any moss growing on my back."

"That's a relief, because I was wondering," she said. Silent seconds ticked away, until she added, "Has it been hard moving so much or do you like it that way?"

He nodded, which was not an answer, then turned and looked at her, and she saw regret or an apology in his eyes and something squeezed in her chest and she had to put down the knife and stand completely still. This would be a perfect moment for Jake to put his arms around her and whisper something sweet, but instead he gathered the shrimp shells and tossed them into the garbage. She wanted to reach out and touch him. No. She kept her hands to herself. Dinner first, then see what happens.

She spread the shrimp on a pan, coated them with a beer-and-melted-butter reduction, added black pepper and Tabasco, and nudged Jake to the side with her hip so she could open the oven door and set the pan in.

Jake worked on the salad. He started with the tomatoes. He tried chopping instead of slicing through the skin and the first tomato exploded, the insides squirting onto the counter and his shirt, leaving a watery orange blotch on his stomach. Celeste laughed and covered her mouth. She had drunk most of her glass of wine and was beginning to feel its heat. She was about to offer to sponge off his shirt when she heard her cell phone ring.

She located her purse on the couch and looked at the display. It was Kristin, the babysitter.

"Adam is at the door and says he wants to come in and see Spencer," Kristin said.

"Oh, God," Celeste said. "What's he doing there?"

Jake glanced up. Celeste shook her head to let him know she had a situation.

"I told him I had to call you first," Kristin said.

"You did the right thing. Don't let him in. Where's Spencer?"

"He went to bed a little while ago, but he might still be awake. Adam asked where you were. What should I tell him?"

"Just tell him I'm out. And tell him Spencer is sleeping and he has to leave immediately. Better yet, give Adam the phone and I'll talk to him, but don't let him in the house."

Celeste could hear Kristin speaking to Adam away from the phone. She couldn't make out the words. She said to Jake, "Adam's there and wants to see Spencer." Jake's face tightened and his mouth narrowed.

A few seconds later, Adam got on the phone. "Where are you?" he asked.

"You're not supposed to be there," Celeste said. "You need to leave."

"Spencer called and asked me to come over."

"I don't believe you—and you know I'll check with him."

"Go ahead and check, Celeste. Check his call log if you want to. What do you think I am, stupid?"

"If he called you, it was a mistake. He's already in bed and can't see you tonight."

"I can send Kristin home, I'll stay with Spencer. I'd like to."

Celeste paced back and forth in Jake's kitchen. "No, Adam, you need to leave right now. It's not fair to Kristin to put her in the middle of our issues."

"You can't keep me from Spencer. I have a right to see my son, Celeste."

She needed to defuse the situation and convince Adam to leave. "You're right, you do, but this isn't a good night for it. Spencer's in bed and Kristin's babysitting. Call me tomorrow and we can work something out."

"Where are you anyway?"

"It's none of your business where I am." *No, don't provoke him.*

Jake was standing behind her now, leaning close to hear.

"Are you on a date—is that it? You're still my wife, Celeste, we're still married. You better not be out with someone else."

"I'm not on a date." She sensed Jake shift beside her. "Please give the phone back to Kristin. I told you we can talk about this tomorrow. Adam, please."

Silence for a moment, then she heard a door closing and Kristin came back on the line.

"He's leaving," Kristin said. "He's getting in his car."

Celeste rubbed her forehead with her thumb and forefinger, massaging the pressure building in her temple. "I'm sorry this happened, Kristin. I should come home."

"No, it's okay. He's gone."

"Did Spencer really call him?"

"I don't know," Kristin said. "We were playing with our phones. Sending text messages and stuff. He was in his room and I was out here."

"All right, call me back if you need to."

She ended the call and noticed smoke curling up from the sides of the oven. She opened the door and a steamy, hot cloud billowed out and the smoke alarm on the ceiling sounded. Jake silenced the shrill chirping while Celeste pulled out the pan and dumped the burnt shrimp in the sink.

They stood among the dissipating smoke, the charred dinner, the wrecked evening. Celeste wished she could press a reset button and start the evening over. Or the last ten years.

"I don't want to make things harder for you," Jake said. "If this isn't a good idea and I'm in the way—"

She shook her head. "This is going to go on forever," she said. "I'll always have to deal with Adam because Spencer is his son. We'll have to live in the same town. We'll have to see each other. There's no getting away from him."

Jake put a hand on her arm. He gave her a tepid smile.

"I need to go home," Celeste said. "In case he comes back." She'd never be able to relax now. She thought of the Super Bowl party, how Adam had swept in and saved the sausages from burning; this time he'd caused the ruin of a meal. In both cases he'd made her anxious and angry. He also made her determined to get him out of her life—but unconvinced she'd be able to. So much for staying optimistic.

"Okay, let's go," Jake said. He didn't try to talk her into staying. Celeste offered to help clean up first. Jake said just leave it.

In the car he turned up the heater, but Celeste couldn't get warm. She crossed her arms and stared out the window. When Jake asked if she wanted to pick another night for their dinner, she said, "I don't know," her tone exasperated, as if Jake had been the one badgering her. Adam was messing up everything, even her ability to carry on a conversation in the car with Jake.

They rode in silence the rest of the way, and the closer they got to her house, the worse Celeste felt. She almost told Jake to turn on Delaware, they could go out somewhere for a drink; she wasn't ready to say good-night to him and be alone.

But she needed to be home.

There were no free spaces in front. Jake double-parked next to Celeste's car and kept the engine running. Her porch light emitted a feeble, milky glow, the bulb wattage too low.

"I can stay and wait with you," Jake said. "That way I'll be here if Adam comes back."

"I don't think he'll come back again tonight. That's not his way of doing things. He prefers to make a big splash and then exit."

"What about your car? I can pick up a battery in the morning and stop over. I don't know much about cars, but I can probably figure out how to replace a battery."

"You're too good," she said. "I don't know why you want to get involved in my mess."

He took her hand and held tight and she felt reassurance flow from him to her. "You'll get past this," he said. "It won't always be contentious between you and Adam. You'll see, it just takes time and then you'll move on, you'll start a new life. I know that's easy for me to say, but it's true."

He was trying to boost her spirits, give her the pep talk. She let herself be swayed. Jake was right: She would get past this; couples and families broke apart all the time and the pieces reassembled in new configurations and life went on and if you were lucky it was better than the life you had before. Maybe that's what Jake was telling her. Maybe by being here he was showing her the door to a better life. Just having Jake in her life hinted that a brighter future could exist.

Jake turned off the engine and they sat in silence. Celeste stared straight ahead. She was aware of her own breathing, her chest rising and falling, a tingling on the back of her neck, Jake's hand mated to hers. Earlier that evening she wondered what she expected or wanted. Now she knew. Now she was ready. The air seemed to shimmer between them, and as he turned to her to speak she reached across and they were in each other's arms and she pressed her lips to his, closed her eyes and swam into a brilliant and needed and wanted connection between them, his mouth melding into hers, tongues touching, and just as she felt herself abandoning caution and opening into him, embracing this seductive sensation and this man, Jake separated from her.

Her lips hummed with heat, her pulse drummed. He looked at her, but it was too dark to read the expression on his face. He said, "I'm sorry, I—" He didn't finish.

Sorry. What was he sorry about? Why had he stopped? She wasn't sure what to say or do next. She didn't want the moment to end but she had to go inside and check on her son, and to preserve and savor the impression of Jake's kiss and to believe that kiss was only a prelude, she gathered herself, opened her door, and whispered good-night.

19

Jake drove down Delaware Avenue and waffled when the signal at Starin changed. First he punched the accelerator and then braked hard, skidding to a stop beneath the red light. He exhaled a long breath and pressed his forehead against the steering wheel and hated himself. His deplorable behavior. His consuming self-interest. He'd been attracted to Celeste from the beginning and found reasons to see her: the lunch dates, walks, visits to art galleries. He latched on under the guise of helping her, because he was alone again, because false hope and physical need propelled him. He knew what came next: He would imagine he loved her—and then he wouldn't know how to scale the emotional wall. And then it would end. He had set himself up for premeditated failure. Come on, look who he'd chosen—another married woman, this one with an angry husband and a vulnerable child. Sure, she was lovely; yes, she was sweet. But he was pathetic. Completely unfair to Celeste, who deserved so much better than him. A few moments ago he managed to pull himself away from her, but already he ached to see her again. Already he wanted her back. And he wouldn't stop himself from pursuing her.

A car horn from behind snapped him back to the present. The light had turned green. Jake sped through the intersection but the driver behind kept close, flashing his high beams off Jake's rearview mirror, punishing him for wasting three precious seconds of his life at a standstill. Jake switched lanes to escape the glare. The driver behind switched, too. When Jake turned onto Masten, the other car followed. Hey asshole, what the fuck. Then he caught a glimpse of the driver in his mirror and adrenaline surged through him.

A hundred yards now until his driveway. Jake considered his options. He could drive past, but Masten dead-ended at the boat launch and he'd have no way to turn around with Adam blocking his way. He could pull over to the side and lock his doors while he called the police. What would he say—he was being tailgated? He knew officers in the Brookfield PD; they'd come to his aid, take his side of any story. Or he could turn into his driveway and deal with this situation, find a way to handle it himself. He had to make the decision, here was his turn. He pulled in and drove up in front of his garage.

Adam followed him in and stopped. Jake searched for something to use to defend himself. His hand found the ice scraper on the floor of the backseat. It had a long handle, a hard plastic edge, a brush along one side. He heard the other car's door open and Jake willed himself to open his and step out. There was Adam, marching right at him. Jake was about to get his ass kicked, or worse. Adam looked primed to explode: pissed off, big fists, someone interfering in his life.

How had he gotten into this? He'd always shied away from confrontation and violence, had been a skinny and bookish kid who didn't emerge until college years, picked near last for any team in gym class, never been in a real fight. Would rather face the humiliation of backing down than get punched in the face. He possessed no fighting skills or any desire to hit or be hit. He believed his revenge against those who bullied him as a kid and shunned him as a teenager had been an MBA and a career that earned him more money than the combined wages of his tormentors, whom he hoped had grown up to be derelicts and convicts. Now the scales were about to tip back the other way, in favor of the tyrants.

Jake squeezed the handle of the ice scraper, kept it hidden behind his leg. The tool felt as substantial as a feather. Adam stopped a few paces away. He had left his engine running and lights on, and the two of them stood in an illuminated arena, darkness surrounding, like mismatched gladiators about to battle.

"Adam. What is it?" He kept his voice neutral and made a point of using Adam's name, hoping to instill a sense of familiarity that might foster civility between them.

"Goddammit, I told you to mind your own business." He pointed his finger at Jake. No civility there.

Jake circled to his right to escape the glare of the headlights. Adam turned and kept them face-to-face. Menace and fear filled his eyes. Not fear of Jake, it couldn't be, but a different type of dread Jake couldn't identify. If he could, he'd find a way to use it to his advantage.

"You fire me from my job and now you're fucking my wife? Is that it?"

"No, that's not what's happening."

"What the hell did I do to you?" Adam demanded. His fists pumped open and closed.

"Nothing. You didn't do anything." Jake stood, legs heavy, the pit of his stomach cold and dense. He needed to find the right words to maneuver out of this.

"I would have run you down that night in the parking lot if I'd known you were going to steal Celeste."

"I'm not stealing her," Jake said. "I've been trying to help her. I got her some work."

"As what—your whore?"

"No. Adam, listen—"

"She's my wife and you stay the fuck away from her!"

Adam moved closer to Jake, a stride long enough to put him within striking distance. Jake stepped back and then said the words without knowing where they'd come from and unable to take them back: "You're the one that should leave her alone. She's through with you, she's divorcing you."

Adam's lips parted and his body appeared to cock like

a trigger. Jake tensed for the blow, considered whether attempting a first strike would be useful. Then Adam lowered his head and stared at the ground, as if he'd dropped something. He made a gasping sound and then another and Jake realized he was sobbing. It was so unexpected that Jake reached out.

Adam's arm shot up and knocked his hand away. He stared at Jake, sniffling. "Fuck you, Atwood. You think you're better than me." Pain and grief spread like darkness across Adam's face. "Celeste and Spencer . . . they're my family. Without them, I have nothing. You're taking away the only thing I have. You're taking my life."

Adam shuffled sideways, out of immediate range. "I know she still loves me," he said. "She needs time to get past what happened. We're going to get back together. We are."

"Okay," Jake said.

The rage returned to his face. "You trying to steal my son, too? You think you can do that?"

"No, you're his father. I'm not trying to steal anyone."

"I'm telling you, stay away from her," Adam said.

"I haven't been—"

"Shut up!" Adam's face twisted and he leaned close enough that Jake could feel his breath. "If I find out you're with her again, I'll come back here and rip your fucking throat out. You hear me? Don't think I won't."

Then he got back in his car and reversed out the driveway, his tires spitting gravel. Jake put his hands to his knees and bent over, desperate to breathe.

20

Saturday morning, Celeste phoned Jake. He didn't answer and she left a message. "Sorry our dinner didn't work out last night—except for the end, that was nice, a little unexpected."

She hoped Jake felt the same way. She wasn't asking more from him beyond companionship, perhaps his arms around her, his lips on hers, a few minutes of wanting and being wanted. Because last night sitting in his car, all she wanted was to be kissed. All she wanted was to lose herself in Jake. She couldn't understand why he had pulled away and apologized to her.

"Anyway, I was wondering if you're still willing to help with my car battery."

She waited an hour; Jake didn't call back.

Spencer wanted to see his friend Peter Beller. Celeste decided to walk with him to Peter's house and then continue on to the auto parts store, another half-mile beyond. It was a good day for a walk: the sun a brilliant golden eye in a cloudless sky, the temperature above freezing, no wind. She could have a talk with Spencer on the way.

"Did you call your father last night?" Celeste asked.

Spencer didn't answer, which was answer enough for Celeste. That, along with his eyes suddenly so interested in where each of his feet landed on the sidewalk.

"It's okay if you did," she said, "I just want to know."

"I guess I did."

"Did you ask Dad to come over?"

Spencer shook his head. "I just wanted to talk."

"So you didn't ask him to come over. What did you talk with him about?"

"I said you were out and Kristin was babysitting."

"Did you tell him where I was?"

"I don't know," Spencer said. "He asked if I wanted him to be his babysitter sometime. I said he can't be my babysitter because he's my father."

"Did you call him because I was out with Mr. Atwood? Did that bother you?"

"He said I could call him Jake."

Spencer let her take his hand while they walked. How much longer would he allow himself to be seen holding his mother's hand? Not long, she was afraid.

"I had a dream that Dad came over. He was going to live with us again."

"He did come over after talking to you, but he couldn't come in because you were in bed and I wasn't home." Spencer probably hadn't fallen asleep yet or was passing through the twilight world between awake and asleep when he heard Adam at the door.

"The part about Dad coming back to live with us—that was part of your dream," Celeste said. "That's not going to happen."

"But he came over to see me."

"He can only visit if he arranges with me first. You know that. That's just the way it has to be."

"I know."

After dropping off Spencer, she continued on to the auto parts store. The walking felt good, her legs strong from running with Emery. Maybe she'd get the new battery in her car and have time to take a run before Spencer got home. She could call Emery and meet her in the park. But then she remembered today was Saturday and Emery would be busy with her family; her older girls had swimming.

At the auto parts store, she tried Jake's number again. This time she didn't leave a message. Maybe he'd forgotten about his offer to help her. Or maybe he was watching her number come up on his display and ignoring her. Had she completely misread what happened last night? There was no mistaking Jake's intent when he was kissing her, but she couldn't blame him if he wanted to avoid her; she'd even suggested as much to him: Why would he want to get involved in her mess with Adam?

She asked at the counter about a battery and the clerk looked up her car make and model, then located the correct battery for her on the parts shelf. He carried it to the counter and asked if she needed anything else.

"They're pretty easy to put in, aren't they?" Celeste asked.

"As long as you've got a wrench. It's usually two bolts on the brace and the nuts on the battery connectors." The clerk was young, early twenties, and could use some hair gel to control his cowlick. "Sometimes the nuts get corrosion on them. It's a good idea to spray them first."

"With what?"

He got her a can of lubricant. "Just spray the nuts and wait a few minutes for it to soak in."

"Thanks." She lifted the battery and set it back down on the counter. "Wow, it's really heavy," she said, thinking of the walk home, almost a mile. "Do you have a bag?"

The clerk put the battery into a thick plastic bag. When she grasped the handles and lifted, the battery formed a tight rectangular outline against the bottom of the bag but didn't rip the plastic. On the walk back she had to keep switching arms and the battery swung like a pendulum in the bag and bumped her legs. She stopped four times to set the bag down and rest. By the time she got home, both her shoulders ached and her shins were bruised from the bumping. She left the bag in front of her car parked along the curb and then popped the hood and searched around until she spotted the battery. At least it was accessible in the front corner. Good thing she'd gotten the spray, because a white, crusty crud covered the nuts like dirty snow. She shook the can and turned her face while she sprayed the bolts on the brace and the two connecters where the cables clamped to the battery. Then she went inside to change into an old sweatshirt and get her tools.

She came back out with three wrenches she kept along with several screwdrivers in a kitchen drawer. None of the wrenches fit. One was too small, the other too big. She tried the adjustable wrench, turning the set wheel and fitting it onto one of the bolts. The wrench kept slipping off. She tried the other bolt. Same thing. She tried one of the battery connectors and the wrench slipped off the nut and the outside of her hand caught on something sharp.

Now she was bleeding. And swearing.

She blotted her hand on her sweatshirt and pushed her hair back behind her ears out of her eyes. She was about to try again when Adam drove up alongside her car, pulled forward, and parked across the street. He got out, waited for a pickup truck to pass, and crossed over to her.

"Hey, what's going on?" He wore his old Taconic State basketball jacket, which still fit after fifteen years. She hadn't seen it in ages.

Celeste folded her arms across her chest, hiding her wounded hand against her sweatshirt sleeve.

Adam leaned in. "You having trouble getting the bolts off? Counterclockwise loosens them."

"Yes, I know."

"Here, let me see that wrench."

Celeste hesitated, about to say no, but what was the point of that feeble protest? She handed Adam the wrench.

"You're bleeding. Are you okay?"

"I'm fine."

He tried to take her hand but she pulled back. "Be sure to clean that cut out," he said. "You get any battery grime in there and it'll get infected."

He examined the wrench. "Here's half the problem—these cheap adjustable wrenches. They don't stay in place."

Despite the cold, he took off his jacket and laid it across the roof of her car. He wore a tight-fitting gray T-shirt underneath, her name displayed on his upper arm. He adjusted the set wheel and fit the wrench to one of the brace bolts, then kept his thumb on the wheel to keep it from moving while he turned counterclockwise. The bolt came right off.

"See, if you hold the wheel with your other thumb while turning the wrench, it stays on better."

He removed the second bolt, then the two battery connectors. Lifted the old battery out and set it on the pavement, nested the new one in place, reinstalled the battery cables and the brace. Tightened all nuts and bolts. Completed the job in about three minutes. Overall, an expert and humiliating demonstration of Celeste's incompetence.

"You know, you don't have to do everything alone," Adam said. "You could have called, I would have helped—no strings attached." His eyes emitted a soft blue light, the way she remembered them from better days. "Don't forget, Celeste, we loved each other once. We spent ten years pretty happily married before I went and screwed everything up."

Something unmoored in her, and she felt her resolve drifting and beginning to weaken. Doubt swirled in her: Am I too unfair? Has he finally changed and begun to right himself? Do I really want to move on from Adam? And then the painful wave struck again: the lying, the gambling, the disappointments. The physical assault and the fear it left in her like an illness she couldn't shake. No, she couldn't trust him, she didn't love him.

"I came over last night because Spencer called," Adam said.

"You can't come here without my permission."

Adam turned and looked at her house, wedged in the middle of the block among other worn dwellings. "I'm here now without your permission. I don't hear you telling me to leave. Or does being on the street and helping you install your battery not count as coming over?"

"You know what I mean."

"Spencer said you were out with your new boyfriend."

"I already spoke to Spencer about what he said."

"Who is he, Celeste?"

She unhooked the stay rod and let the car hood slam shut. She put the old battery and spray can into the plastic bag, left the bag at the curb, and started up to her house, Adam on her heels.

"You better not be whoring around. I won't stand for that."

She spun around and almost slapped him except she was afraid he'd hit her back. "Get over it, Adam. I'm moving on with my life and you need to do the same."

"Doesn't matter. I know who your big hero is. He's not so tough after all."

What did that mean?

"I saw you with him, I saw you sitting in the car. You were so wrapped up you didn't know I was right across the street."

They stood at her front steps now.

"I want to see Spencer. That's what I'm here for."

"He's at a friend's house."

"What friend?"

"You want to see Spencer? Fine. A visitation agreement will be part of the divorce. Then you'll have your rights to visit with Spencer. Until then, stay away from me. And stay away from Spencer. I've already made that clear."

He grabbed her by the arm, his hand constricting around her bicep, pinching her muscle to the bone.

"Ow! Let go, you're hurting me." She tugged and he gave her another squeeze, then released her. She rubbed her arm.

"You can forget about seeing Spencer," she said. They were at a standoff, glaring at each other. She wanted to go inside but he might follow her, so she returned to her car and got in. The engine started right up. She drove off, leaving Adam standing on the sidewalk.

21

Allison Chambers sat at the next desk in his class and sometimes they lent each other an eraser or hung out at recess on the monkey bars, and now every day after school they walked home together for the first few blocks as far as Tioga Street, where Allison turned and Spencer continued on Westin and Kathy kept him company the rest of the way. Most days he and

Kathy played the alphabet game. By the time Spencer reached Amherst Street they would be up to *W,* sometimes *Z,* with only half a long block remaining to his house, and he often raced Kathy the distance and sometimes let her win but usually he won or they tied.

Today he dragged along, his backpack heavy from the three rocks Mrs. Moore allowed him to take home. The class had finished the unit on geology and she had given him the samples of obsidian, marble, and shale displayed in the classroom so he could use them for his science fair project. Each one was about the size of two of his fists and combined weighed down his pack a lot. Plus he had his math book and spelling notebook and his empty lunch box in there. He could hardly get the zipper closed. And he had to carry his trumpet case; today was lesson day.

He had just finished with the letter *T—T my name is Thomas and my wife's name is Teresa, I come from Tarrytown and I'm selling toilets*—and was almost to the intersection at Amherst when a car that looked a lot like Dad's pulled to the curb and the window on the passenger side rolled down.

It was Dad.

"Spencer, hey Spence." Dad leaned across the seat toward the open window.

Spencer stopped, then approached the car. His mother had drilled in him like a million times that he should never ever respond to anyone calling out to him from a car while he was walking home. He shouldn't even look at cars going by on the street.

But this was Dad. This didn't count.

He went up to the window and Dad reached out and touched Spencer's cheek and he flinched for a second.

"What's up, buddy? I thought maybe we could do something together."

Spencer glanced back over his shoulder toward the corner at Amherst. He was only a few minutes from home.

"What do you say? Get in."

"Mom said I had to walk straight home after school."

"Of course you do, I just talked to her. I told Mom I'd pick you up and we'd have a few hours together and then I'd drop you back later."

"You told Mom I called you," Spencer said.

"You didn't get in trouble, did you?"

"I didn't tell you Mom was on a date. I just said she was out with someone."

"Sure, sure. Come on, let's go. Get in."

Spencer shifted his trumpet case to his other hand. "I have to do my homework first."

"We'll do your homework later—and I'll help if you want."

"I have to practice my trumpet."

"Yeah, I'd love to hear you play. Here, give me that backpack."

Dad opened the passenger door. Spencer slid off his backpack—that felt good—and handed it to his father.

"Whoa, that's heavy, what have you got, a bunch of rocks in there?"

"How did you know?" Spencer started to open the rear door.

"Come on, sit up front with your dad."

"Mom says I should sit in back because of the air bags."

"You're a big boy. Ten. You're double digits from now on, until you're a hundred years old." Dad heaved his pack into the backseat. Spencer got in front.

"What should we do? I know, let's go bowling. I passed by the bowling alley on my way and remembered how much fun we used to have. Right?"

Spencer examined the floor mats. He did remember

having fun bowling with Dad, but Spencer sensed betrayal of his mother now. Although if Dad already talked to her, then it must be okay.

Adam put the car in gear and pulled away from the curb. "What do you say? Bowling?"

Spencer spoke into his window, which returned a vague, ghostly reflection of his face. "Mom said you hurt her."

"What?"

This time he addressed the dashboard. "Mom said you grabbed her by the neck."

Oh, Jesus. What the hell has she been telling him?

"Do me a favor, Spence, tell Mom if I hurt her in any way, I am so sorry. If I did, it was completely an accident. I would never hurt Mom. Will you be sure to tell her that? I already told her myself, many times, but can you tell her, too? That I'm sorry, I would never hurt her."

"She had a bruise on her neck. I saw it. You choked her."

Adam sighed. He'd like to choke the bitch right now. "Spencer, have you ever been angry at someone, or in an argument with a friend or classmate, and maybe you wanted to push that person or something?"

"I hit somebody on the bus," Spencer said.

"Well, then you know. And you also know it was a mistake. Mom and I had an argument and that's what happened. It was a mistake, and like I said, I'm really sorry, and it will never happen again."

"And you won't hit me again?"

"Hit you? I never—" Oh, Christ, that one time he'd given Spencer the back of his hand at the dinner table because he wouldn't stop playing with his food. And the way Celeste had jumped up and screamed as if Adam had pulled a gun and shot his son. He'd meted out a small spanking that a generation ago would have seemed soft and now was practically a crime. Yes, it was a mistake—and no one would let him forget it, even though more than a year had passed since then.

"I will never hit you, I promise you that," Adam said. Then he added, "It's good you brought this up, because Mom asked me to talk to you. Explain the situation, you know, father to son." He gave Spencer a moment to process this information. No doubt, it was a lot for a ten-year-old.

"Did Mom tell you I came over and put a new battery in her car?"

"She said you're still a gambler and won't stop. She said you can't control yourself and that's why you hurt her."

He gripped the steering wheel tight enough to yank it off. The color from his knuckles drained. How was he going to get through this? How to undo the damage? He had to, or Spencer would turn against him forever. He couldn't lose his boy. Never. Not Spencer.

"That's another thing we need to talk about," Adam said, keeping his voice controlled and even. "You know how when someone is sick they don't always get completely better right away? Remember when Grandma had cancer? That was a really hard time. The doctors treated her cancer and we all thought Grandma was better, but then the cancer came back and the doctors had to treat her again."

"Grandma and Grandpa sent me a hundred dollars for my birthday," Spencer said.

"Yes, that's really generous of them. They love you so much. And Grandma, you know, she's been sick."

"But she's better now, right?"

"The doctors gave her more medicine and now the cancer

has gone away again. Now she's better and we hope she stays that way. But the cancer could come back, that's the way some diseases are. We hope it doesn't happen, but if it does, the doctors will help her again."

Adam put a hand on his son's knee. Spencer's leg tensed.

"I'm telling you this about Grandma because I have a disease, too. Gambling, that's a disease. It's an illness. It's one of those diseases like cancer that starts without your even knowing, and by the time you realize you have it, you're pretty sick. I saw doctors and they helped me get better, but then the disease came back, just like it did with Grandma."

"Are you going to die?"

"No, no. It's not that kind of disease. I'm healthy again, and I plan on staying that way."

Adam hadn't placed a bet since the disaster with the Taconic game. He'd thought about it a few times, but then the thought would fade. Maybe that was the hump the doctors had talked about at Glendale, the need waning. He'd gotten over it. Besides, he couldn't go anywhere near his bookie. He'd been waiting for Vincent Canto to track him down with a couple of guys for that twenty-five grand, although Canto didn't know where to find Adam—he lived with his parents in Chappaqua and he sure as hell wasn't going back to GA meetings at Holy Trinity or ever showing up at Mario's again.

What troubled him now more than the gambling urge was his anger toward Celeste. He couldn't help thinking Celeste was poisoning Spencer with a lot of misinformation and ruining Adam's chances for reestablishing a good relationship with his son. What boy needs to be told the father who loves him is violent and out of control—when, in fact, Adam was doing his best right now? He may not be the perfect father, but he loved his son. He missed Spencer even more than he missed

Celeste. And Celeste was so insistent on keeping Adam away from Spencer he was forced into tactics like intercepting his son on his walk home from school just so they can spend an hour or two together. The attorney his father hired for him, Howard Jasper, told Adam the court would ultimately determine Adam's access rights to Spencer, but Adam believed the more the lawyers got involved, the worse the chances he'd ever get his family back. Lawyers were for people who couldn't solve their own problems, who weren't intelligent enough or committed enough to their goals. Some things needed to be worked out between people, and his and Celeste's marriage was one of them.

Celeste put on her coat and stepped out on the porch. She didn't need to watch Spencer walk down the block every day, but she loved waiting for him and then seeing him—that first glimpse every afternoon filled her with joy. Many mothers couldn't be at home for their kids after school; they worked and sent their kids to after-school programs or let their kids come home alone. Celeste could never do that. She would live her entire life in this house, keep her thermostat turned down, and pay bills late rather than not be here for Spencer every day. Her son was going to grow up knowing he meant everything in the world to at least one of his parents.

The rules she'd set with Spencer: Walk straight home after school. No long cuts. No dillydallying. Obviously no talking to strangers or getting in or near anyone's car.

So where was he? He should never be later than 3:32 but here it was 3:35 and no sign of him.

She called Spencer's cell number. No answer. She started to walk down Amherst, following the route Spencer took home.

At the corner she turned right onto Westin and still didn't see him. She picked up her pace and got to Brookfield South Elementary and still no Spencer. She searched in back on the playground and stopped in his classroom and asked Mrs. Moore if she knew where Spencer had gone after school.

"I thought he just went home," Mrs. Moore said. "I haven't seen him. Is everything okay?"

"I don't know." She went to the office and asked the secretary if she'd seen Spencer Vanek or if maybe he'd taken the bus and gotten on the wrong one, forgetting which one was his since he'd been walking home recently.

"We didn't get a call from any of the drivers," the secretary said.

Suddenly the acid rose in her throat, and the horrible thing every parent feared ran like a film reel through her head—*Hey, boy, do you want some candy? Hey, can you help me find my lost dog?*—even though the chances of the horrible thing happening were so small; a child in Brookfield was more likely to die in a car accident or be struck by lightning. Still, a risk was a risk, and if the horrible thing struck, it didn't matter what the odds were leading up to it, and Celeste would never forgive herself for allowing Spencer to walk home.

Maybe he'd gone home with Peter Beller. Although Spencer would never do that unless Celeste had made a plan ahead of time with Peter's father. She was about to call the police and report that her son was missing, but just then her cell phone chimed. Thank God. It must be Spencer with some crazy explanation for why he hadn't come home after school.

She fished her phone from her coat pocket and saw Adam's name on the caller ID display. *Please*, not now, she thought—but then realized what had happened to Spencer.

First thing when they arrived at Del Lanes, Adam told Spencer he wanted to call Mom to let her know where they were. "Go pick out a ball," he said to his son. "Don't get one too heavy."

Spencer set out for the rack that held the colorful, lightweight balls.

Adam closed his eyes for a long blink to compose what he wanted to say. This wasn't going to be easy; she was going to be pissed. He pressed to call Celeste's number.

"Adam?" she said. She sounded out of breath, panting.

"Guess what? I ran into Spencer on his way home from school and we decided to spend a little time together."

He held the phone away from his ear as a sound somewhere between a growl and a scream came back at him. "Oh my God, Adam, do you know what you just put me through? Do you have any idea how I felt when Spencer didn't come home and I couldn't find him? I was panicking."

He could hear her crying on the other end. Her reaction was worse than he'd anticipated.

"It was only a few minutes," Adam said. "That's why I'm calling you."

"A few minutes? He should have been home a half-hour ago. I had no idea what happened to him. I was about to call the police."

They'd never had the same concept of time. Celeste tended to be punctual to a fault—never late, often early—and intolerant of Adam's more relaxed interpretation of time.

"Where are you?" she demanded. "You ran into him? What does that mean? Put him on, I want to speak with him."

"Slow down, everything is fine."

"Nothing is fine! You can't do this, Adam, I mean it. You can't take him without my permission. This is going to have consequences."

It was his turn to growl. "If you're not going to let me see Spencer, then I'll do it my way."

In the background, someone rolled a strike. The pins crashed and the bowler yelled out.

"What was that noise? Where are you? I want you to bring Spencer home now."

"I'll bring him home when I'm good and ready."

"No. Bring Spencer home right now. I'll call the police and have you arrested if you don't."

"Call the fucking police, I don't give a shit." He ended the call.

Spencer walked over to him with his ball, a shiny, dazzling planet of blue and yellow swirls, which he handed to Adam and asked if it was okay. Adam was vibrating from his argument with Celeste, the rage like a drug in his veins. He took a few breaths to steady himself, then held Spencer's ball. It felt about as heavy as a balloon. "Perfect," he said. "Let's bowl."

They traded their sneakers for bowling shoes.

"Do you want the gutter guards up?" Adam asked.

"I don't know."

"I could use them, I hate rolling gutter balls."

"Okay," Spencer agreed.

Adam asked the cashier to put up the gutter guards, then he and Spencer started bowling. He pushed his conversation with Celeste out of his mind, and simply enjoyed playing a game with his son. Adam could bowl without embarrassing himself—he usually rolled a 150 or higher—and obviously didn't need the gutter guards. But Spencer's ball caromed off one guard and then the other for the first few frames. Adam reminded him to balance the ball in the palm of his non-rolling hand, line himself up with the marks on the alley floor, and perform a simple three-step approach before squatting and releasing the ball and following through. Always end with your arm up high. He went over the motion with him a few times, and being this close to Spencer—holding his arms and guiding his movements, absorbing the warm radiance of his son—Adam felt his own heart melting. By the end of the first game, Spencer had gotten a spare. Final score: Adam 162, Spencer 49.

"I'm so bad," Spencer said. "I stink at bowling."

"What's the matter—you did great. It's like any game, you have to practice if you want to get better. You know that. Come on, we'll play another. But we should get a snack first."

Adam got an order of French fries and two Cokes. They sat at a table against a half-wall perched above their lane, and Adam asked Spencer who he was hanging out with from school these days.

"No one too much."

"What about that boy, Peter—are you friends with him still?"

"Sometimes."

"Do you still have your other friend? The pretend one."

"Kathy," Spencer reminded him.

"Can I ask you something, Spence? How come you have this imaginary friend? I mean, where did she come from?"

Spencer sipped the soda through his straw. He looked directly at Adam, his face serious and thoughtful. "She just comes. She shows up in my mind and I can see her there."

Adam nodded. "Sure, I know exactly what you mean." He had been the same way: how one second his mind could be empty of thought or focused elsewhere, and the next instant he was gambling. Or losing his temper and lashing out.

It was like he didn't have a choice, he didn't decide. It just happened.

"You know how much I love you?" Adam said. "I can't tell you how much, it's so much." He started to choke up and he waited for Spencer to say something back, but his boy just sat there sipping soda.

Adam battled back the surge of emotion. He squirted more ketchup on the fries. "It's good to have time for just the two of us. Don't you think?"

"Mom said I wouldn't be seeing you much anymore."

Again he fought a welling of tears. "Of course you're going to be seeing me," Adam said. Then he added, "In fact, you're going to be seeing a lot more of me than you have been. A father and his son need to spend time together, don't you think?"

Spencer nodded neutrally. He reached for a French fry.

Adam said, "You know, if anything ever happened to Mom, you'd come live with me at Grandma and Grandpa's."

Spencer stopped chewing. "I thought Aunt Chantal was my guardian."

"No, with me. You'd live with Aunt Chantal only if something happened to both Mom and me at the same time. But don't even think about that."

Spencer lifted shiny, wet eyes to his father's face. He was about to cry. "What's going to happen to Mom?"

"No, no, no. Let's forget all this talk," Adam said. "I shouldn't have said anything. What do you say, let's bowl another game."

22

She did end up calling the police, and two Brookfield police officers, both younger than Celeste, showed up at her door with dark blue uniforms, buzzed hair, and belts thick with tools and weapons. They looked official and righteous and powerful and did absolutely nothing on her behalf. They informed her that because Celeste had no legal separation or custody agreement in place, Adam had just as much right to be with Spencer as she did, even though Celeste had been distraught when her son didn't come home and Adam had taken him without letting her know. No law had been broken, no order of protection violated, no threat issued, no act of violence committed. One of the police officers handed Celeste a business card and suggested she contact the Social Services Department if she needed assistance working out her personal situation. The entire encounter proved pretty embarrassing. Then, just as the officers were leaving, Adam pulled up behind the police cruiser and Spencer got out of the car and strapped on his backpack and picked up his trumpet case. Adam waved out the window and drove away.

Spencer came slowly up the walkway, eyeing the police car and then the two policemen standing on the porch. One of the cops leaned down and said to Spencer, "Was that your father?"

"Yeah."

"Are you okay?"

"I'm fine?" More a question than an answer, his face a bundle of confusion.

The two officers left and Celeste took Spencer inside and

settled him at the kitchen table. She put a pan of milk on the stove to make hot chocolate.

"Why did the police come, Mommy? They scared me."

She kept her voice calm. "When you didn't come home from school, I thought something might have happened to you. I called your phone."

"It was in my backpack."

"You have to keep it where you can hear the ring," Celeste said. "I had no idea where you were. You should have called me if you weren't coming home right away."

"Dad said he talked to you."

"Only after I walked back to school and asked the secretary and Mrs. Moore if they'd seen you. And after I called your phone and got no answer."

"Are you mad at me?"

Celeste sat down across from him. She took his hand. "No, honey, I'm not mad at you, but I was very concerned when you didn't come home."

"You're mad at Dad?"

"I'm definitely angry with your father. He knew I'd be worried." She lifted his backpack off the table and set it on the chair. "What's so heavy in here?" She opened the pack and picked out the rocks, placing each on the table.

"Mrs. Moore gave them to me because I wanted to do my science fair project on rocks."

"That was nice of her."

"But now I changed my mind. I want to do it on gambling disease instead."

Celeste got up to turn off the burner under the pan of milk, giving her a few extra seconds to determine the right way to respond. But there was no clear right way when facing this unknown territory. It was like navigating an uncharted river:

You have no idea what you might find around the next bend—smooth water, or rapids, or waterfalls. The one thing you did know is the current flowed in one direction only, there was no traveling back upstream; you were destined for what lay ahead.

"I don't think that would be considered science," Celeste said, choosing her words carefully. "Aren't you supposed to ask a question—such as *How are rocks formed?*—and answer it? You already have a really good science question."

"I can ask how doctors treat gambling disease. Dad said he has it, but he's getting better now, like Grandma's cancer."

She sat across from him again and waited until he met her eyes. "Let me explain something, honey: What your father has is nothing like Grandma's cancer. Not at all. She had a disease she had no control over and could do nothing to prevent. Your father doesn't have a disease. He didn't contract or catch anything that made him sick. He made a *decision* to gamble. No one makes a decision to get cancer. Do you understand the difference?"

That was one of the things that bothered her about the Glendale Wellness Center. Its philosophy was to treat compulsive gambling as a disease. You take that perspective and now you have a medical problem to deal with, as if Adam had a damaged organ instead of weak self-control or a destructive habit. One aim of this approach was to make others more sympathetic to sufferers, but Celeste's capacity for sympathy had been exceeded. What was next? Choking and assault as a medical problem?

It wasn't only at Glendale that gambling was considered a disease. Just last week, Eva Vanek had visited Celeste and Spencer. She said she wanted to see for herself where her daughter-in-law and grandson lived, but from the way she hugged herself and averted her eyes—her gaze constantly flicking around, settling on nothing—she acted as if she didn't want to see anything. Celeste served a banana bread she'd baked and Eva chatted with Spencer about school and friends and music, and when he ran out of things to tell her he excused himself and went to his room to write his spelling sentences. That's when Celeste told Eva her hair was growing in nicely and asked how she was feeling now that the chemo treatments were over.

"I feel ages younger than I did last year at this time," Eva said. "I think we've beaten this awful disease back for good."

"I'm so relieved to hear that."

"You know what was the best medicine throughout the ordeal? My family. Having Joseph by my side the whole time, and the kids, of course. Cori and Ben visited every month, and Adam, well, he's there for me."

Celeste offered a sympathetic smile and let the silence drift between them. Then Eva, a hint of bitterness in her voice, said, "I wish you could see that Adam is every bit as ill as I was, that he, too, is in the throes of an insidious disease, and he needs the kind of support from his family that I had from mine."

"I understand what you're saying," Celeste said, a response that neither agreed nor disagreed with Eva's statement. She wasn't going to argue with a frail old woman who'd battled cancer for the past two years. She wasn't going to counter Eva's claim about her son suffering in the grips of a disease by telling her Adam was weak and self-destructive and had attacked and choked her—what good would that do? What mother wouldn't roar back in defense of her son?

But speaking with her own son now called for a different approach.

"Every time your father placed a bet he made a decision," Celeste said, mixing in the cocoa powder and setting the cup of hot chocolate in front of Spencer. "It wasn't a disease that caused him to act. He could have said no. He could have decided his family was more important than a bet he was making. But he decided to gamble instead, and that's the choice he made and kept making until he lost all the money we had, until he lost his goodness, lost us."

Spencer blinked hard a few times and stared back at her and didn't say anything.

"I'm sorry, I know this is hard to understand and accept about your father. You shouldn't have to go through this, it's so unfair to you."

"It's unfair to you, too," he said.

She eked out a smile and leaned over and kissed the top of his head.

"I guess I'll still do rocks," he said. He picked up the cup Celeste set in front of him and blew on the surface to cool the steaming cocoa. He took a tentative sip.

"Dad said if anything ever happened to you that I would live with him."

"*What*?" Her voice near a whisper. What did he mean *if anything happened to her*?

"He said I'd only live with Aunt Chantal if something happened to both you and Dad at the same time."

"Nothing is going to happen to me," Celeste said. "You don't need to worry about that. There's no reason to even think about this. I don't know why Dad mentioned it to you."

"But is it true—I'd live with Dad if anything happened to you? Does that mean if you died?"

She needed to do something with her hands. She reached and brushed his hair off his forehead, told him not to think that way, she wasn't about to die, nothing bad was going to happen. The next day she called her attorney.

Iris Mair's office occupied the rear of the first floor of a wooden Victorian two blocks off the commercial district in Brookfield. A wooden sign attached to an iron pole planted in the front lawn had the words *Iris P. Mair | Family Law* engraved in gold lettering on a navy background. Inside, her furniture consisted of an oak teacher's desk and laptop computer, two floor-to-ceiling bookcases with law books arranged at every angle, and a round wooden coffee table circled by three armchairs. Heavy red drapes were pulled back to let in the afternoon sun, which cast a long, bright rectangle on the wall opposite the window.

Celeste sat in one of the chairs, Iris across the table from her in another. Iris was barely five feet tall, thin as a reed, with tiny and perfectly proportioned features like those of a doll. Her eyes were dirt brown. A pencil-line scar ran from the inside corner of her right eye, down along the valley of her nose, ending at the top of her upper lip, from the time she'd tripped and fallen through a glass patio door in the days before safety glass was used. The scar could possibly be mistaken for an age line, and might one day, but Iris was too young for such an age crease—a few years older than Celeste, although she looked five years younger—and there was no matching line on the other side of her face.

In college, Iris had been friends with Celeste's sister. Chantal told Celeste she'd accompanied Iris when Iris went for an abortion, and her friend promised to repay that act of kindness someday. Years later, she did so by accepting Celeste as a client, at a significantly reduced rate, even though Iris was a sole practitioner and already burdened with a full load of divorce cases and other family matters.

Celeste was explaining about Adam taking Spencer on the walk home from school, causing an hour of harrowing panic and confusion and prompting her to call the police when Adam wouldn't return her son. While Celeste was talking, Iris's desk phone rang, immediately followed by her mobile phone, which rested on the table between them. Iris picked up her cell to read the display.

"Don't ever think the police are on your side," Iris said, returning her attention to Celeste. "They are loath to get in the middle of domestic arguments, which are some of the most dangerous situations police face. People get very emotional when love goes wrong. They can quickly turn violent."

Iris typed a response to whatever message she had just received and hit the Send button.

"Sorry," she said. "I've got a couple of cases coming to court this week. Where were we?"

Celeste then recounted the story about Adam telling their son that if anything happened to Celeste, Spencer would live with his father. She knew a threat lurked in that comment's shadows. Adam was using Spencer to deliver the message. And frankly, she was getting scared—as was Spencer. Imagine being ten years old and having to hear that.

Iris's first reaction to Celeste's story was to commiserate. "You've been through an awful experience," she said. "This must be so hard on you." Then she put Celeste's feelings aside. "But the fact is the police responded appropriately and Adam acted within his legal rights. True, his actions could be construed as aggressive for not letting you know he was picking up your son, but Adam's lawyer will argue that it was simply a miscommunication. The other thing—what Spencer said about living with his father if anything happened to you—that information was delivered secondhand from your child, so it's hearsay. We don't have the benefit of context here. Sure, you can see the threat in that remark, and I do, too, but someone else might interpret it as factual information clarifying custodial rights in the event of a tragedy."

"He was threatening me—I know it," Celeste said. She gripped the arms of her chair and leaned closer to Iris. "He even came by demanding to see Spencer and accusing me of *whoring around.* Those were his words. I can't believe he said that."

Iris's mobile phone sounded again. This time she held up one finger to Celeste and said, "Hold that thought, I need to take this." She stood and turned away from Celeste and spoke rapidly to the caller. Celeste felt a little miffed that Iris wasn't completely paying attention to her.

When Iris got off the phone, Celeste said, "The bottom line is I need the divorce to go through quickly, and I need full custody of Spencer."

"It's going to take more time," Iris said. "This attorney Adam has—Howard Jasper—he knows all the tricks. Adam has clearly asked him to delay the divorce as long as possible."

"There has to be something we can do."

"Well, there is," Iris said. "When you first met with me about the divorce, you said Adam had choked you. I suggested you file for an order of protection, but you decided not to."

The idea had sounded so severe. At the time, she was still granting Adam some semblance of compassion—he had lost control and hadn't meant to attack her, she didn't want the police involved, and she had just made the decision to divorce him and was getting used to the idea. Plus she hated being labeled a victim. Now she realized that whether Adam had meant her harm or not wasn't the issue. The issue was that one uncontrollable moment could be followed by another, and Adam picking up Spencer unannounced and making an innuendo about something tragic happening to Celeste actually amounted to a forced abduction and a real threat. It wasn't only herself she had to protect, but Spencer, too. Especially Spencer. The truth was, she would never get that slap out of her mind, when Adam's hand darted out and struck Spencer on the side of the head. He had hit their child—hard. And from where one act of violence originates, others spawn.

"I should have taken your suggestion," Celeste said.

"You still can," Iris said. "If there is any evidence of violence, even if it occurred in the past, you can go to court right now and get an emergency temporary order of protection. Judges err on the side of caution and will grant your request—at least until a hearing is set."

"And then what happens?"

"A judge will decide if a permanent order of protection is necessary. But either way, you're serving notice to Adam: He will be held accountable for his actions."

"How can I prove what happened?" Celeste said.

"I remember you mentioned that someone intervened. So there was a witness?"

"Yes. His name is Jake Atwood. He works at this company, GeoPol, where Adam attacked me. He was walking out to his car in the parking lot and saw everything."

"He stopped Adam from choking you?"

"He came right up to us and made Adam back off. He saved me."

"Can we get him to testify on your behalf at a hearing?" Iris's phone chimed and she picked it up and typed a quick reply.

"I'm sure he would. I've seen him a few times since then, and he helped me get work from his company."

Hopefully Jake would testify. Celeste hadn't heard from

him since Friday night when their dinner was ruined and they shared that spontaneous kiss after he drove her home. She had called him the next morning, twice, but he didn't answer his phone either time and had yet to return her calls. She knew why. He didn't want to get involved with her because of Adam and because Celeste came with the baggage of a child. A woman, a mom, harassed by her soon-to-be-ex-husband? Now there's a prize. Plus Jake had already made pretty clear what a relationship with him entailed, although just because she kissed him and wanted to again didn't mean she needed a commitment from him. Desire had its own agenda, its own schedule—not always clean and not always tidy, but always demanding. You just can't control some things. But she couldn't explain any of this to Jake unless he returned her calls.

"The first thing to do is get the temporary order," Iris said. "Then the judge will schedule a hearing where both you and Adam—and me, of course, and Howard Jasper—will be present. At that time, Mr. Atwood can present his testimony and the order of protection can be extended."

It sounded like a good plan to Celeste.

"I should warn you," Iris said. "Divorce proceedings are heard in the Supreme Court, but a domestic order of protection is handled in Family Court. There's a big difference. Family Court is like the emergency room for poor people seeking legal remedies. Although domestic violence crosses every demographic, people with resources usually can work out their issues through attorneys and reasonable negotiation, but if you can't, you come to Family Court."

Iris's phone rang yet again.

23

Sara pushed through the bathroom door, opened the toilet lid, and vomited from a standing squat. Not much came up from her empty stomach: a few orange droplets splashed on the rim, a sticky stream clung to her mouth. She lowered herself to her knees and hugged the bowl and felt Connie's hands on her shoulders, holding back her hair. This time she dry-heaved.

"Jesus, what's wrong?" Connie asked. Shaving cream covered half his face.

She cleared her throat and spit, then ripped off a length of toilet paper and wiped her mouth. She dropped the wadded tissue into the bowl and flushed.

He put his palm on her forehead. "You feel warm. I think you have a fever."

"I'm sweating from puking." She did feel like crap: achy and hot, her stomach a speeding roller coaster.

Typically, it was Connie who suffered the maladies: the upset stomach, the cough, the headache, the dizzy spell—every twinge and ache signaling the next heart attack, his impending demise. He was so afraid of dying, Sara thought, he almost wanted to get it over with so he wouldn't have to live with the fear. Those times when he was sick or thought he was, Sara had to counsel him more than she had to nurse him, talk him down from the ledge of despair.

Today was his turn to provide counsel.

"Do you want me to call the doctor? Should I take you in?"

"It's nothing, just a stomach bug maybe."

"There's a lot of flu going around right now. Almost a third of my class is out. You should stay home today."

"No, I already feel better now that I've thrown up." She stood and held onto him for support.

By the time she got to work she felt good enough to snatch one of the pastries from the box of baked goods that appeared in the break room every morning. She was eating an apple turnover at her desk when her phone rang and Falcone said, "Montez. Get in here."

Now what? She could never tell what he wanted from his tone alone; he spoke in only two notes: gruff or grumpy. He could be in the sweetest, most generous mood and he would still bark like a guard dog.

Falcone remained seated, elbows on the desk, hands folded and tucked beneath his chin. He did not offer Sara a chair. She remained standing, facing him. He studied her, his eyebrows squeezed and arched into question marks, as if she had been the one to request a meeting and he was waiting for her to begin.

"Remind me why we hired GeoPol for a job of such high importance?" he said.

This again. "Is there a problem I don't know about?" she said. "The address matching rates have improved to acceptable thresholds since they updated their software. We're on schedule and adding new data feeds from other jurisdictions."

"Let me put it this way: How did GeoPol win this contract?"

Okay, he wanted her to repeat an answer he already knew. It was like he was playing the cop who rephrased the same question a dozen different ways to trip up a suspect during interrogation. She'd always liked that game, the semantics of it, watching her prey fret and squirm. Now, at the other end of the questioning, it wasn't as much fun.

When she didn't immediately answer, Falcone said, "If I recall, their bid was uncannily close to what we budgeted for the project. Just under. It was a no-brainer choosing them, wasn't it? And their technical approach—a perfect fit for our architecture."

"Yes, that's why we hired them. Can I ask why we're rehashing this?"

"And Jake Atwood. What a presentation he gave. We were all floored by how well he knew our requirements, anticipated our questions. He was so prepared, so smooth. You'd think he was a Hollywood actor reading lines."

Her insides began to heat up again. Maybe she did have a touch of the flu. She tasted the apple pastry she had so recklessly eaten a short while ago.

"Do you know Jay Palmer from Oracle?" Falcone said.

"They bid on the project. He was their technical lead."

"I had a conversation with him. He mentioned he saw you at the LawTech Conference in the fall."

"I saw a lot of people there." What difference did it make where she ran into Palmer? Of course she would have put the proposal request out to a company like Oracle, and of course they'd submitted a bid.

"Not exactly at the conference," Falcone said. "He said he saw you in the hallway of the hotel. And you were . . . well, he described the activity you were engaged in with more detail, but I don't need to, it's hard enough purging the image from my mind. Not that I don't think you're an attractive woman, detective, I just don't like to picture you in certain ways."

She glanced at the chair in front of Falcone's desk, wishing she could collapse into it.

"Anyway, according to Palmer, you were 'making out' with Jake Atwood from GeoPol and doing something with your hands as well."

It was like he kicked her in the stomach. For a second she thought she might vomit again right here. One of her knees wobbled and she had to right herself.

Falcone let out a short laugh, more of a cough. He stared her down and said, "You're seen swapping spit with a GeoPol executive and two months later the company submits the perfect proposal. At the time, we all think, well, that GeoPol, they're the little engine that could, the long shot that actually came in."

He paused and waited for her to jump into the conversation. She tried. "They're getting the job done. Four jurisdictions are already contributing live data, with more coming on every day. They're on schedule and on specification."

"Not anymore. We're paying GeoPol a kill fee for work performed and handing the project over to Oracle to complete."

"But why? The project is going smoothly. They resolved the address matching issue, they're bending over to please us."

"Please. Do you have to say *bending over*?"

"We wouldn't have hired them if they weren't qualified."

"They're done."

"Do they know that?"

"And so are you," Falcone said, ignoring her question. "It's called ethics, and we try to abide by them here. You're suspended from CompStat pending an internal investigation, after which, depending on the outcome, your employment may be terminated."

"I'm retiring in October, I'll have twenty years in," Sara said.

"This is CompStat. Maybe you should have thought of that before you threw integrity out the window."

Her head felt swimmy and thick. "Preferential treatment for contracts is how most business gets done," she said. "Connections, relationships . . . that's the foundation of business." It was something Jake had told her, and it sounded extremely lame coming out of her mouth right now.

"That's not how the NYPD does business, not when you've got oversight committees and ethics panels studying every penny we pitch out the door," Falcone said. "You made a big mistake, detective. I don't know if it was due to love or lust or stupidity, but it wasn't due to honor and integrity and respect for your position."

She wondered if she should beg forgiveness, but Falcone was not the forgiving type. Once he set his teeth, he chewed you to pieces. Maybe try for the pity play: her husband had lost all affection for her, she was desperately lonely, she just happened to get involved with someone who became a customer. Who else was she going to have an affair with? A cop? God, no.

"We have a record of your correspondence," Falcone said. "Some of the e-mails you sent Atwood during the bidding phase contained internal, confidential documents."

She deserved to go down for being such an idiot—you'd think she'd know enough about covering her tracks. Too late now. But she couldn't risk getting suspended, not with retirement coming up, not with how she'd been working overtime for the past year and a half to get her wages up and her monthly retirement benefit higher.

"I can tell you something about integrity in the CompStat division," Sara said. "My husband Conrad just completed a survey of retired commanders who worked under CompStat. More than half of them were cooking the books to make crime rates look lower. They underreported crimes, they downgraded major offenses to lesser crimes. It's all there in the survey."

She could see Falcone take in a breath and hold it, his chest expanding. He exhaled and said, "Everyone knows there were kinks in the system early on. This has nothing to do with the issue at hand."

"If the *Daily News* knew about this, I don't think they would call it 'kinks in the system.' Neither would the *New York Times*. Or the *Post*. And it wasn't just early on—it's still happening."

"What—are you threatening to expose this survey to the media?"

"That's what Conrad wanted to do, but I talked him out of it. With all the positive press the mayor and police are getting for low crime rates, this would be a terrible disclosure. And it won't help when budgeting rolls around."

Falcone shook his head in a sad, dismissive motion. "I've been completely wrong about you. I used to think you were a professional, a person of trust."

"We're all supposed to be. But if that was the case, no one would be fudging the crime stats."

"What is it you want? You want GeoPol to finish the project? It's that important to you?"

At this point, she'd sacrifice GeoPol like a lamb, no offense, Jake.

"I don't want a suspension on my record," Sara said. "I just want to last until my twenty years are in so I get full retirement benefits. I can get Conrad to keep quiet about his survey, but I can also get him calling every media outlet in the city."

"Jesus, you're serious about this."

She said nothing. She'd known Falcone for six years, had worked under him for two—but she had to save herself first.

Falcone turned away and addressed the wall. "I don't care what you do until October, but don't let me see you around here. Go back to homicide and spend your last months there. I'll even sign the transfer papers."

24

Jake paddled halfway across the river into a fiery sun descending behind a mountainous range of dark clouds. Within minutes the wind accelerated to a gale and the water churned and a snow squall struck him head-on. He was protected except for his face, which endured a thousand lashes. He turned the kayak and headed back; at least he thought it was back. The snow obliterated the riverbank and the lights on the railroad trestle marking the entrance to the Vloman Creek. The sudden chop tossed the boat and he missed strokes with the paddle. His nose ran and his eyes teared and his arms ached as he flailed at the water.

He became disoriented, unsure which direction he was headed in. He knew the panic of being lost on the water. In high school he'd been on the crew team, his one sport in a college prep school that required all students, even the brainy graceless ones like him, to participate in athletics. He sat in the third seat in the lightweight eight-man boat in a sport that required timing and effort and endurance but not a lot of athleticism. One early spring practice they were rowing in a dense fog and the coxswain mistakenly steered their shell through an opening in the break wall of the Black Rock Channel and into the Niagara River. Outside the calm of the protected channel the current swept them along. The coxie realized his error and shouted to his crew to turn the boat around. Port up and starboard back. Stroke. Stroke. Stroke. They turned sideways and then straightened and fought the current, rowed harder into the mist than they had in any competitive regatta—fear will give you that superhuman strength. Jake could hear the kid behind him starting to cry. They were a team of eight boys with oars, seated in a straight line, and rowing in unison, yet Jake understood it was every man for himself. He had visions of being swept twelve miles down the river and over the falls, impossible to go that far without rescue but tell that to the fifteen-year-old in the boat. They finally made their way back into the channel, exhausted and exhilarated for overcoming their brush with disaster, only to get chewed out by the coach puttering through the fog in his motorboat: *Where the hell have you been!*

As suddenly as the squall had appeared it passed and the sun returned in time to set in scarlet splendor. The wind had blown him a hundred yards south of his marker. He worked upstream, breathing hard, hands and arms numb, back twitching. He angled into the Vloman and paddled to the dock. He'd been out less than thirty minutes but had put in the workout of two hours.

He shouldered and carried the kayak up to the garage and racked it on the berth above the canoe. He toweled his frozen face and stripped his outer layers. Once inside, he switched on the fireplace. When he first moved into the house he was disappointed that the fireplace burned natural gas controlled by a dial, but he couldn't disparage the quick surge of heat and flame that warmed him now. You had to look twice to realize the logs and glowing coals were fake. There was even a feature that emitted the scent of a wood fire.

He poured a glass of bourbon and added a single ice cube and settled himself on the couch facing the fire. He opened his laptop again. He had a presentation to complete for the Toronto Police Service, a $1 billion law enforcement agency that could become GeoPol's first customer in Canada. The door in Toronto was nudged open because word had spread about GeoPol winning the NYPD contract, but now that project had skidded to a halt, putting the Toronto deal in the must-win category and Jake on the hook to bring it home. Was there a married woman on the Toronto team he could sleep with? Stop.

After Sara had called and said the contract had been canceled because news of their relationship had leaked, Jake tried to apologize, but Sara wouldn't allow it.

"I'm as responsible as you are, Jake, if not more," she said. "And I'm not sorry about what happened—you and me, that is. I told you before and I still mean it."

He might never see her again. "I'm not sorry about that, either," he said. Although he was. He'd lost both a lucrative contract and most of his self-respect, with the pitiful remains of his integrity flittering away for his reckless pursuit of Celeste. This last week had been a long and lonely one.

He stared again at his first slide outlining the Toronto meeting agenda, the same slide he'd abandoned to paddle the kayak and clear his head, but still he struggled to focus, and this was his reputed strength: telling the company story, the compelling reason for doing business with GeoPol, all based on facts, figures, analysis, charts. Yet he couldn't muster up the conviction that any of it mattered. The one thing he'd always been invested in—his career—now felt like a chore, an annoying responsibility. He spun the globe next to him, stared at the colorful countries and blue oceans passing by until the rotation stopped. Every distraction picked at him: another gust of wind, the low hiss of the fireplace, the refrigerator hum. He'd been this way for days, accomplishing nothing, rescheduling a meeting in Pittsburgh, waffling on this Toronto opportunity, letting his inbox pile up.

Earlier in the week he had been summoned to a special meeting with the executive team and board of directors and told to explain himself about the NYPD. He insisted his personal life did not interfere with business decisions. He claimed GeoPol could have won the contract without his getting inside information, although no one fussed about how he'd gotten the contract, only that it had been canceled. Jake promised he could make up the lost revenue with new clients. He had a proven record of success, and the board decided to let him stay on and prove it again.

So he'd better get serious about his pitch to Toronto. Better start feeling it mattered. But now another distraction: the outdoor motion light flicking on and tires crunching on the gravel driveway.

He went to the window and watched Celeste step out of her car. There, now he felt something.

She stood there for a moment, as if trying to make a decision. The breeze swept her hair across her face and she pushed it back behind her ears. She studied his house as if looking out to sea for a lost ship carrying her loved one. Without warning, longing and shame crushed him. Longing because he missed her, shame for not responding to her calls and the message yesterday saying she needed to speak with him.

She took the steps quickly, in a hurry or wanting to reach her destination before she changed her mind. He met her at the door. She spoke before he could. "I'm sorry to pop over like this but I need to—what is it?"

She must have seen the torment in his expression.

"I should have called you back, that was pretty juvenile of me."

"It's okay, that's not why I'm here."

She looked beyond him into the room, to the couch and coffee table where he had his laptop. Why had he never noticed the way her tapered eyebrows framed her perfect green eyes? The splash of freckles on the bridge of her nose? The arc of her upper lip? He should have memorized such details so he could recall them later, when he was old and alone and a tender daydream might soothe his pain.

"I'm interrupting your work," she said.

He stood back and let her in. "No, please. I wasn't getting anything done."

She kept her coat on and sat with him on the couch in front of the fire and he offered a drink like his own. "I can't stay long," she said.

"Where's Spencer?"

"Having dinner at Emery's. I took a chance you'd be home on a Sunday and came over without calling because . . ." She didn't need to finish her sentence: because you didn't return my calls.

"I saw Adam," Jake said.

Her forehead contracted, her fine eyebrows skewing. "You did? When?"

"He followed me home from your house. He must have been waiting nearby to see who you were with."

"Why? What did he want?"

"He said you two were getting back together, and if that's the case, I wanted to stay out of the way."

She blinked and let out a breath like a sigh. "If you know me at all, you know Adam and I aren't getting back together. If you don't want to see me, please don't use that as your excuse. Tell me anything but that."

"I do want to see you. But I don't want to do wrong by you and I'm afraid I will someday. You deserve better."

"Someday is later, Jake, and I'm not thinking about then," she said. "I need to get through today. And tomorrow, and next week. You're my friend and that's why I'm here. I've come to ask you a favor . . ." She trailed off, her face burdened with indecision and doubt. "But I guess this isn't a good time."

"Tell me." He got up and poured her a drink, even though she hadn't wanted one. Celeste sipped and suppressed a cough. She gazed at the fire for a moment and didn't speak.

"What favor?" Jake said.

She spoke to the fireplace. "I have a court hearing about an order of protection against Adam, and I want to ask you to testify about what happened the night Adam choked me."

Jake hesitated. Go on record denouncing Adam Vanek. Swear under oath that Adam attacked his wife. The next time Adam came after him, Jake would need more than an ice scraper to fend him off. The next time . . . there was more than one reason Jake hadn't returned Celeste's calls—there was also that promise about having his throat ripped out. He felt like a coward.

When he didn't respond immediately, Celeste said, "My lawyer told me if there was a witness, the court will grant my request. I already have a temporary order, but now there has to be a hearing with both parties in front of a judge. He choked me—you saw it yourself. But even more than that, he took Spencer the other day. Adam drove by in his car and picked Spencer up while he was walking home from school. I had no idea what happened to him. And then . . . well, I'm afraid, Jake. Adam's making these threats."

Yes, Jake knew about the impact of Adam's threats. "This is his way of working things out with you—taking Spencer and menacing you?"

She took another sip of the drink he'd made her, then set the glass on the table and pushed it away. "He's so angry at me. He knows I don't love him and am ready to move on and he refuses to accept it. I don't know what else to do."

"Did he do anything to Spencer?"

"Adam told him if anything ever happened to me, Spencer would live with him." She looked up at him, her eyes apologetic, as if admitting a mistake. "I understand if you don't want to. I know I'm asking a lot."

"Nothing's going to happen to you," Jake said, then rephrased it: "I won't let anything happen." A sense of conviction and devotion filled him and he understood he could not say no to her, despite his own history and Adam's threats, and this sudden realization expanded his emotional range into unfamiliar territory. He felt a stone deep in his belly and unexpectedly thought of his first girlfriend. He was in his second year at Colgate, finally maturing out of his awkward years and developing an aura of restrained intelligence, a scholarship student majoring in economics. Jessica was a tall, gangly pothead who came from a wealthy Boston family and studied anthropology. She lived upstairs in the same dorm and Jake helped her with statistics homework and then started sleeping with her; she was his first sexual and emotional experience and he glommed onto her like a glue stick. When she dumped him, because she had a boyfriend at home, he almost threw up on the floor of her dorm room. His stomach churned for the rest of the semester, he lost weight he didn't know he had to lose, he got his one and only C in college. He swore he'd never let someone get to him like that again and no one has since, but now sitting here with Celeste he wondered what his stomach might do.

Celeste leaned into his shoulder and he put his arm around her. It had been almost a week since they sat together in his car and that was the last time Jake had touched another person. The weight in him lifted and he felt calm and steady again.

"The hearing is Thursday at 11:00."

They talked in each other's arms. "The timing works. I'm going to be in Atlanta tomorrow, but I'll be back Wednesday night. And then I leave for Toronto late Thursday."

"You just have to tell the judge what happened, about Adam choking me and how you stepped in and saved me. My lawyer's name is Iris Mair. She'll want to talk to you beforehand to get your side of the story."

"Give her my number, have her call me."

"You did save me that night, Jake. You know that, don't you?"

He took a long swallow of his drink, draining it to the ice. Then he lifted her chin and kissed her briefly. He wanted to keep holding her. "Can you stay for a while?"

"I have to get back to pick up Spencer." She withdrew from his arms and sat up. "I can't believe Adam followed you home that night, that he was out there and we didn't notice him. What else did he say to you?"

"He thinks we're sleeping together."

"I know. He can't believe we're not."

They locked onto each other's gaze and Jake sensed they had just come to an agreement, one to be consummated at a future date. He said, "So did you get your battery fixed?"

Her face colored, as if he'd said something to embarrass

her. She glanced at her hands and back up. "Yes, I got a new one in."

"That's good," he said, nodding, waiting for her to go on with whatever she was holding back, some humorous anecdote about trying to get the battery installed. Another private joke they could share. But she had nothing to add.

25

Adam ordered a draft beer and asked for a menu.

"Haven't seen you in a while," the bartender said.

Adam knew him: Mike. He had a head of wiry gray hair and a matching beard. He wore a white shirt with yellow stains ringing the collar and cuffs and a black tie.

"I've been pretty busy," Adam told him.

"I say good for you. You don't know how many guys come in here telling me they lost their jobs. And those are just the ones who come in."

How about losing your job *and* your family—you got any guys telling you that?

Adam had kept away from Checkers since his stay at Glendale. One rule of rehab was to avoid all gambling establishments—not that Checkers was a casino or hosted backroom poker games, but plenty of bets were laid and money passed here. The weekly football pools, the March bracket, the scratch-offs for sale from the vending machine. Eight flat screens hung from the walls; no matter where you looked, a game was being played, a score kept. Adam scanned the room and counted two college basketball games, an NBA game, two

NHL games, a soccer match broadcast from Europe, a downhill ski event, and a curling match. Curling? How did that sport get popular? If you could even call it a sport: a cross between bowling and shuffleboard, played on the ice with brooms and stones. Did people bet on it? Sure they did. If the outcome was uncertain, somebody would wager.

But Adam hadn't come here to gamble; the urge for action that once pumped through his veins had subsided. He didn't know whether to attribute it to Glendale or GA or his huge fuckup on the Taconic game-fixing scheme—or none or all of the above. The craving simply ebbed, inexplicably, which unfortunately made him feel less in control, not more. The gambling beast had a life of its own, now asleep, and coming into Checkers was practically trying to shake it awake. Maybe that was one of the reasons he was here—to test or confront the gambler in him—but he also wanted a familiar place to grab a bite to eat and hang, to feel like part of a community. He studied the faces around the bar and in the booths; almost all guys in here, a few women out with their men. Sports fans, like himself. Some bettors, some not.

He met eyes with one guy he recognized at the end of the L-shaped bar, but Adam couldn't place him. A thick, bruiser type, remains of his hair cropped close to his skull. From the Y? Probably just another dude getting out of the house to have a few beers and watch the game and park his worries aside.

That was Adam's intent, anyway.

To think a police officer had shown up at his parents' house and presented him with an emergency order of protection. His mother had been home at the time and answered the door. She called for him and stood by his side, shaking and stunned, as if the police had come for her and not Adam.

Afterward, Adam had to guide his mom to a chair. She sat

speechless, her face drawn and creased, the light draining from her eyes, her son finishing the job the cancer hadn't.

"Mom, she's lying. She's doing this to punish me."

He read over the documents, three of the boxes checked off from a long list of offenses: *Assault in the second or third degree. Reckless endangerment. Family offenses against a child.* He could not come within one hundred yards of either Celeste or Spencer. The length of a football field.

His mother found her voice, but it was toneless. "You must have done something to warrant this."

"I took Spencer bowling without asking her," Adam said. "I'm his father, right?"

"What about the assault?"

No answer.

The papers slipped from his mother's hands and scattered on the floor. "I've been judgmental of Celeste. I've been defending you to your father," she said. "Now I don't know why."

He shouldn't have taken Spencer like that, but how else would Adam get to see him? Ever since the choking incident, if he asked Celeste about seeing Spencer, she said no. Negotiating through his lawyer would lead in one direction only: divorce and custody arguments. Adam was simply a dad aching for his son. Dad and lad. Sad dad. Bad dad. Mad dad. Whatever. Mr. Tiger Shark Attorney Howard Jasper told him Celeste didn't have a prayer to maintain the order of protection, and was only firing a shot over Adam's bow for the divorce battle, hoping for a settlement in her favor.

Jasper had obtained a copy of Celeste's petition. "I think her action is mostly related to your taking Spencer that day," Jasper told him, prepping Adam for the upcoming hearing. "And if she's basing her claim on the fact that you picked up your son after school, when there is no legal separation or custodial or visitation agreement in place, we will destroy her."

The problem: Adam didn't want to destroy Celeste. Even though she was a bitch for the way she treated him, and a slut for fucking that Atwood, he was still married to that bitch and slut and she was the mother of his son. And he wanted them both back. That was the only urge eating at him now. How could he reconcile that desire with Jasper's proclamation they would destroy her?

But he didn't have much choice. He had to appear in court and defend himself against her allegations; otherwise, she'd likely be granted the permanent order of protection, which would be the worst possible turn of events. Once a restraining order was issued, having it rescinded was like trying to get a river to flow upstream.

So he'd put on his best suit, polish his wingtips, show up in Family Court, and let Howard Jasper work his legal voodoo to protect Adam's rights. But for now, he'd order the burger with Swiss cheese and sautéed mushrooms and try not to worry. He'd sip his beer, which tasted cold as snow going down his throat. He'd watch the hockey game on the screen in front of him: Rangers and Sabres, tied late in the third period, which practically guaranteed overtime and perhaps a shootout to decide the outcome because neither team would risk a mistake now.

Just as Mike delivered his food and Adam took his first bite of burger, a guy sat down at the stool next to him and put two twenties on the bar. Adam moved his own money closer—a twenty and some bills and change from the other twenty he used to pay for the beer. He had to ask his parents every day for a little spending money. Twenty or forty bucks at a time, that was all they'd give—he was like a little boy getting his allowance. *Now, Adam, don't go out and spend it all on candy or gambling.*

He desperately needed a job. He hoped to get an interview with a company that sold alarm systems to businesses, but if a potential employer called GeoPol to find out why he'd been let go, Adam would never get another job. He needed employment to demonstrate his ability to financially support Celeste and Spencer again, to make himself essential to his family. And he needed to come up with the money to pay Canto, who'd left two menacing voice mails on Adam's cell phone this week. Adam couldn't hide from Canto forever. But where was he going to get $25,000? He'd have to resort to sending Vincent Canto to see his father to get paid.

"Who's winning?" the guy next to him asked. He was a big man, like Adam, not as tall but wider around the middle, probably a powerhouse at one time who let himself go soft.

The score displayed right there on the screen: 3–3. "Tied," Adam said, taking another bite of his burger. Juices ran down and he wiped his chin with a napkin.

"Go Rangers, baby," the guy said.

Adam had never been passionate about any one team or player, just the final score. Just the action. The betting line. But he did have a soft spot for the Sabres because their leading scorer was named Thomas Vanek, a kid from Austria, right next to where Adam's grandparents had been born in the Czech Republic. Adam didn't know anyone else with the last name Vanek. Maybe he and Thomas Vanek the hockey player were related somehow. Although hadn't Adam's father recently questioned whether his son was really a Vanek? A disgrace to the family name is what his father was actually saying.

"You like the Rangers?"

"Sabres," Adam said. "Don't *panic* . . . here comes *Vanek*!" He repeated the line he'd heard announcers say, one that Spencer would shout out back when they pretended to be broadcasters together.

"What are you, from Buffalo or something?"

"Nah."

"Well, your boys are going down tonight."

Adam gave a shrug. "Could go either way," he said. There was a minute left in the game, the two teams trapping each other in the neutral zone, playing for overtime so they'd at least come away with a point in the standings if either lost in sudden death.

The Rangers fan took a long slug of his beer and set the glass down, then slid one of his twenties in Adam's direction. "Twenty says if it goes to overtime or shootout the Rangers win."

Adam leaned away, as if the money were a dangerous snake. No way. But . . . If he was lucky, he could turn his own twenty into forty, then maybe that forty into eighty. He felt the beast begin to turn inside him, stretching, yawning, waking up.

"I don't know much about hockey," Adam said.

"You know about Vanek. He ain't exactly a household name."

Regulation ended, the players were lining up for the overtime face-off. He noticed the familiar guy at the end of the bar again, peering Adam's way while talking on his phone. Adam still couldn't place him.

"Twenty bucks?" the Rangers fan said. "Going once, twice . . ."

"Sure." Adam put his twenty on top of the other, a quick slapping motion. The desire for action hadn't compelled him; it had been support for his name: Vanek. A player for the Sabres with his last name. It didn't make sense as a reason to bet—not that gamblers needed a reason—but here he'd done it.

He looked up and the guy across the bar had a grin smeared across his face. Who was he? Then a bubble popped in Adam's throat; he swallowed a belch.

"Wait a sec, I changed my mind," Adam said.

"The puck's dropped, you can't change your mind. A bet's a bet."

"Fine. Whatever." He motioned the bartender and asked for his check. He finished the last of his beer, paid, and left a tip.

The Rangers fan said, "Fuck!" The Sabres had just scored to win the game, less than two minutes into overtime: Thomas Vanek on a slap shot from the top of the left circle.

"You win," the guy said, pushing the two twenties toward Adam. "Your boy Vanek."

"I said I changed my mind." He picked up only his own twenty and left the other one there, then made for the front door.

The guy he'd bet followed him. "Hey, pal, wait a minute—I pay my debts fair and square. This is yours."

He was surprised to walk out into a heavy snowfall, the fat flakes swirling in the lights of the parking lot. They'd gotten hardly any snow all season, just cold rains and sleet. In the hour that Adam had been in Checkers, more than an inch had accumulated. He started toward his car and slipped, but regained his balance before he went down. He continued with a skating motion, not lifting his feet, leaving long dashes as his tracks.

His car was in the back, behind the building. The snow had muffled the world, the only sound the exhaust fan from Checkers, pumping the aroma of fried food into the winter night.

The guy from the bar called to him again. "Hey, you want your money or not?" He was standing outside the door.

Adam clenched his cuff and started brushing off his windshield with his coat sleeve. A car pulled into the back and Adam squinted at its headlights, then turned away from the glare. The lights went off and the car stopped, blocking Adam's exit path.

Adam recognized the vehicle and his heart bumped hard. A few seconds passed, then three doors opened. Vincent Canto got out of the back and his driver, Wally, came around the front. A third guy emerged from the passenger seat. A fourth approached from the side of the building—the bruiser Adam had seen talking on his cell phone in the bar.

Four of them, one of him. *Don't panic . . . here comes Vanek!*

"It's okay, I've got the money," he said, speaking to Canto, ignoring the others, who began to circle him.

Canto said nothing, held his hand out flat, palm up.

"In the glove compartment," Adam said. He had his father's business card in there and would offer it to Canto, telling him where to collect. He opened his door, but one of Canto's guys grabbed him by the arm. Adam didn't resist.

Canto leaned in and opened the glove compartment, felt around, came back out. "There's no money in there. Is it invisible?"

"I don't have it with me," Adam said, "but I can get it. Vincent, you know I'm good for it."

"Time's passed for that." Canto stood back from the other three.

"Come on, Vince. Be reasonable."

"I've been more than reasonable," Canto said. "What do you say, gentlemen, haven't I been reasonable?"

Adam scanned the faces, the expectant leers. He glanced at their hands: already molded into fists. He didn't see any weapons, although that could change quickly. A pipe, a knife, or a gun could easily appear from the inside of a coat.

One of them moved to Adam's left and stepped closer to him.

"Vincent, we were partners," Adam said. "I helped set up Elevet. Doesn't that count for something?"

"It counts for $25,000 you owe me."

"Please." The burger rose in his throat. Then, "I won't just stand here."

"Didn't your momma teach you how to take your medicine?" Wally said.

Adam struck first. He fired his elbow into the face of the man behind him, connecting with a solid, crunching blow. The other two jumped him. One crash-landed fists on his head and Wally dove at his legs. Adam fell on the ground next to his car and tried to roll underneath it but the one whose face he had elbowed stomped on his balls, a direct, paralyzing hit, and then they had his arm levered between the wheel well and the pavement. The boot came down and his bones snapped like dead tree limbs and volts of pain surged through him. He stared up at the oily undercarriage of his car, his eyes unfocused, then turned his head and vomited.

They grabbed his legs and dragged him out, his broken arm flopping uselessly at his side, vomit coating his mouth and chin. Someone leaned down close to his face. It was Canto. His breath smelled like mint and beer.

"Next time, it's the other arm. Then we start on your legs.

And when you've run out of arms and legs, you've run out of time. And then you're dead."

Canto cleared his throat and spat in Adam's face. "There you go, *friend.*"

26

Two armed sheriff's deputies sat behind a desk in front of a room lined with wooden benches like rows of church pews. The people sitting on the benches, waiting for their court appearances, they didn't look like churchgoers. They were sullen gangbangers wearing weird medallions on chains around their necks and baseball caps with brims turned backward; overweight women outfitted in baggy clothes; a group of men and women conversing angrily in Spanish; some steroid-soaked brute wearing a sleeveless undershirt and a swastika buzzed into his hair. Plus a few men and women wearing suits—the lawyers. Celeste had worn a suit, a matching navy jacket and pants. Maybe she would be mistaken for one of the attorneys.

"Come on, over here." Iris took her elbow and guided her to a bench at the far end of the waiting area.

Celeste surveyed the room again. Adam had entered and stood next to a water fountain in the rear of the room with Howard Jasper. Adam had worn a suit, too, but one sleeve was empty and his left arm was folded across his body in a thick cast and sling.

"Look at that," Celeste said.

Iris followed Celeste's gaze. "I've seen people fake injuries to gain sympathy from the judge. Happens all the time. But usually it's the other way around—the person claiming assault puts on makeup to imitate bruises or wears some kind of sling or brace."

"Why would Adam fake an injury?"

"Celeste, do not underestimate the other side. Especially a side represented by Howard Jasper. That man is a predator, but don't worry—we've got them."

Adam caught Celeste staring at him. He gave her a long, glazed look, then averted his eyes, as if he were embarrassed to be here, too.

Suddenly she felt she'd made a mistake. This wasn't the way for her and Adam to resolve their problems, in the bowels of Family Court, the so-called legal emergency room for the poor and underprivileged. Was it too late to change her mind? But then she remembered: He'd assaulted her, threatened her, taken Spencer. He showed no signs of letting up or leaving her alone or listening to reason—and she'd demonstrated no ability to alter his behavior. Her husband, the man she had once loved and promised her life to, and now it's come to this: seeking legal protection from him. It was still hard to believe they couldn't work this out reasonably, although now, for Celeste, *reasonably* meant a quick divorce and full custody of Spencer.

The door to the waiting area opened and Jake stepped in. He scanned the room and she saw his expression of wary puzzlement and guessed he had the same response she'd had—*I've come to the wrong place.*

Jake walked over and Iris stood and shook his hand. He had expected her to be more physically imposing: Her voice had been crisp and persuasive over the phone when she called to ask about his witnessing Adam's assault on Celeste, yet here stood a woman with delicate features and modest stature. He'd known others like her in the corporate world—a wisp of a woman who appeared meek but roared like a lioness. The type of person everyone underestimated, until she devoured you.

"Thanks for being here, Jake," Celeste said. He took a seat on the bench next to her.

"We about ready to go?" he asked.

"Running late, as usual," Iris said. "Probably another twenty minutes."

The door opened and the court officer entered and called for Maria and Hector Ramirez. The group that had been speaking Spanish stood and went into the courtroom. One of the women was pregnant and waddled behind the others.

"We're up after them," Iris said.

Jake spotted Adam at the far end of the room, staring back at him with his brow creased and lips flattened into an angry grimace. Adam leaned and said something to his lawyer, who quickly shot his eyes at Jake. They spoke back and forth.

"Don't worry about him," Iris said.

"I'm not worried."

"He's a bully and you're helping protect his wife."

His wife. Celeste sat with her hands folded in her lap, top teeth chewing bottom lip, staring straight ahead at the courtroom double doors. Although Jake had told Celeste he wouldn't let anything happen to her, he wondered how much he really was helping protect her by giving his testimony. Even if the temporary order of protection was continued, would a signed piece of paper and the threat of arrest deter someone who wanted to do harm? Would Jake be able to protect Celeste if Adam came after her?

They waited in silence. Iris Mair walked over to the window, where she fingered away on her phone, rapidly exchanging messages with someone. Jake checked his watch, and a few minutes later looked at it again.

"Are you pressed for time?" Celeste asked.

"No, I'm okay. I have to catch a flight out of Stewart to Toronto at three," he said. That gave him four hours, but he needed to return to the office where he'd left his laptop and papers, meet with Ray to go over their strategy, and then stop at home to pack an overnight bag.

"Spencer's science fair is tonight," Celeste said. "If you weren't going out of town I'd invite you to come."

He was pleased she extended the invitation. "I'm sorry I can't make it. Tell him I wish I could have seen his exhibit."

The courtroom door opened and the court officer stepped out, followed by the Hispanic family, all of them now subdued, heads down, as if exiting a disappointing movie.

"Celeste Vanek, Adam Vanek," the officer called.

The courtroom was smaller than the waiting room, with three long tables forming a U around the judge's bench and a desk to the side for the judge's clerk and court reporter. A few chairs filled a narrow row behind a half-wall in the rear of the room, although no spectators attended.

Judge Gerald Kennedy sat behind his raised dais. To Celeste, the judge resembled Adam's father: about sixty, with a wide forehead, pronounced nose, broad shoulders. He wore a black robe over a white shirt and blue tie.

Iris, Celeste, and Jake took seats at the table to the left of Judge Kennedy; Howard Jasper and Adam sat across on the right. The court officer closed the door and stood with his arms folded at the back of the room.

"Let me remind everyone this is a hearing to determine

the continuance of a temporary order of protection against Adam Vanek," Judge Kennedy said. "Testimony will be heard from the plaintiff and a response, if desired, from the defendant." He glanced down at a sheet of paper. "Ms. Mair, if you will."

Iris remained seated. It wouldn't be one of those hearings where the lawyers pace dramatically in front of the witness stand, asking leading or trick questions.

Iris said, "We are requesting the court to continue the order of protection against Adam Vanek because the defendant has a demonstrated history of violence against the plaintiff and has continued to make threats against her."

"We'll hear from Ms. Vanek first," Judge Kennedy said.

Celeste was sworn in and asked for her testimony. She sipped from a water bottle to wet her mouth and began to recount the story about Adam choking her that night at GeoPol. How she had walked into the building to look for Adam because he hadn't shown up at their appointed meeting place to take their son for a sleepover to celebrate his birthday. As soon as she saw him, she knew he'd been gambling and she confronted him.

"At first he denied it," Celeste said. "Then he asked me to give him another chance. When I tried to leave, he grabbed the back of my coat by the collar. He spun me around and pushed me against the wall and started twisting my collar."

She paused and glanced over at Adam. His eyes were fixed on the court reporter's hands typing Celeste's testimony into a laptop. The typing ended a few seconds after Celeste stopped speaking.

"And then what happened?" Iris prompted her.

"He twisted my collar so hard I couldn't breathe. I was choking." Then she remembered how Iris had told her to phrase it: "He was choking me," she added. "I felt like a rope was being tightened around my neck, suffocating me"—another line from Iris. "And then I heard someone call out to us from the parking lot. He yelled for Adam to let me go."

"Who was this person?" Iris said.

Celeste indicated Jake. "Mr. Atwood. He saw Adam choking me and told him to step away."

"And did he?"

"Yes. Well, not at first, but when Mr. Atwood called again and got closer, Adam stopped."

"And what did you do?"

"I couldn't do anything, I was coughing, I was trying to breathe," Celeste said. "Then I left. My son, Spencer, was waiting in the car and we drove home."

"What has your relationship been like with your husband since that night?"

Celeste explained she hadn't had much contact with Adam, but on several occasions Adam showed up at her house insisting on seeing Spencer or wanting to speak to Celeste, and he always seemed angry, which caused her to feel tense and afraid that he might assault her again. On one other occasion he grabbed her by the arm in a violent way. On another day Adam took Spencer while her son was walking home from school and she had no idea what had happened to him. She thought he'd been abducted. Well . . . he had been abducted.

When Celeste finished, the judge said, "Your son lives full-time with you, is that correct?"

"Yes."

"Although at this point there's no legal separation or visitation agreement in place?"

"No . . . not yet."

"Excuse me, your honor," Iris Mair said, rising from her

chair. "We've been attempting to negotiate formal custodial and visitation rights with the defendant, without much cooperation, I might add."

"Do you have a date scheduled in Supreme Court?" Judge Kennedy asked.

"We're hoping to avoid judicial arbitration in the matter."

Judge Kennedy said, "I'd like to get Mr. Atwood's testimony now and a response from the defense and rule on the order of protection, and then we can address visitation and custody. Mr. Jasper, would you hold your questions until we've heard from Mr. Atwood?"

Jasper stood. "That's fine, your honor. We'll wait."

"And you can stay in your seat," the judge said.

Jasper sat back down. He reminded Celeste of a politician—his hair meticulously groomed, his suit perfectly cut. She wondered if he was wearing a little makeup to brighten his eyes.

"Mr. Atwood," the judge said. "Please state your name for the record."

Jake stood, as Howard Jasper had. "Jacob Atwood."

"You also can remain seated," the judge said. "Why does everyone want to stand today?"

Smiles all around. This was going to be like paddling with the current, Jake thought.

"Go ahead, Mr. Atwood," the judge said.

Jake recounted the events just as he had to Iris Mair over the phone: how he'd left the office and was walking through the parking lot, had first noticed the boy sitting alone in the car, then heard the commotion by the back door of GeoPol and saw Adam choking Celeste.

"Celeste had her hands on his arms as if trying to break

his grip. I shouted out for him to let go. I had to shout several times."

He paused at that point, as Iris Mair had coached him to—stop at the dramatic moment.

"How would you describe Ms. Vanek's condition?" Judge Kennedy asked.

"She was struggling for breath. She appeared terrified," Jake said. "I could see her expression. She was afraid—but also relieved that someone had come to her aid."

"There is no question in your mind that Ms. Vanek was being choked."

"No, your honor. No question at all."

"Thank you," the judge said. "The court appreciates your coming here today and providing your testimony." He faced Howard Jasper. "Mr. Jasper, do you have any questions for Mr. Atwood or Ms. Vanek?"

"Yes I do, your honor. Thank you." Howard Jasper adjusted his chair to face Celeste directly. "Mrs. Vanek, I'll start with you. The alleged choking incident you described occurred on January 6 of this year, is that correct?"

"It wasn't alleged," Celeste said. "It was real."

"I'm sorry. But it was January 6?"

"Yes."

"That was almost eight weeks ago. Why did you wait all this time to ask for an order of protection?"

Iris leaned toward Celeste and whispered. "Remember what we said—your growing fear at his continued threatening behavior."

"At first I thought it was an isolated incident because I'd caught him gambling, and so I let it go because Adam has a lot of problems and I didn't want to add to them. But then he started saying things that began to frighten me. And he took

Spencer without my knowledge and I was afraid he might hurt him, or me again."

"Did he make specific threats?" Jasper said. "Did he tell you what he would do?"

"Not exactly, but—"

"Thank you, Mrs. Vanek," Jasper interrupted, stopping her midsentence.

But Celeste had more to say. "He told Spencer that if anything ever happened to me—like if I were to die—then my son would live with him. Adam told my son to let me know that. He used our son to deliver a threat to me. And he frightened our son."

Howard Jasper looked surprised by her statement, but he recovered immediately. "And is that true," he said, "that if anything happened to you—anything tragic—that your son would live with his father?"

Celeste nodded. "Well, yes, but—"

"Just to be clear, has Mr. Vanek specifically threatened you in any way since the one incident in question? So that we get the facts straight, Mrs. Vanek. The one incident—the one you said earlier you believed was an isolated incident—those are your words: *isolated incident*—the one with your coat collar. We've heard about that, but we want the whole story. Has he struck you or assaulted you in any way since that night?"

"He grabbed me by the arm once, hard enough to leave a bruise. And when we were living together he grabbed me and pushed me several times and struck Spencer."

"He took hold of your arm," Jasper said. "Okay. Yes, that's in your written statement. Also in your statement you claim to feel threatened in his presence, that Adam—" Jasper stopped speaking and removed a pair of glasses from his inside jacket pocket and slipped them on. He read from a sheet of paper.

"That he 'told me in an aggressive tone I was his wife and I'd better not forget that or forget he had a right to see his son anytime he wanted, and if I continued trying to break up our family he would have to do something about it. Whenever we interacted, it was always an argument, always tense. He always seemed to be threatening me. I was constantly afraid.' "

Jasper set down the paper. "That's directly from your statement, isn't it, Mrs. Vanek?"

Celeste nodded. "That's right."

"So your interactions were always tense. You always felt threatened?"

"I did, yes."

Jasper picked up a second sheet of paper. "My client said that on Saturday, February 17, he installed a new battery in your car. Is that correct?"

Celeste first looked at Jake, who blinked and opened his mouth as if about to answer the question for her; then she turned to Adam, who still wouldn't meet her eyes.

"Mrs. Vanek—did your husband install a new battery in your car for you?"

"Yes." Barely a whisper.

"You allowed him to do that?" Jasper said. "You weren't afraid he might try to choke you with, for instance, the jumper cables?"

"I don't have jumper cables." Useless statement.

"Mr. Jasper," the judge said.

"Sorry, your honor," Jasper said, a thin smile on his face.

Celeste felt herself sinking. "That was the same day he grabbed me by the arm."

"And at that time, did Mr. Vanek express to you his desire to reconcile your differences and live together again?"

Celeste hesitated, thinking back. "I don't know."

"You don't know or you don't remember?"

"I'm not sure what the difference is—I don't know and I don't remember. Adam's done that a number of times."

She heard Iris sigh next to her.

"So on a number of occasions, your husband has made known his desire to keep your marriage intact—although that's not your desire."

Iris spoke up before Celeste could respond. "Your honor, the current state of their marriage is not related to the need for an order of protection against Mr. Vanek's violent and aggressive behavior."

"I agree," Judge Kennedy said. "Let's move on, Mr. Jasper."

"Yes, I'm sorry. One last question for Mrs. Vanek. After your husband allegedly assaulted you on January 6, did you seek medical care afterward?"

"No."

"You had no injuries—no bruising, no pain, nothing that would require medical treatment?"

"I was bruised—and I was in pain—but I didn't see a doctor. I just wanted to get my son home."

"I see," Jasper said. "That's all for Mrs. Vanek. I have a few questions for Mr. Atwood."

"Go ahead," the judge said.

"Now, Mr. Atwood. You are employed by GeoPol, where this incident occurred. Were you acquainted with Adam Vanek, who was also employed by GeoPol?"

"I didn't know him."

"Not at all?"

"He might have looked familiar, but GeoPol has over one hundred employees, I don't know everyone."

"But Adam Vanek is no longer one of those employees?"

"No, he isn't."

"That's because you terminated his employment, didn't you?"

"The company terminated his employment, I didn't personally," Jake said. "GeoPol has a zero tolerance policy about violence in the workplace. Mr. Vanek was let go because he damaged company property and assaulted Celeste—I mean Ms. Vanek—on the premises."

"Yes, Mrs. Vanek," Jasper said. "What is your relationship to Mrs. Vanek?"

"I didn't know her."

"I mean your current relationship—are you complete strangers other than your being a witness to the events on January 6?"

Jake hesitated a beat before answering. "No."

"Have you seen Mrs. Vanek on any occasion other than the night of January 6?"

Celeste could see him trying to frame an answer in his mind before speaking. He said, "I've seen her since then."

"Are you in a relationship with her? A sexual relationship?"

Jake didn't respond.

"Mr. Atwood," Jasper said again. "Are you or are you not in a sexual relationship with Mrs. Vanek?"

"No, I am not. We've become friends."

Jasper shook his head as if Jake's answer disappointed him. "Friends? The kind of friends who share passionate kisses?"

Iris leaned close to Celeste and shielded her mouth. Her voice was a hiss: "You didn't tell me about this."

"I told you we've seen each other a few times," Celeste whispered. It was probably a statement that Iris didn't catch because she'd been harried that day, and on and off her phone throughout Celeste's entire meeting with her.

Iris Mair spoke up. "Your honor, this is not relevant to the fact that the assault took place."

"I believe Mr. Jasper is trying to establish the credibility of the witness's testimony," the judge said. He appeared more interested in the proceedings now.

"Exactly, your honor," Jasper said, then produced a photograph from an envelope. "I'd like to submit this photograph to be included as part of this hearing's record." He turned and held it up for the court to see, then advanced a few steps and handed it to the judge.

The judge studied the photo, then looked at Jake, then Celeste, his face like a stern headmaster.

"This photograph was taken by my client with his camera phone," Jasper said. "It clearly shows Mr. Vanek's wife and Mr. Atwood engaged in what I can only conclude is a passionate kiss." He took a second copy from the envelope and handed it to Iris. She looked at the photo, let out a breath, and dropped it on the table in front of Celeste.

The photo was grainy and taken from a distance and the car window distorted their figures somewhat, almost imparting an artistic effect, but yes, there was Celeste kissing Jake, their arms around each other, the moment captured and recorded by Adam the night he'd lurked nearby waiting for her to come home.

Jasper continued, addressing the room and not Jake directly. "This witness, whose only purpose here today is to corroborate the plaintiff's story—a story that conflicts considerably with my client's version of the events, in which we claim there was no choking, just a holding of the plaintiff's coat to prevent her from running off before my client could explain why he was late picking up their son—as I said, this witness, whose testimony is so critical to the plaintiff's version of events, is evidently in some kind of romantic or sexual relationship with the plaintiff."

He paused, dusted his jacket lapels with his palm, then added, "I think we must seriously challenge the credibility of this witness."

Celeste and Jake both turned to Iris: *What do we do now?* She looked down at her papers, as if the answer might be there, her face blooming with anger.

"Your honor, I'd like to sum up the situation now that we have additional relevant facts in front of us," Jasper continued. "Mrs. Vanek is seeking a continuance on a temporary order of protection because she fears for her and her son's safety following her claim of assault by her husband on the night of January 6. Choked, she alleges, and injured, although she did not seek medical treatment. Mr. Atwood here was a witness to that event—Mr. Atwood, who after the night of January 6 and the firing of Adam from his place of employment began a relationship with Mr. Vanek's wife. Now, many weeks later, Mrs. Vanek decides to seek an order of protection against her husband."

He paused, took a deep, satisfying breath, and waited for the court reporter to catch up on the keyboard. "Your honor, I believe you are being taken advantage of. Mrs. Vanek may have a challenging marriage, she may not love her husband anymore, but clearly she is fabricating, exaggerating, and in collusion with Mr. Atwood in order to use this courtroom to achieve her ends. I request that you vacate the temporary order of protection immediately."

Iris Mair began to speak, but the judge cut her off.

"Hold your thoughts, Ms. Mair," the judge said, his voice firm. He leaned forward and crossed his arms on the desktop. He locked his eyes onto Celeste. He said, "I've been serving on this bench for fourteen years, and it's pretty clear to me that you, Ms. Vanek, are grossly overstating the perceived threat presented by your husband to you and your son. I've seen too many mothers come into this court hoping to exact a personal vendetta against their husbands and the fathers of their children."

Now the judge turned to Jake. "However," he said, "I do not often see them bring their new boyfriends along to help substantiate their tales. I do not appreciate my court being used in this manner. I am vacating the temporary order of protection as of this moment." He turned his attention to the attorneys. "As for asset distribution and custody arrangement, that is a matter for the Supreme Court, although as part of my judgment today I will grant both parties ten days to negotiate a settlement. Otherwise you will both be found in contempt. In the meantime, for the best interests of the child and to avoid any disruption or use of the child as leverage against each other, Spencer Vanek will stay in custody of the mother."

He turned in his chair to address Adam. "Mr. Vanek, do you understand that over the next ten days until a settlement is negotiated or you appear before the Supreme Court that you will suspend your visitation rights?"

Howard Jasper whispered something to Adam, who then responded to the judge, "Yes, I understand." They were the first words spoken by Adam in the courtroom. Up until now, Jasper had done all the talking for him.

"It appears you're somewhat incapacitated at the moment, anyway," Judge Kennedy said. "May I ask how you injured your arm?"

Celeste remembered what Iris had told her about litigants faking injuries. She almost expected Adam to claim she'd done something to hurt him, making her out to be the violent one who'd committed assault, which would only pile on the lopsided defeat they were enduring here.

"I slipped on the ice," Adam said.

"I see. Sorry to hear that. Okay, we're done for now," the judge said. "Dismissed."

Then it was over. Celeste and Jake sat speechless, staring in opposite directions, while Iris stammered about how Celeste should have informed her about her personal relationship with Jake, at which point Jake cut in and said, "If it was so damn important, why didn't you ask about it? Isn't that your job—to prepare your clients?" And that shut up her muttering.

Celeste watched Adam stand and shake hands with Howard Jasper, using his left because his right was immobilized. Jasper had a broad smile on his face, but Adam looked dejected, as if he'd lost. On the way out, in the hallway, Adam called her name and she halted, told Jake and Iris she'd catch up, and waited for them to pass.

"I didn't want to do this, Celeste," Adam said. "But you made me."

"I didn't make you lie." She spoke between clenched teeth.

"That was the lawyer, but we don't need lawyers," Adam said. "I told you we should have worked this out ourselves. We still can, you and I. It's not too late."

She motioned to his cast. "Is your arm really broken?"

Jake and Iris waited nearby, each of them looking out a separate window, not speaking to each other.

Adam lowered his voice. "I warned him to stay away from you," Adam said.

"It's not up to you what he does—or what I do."

"You can't fight me, Celeste," Adam said. "You won't win. If you divorce me, I'll get Spencer. You don't believe me? Just look what happened today."

"You'll never take Spencer from me. I promise that will never happen."

"You can learn to love me again."

She threw up her hands and dropped them. "Adam, I did love you once. I wouldn't have married you if I hadn't. We wouldn't have had a child together. And I stuck by you for a long time, waiting for you to get past your gambling. But you only got worse. And you got violent. You hit our son, you grabbed me, you choked me, you used Spencer to threaten me. I'm not going to learn to love you again. When are you going to get it: I want you out of my life."

He flinched, as if she'd struck him. "You shouldn't have said that, Celeste. And you shouldn't have gone after a restraining order." His face hardened. "You're going to be sorry."

He turned and started down the hall. He slowed in front of Jake, gave him the finger, and walked out.

PART 3

The Coolest Kind of Rock

27

Connie shifted in his sleep but did not wake when Sara got up from bed. She went to the hall closet, reached into her coat pocket, and located the package. The bathroom was dark except for the blue nightlight to guide Connie's nocturnal trips to urinate. She shut the door and flipped the switch for the overhead. After she'd bought the kit, she walked around with it in her pocket for two days, turning the box over in her hand, fidgeting, rubbing the packaging like some charm or talisman. She hadn't been ready.

Now she was. Nothing had happened to elevate her sense of urgency, except time ticking and again rousing before dawn in her state of queasy anguish, not puking but wanting to.

She opened the box and tore the plastic wrapper, held the stick in place while she sat on the toilet and peed. She set the stick on the sink and waited. The test was nothing more than a formality, but an investigation was often exactly that. Sometimes you worked backward from the conclusion and collected evidence to close the gaps. She had never been pregnant but understood her morning nausea, the source of her headaches, why her breasts were tender, period missed. Why she'd gained five pounds. Jake had used a condom the first few times but then she asked him not to so she could completely immerse herself in betrayal. It was part of the attraction, if you can believe that. She trusted when he said he was healthy. She told him she couldn't get pregnant, had never used birth control in her life.

She had no idea how to tell Connie and hoped having a prop such as this test-stick result might help her navigate the way, although the backlog was growing of what she needed to tell her husband. She hadn't mentioned to him yet about her eviction from CompStat and transfer back to homicide, still trying to determine the best way to position the change. She'd already cleaned out her desk at One Police Plaza and moved her box of junk back to the Tenth, where her old CO, Paul Krewski, had made room for her while they waited for the paperwork to be processed. She'd spent the last week perusing cold case files, offering a fresh set of eyes on stale reports. One of the first cases she examined had her name as lead investigator: Vincent Canto, who murdered that jockey at Belmont, but other than locating him in Brookfield, there was nothing new for Sara to go on.

But how to tell Connie. Yesterday, he had come home with flowers for her, an array of brilliant tulips wrapped in cellophane. Conrad Fulton had actually given his wife flowers. She didn't ask him why. It wasn't her birthday, not their anniversary—not that those occasions had warranted flowers in the past. Except for one time, on their first anniversary, Connie had given her a dahlia plant thick with blooms, the national flower of Mexico, which lived for years on their windowsill yet never flowered a second time. But those tulips yesterday—their colorful petals pressed her heart. And look how she was about to reward him. Justice was an elusive goal. For every wrong righted, another wrong stepped up to take its place.

She peered at the stick. The blue plus sign emerged from the white background like an apparition beckoning her. As if on cue, her stomach churned, and she leaned toward the toilet.

But this was not nausea, it was the acrobatics in your belly when you cannot reconcile the rapture and the fear, your entire body electric and hot because a dream has just come true, but not without a steep price to pay.

Sara had expected to have a baby at age twenty-five, then at thirty, even thirty-five, but not at forty-two, although there were plenty of new mothers that age pushing strollers around the streets of Manhattan. Connie had bowed out of their quest first, surrendering after a year of drug injections into Sara's thigh and ovulation testing and sperm counting and scheduled sex, telling her she was all he needed. By then she was working homicide, spending her days solving the dark side of the human puzzle, and at the end of many of those days she wondered if bringing children into the world was irresponsible, wondered, too, if she'd be a terrible parent because to keep from going batshit she had adopted a fatalistic attitude and cracked jokes with her colleagues over mangled corpses. She and Connie weren't abandoning the idea of starting a family, but given their tempered enthusiasm they toned down the extreme measures to get her pregnant. What will be will be. Eighteen years of unprotected sex—very little of it the last three years—and nothing had happened, not even a missed period. Until she slept with another man.

Now she held in her hands evidence that the reason she'd never gotten pregnant was due to Connie's physiology, not hers. But this wasn't an *I told you so* situation, it was an unbearable one. So you can't just cleanly end an affair and be done with it. If she had discovered she was pregnant while still seeing Jake, she would have told him and together they could have decided what to do. She might have left her husband. She might have had an abortion. She might have—

—My God, she had a baby growing inside her. Of course

she hadn't told Connie about Jake. Another item on the disclosure backlog. And now, for a baffling instant, she believed she might not tell him about her pregnancy. She could terminate and Connie would never know, Sara's mistake with Jake simply that: a misjudgment during a time of weakness and need, not one to advertise, now put behind her.

Sara wrapped the packaging and stick in toilet paper and tossed them in the wastebasket. She returned to the bedroom to get dressed, cold now in just her T-shirt and bare legs.

Connie's eyes were open and he watched her from the bed.

"Come here," he said.

She stepped closer. "You're awake."

"I mean here." He pushed back the covers for her to crawl in. She hesitated, then did as he asked, and he pulled the blankets back up as if he were tucking her into an envelope. When he started stroking her shoulder, she froze in place. He moved his hand along her arm in sweeping waves up and down, what she'd wanted for months, years—to be caressed by her husband—but he picked this of all mornings to search and rescue their lost intimacy. His hand reached between her legs and fondled her hair, a finger tapped.

"Don't," she said.

"What? I want you." He put one leg over her and kissed her neck, then her ear.

She faced him and tried to cross her knees. There was just enough light to see the intent in his eyes. "What are you doing?"

"What does it feel like?" His hand slid beneath her, cupped a cheek of her ass. "I've missed you, I don't know where I've been for so long."

"Connie, wait. Connie—" How do you broach these

subjects with your husband whose body has been taken over by a romantic marauder?

"I love you, Sara."

"Are you sure it's safe? I mean, your heart. Morning is the most stressful time, the doctor said. You don't want anything to happen while we're . . ."

He giggled, as if she'd told a silly joke. "You're more worried than I am." He moved on top of her; she adjusted his weight and opened her legs.

28

When Celeste's father died suddenly, Chantal was away at her first year of college and her mother so distraught that the sad task of making phone calls fell to Celeste, just fifteen years old. She made the first call to get her sister home and then moved on to aunts, uncles, family friends. She reported the tragic news simply and succinctly, functioning on autopilot, holding her own pain and grief in check, at least for the moment, and performing so well she almost questioned the truth of what had happened: Had her father really just been electrocuted rewiring a warehouse?

Celeste remembered that experience now while talking to Chantal, the day after her court hearing, telling her sister that the judge had rescinded the order of protection. Chantal's response was to insist that Celeste get up to Burlington as soon as possible—today, even.

"I'm okay," Celeste said. "I'm not about to make any

dramatic decisions. I just wanted you to know what happened." Yet her sister had been perceptive: After Celeste's defeat in court and with Jake having flown off to Toronto, one of Celeste's first thoughts was to simply leave town to escape from Adam and his threats.

"Sounds like Iris wasn't prepared very well," Chantal said.

"I think she's really busy, and she thought this would be a straightforward hearing."

"I shouldn't have recommended her."

"No, I don't blame you for that." Chantal hadn't exactly recommended Iris Mair, just passed her name on as someone she knew from college who owed her a favor. The last thing Jake had said to Celeste as they left the courthouse was that she needed a better attorney, one who put more effort into Celeste's case. When Celeste told him she couldn't afford a better attorney, he said, "You can now," his voice determined and reassuring. Amazing. He wanted to stick with her, even after being humiliated at the hearing and falsely accused of colluding with Celeste.

Next she called Emery. "The judge thought I was lying about Adam threatening me," Celeste said. "Even about the night he choked me. His lawyer destroyed the credibility of Jake's testimony as a witness."

She explained how Adam had taken a photo of Celeste kissing Jake.

"So you *are* seeing him?"

"Not exactly . . . I don't know. He's really done a lot for me," she said. Their relationship status remained to be clarified—in her mind, if not the judge's—yet she felt no sense of urgency in that regard, although she wished Jake was still in town and easily reachable. At the same time, after what happened in court, Celeste had to consider whether pursuing a relationship with Jake would harm her chances of getting full custody of Spencer. If that were the case, she'd have to stop seeing him.

"The judge lectured me about trying to take advantage of the system," Celeste said. "He basically said fathers are getting screwed in courts, usually by vindictive wives."

"That's so absurd. You're the one who got screwed."

Just then her call waiting sounded. She looked at the display: Jake.

"Why don't you come over and we'll take a run?" Emery said. "I can drop Maya at the sitter's and we've got time before school gets out."

She could use the exercise and release, but Celeste hated running in the rain—her feet got wet and her socks bunched up and she ended up with blisters. And the forecast called for a change to freezing rain, which would make running treacherous.

"Not today," Celeste said. "The weather's supposed to get worse and I've got this project I need to work on."

"You sure? You'll feel better."

"Maybe tomorrow."

"You know we're here for you," Emery said. "Both Stephen and I are. Whatever you need."

"I know, and I really appreciate it." She said good-bye and checked the message from Jake. He was about to board his plane home. She called him back, got his voice mail, and the phone tag game was on.

Celeste turned on her computer to check the weather before starting work. The radar map showed the storm inching up the Eastern seaboard, with Brookfield sandwiched in a narrow band of freezing rain between snow to the north and rain just south.

She got up from her desk and stepped out on the porch. The rain had already changed over. Silver shards of glass fell from the sky. Frozen rain pinged off the hoods of cars, hissed in the trees, pattered against the ground. Fine. Okay, everyone get cozy, stay inside, and wait it out.

Wait it out—which was what Iris Mair had told Celeste she needed to do. Iris said even though the order of protection had been rescinded, Adam may have gotten the message that his behavior had to change. Celeste doubted that. If anything, Adam was changing for the worse. There must be more she could do besides wait—that and retain a more effective attorney.

She searched for "denied order of protection" on the Internet. There were about four million results. She scanned the first page and the listing that grabbed her attention was about a judge in California who denied an order of protection to a woman and her nine-month-old baby. She clicked on the link to read the article. The woman claimed her ex-boyfriend had pushed her two different times and knocked her down once. Yes, Celeste could relate to that. And then the ex-boyfriend wrote her a long e-mail, a rambling, crazy story about a father who wanted his family back so badly and if they didn't return to him he'd kill them all so they could at least be together in death. The woman had printed out the e-mail to show the judge, but it had been sent from an anonymous account and could not be verified. Of course the father denied everything; he said the woman was falsely charging him and scheming with her new boyfriend to keep him away. The judge accused the woman of lying in his court. He denied the restraining order and the mother had to make arrangements to hand over the son for visitation. When she met her ex-boyfriend for the handoff, he shot the baby and the mother, then killed himself.

Celeste tried to swallow past the gritty sandpaper in her throat.

She couldn't stop reading and continued to the end of the article. The judge was quoted saying that as horrible as he felt about what happened, he had ruled based on the evidence and the woman had not presented a credible case.

Her heartburn rapidly spread to her chest, down to her stomach and pelvic region. It rose up and her head began to hurt. The more she thought about it, the more she convinced herself Adam was capable of anything. Hadn't he assaulted her? Didn't he believe Jake was her new boyfriend and they were conspiring against him? Hadn't he threatened her after the court hearing, telling her she'd be sorry? What would happen the next time Adam came for Spencer—would he kill them all?

Stop it. Stop. You're getting hysterical. Control yourself. Adam would never do anything like that California man did. Ruin himself with gambling? Yes. Assault her? Yes. Take Spencer without her permission? Yes. But not murder. Not Adam. How could she even think this way?

She forced her attention back to work. She had a new assignment from GeoPol: designing a full-page, four-color ad for *Law Enforcement Technology* magazine. To help get started with ideas, she flipped through back issues of the magazine Margo Roberts had sent over, studying ads for security and surveillance cameras, body armor, weapon holsters, eye protection, firearms, communication devices. The ads were compelling because each piece of equipment seemed indispensable to Celeste, a must-have product—even for an average citizen like her. Could just anyone buy this stuff for protection? Could—

Stop. It was if she were deliberately trying to scare herself. To imagine the unimaginable. Focus. You've got to focus. You've got a deadline on Monday.

Her phone chimed and she expected a text message from Jake, but it was the school notification system announcing that school was closing at one o'clock due to the ice storm and all students must either be picked up or ride home on the bus—no walking today.

A minute later she got another text message, this time from Jake. "Flight delayed, bad weather in NY, I have something for you."

She wrote him back: "I wish you were home safe."

Jake had devoted hours to preparing his presentation, but within minutes of showing up at the Toronto Police Service he understood that GeoPol had no chance to win the business. Toronto's project lead, a lanky, claw-nosed tech manager named Atticus Toor, asked Jake right away why GeoPol had been removed from the NYPD project. Jake had prepared a response for that question: A change in project management at the client led to a different direction and a new vendor—but his explanation was met by blank stares and a few ironic grins. They'd already heard the rumors. Jake concluded that his presence today was merely to satisfy Toronto's internal requirements to vet proposals from at least three vendors before making a selection. GeoPol offered them an easy one to check off, reduce their workload, and narrow the list.

He could have excused himself at that point, but he pressed on, in case by some miracle he'd misread the mood in the room and GeoPol could still be under consideration. He spoke to his slides, mustered up as much enthusiasm as he could, and left behind copies of the GeoPol proposal, obviously headed directly to the shredder.

After leaving police headquarters, he ramped onto the

highway in the wrong direction and didn't notice for twenty miles because he was replaying his meeting, trying to come up with a different outcome (there wasn't one), and wondering how GeoPol would replace the lost revenue from the NYPD. More likely the board would replace him, which would force him to find a new position in another company located in a different city. He'd have no problem securing new employment, but for the first time in his career the idea of moving repelled him. For the first time he felt someone holding him in orbit.

He finally noticed he was driving north along the flat patchwork of rural Ontario. He got off at the next exit and searched for the entrance ramp heading back south. A road sign caught his attention. He steered to the shoulder and backed up. The sign said: CELESTE, with an arrow pointing straight ahead. Below the sign, bolted to the same pole, was a wooden plaque with the hand-painted words *Heaven Ahead.*

Jake got out of the car and clicked three photos of the sign. Then he drove toward the horizon for five minutes until he reached the town of Celeste, Ontario, which amounted to a country crossroads with a drugstore and a gas station/diner. A cluster of modest brick houses extended in each direction from the intersection. It looked like the kind of town where you were born and lived your entire life. Possibly some people moved away and afterward became local legends simply because they had set sail for new horizons and did not return.

He stopped at the diner to buy a coffee to go. Two elderly men sat at the counter by the door and they swiveled slowly on their stools and squinted at Jake, studied him for a moment, and turned back when they didn't recognize him. The waitress was young and pretty and pregnant. When she handed him his change, she smiled and showed Jake a skewed front tooth and a faint glow of anticipation or hope on her face. Her round belly pressed into the counter. "What brings you to Celeste?" she said. "You're not from around here."

"I took a wrong turn and then saw the sign down the road that said *Heaven Ahead*, so I thought I'd check it out." To be kind, he added, "Seems pretty nice."

The waitress snorted and lowered her voice, so the two men at the counter couldn't hear. "More like hell," she said. "I'm leaving as soon as my baby is born."

Jake nodded and gave her a sympathetic smile. "Good for you."

He thanked her and rushed back to the airport, running late now for his flight. He returned his rental car and inched through the security line only to learn his flight was delayed due to a storm on the East Coast.

To pass time he wandered the terminal and came across a kiosk where you could upload images and print photos. He plugged in his phone and printed all three photos of the sign *Heaven Ahead* in five-by-seven size, picked the best one, and bought a picture frame in a gift shop. He slipped the photo into the frame and zipped it away in his laptop case. He thought the photo might cheer Celeste, who'd been understandably upset after the court hearing yesterday. He'd spent thousands of dollars on gifts for women in the past, but none of the gifts were as special as this one. None of the women as special as Celeste.

When the time came, Celeste waited by the window for the bus, which arrived late, and she stepped outside when Spencer got off. The sky continued to spit frozen rain and every surface was coated now.

"Be careful, it's icy," she called from the porch.

"It's fun." He skated along the walk and grasped the wobbly handrail coming up the steps. Just as he reached the porch there was a loud crack and they looked up to see a limb on the tree across the street splinter from its trunk and thunder to the ground. The smaller branches exploded and scattered. Spencer threw himself at her and she hugged him.

"It's okay, it's just a branch falling," she said. "The ice is building up and making them too heavy." But the noise had jolted her, too; she was still anxious from reading about the denied order of protection case out in California.

Once inside, they heard another loud crack and crash. She kneeled on the love seat cushions and faced the window. A tree limb had landed on the roof of a car across the street. She looked above her own car and saw it was out of range of any overhanging trees.

"Come here, sweetie. Come sit with Mom." Spencer sat and she drew him closer and smelled his sweet hair; he'd used her shampoo again this morning. Holding her son grounded her and made her better. Calmer. But not for long. Over the next hour they heard more cracks, like booms of thunder—some close by and others distant—and each one gave her heart a little jump. Limbs broke and fell, revealed stark white wounds, littered the lawns and street with debris. After one loud thud, the lights flicked off and the furnace shut down. In minutes, a quiet, dusky gloom descended over the house.

Because his mother had taken the train into the city with his father earlier that morning to meet her lady friends for lunch and shopping, Adam had the house to himself. He sat and watched the storm from the leaded-glass window in his father's study, a wood-paneled, book-lined space with a desk and two stuffed chairs. As a child, he had not been allowed in the study unless his father summoned him to issue advice or lecture him, but when no one was around Adam would slip in and poke through his father's desk drawers and shelves. He never found anything of interest and couldn't understand why the room was off-limits. Even now there was nothing to hold his attention, but he still experienced the feeling of sneaking around where he wasn't allowed.

The house phone rang. It was his mother. "It's only rain down here, although I heard there's an ice storm up there," Eva said. "Did we lose power?"

"No, we're fine."

"Your father and I have decided to stay in the city tonight at the firm's apartment. The news reports say to keep off the roads. Will you be okay on your own?"

"I'm fine, Mom." God, why did she have to treat him like a child?

"If the power goes out, I have candles and flashlights on the top shelf in the coat closet. How's your arm feeling? Don't take more pills than the label says."

"I'm not taking any of them," Adam said.

What a week: the hospital, then Family Court. At least he hadn't languished too long on the ground in the parking lot after getting his arm stomped. The guy at Checkers who'd come out to give Adam his money from their hockey wager saw what happened and called 911. Adam rode to the hospital in an ambulance, his arm secured in a plastic splint by the paramedics. He phoned his parents from the emergency room, and when they arrived, he put together a story about slipping in the snow while brushing off his car and landing with his arm caught underneath him.

His father eyed him with suspicion. "I talked to the police," he said. "They're standing right outside. They said a witness saw you attacked by several men in the parking lot."

Adam groaned. He lay on a gurney in the emergency room, his arm braided on itself, waiting for surgery. He'd been given a shot of painkiller, which wasn't helping much.

"Does this have anything to do with your owing someone money?"

"Dad, not now."

"Did you tell them what to do if they want to get paid?" his father said. "Did you give them my card and tell them to come see me?"

He spent the night in the hospital. The doctors called his injury a clean break, no shards or grains of bone that would haunt him later, and now titanium screws held together both his radius and ulna. The first day home he'd taken the Percocet, but it gave him a buzzy, disoriented feeling, as if his head had separated from and floated above his body. He preferred the wincing pain. The anger. The despair. He'd taken a couple pills before the court appearance so he could control his facial expression and he ended up in the clouds, hardly able to follow the proceedings, which didn't matter, since Howard Jasper ran the entire show like a master of ceremonies at a banquet.

Funny enough, Jasper had been delighted when he saw Adam's arm in the cast and sling—it would foster sympathy from the judge, he said. And Jasper had been delighted with his own performance in court and especially with the judge's ruling. Naturally, Adam's parents expressed relief that the order of protection had been rescinded, although they were upset about Adam having to appear in court in the first place. They didn't know whether to believe their son's claim that Celeste acted out of vengeance to keep Adam from Spencer. Celeste had never seemed like the vindictive type, his father said. She'd been the reasonable and mature one throughout this ordeal. Fine, don't believe him.

For Adam, what should have been a victory was only another step down into darkness. He felt completely defeated, pointed in the wrong direction and unable to turn around or even stop. He had no desire to meet with Howard Jasper again, this time to "go over their strategy" for the divorce settlement. Jasper had warned Adam that it would be a challenge to be awarded joint custody of Spencer, despite the order of protection being rescinded. Even visitation rights might not be favorable, given Adam's history of gambling and violence.

But no one was going to tell Adam he couldn't be with his son. Celeste may be leaving him behind for another man, she may never come back to him, but she wasn't taking Spencer with her. His son was all he had left in the world. One way or the other, Adam would be with his boy.

He called Howard Jasper to let him know he was done.

"Adam, I hope you're staying off the streets in this storm," Jasper said. "We're still meeting tomorrow, right?"

"I'm not going to court again."

"We hope that's the case, although negotiating with Iris Mair is like trying to reason with a rock, but don't worry, we'll figure out a way to handle her again."

"No more lawyers running my life," Adam said. "I'm working out my own problems from now on."

"Excuse me?"

"I don't have time for this shit. I could be dead before I see my son again." He was thinking about Canto, who would be hunting for him again—one limb at a time.

"Take it easy, Adam. Did something happen you want to tell me about?"

"I'm just saying: no more lawyers. I'm through."

"With all due respect, young man, I don't think that's a wise decision," Jasper said. "Now more than ever you need legal representation. And technically, I'm being retained and paid for by your father. What does he say about this?"

Adam hung up.

He sat by the window and brooded, watched the world turn to ice. The day waned, and he didn't realize the power had gone out until he went to switch on a light. He tried another. Nothing. He forgot about the candles and flashlights his mother had mentioned, and as darkness filled the house, panic engulfed him: the sensation of being buried, light dying, world ending.

Halfway through the return flight the plane hit turbulence, a sudden plunge and recovery that jostled Jake's stomach. He had been dozing—or trying to—and he sat upright and stared out the window at a dark gray void.

The plane lurched again, and the murmurs of anxious passengers filled the cabin. The seat belt sign turned on. A flight attendant announced over the loudspeaker that everyone should return to their seats.

Jake sat in the bulkhead. A carpet of alternating blue and orange swirls adorned the wall in front of him. Next to him sat a preteen girl traveling alone. An attendant had helped her find her seat when the passengers boarded and she'd kept her eyes closed and earphones on the entire flight. Jake glanced her way. Now her eyes were wide open and round as marbles, and she stared straight ahead, knuckles white on the armrests. One earbud had fallen out.

"It's just turbulence, happens all the time," Jake said. "You get used to it after a while."

She didn't respond or turn her head.

The plane dipped and tipped for fifteen tense minutes, and then the captain came on the PA system and announced in an annoyingly optimistic tone that Stewart Airport would be closing due to ice and their flight was being rerouted to LaGuardia, where the precipitation was only rain.

Collective groans up and down the aisle replaced the nervous mutterings of a few moments before. Risk our lives with a dangerous landing, yes; inconvenience us, no. Now Jake would have to rent a car to drive through the storm from New York back up to Stewart to retrieve his own car. It would be close to midnight by the time he got back to Brookfield. He had hoped to stop by Celeste's this evening; now he wouldn't be able to see her until tomorrow.

But then the captain's voice came back on. "I've got a correction and some good news, folks. Change of plans. We're so close to Stewart they're going to keep their lights on for us before shutting down. We won't be diverting to LaGuardia after all. Our approach might be a little bumpy, but we'll have you on the ground soon."

Hopefully not in flaming pieces. Was this good news or not—trying to squeeze in one more landing before closing down an airport due to dangerous ice buildup?

A sudden drop in altitude sent his stomach into his throat. The plane rocked and corrected to level. Jake glanced again at the girl sitting next to him. Her eyes were closed now, but her grip on the armrests hadn't relaxed. He should say something reassuring to her again, but at this point he could use someone to do the same for him.

Adam backed out of the garage and the car slid beyond his control down the driveway and into the road. Fortunately, no other cars were coming. Probably foolish to drive in these conditions with only one useful arm, but he had no choice. He reached across his body with his left arm and worked the gearshift into drive.

The roads were slick and glossy. He drove slowly and tagged fifty yards behind a salt truck, its golden lights blinking in the night. He passed a utility crew that had closed off one lane of the road to repair downed power lines. A flagman waved him forward.

He continued until he reached the outskirts of Brookfield and then the business district. The signal at Passaic and Delaware was out, all the buildings on one side of the street dark, the other side lit, including the neon sign blazing in front of Mario's. He pulled to the curb in a no-parking zone and got out. He baby-stepped across the icy sidewalk to the front entrance. Inside the bar, the doorman and one of the dancers sat at two stools, but there was no one to dance for, no one to card at the door or toss out for lewd behavior. The place had an abandoned feel, even the perverts staying home on a night like this.

Adam walked around the stage toward the back. A guy at the last table stood up and blocked his way to the office down the hall. Adam recognized him from his fattened, stitched lip: the goon he'd elbowed in the parking lot, the one who'd broken his arm. When he sneered at Adam, only one side of his mouth moved.

"Tell Vince I'm here to see him," Adam said.

The guy gave him the kind of hard, superior stare that let Adam know he didn't have to do anything Adam told him to do; then he disappeared down the hall and through the office door. A moment later one of the dancers came out wearing a silky robe that barely covered her twat. Her legs were as long as Adam's. Without a glance at Adam, she walked past him and into the bar.

The guy with the bent mouth poked out from the office and motioned with his head for Adam.

Canto sat behind a desk with a laptop open in front of him. A toothpick rolled on his lips. He took a long look at Adam's arm, then met his eyes, his stare blank, as if Adam were a stranger. Bent mouth closed the door and leaned against it.

"You come looking for me on a night like this, you must have something special for me," Canto said.

Adam opened his wallet and offered Canto his father's business card. "I can get your money, but you have to contact my father for it."

Canto took the card, read the name in a low, dead voice. "Joseph Vanek." He dropped it on his desk. "Are you fucking with me? You want me to collect from your *daddy*?"

The bent mouth snorted.

"It's the only way I can get your money. Just call the number, he'll take care of it."

"AV, you've lost your goddamn mind. I'm not calling your father."

Adam held out his left arm, palm up. "Then go ahead, this one's next. That's the only option I've got."

Canto sighed and shook his head.

"I'm offering you a way to get paid," Adam said.

"Jesus Christ. Go away, would you?"

"Please, just call the number. You can have your money."

Canto studied the card again, then put it in the top drawer of his desk. He returned his attention to his computer. Adam started to speak again, but Canto cut him off. "Out," he said.

Bent mouth held the door for him and followed Adam into the hallway, close enough behind that if Adam stopped, the guy would bump into him. Adam veered to the bar and the guy plopped back into his seat at the rear table.

Adam ordered a bottle of Bud, paid, drained half in one long swallow, then returned to the table.

"Now what?" the guy asked, his voice mumbled and cottony.

"How'd you like the other side of your mouth shut?"

"Huh?"

It wasn't a perfect strike because he had to swing left-handed, but he connected with the cheek and jaw. The bottle shattered and beer sprayed them both. The guy fell over the back of his chair, his face cracked and bloodied. Before anyone could react, Adam was out the door, sliding to his car. His tires spun like pinwheels on the ice, then grabbed enough to accelerate.

Probably a mistake, but how much abuse was he supposed to take? That fuckface had broken his arm. Besides, Canto could get his money now.

Celeste saw Jake's name on the display and answered after the first ring. "Jake, are you back?"

"I just got home. There was a long delay because of the storm. How are you?"

"Our power is out," Celeste said. "I think a tree branch knocked down the lines."

"Half the county is out. It was like driving through a ghost town. How cold is your house?"

She checked the thermostat and squinted at the readout. "Fifty-six," she said. "And we're down to one candle and our flashlight batteries are low."

She walked into the dark kitchen, leaving Spencer huddled around the candle with the afghan over his shoulders.

"It was only one day but it felt like you were gone so long—" She stopped because she felt like she had to burp. Then the pressure mounting inside her unexpectedly burst and she started spewing a chaotic, disjointed story about the woman in California who'd been denied an order of protection and was murdered along with her baby by her ex-boyfriend and what if Adam . . .

"Celeste, slow down," Jake interrupted, talking over her. "I'm not following you. Who is this woman you're talking about?"

She paused and took a few breaths. Now that she'd erupted, her tension had released. She started again, telling Jake the story, more slowly this time.

"I know what happened in court was painful," Jake said. "But you're talking about an incident that has nothing to do with your situation. Think of how rare it must be . . . otherwise the story wouldn't have made the news."

"I know, you're right," she said. "I got carried away. But we're alone here and—" Just hearing Jake's voice made her feel steady, more secure. She felt foolish for her outburst. "—I'm sorry," she added.

"I want you to come to my place tonight," Jake said.

"You think we're not safe here?"

"No, I think you're facing a cold and dark night. My lights are on, the furnace is running, it's warm."

"I've got Spencer. And it's almost his bedtime."

"I meant both of you, of course. There's a double bed in the second bedroom. You and Spencer can sleep in there. Really, Celeste. I want you to come."

"I don't know. The roads are bad. They're saying on the radio that everyone should stay home."

"I'll come and get you," Jake said. "The storm's letting up."

"Jake, are you sure?"

"Yes, I'm sure. I'm on my way."

"No, that's okay, I can drive, that way I'll have my car. And Jake? Thank you."

Celeste got off the phone and told Spencer they were spending the night at Jake's house. He immediately protested. "I want to stay home. *Please.*" He latched onto her waist as if serving notice that he would need to be dragged out the door. "I don't want to go. I won't go," he said.

Now what? Spencer had been cautious and hesitant since the afternoon Celeste had called the police about Adam taking him. He'd lost his enthusiasm for outings, he wanted to stay home after school and on weekends, he didn't want to see his friends. Celeste hadn't told him about the court hearing for the order of protection; she didn't need to share everything, not when her son seemed so overwhelmed.

She hugged him for a moment, then extricated herself. "It's cold in here—and dark," she said. "Our last candle is almost burned down and then there's no light at all. No nightlight, our flashlight is almost dead. No heat. You can already see your breath."

"How come his house still has lights and ours doesn't?"

"It all depends on which power lines get knocked out." She moved while speaking, packing toothbrushes and Spencer's pajamas in an overnight bag.

"I'm not cold," he insisted, although they both had been wearing their coats and hats for the past few hours.

"Jake really likes you, that's what he told me. He invited us over."

"Why do we have to?" He was pleading with her now.

She noticed the science fair project he'd brought home from school after last night's event and staged on their kitchen table. "I have an idea," she said. "Why don't you bring your rock exhibit and you can show Jake? He seemed pretty interested in rocks when you two were talking."

Spencer mulled this suggestion over for a moment. "The poster and the rocks?"

"I'm sure he'd want to see the whole thing."

They were out the door two minutes later, Celeste carrying the overnight bag and Spencer holding his poster and lugging the three rocks in his school backpack.

The cars along the street were encased in ice, unrecognizable, as if frozen in place for years. Every house dark and abandoned-looking, like some apocalyptic movie set. The roof of one car had been caved in by a tree limb. Branches littered the street. Adam pulled into a vacant spot right in front of Celeste's house.

He slid over the slick sidewalk and onto the patch of lawn. There were footprints in the crunchy grass. He maneuvered the frozen porch stairs one by one, stabilized both feet on each tread before attempting the next.

He rang the bell. No answer. Cupped his hands against the window. Completely black. No light from candles or flashlights. Had they gone to bed already? He rang again. Tried the handle. Then he considered the jumble of footsteps broken through the crust on the lawn, the parking spot he'd found out front with the dry pavement exposed due to a recently departed car.

"Celeste!"

With his good hand he pounded on the door.

"Goddammit, Celeste! Open this door!" *You fucking bitch you cunt.*

"Spencer!" he yelled. "Spencer!" He punched the door with his fist, then delivered a single blasting kick, but the lock held and the impact jarred his ankle. He lost his balance and grabbed the doorknob to stay on his feet. "I want my boy!" He almost started crying. "I want you!" Check that: He was crying.

29

Jake was waiting for them in the open doorway to his garage. "Come in through here, the stairs are slippery. How are the roads?"

"Most of them have been salted now, so not too bad," Celeste said. "I drove slow." She carried the bag and Spencer had his backpack and folded poster.

"What have you got there?" he asked Spencer.

"My science project about rocks. Want to see it?"

"You bet I do, come on in."

"Are those your boats?" Jake's car occupied one bay of the garage; the other contained two racks holding the kayak and canoe.

"Yes, they are," Jake said. "Someday I'll take you out in the canoe. We can go in the Hudson River when the water is calm and you can see all the way to the Tappan Zee Bridge."

"Would I wear a life jacket?"

"Of course, those are the rules."

Jake moved the block of kitchen knives to clear space on the island countertop. Spencer unfolded his poster, angling the three sides to stand the cardboard upright. He had written a list of bullet points describing the characteristics of the three types of rock: igneous, sedimentary, and metamorphic. Although he'd drawn guides with light pencil and ruler, his words in colored markers still slanted downward across the poster, but at least he'd done the work himself, unlike some other projects Celeste had seen at the fair, which were obviously spruced up by the hands of parents.

Next, Spencer opened his backpack and placed the three rocks in front of the panels. He proceeded to read his bullet points out loud, saving his favorite for last: the igneous rock obsidian. Did Jake know that obsidian actually was a form of glass? Did he know Indians used obsidian to make arrowheads and today it's used for surgical scalpels?

"Who would have known all that about obsidian?" Jake said.

"It's the coolest kind of rock," Spencer said.

"I can see why you like it. May I?" Jake hefted the shiny black rock in his hand, one side cut smooth and ending in a rounded tip.

"We're going to Howe Caverns," Spencer said. "They're having Rock Day on May 21, and you can bring any rock and have it analyzed and even study it under a big microscope. Then we get to tour the caves. There's even a boat ride, I saw pictures on their Web site. Do you want to come with us? It's May 21."

"If it's okay with your mom."

"Promise you will?"

Jake raised his eyebrows at Celeste. "Don't badger him, Spencer," she said. "May is months away. You can ask him again when the time gets closer."

"I'll come," Jake said. "I want to. I've never explored a cave."

"Awesome!"

"Okay, it's time for bed," Celeste said to Spencer. "Look how late it is."

The sheets in the extra bedroom were flannel, the comforter stuffed with down. On the nightstand stood a lamp that responded to hand taps, three different settings, the lowest one emitting a soft glow. Spencer tapped the light about a hundred times until Celeste finally told him to choose one setting and be done with it.

She tucked him in up to his chin. "Didn't I tell you this would be better? It's cozy and you have a nightlight."

"Will you stay until I'm asleep?"

She settled next to him on the bed, but remained on top of the comforter to keep from getting too warm and comfortable and falling asleep herself. She heard Jake moving around in the other room, opening the refrigerator, getting down a glass, making himself a drink. Make me one, too, she thought. I'll be right out. She stroked Spencer's forehead, and he rolled to face the wall. After a few minutes, his breathing changed and she started to get up.

"I'm still awake."

"I'm right here." She put her head back down on the pillow. She understood that Spencer would take longer to fall asleep here, even though it was after ten o'clock, well past his regular bedtime. She remained still for a long time and heard

Spencer whispering, but she couldn't make out the words, and finally he said, "You can go now. Kathy will wait with me until I fall asleep."

"I don't mind."

"Good-night, Mom."

She kissed him. "I'm right outside your door in the other room. I'll come to bed soon."

She left the bedroom door open a crack on her way out. Jake sat on the couch in front of the fire, waiting for her, a drink on the coffee table in front of him, his computer on his lap. She picked up his glass and took a taste.

"It's bourbon, you want one?"

"Don't get up—I'll just share yours."

She sat next to him. He moved his laptop to the table.

"Everything okay? You were in there so long, I thought you fell asleep, too."

"Spencer had a little trouble settling down."

"The storm's over," Jake said. "I was just looking at the radar map and it's clearing. But who knows how long your power will be off."

"Don't worry," she said, and laughed. "We're not moving in." He took her hand and she put her feet up on the coffee table. She noticed a tiny hole in the ankle of her sock, a dot of pale skin surrounded by dark wool, a pinpoint star in a black sky. She crossed her other foot over her ankle. Jake angled his leg toward hers.

"What about you? Are you settled now?" Jake asked.

"I guess I got a little hysterical about that woman and her baby in California. It's a horrible story, but you're right, it doesn't have anything to do with me."

"You've been through a lot and you've handled it all really well. And I'm telling you everything is going to be fine. I know I said that before, but I mean it. I'll do everything I can for you."

At this moment, sitting next to Jake on the couch, she believed him: *Everything is going to be fine.* She'll get a better lawyer and return to court and fight for justice and move on with her life. Yesterday's defeat will become nothing but a blip in the distant past.

"I'll be right back." She got up to check on Spencer. She peeked in the room and then closed the door until the latch clicked. She took her place again on the couch next to Jake. "Sound asleep," she said. "He'll be out for the night now."

"I loved seeing his face when he was telling me about his rock project. He was so excited."

"I don't know if it was a good idea telling him you'd come to Rock Day. It isn't until May, and Spencer's pretty sensitive. He'll remember you promised."

A flick of hurt streaked across Jake's face. "I plan on sticking around. Unless you don't want me to."

She wanted him to—but she wasn't about to expect or assume anything. When you're trying to navigate day by day, a few months into the future can feel like a millennium away. "Thank you for having us over," she said. "It would have been a long, cold night at my house." She took another sip of the drink and passed the glass to him.

"I have something for you," Jake said. "A present—it's nothing, really, just a . . . you'll see."

He went into his bedroom and a moment later came back and handed her a plain white paper bag, the kind you get from a stationery store. She slid out the frame and studied the photograph, read the words. "Is this a picture of a road sign?"

"The town is called Celeste and the other sign—*Heaven*

Ahead—was bolted to the post below it. I saw it when I was lost driving in Ontario and I stopped to take a picture."

She held the photo close to her. "I could have gone to a hotel," she said. "Or I could have driven to Vermont to stay at my sister's or to Emery's. But I wanted to come here. I wanted to be with you."

"I thought you might not want to after what happened in court. My testifying for you completely backfired."

"It's not your fault—we were ambushed and Adam's lawyer was a lot better than mine. Jake, it means so much to me that you were there."

She set the frame down and reached and drew him closer. They held each other, not moving, her face pressed against the side of his. He had offered her warmth and companionship and a feeling of security and that was what she wanted tonight. She deserved this comfort, she welcomed the physical craving stirring in her. She didn't believe any harm could come from what she was about to do. Jake felt exotic and foreign in her arms, his shape, his texture, his scent all novel to her. She wanted to seduce him and be seduced and she knew from the moment Jake asked her over tonight he was inviting her for this, and she was accepting.

His hold on her tightened and she found his mouth and kissed him and felt herself softening and melting inside, shedding stress and anxiety and making room for him, and she heard the sound of pleasure she made deep inside herself. She gave herself over to him—finally; they were moments away, and she was flushed, she was ready, and Jake's hand slid down her and reached under her shirt and his fingers traced her curves and she kissed him harder, and then a beam of light waved across the front window and into the house and the spell of desire broke.

A car door slammed.

Jake sat up. "Someone's here," he said.

30

Jake stood in the half-open door. Celeste remained behind him, straightening her top, smoothing her sleeves. Adam appeared composed, none of that black hate in his eyes, yet Celeste experienced a sense of revulsion at seeing him and felt a prick of anger, as if Adam knew exactly the moment he'd interrupted and had come here intent on stopping them.

"I need to talk to Celeste."

"She doesn't want to see you," Jake said. "You're not welcome here."

"I have something to tell you, too," Adam said. "I want to apologize for following you home that night. I wouldn't have hurt you, I was just upset, I shouldn't have done it."

"Okay." No forgiveness in Jake's voice.

"Can I come in? My arm, it hurts more in the cold."

"No."

"A couple minutes, that's all I need."

"It's okay, Jake. Let him in," Celeste said. She retreated a few steps into the house and exchanged a glance with Jake, letting him know they could handle this together. Look at Adam: his face long and forlorn, shoulders hunched, arm wrapped in the thick cast and sling. To think just hours ago she'd been terrorizing herself with thoughts of Adam turning murderous on her. Celeste pitied him, she realized. He was hurt, lonely, and lost—but there was nothing she could do for him anymore.

Her decision about Adam was behind her, and she could be generous now.

Jake hesitated, as if about to protest, but then stepped back, and Adam entered and stood inside just enough for Jake to close the door. Adam surveyed the room, eyes roaming. He spent a long minute staring at Spencer's rock exhibit on the kitchen counter. The ice edging his boots melted onto the floor.

"I'd like to talk to Celeste in private," Adam said. "It's personal, between us."

"This is my house. If you want to speak with Celeste, you do it with me here."

Adam turned to Celeste, apparently resigned to accepting Jake's conditions. "Where's Spencer?"

"He's asleep."

"You brought him here." His voice turning into an accusation now.

"My power was out, it was cold and dark and . . . I don't need to explain to you. You won in court, Adam, what more do you want?"

"I'm not going back there again. Not for custody, not for divorce. Nothing."

The disgust surfaced again. Of course it would be like this—how could she have expected otherwise? A moment ago she almost felt sorry for him; now she just wanted him to leave. "Adam, why are you here?"

Jake moved to one side, his eyes on Adam.

"I'm not coming back to you," Celeste said. "We've been through this over and over. What do I have to do to make you understand?"

"I'm not here for *you*! The fuck with you!" Adam shouted. His eyes blazed past her, toward the hallway, the bedrooms, where Spencer was asleep.

"Hey! Whoa, whoa," Jake said, moving between them. "That's enough. You'd better leave." His hands trembled; he was afraid, and it made Celeste afraid, too.

"I want to see my son." His voice calm again. "I'm here to see Spencer."

"I told you, he's asleep," Celeste said. "You have to stop, you can't keep doing this."

Adam darted his attention back and forth between Celeste and Jake. "I'm not leaving without Spencer."

"What? That's impossible. No—you're not taking him," Celeste said.

"I want my son!" he shouted.

Jake stepped forward. "Listen, you have to—"

Adam spun on him. "I told you to stay the fuck away from her!"

Jake held up his hands as if to show he was doing exactly that, staying away, and when he did Adam kicked him, his boot rising fast and hard and high, the thick sole slamming him in the ribs. Jake stumbled backward from the blow, tripped over a standing lamp, and crumpled to the floor.

Adam started toward the bedroom where Spencer slept. Celeste quickly moved in front of him, blocking his way in the galley between the kitchen counter and island. "Adam, no, stop—" His open hand struck her chest and she fell against the edge of the granite and her arm knocked over the block of knives, which scattered across the counter. She regained her balance and grabbed the handle of one of the knives and held the blade out in front of her, having no idea what she would do and unable to steady her hand. *Jake, please get up, help me.* Adam slapped her arm and the knife clattered to the floor. She yelled out and the next instant he had her by the throat with one hand.

Jake pulled himself to standing, using the wall for support. With each breath came a sharp pinch in his chest. He heard the struggle and saw Celeste on the floor, one leg extended, the other bent at the knee tick-tocking back and forth, Adam's broad shoulders and back looming over her like a bear, his free hand extended down, locked on Celeste.

For a few seconds he stood there a paralyzed witness, unable to comprehend what was happening, and then he bolted forward as if pushed from behind. He grabbed a rock from the counter—the dark, glassy one that caught his eye, the dense one with the hard rounded tip—and without thought or deliberation he windmilled his arm in one swift arcing movement, coming down and striking the back of Adam's head with all his strength near the top of the skull where the hair was full and thick. There was a muted smack, like gloved hands clapping, and Adam released an explosive grunt of air—his skin split, bone shattered, a ragged gash of pink appeared followed by a bloom of red and he collapsed on top of Celeste.

She coughed and hacked, pinned beneath Adam, and Jake pushed Adam to the side with his foot and reached for Celeste's hand and helped her up, still holding the rock in one hand. Her eyes had changed into dark, fluid pools and he saw fear flooding into them. "Jake. Jake," she repeated, crying now, gasping, her face smeared with tears and snot. Coughing again. Then she looked down. Blood seeped onto the floor and spread out around Adam's head. She immediately dropped to one knee, then just as suddenly pulled back and stood. She hadn't touched him. He made no movement. "He's dead," she said, her voice low and plaintive. "Is he dead?" This time a question.

"I—I don't know." His breath came in short gasps.

Then Adam's arm moved, and one of his feet, a low groan drifted up, and they both leaned closer to him.

"Do something," Celeste said. "We have to do something."

"I'll call for help," Jake said. He looked at the rock in his hand; that wasn't his phone. He couldn't figure out what to do next.

And then: "Mommy?"

Spencer stood in the doorway to the bedroom. "Mommy? I heard a noise." Eyes half closed, rubbing with his knuckles.

Adam was hidden from view behind the kitchen island. "I'm here," Celeste said. She wiped her face with her sleeve and hurried to her son. "I'm here. I'm coming."

She shepherded him back into the bedroom and closed the door behind her without looking back.

Alone with Adam now, Jake stood over him, the chunk of obsidian heavy in his hand. For a moment he did nothing but listen. No sound from Adam. He lay motionless, bleeding. There was the sigh from the fireplace, the patter of rain on the porch roof, silence from the bedroom. His own pounding pulse and shallow, rapid breathing, a sharp stab with each inhale—had that kick cracked one of his ribs? The force of Adam's blow had knocked the wind from him and put him down; he'd struggled to recover. And then reacted by instinct.

"You fucker," Jake mumbled. "You fucking—" He heard a bass murmur, a distant moan. One of Adam's legs moved, straightening, then an arm. His face slid forward an inch on the floor. Nothing. Silence. Fingers twitching. The mouth opening, closing, threads of blood hanging from the corners of his lips.

Do something, Celeste had said. *We have to do something.*

He must call for help. Find his phone. He looked around the room. Every object appeared to have sharp edges: the countertop, the furniture, even the walls. He felt cold and folded in on himself, as if trying to hide.

Adam released a gasping wet breath. Jake squatted near his face. "Adam?" Jake said. No response. The labored, erratic breathing. "Vanek," he said.

"Ccssspp . . . ssp . . . sp . . ." A surge of blood pumped out, pooling around his head. The sight of it thrust a spark up Jake's spine. "Die," Jake said softly to him. "Die. Leave us alone." The spark became a hot, insistent itch inside him.

Adam motionless and silent again. Then Jake raised the rock and held it over Adam, waiting for him to move, listening for the feeble wheeze. The rock grew heavy. His hand began to shake. No. No. What are you doing? He lowered his arm.

Jake looked once more toward the closed bedroom door, mother and son sequestered safely inside, protected from this animal sprawled at his feet. He turned back to Adam and brought the rock up and down again, one quick hammering movement, leading with the pointed side, aiming for the same glistening target on the back of Adam's head, closing his eyes at the last instant and hearing the sickening crunch.

31

"You were having a bad dream," Celeste said. "Try to go back to sleep."

"I want to go home."

Me too. I want to go home.

Spencer burrowed under the blankets and curled his fists under his chin. This time Celeste got under with him. "I was dreaming about Dad," Spencer said. "I heard him."

Her heart knocked, as if seeking a way out of her—anywhere but in here, anything but this, yet she forced herself to focus on Spencer and speak in a gentle voice. "You know dreams aren't real." She wanted to stroke his face or hold him, but couldn't get her arms to cooperate; they wouldn't stop trembling.

"Are you cold?" Spencer asked.

"A little." He climbed on top of her in that way he hadn't done for years and latched his arms to her shoulders. She felt his warm breath on her neck and soon her shivering stopped. She shifted his weight to free her arm and used two fingers to explore her throat where Adam had clamped onto her. Just one hand Adam had used, a hand the size of both of hers, the strength in the one arm more than she could fend off. He was on her faster than she could blink, cutting off her words, and she fell to the floor and fought against the snake on her throat and she didn't recognize Adam, his face just inches from hers, his eyes fierce and hot and his mouth twisted and spitting and babbling words at her . . . could he be saying he loved her? Or he hated her. *You, you, you*—she heard that much coming from him, but from a stranger, a madman, not the man she'd fallen in love with years ago or married or made love to or had a family with, but a beast that had been stalking her and now was killing her to get at their son and what would he do to Spencer? And then there was a flash of movement behind Adam, Jake striking him, a sound like ice cracking, and he collapsed on top of her, a heavy, crushing mass. She twisted and writhed to get out from under him. None of that had been a dream.

And now she huddled in bed with her son and heard

noises from the other room. Was Jake giving Adam first aid? Had he called for help? That wound, his head . . . she'd only dared a glimpse, but all that blood—he had to be badly hurt. Or already dead. She had to get out there and help, but she couldn't leave Spencer now.

She listened for sirens. For car doors. Shouts and commands, someone taking control. What would she tell her son now when the knock came at the door?

She heard a rubbing or dragging noise. And then again. She needed to get up and see what was happening. Was that the door that just opened?

"Mommy, you're squeezing too hard."

"What? Sorry." Spencer squirmed and settled himself on her again, his heat spreading to her, and soon their breathing synchronized and Spencer fell asleep. There. At least she'd done that right; she got her son back to sleep, and whatever he was dreaming had to be better than what waited beyond the bedroom door when he woke up. She would stay a few more minutes and then slide out from underneath him. She would open the door and deal with the nightmare. Except she couldn't make herself move.

Jake cleared his mind to concentrate on the next task and not dwell on the previous one. He hefted one of Adam's feet and dragged him across the floor. Like moving a piano—an unforgiving, intimidating weight. He bent at the knees to leverage his legs and back, pulled, repositioned himself, and repeated. His ribs speared him with each move. A smear of blood trailed on the floor and Adam's coat bunched beneath him, creating more resistance. His cast snagged on the leg of a counter stool. Jake reached down and freed the limb and rotated the body to pull on the arm. The cast provided a better handle and the coat flattened out beneath him. Jake got the front door open and maneuvered Adam onto the porch. He paused and caught his breath and rolled him twice to the edge, then pushed with his foot to bump him down the stairs. The sensor detected the movement and the light over the garage flicked on. Jake came down the stairs and dragged Adam along the icy ground until he lay beneath the porch railing hidden from view of anyone looking out the window.

Done. At least this task: move Adam so if Spencer came out of the room again he wouldn't see his father's bloody corpse sprawled on the floor. No child should see that.

A light rain continued to fall, the regular kind, not icy but wetting the surface of the ice already on the ground and making any movement hazardous. The wind had shifted and the air felt warmer on his face. Adam was positioned on his back, his cast set at a right angle over his chest, eyes mostly closed although a fingernail of the whites gleamed at Jake. His left arm was raised over his head as if to wave—*Good-bye, see you in hell.*

No time for thinking that way. He believed Adam would have died from the first blow or perhaps survived with a short-circuited brain, leaving him sentient as a plant. But the fact in front of him was Adam dead and Jake responsible. He'd chosen a treacherous path he could not backtrack from, and the path required him to take further action.

He went back inside. He'd never seen a crime scene except in photos and on television, but he was standing in one now. There was work to be done. He found a towel in a cabinet drawer and wiped the floor from the kitchen to the door, stopping once to wring the towel out and rinse it in the sink, watching blood mix with water and swirl pink down the drain. He remembered once as a kid cleaning up after painting with watercolors at school and seeing this exact pink color and pretending it was blood. If only this were pretend play now. He doubled over his work with a clean towel, then threw both towels into the fire, where they smoked and sputtered. Mistake. He shouldn't burn anything in a gas fireplace.

He picked up the fist of obsidian. Bits of hair and flesh stuck to the black surface. His gut protested, but he would not allow himself to be sick. He rinsed the rock under the faucet, scrubbed it with dish soap, rinsed again. He ran the hot water to flush the trap. He dried the rock as best he could and replaced it on the counter in front of Spencer's poster. *May I present Exhibit A.*

The bedroom door remained closed.

Jake collected the spilled knives and replaced them in their allotted slots in the knife block. He righted the lamp he'd knocked over when Adam had slammed him with that kick. There. Everything back in order. A tidy house. Although any third-rate CSI would find gobs of evidence. Adam's fingerprints could be anywhere. DNA as prevalent as dust. Look, his own clothes—his coat stained with blood, covered in fibers. They would need to be burned as well.

He put his ear to the bedroom door, heard nothing, and interpreted this as a message from Celeste for Jake to take care of this side of the door, while she handled her side. The question was what to do next.

Celeste sat up. It didn't seem possible she had fallen asleep. Or was her response a natural one, her shocked system retreating into unconsciousness as a survival mechanism? A special skill of hers, falling asleep during times of duress. She had nodded off during her father's funeral; she'd been kneeling at the time, between her sister and her mother, in the first row of the church, while an altar boy swung the incense decanter on its chain and the priest recited prayers over the casket. The smell and smoke of incense got her, burned her throat and stirred her stomach, and she sat back in the pew and a moment later was asleep; her mother woke her for communion. She slept almost twenty hours after she and her painter boyfriend broke up, for twelve hours the night she discovered Adam's gambling and would have slept more if Spencer hadn't woken her up the next morning. After Adam attacked her at GeoPol, she'd gone home and slept soundly in the bed with Spencer, even though she'd been worried Adam might show up at her house that night.

At some point Spencer had rolled off her and now slept near the edge of the bed. Celeste got up and stood at the closed door. Listened before opening it a few inches. "Jake?"

No answer.

She opened the door enough to slip out and closed it behind her. She was afraid to approach the kitchen island and face what she'd left there. She wanted to climb back into bed with her son and escape into sleep again. She managed a few steps. A few more.

The kitchen appeared normal. The knives arranged neatly in their block. The lamp righted. The rocks lined up in front of the poster display. No one lay sprawled on the floor. For a few surreal seconds she believed she had dreamed it all, a nightmare, just as she'd told Spencer he had. Please, just a few more minutes of this fantasy.

Sorry, no. When you awakened from nightmares, your terror subsided, your soul recovered. This didn't happen for Celeste. The aching dread remained. An acrid smell hung in the air, something burning in the fireplace, smoking and smoldering, a wet, bitter scent.

She peeked in Jake's bedroom: the bed empty, blankets smooth. She returned to the main room and looked out the window. There was Adam's car parked behind hers, the first real proof she hadn't been dreaming. She put on her shoes and coat and stepped outside. She found Jake standing to the side of the porch, Adam next to him on the ground.

"What are you doing?" She stood under the protection of the porch roof.

He looked at her, his eyes flat and distant. "He's dead."

She could see that, but still his pronouncement stung her, from the inside out, a pain deep in her chest spreading out in sharp, tight eddies. She tried to speak and her voice lagged, stuck, then the words escaped. "You had to . . . you saved me. You protected Spencer."

Adam had been strangling her and then would get to Spencer. Like that father in California, the one who'd killed his family—Celeste hadn't been overreacting after all. "He might have killed me . . . he was going to take Spencer."

Jake didn't respond.

"Did you call the police?"

Jake shook his head slowly. "Too late for that."

"Why? We need to explain what happened, how he attacked us, and then how you—" She stopped. Waited for Jake to take over the story and fill in the details. Confirm he took heroic measures to save her. Performed the ultimate act in a string of courageous acts on her behalf: stopping Adam's assault of her at GeoPol, finding her work, being kind to her son, testifying in court, showing her affection. And now this: saving her life.

But Jake didn't fill in the story. She said, "I don't understand. Why did you bring him out here? And inside—you cleaned up."

"I was afraid Spencer would come out again. I couldn't let him see his father like this."

Oh, he'd done it for Spencer. Yes, now she understood. Celeste couldn't tell if Jake was crying or his face was wet from the drizzle. "We need to call the police," she said. "We need to tell the truth about what happened."

Jake took an audible breath before he started speaking. He held one hand against his ribs. "Didn't you just tell the truth in court? Didn't you testify to what happened when Adam choked you last time? When he took Spencer off the street?"

Yes, she had. But—

"I can tell you how the police will see this." Jake made his way up the stairs to the porch. He stood close, but did not touch her. "You just had an order of protection against your husband rescinded. The judge was convinced you were scheming with your boyfriend who claimed he witnessed Adam choking you. The judge believes we made up the assault story to get a restraining order that would keep Adam away—but you couldn't keep him away, not legally, not in any way. He wouldn't leave you alone."

A flat of ice slid off the porch roof and splintered on the ground next to Adam.

"Now you must return to court to establish binding custody and visitation arrangements. But here's what the police will see: Celeste Vanek didn't want to go back to court. She'd been defeated there once, she was afraid it would happen again. What she wanted was for Adam to go away, leave her and her son alone, but he wouldn't. He wouldn't give up his wife. He wanted his son."

"I was ready to go to court. It was Adam who said he wouldn't," Celeste said. Pointless.

Jake spoke with an oratory flair, as if he were the prosecuting attorney. "Adam Vanek was forced to sneak off with his son in order to see him because his wife wouldn't allow it. Sure, he had problems. Sure, he'd made a mess of their lives. He was a gambler, he had a temper—but he wasn't a criminal. He didn't deserve to die. He didn't deserve to be murdered by his wife and her lover."

"*Murdered*—that's not true. Why are you saying this?" She grasped the railing for support.

"Because that is what the district attorney will see. Adam didn't deserve to be murdered, but that's exactly what happened when he showed up one night where his wife was hanging out at her boyfriend's, with Adam's only son sleeping in the other room, Celeste living her tidy new life—except for her husband, of course, who wanted his son, who wanted to patch things up with his wife. That wasn't so tidy. That problem wasn't going away."

"You're turning this around," she said. "You're making up a story that didn't happen."

"Okay, so what did happen? I acted to protect you, protect your son, right? I had to . . . I wanted to. There was nothing else I could do other than physically stop Adam. But now Adam's dead. Justifiable homicide, it's called—I came to your defense. Except there are no witnesses—well, we're the witnesses, Celeste. You and I. And we know how well that worked last time, when trying to corroborate the story of a simple assault."

She hated what he was saying, but he had her attention.

"They will go after us," he said. "I know this. I know how the police think: They pursue the obvious solution and most of the time they're right. And you've seen how the courts work. In the end, we will go to prison."

She stared into the distance at the ice-crusted trees and the creek at the bottom of the slope. The rain had stopped and a mist grayed the night. She said, "You figured all this out and then decided to . . . Jake, no. We need to call the police. I'll tell them you acted to protect me. That's what you did—you had to, just like you said. You were defending us."

"I haven't saved you yet, Celeste."

"Jake, we haven't done anything wrong. We haven't. And if we call the police they'll know we haven't done anything wrong. But if we don't—"

He spoke over her. "You call the police, they'll bring an investigative team, and you can be sure Spencer will wake up again. This time it will be more than a noise that wakes him. He'll see the police and you'll have to tell him what happened and it won't be pleasant, this story about how his father attacked you and I used his favorite rock to crush his father's skull. That's a story that will stay with him for a while—and that's just the beginning. Wait until the charges get filed, wait until they take your son away from you. And they will—they will take Spencer."

Part of her couldn't believe what he was telling her, refused to accept the direction of events. It was too impossible. Adam dead. A crime committed. Adam was the only one who'd committed a crime. He's the one who'd attacked them.

She glanced down and saw the crushed back of Adam's head, hair matted with blood. Quickly looked away. It had to be someone else, or just a shape, not a person at all. She spit out a thought she hadn't meant for words: "You hit him so hard."

He stared at her with what she thought was pure anger.

"I'm sorry, I didn't mean that."

"I did hit him hard."

She turned to go inside. "I'm calling the police. I have to."

"And then I hit him again."

She was at the door. She didn't understand. "Celeste, I hit him a second time," Jake repeated. "With the rock. I killed him." As soon as he spoke his eyes lost their intensity. She tried to think back. Adam had been on top of her, she hadn't seen Jake strike him. How could she know how many times Jake hit him?

"When you were in the bedroom," Jake added. "I struck Adam again while he was already down."

She couldn't make sense of what Jake said. "I had to go in to Spencer. He called for me. He said 'Mommy.' "

"Adam started moving. He made sounds, but he was hurt bad, he was bleeding a lot. You were right—he was never going to stop. He was going to keep coming after you, just like he was going to keep gambling. I wanted to stop that. He was ruining your life, he was ruining . . ." *Us.* He had no right to say it. There was no *us.*

"Maybe he would have died anyway," she said. Pleaded. She felt sick and unsteady. "Why, Jake?"

"I wanted him gone. I had to show you that I—" He didn't finish.

That you what? Show me what?

"What do we do?" she said.

He stood straighter, spoke now with assurance. "There's only one thing we can do. Adam will disappear. No one will know what happened to him. You said yourself he used to go away for days on gambling trips. This time he doesn't come back."

"Disappear? You mean hide him?"

"Not hide him, make him vanish."

"No," she said. "You were defending me, you had to hit him."

"Celeste, trust me. We need to do this. You call the police now, the evidence will be right in front of them."

He tried to take her hand but she pulled away and hurried back inside, expecting Jake to follow her, but he didn't. She opened the door to the bedroom and located her overnight bag on the floor and found Spencer's clothes where she had folded them on the dresser. She stuffed them in the bag, her mind intent on escape, getting as far from here as possible, and then she stopped and looked at Spencer, sound asleep, in the exact position she'd left him on one side of the bed. Her only child. Her angel. The one person in her life she would do anything for, go to any length to protect. As would Jake, apparently.

What was she supposed to do? Wake him up and carry him out past his father's corpse and drive him home in the middle of the night? Or call the police? She could do it now; her phone was in her bag. She hesitated, trying to decide. There was no simple answer. Although Jake was right about one thing: A few minutes after the police arrived, Spencer's life would change forever. He would wake up and discover that his father was dead and the police would ask him questions, too, about what he'd seen or heard. Who knows what his answers would be? And Jake was also right about how the police would interpret the events: the estranged wife and her new lover knocking off the husband. A story as old as time. As fresh as tonight. And they weren't even lovers yet.

32

Burial meant driving to a remote area—a field or forest or ravine—breaking through the ice, and hacking away at the frozen ground. It would be difficult work. The grave shallow. Transportation risky. Plus, buried bodies were almost always found, eventually. Hunters came across corpses, dogs sniffed out remains, construction crews scooped up skeletons in excavators.

Which left the river as the best option. Jake knew about bodies dumped in the water from one of his postcoital chats with Sara when he'd enticed her into telling war stories about the homicide beat. There was the time she told him about floaters, how a body disposed of in water initially sinks, but as decomposition sets in the internal cavity fills with gases and the corpse rises like a helium-filled balloon. Cold and deep water can delay the decomposition process, prevent the body from surfacing for months, or give the current a chance to wash it out to sea. A body weighted down is most likely gone forever, it settles on the bottom and never reappears, it feeds a school of fish. You sink a corpse and there's no body, no crime. Just a statistic: one of the fifty thousand people who go missing each year in the United States.

He opened the garage door and lifted the canoe off its rack. He struggled to balance the boat, and one end scraped the floor. His ribs protested, but the pain had almost become his companion and motivation. He walked the canoe outside and guided the aluminum keel down the icy slope. The boat slid along as easily as through water. The gray sky hovered over him, backlighted by a full moon hidden behind the clouds, enough illumination for Jake to see, not enough to feel exposed. At the end of the dock he lowered the bow and then the stern into the water and secured the line to the dock cleat. He went back and located supplies in the garage: a crowbar, a length of rope hanging from a nail, a folding knife in a toolbox. Then he hunted along the creekside until he found a mostly round rock he guessed was the right size. He wedged it free with the crowbar and tried to lift it. The rock must have weighed fifty pounds or more, ideal for an anchor but too heavy to carry the distance. He resorted to rolling the rock like a snowball until he got it positioned on the dock next to the canoe. He went back for Adam. He paused before touching him, but there was no other way. The cast made a convenient handhold and Jake dragged him along the ice, stopping twice to rest and tenderly feel around his ribs. He pushed the pain aside and returned to work, his breath steaming the cold air. He angled Adam into position, and now it was time for the rope. He wrapped the rock as if winding a ball of twine and he roped the body, lifting up one side, passing under, then stepping over and lifting up the other. Two more times around. Almost like he'd done this before. He cut the extra rope, slipped the knife into his pocket, and tied the end of the rope to one of the loops with a square knot—the only knot he knew. He tugged at his work and believed it was secure. Adam would sink and disappear.

"What do you need me to do?" Celeste said.

He jerked around when she spoke. He'd been absorbed in his work and hadn't heard her come down from the house. "You scared me," he said.

"Now we're both scared." She crossed her arms as if hugging herself and fixed her gaze on the black water, the bend in the creek that led to the river. "What should I do to help?" she repeated.

He was grateful for her offer, and for not calling the police. He had kept at his task knowing he couldn't control her, having no choice but to accept the risk and hope Celeste trusted him.

"You should go back inside and be with Spencer. The less you know, the better. You won't be able to answer questions if anyone asks them."

"We're either in this together or we're not," Celeste said.

She was right, of course: He and Celeste were now irrevocably bound together, in what way he didn't know.

"Tell me what you're doing. Tell me the plan."

Yes, the plan. He took a long breath. With the canoe in the water and the rock tied to Adam, she could already see this part of the plan. He explained to her why he chose the river and not the ground, and her face grew stiff and pale as he spoke of dogs rooting out shallow graves and gases inflating the abdominal cavity, but she bit her lip and listened to what he had to say about how he would sink the body and Adam would vanish forever and somehow they would go on with their lives.

"But you should go back inside," he told her again. "I can handle this part myself and then we'll talk about the rest when I get back. This is the first and most important thing."

"How long will you be gone?"

He guessed fifteen minutes out, fifteen back. "A half hour. Maybe a little more."

"I'll be waiting for you."

Jake arranged Adam lengthwise near the dock's edge, just above the canoe. He maneuvered the rock on top of the body. He paused and listened. Quiet except for a breeze that rattled the thin, icy branches in the trees. The storm had moved on.

He rolled Adam once and his body thudded with the rock into the canoe, clanging against the aluminum. The boat wobbled and settled. Adam's legs rested along the top of the yoke, the torso and head in the bottom of the keel. Jake shoved the feet off the bench and settled himself in the stern, lifted the line from the cleat and pushed away, using the paddle against the dock.

He felt the weight of his load as he paddled around the bend in the Vloman, the canoe sitting low in the water, each stroke an effort. He ruddered to straighten the bow and steered beneath the railway bridge, its dark trusses a skeletal network overhead. The canoe emerged on the other side into a thick, steely fog, and Jake alternated strokes starboard and port, the pain in his ribs pulsing now and he remembered the night he'd paddled his kayak with his skinned elbow, also thanks to an encounter with Adam. But Jake got the best of him this time—an irreverent thought that popped unbidden into his mind and one he quickly banished.

The current pushed him downstream and the canoe swayed and bumped in the frothy chop. Water splashed into the boat. The weight in the keel minimized the rocking but made steering control squirrelly. He was cold and wished he'd worn gloves and a hat. He paddled for ten minutes and made insignificant progress. After another five minutes he stopped. He set down the paddle and scanned all directions. The opposite bank was hidden in the fog, the near bank a murky blur, the train trestle a black smudge with seeds of red lights blinking on and off. A foghorn mourned in the invisible distance. He couldn't be halfway across, but the time had come. He was drifting steadily downstream and the trip back would be cruel against the current. He got to his knees in front of Adam's feet. He lifted one leg up on the gunwale and the canoe leaned to that side. Then the other leg. More lean.

He realized his mistake: He might not be able to lift and push Adam over the side without capsizing the canoe.

The boat rocked and swayed in the water and the motion made him nauseous; he was wet now and his muscles began to stiffen in the cold. He tried to think of an alternative. The canoe continued to drift in the chop and brushed by a buoy marking the shipping channel. He was wasting time. It wasn't just this mistake that gnawed at him but others he must have already made and would make moving forward. He needed to be more careful, examine from every point of view, analyze all possibilities. He remembered something Sara had told him once: There were a hundred ways to screw up while committing a crime, and if you accounted for half of them, you were a genius. Where did that leave him?

Come on, what's the plan? Any decision he made was a gamble. There was nothing to do except try to get him over the side. If the canoe tipped he probably could right it and climb back in. He'd be drenched, but the effort of paddling would keep him warm and hold off hypothermia.

He secured the paddle beneath the yoke and squatted and positioned himself in the middle of the canoe, legs spread. He grabbed the gunwales for balance and waited for the boat to steady, then worked his arms under Adam's back and stayed in that position, wondering again about an alternative. There was none. He found two handholds on Adam, inhaled deeply, and heaved to send him up and over the side. The canoe immediately capsized.

Jake fell in the river on top of Adam, and the cold water stung him like a cattle prod. For a moment the canoe and Jake and Adam were jumbled together in the water. The rock tied to Adam had caught under the seat and the rope pulled taut when the body began to sink. The canoe was upside down, already half-submerged. Jake clung with one arm to the wide, slippery keel and with the other he reached and tried to free the rock wedged beneath the seat. Adam's weight pulling on the rope made it impossible to dislodge or even move the rock using only one arm. Jake let go of the boat and held tight to the rope under the water with both hands. A splash of water got into his lungs and he spit and coughed. He balanced in a squat with his feet on top of Adam, who was just below the surface and connected by the rope to the rock. He fought for breath, heard his own rapid panting. With one hand he fished in his pocket for the knife and opened the blade with his teeth. He sawed at the rope back and forth many times until it severed with a jerk and the canoe shot away and the body disappeared below. Without Adam for support, Jake went under again. He pushed down with his arms and kicked and struggled to the surface. He tread water and rotated in search of the canoe. He spotted a sliver of its hull ten yards away and then that was gone as well, sinking alongside Adam.

The water was debilitating in its chill, the air even worse. He felt heavy and exhausted with his clothes and boots on. He huffed and panicked for seconds while seeking his bearings and the direction he needed to swim. There: the blinking lights of the trestle, a faint red glow in the mist, but too far north. He couldn't get that far. Just reach the near bank—that was his only objective. He was a decent swimmer and knew the crawl, the sidestroke, and the breaststroke. He started out with the crawl and the river slapped back at him and his hands and face grew numb. He swallowed water. He flailed spastically, ribs stinging, wasting his energy. He switched to the breaststroke, which he executed more like a doggy paddle now that he was tiring. It seemed he was making no progress and was going to drown and sink with Adam, the two of them sharing a watery grave. That thought alone renewed his strength. Keep swimming, he told himself. Keep swimming. Or Celeste will be waiting a long time for your return.

He swam and struggled for what felt like forever and finally his foot found the soft bottom, as if he'd stumbled upon a miracle cure for an affliction that was killing him. Thank you. Thank you. He could stand, and then walk, his legs leaden and stiff. He emerged from the water like a creature from the deep, staggering, stooped and dripping, his clothing sodden rags. He collapsed on the bank and cracked through a wafer of ice and settled into the mud, but he couldn't rest or he would freeze to death. He willed himself to his feet. He was far downstream from his house and began to walk along the edge of the water. In the open air he began to shiver so uncontrollably he feared he was having some kind of seizure or attack. His jaw hammered up and down, his back clenched, the pain in his ribs burned like coals in his chest. He forced each foot forward and picked his way along a deer path just worn enough to navigate at night. Ice painted the ground and he slipped and went down, stayed for a few moments staring up at the shrouded heavens. He wished he could see stars, for some reason believing they would reassure him. He admonished himself for his lack of balance and demanded he pull himself together and keep going. Back on his feet. One step and then another. Count ten steps and count ten more. At one point the brush became too thick and he waded into the water, dragging his feet through the shallows, no longer feeling the cold. On and on he trudged.

When he reached the mouth of the Vloman and the train trestle, he realized his stupidity in not climbing up and walking along the tracks earlier. His thinking must have been impaired or else he was determined to punish himself by doing things the hard way. But there would be time later to flog himself. He reached the tracks and crossed the trestle and then started through the trees, grasping at trunks for support. His house came into view and he felt a surge of relief and energy. A lighted window was his beacon. He stepped faster. He'd made it.

The reprieve lasted the few seconds for him to notice Adam's car parked in his driveway.

He approached the car slowly, circling around back, as if it might be booby-trapped. For the first time he thought about the keys, whether they were at the bottom of the river in one of Adam's pockets. Jake had never checked. Idiot. Yet another potentially fatal mistake. He was so unprepared, so beyond his skill set, nowhere near the genius he needed to be.

He peered into the driver's window at the steering column. A set of keys hung from the ignition slot. He waited for blessed satisfaction and received none. This is what he told himself: He loved Celeste. She was inside his house at this moment—frightened, yes, but warm and safe. He'd made that possible for her. Adam Vanek was and would continue to be an unrelenting and uncontrollable menace to her and to Spencer—and to Jake, to their being together. And so Jake destroyed the dragon. He summoned up a primal act he would have sworn himself incapable of performing—he was a business executive, for God's sake, an office prince with a fat wallet and thin arms. He'd never committed a violent act against another human being in his entire life, but now he'd committed the ultimate act. The lowest form of humanity, that's what Sara called murderers.

He turned from the car and lowered himself until he sat on the frozen ground. He buried his face in his hands. He was cold and stiff, yet the shakes struck again, as if he were shrugging his shoulders over and over, and now he blubbered like a baby. What had he done? He knew what he'd done. He'd chosen to do it. He would allow himself to weep, just this once, and not again.

33

When Jake left in the canoe, Celeste went back inside to wait. Again she debated the idea of packing and leaving, driving straight through to Burlington. But this weighing of options was inconsequential, a way to pass time until she came to terms with the decision she'd already made to trust Jake, although it felt less like a decision and more like a stroke of fate.

She found Jake's bourbon and poured herself a glass, swallowed a fiery sip, and dumped the rest in the sink because this was no time to get drunk. She checked on Spencer three times, and three times he hadn't moved. She watched the clock and chewed her nails and when Jake had been gone too long she began to worry. She couldn't see anything from the window and couldn't leave the house to look for him in case Spencer woke up and called for her. She waited thirty minutes past the time he said he'd return and couldn't wait any longer, so she stepped out on the porch and heard a noise like an animal snorting and found Jake hunched on the ground next to Adam's car, soaked and shaking. Nodding, mumbling—his lips blue and his face drained of color.

He couldn't speak and she helped him stand and she got him inside and into the bathroom. She turned on the overhead heat lamp. His fingers could not handle the buttons of his shirt or the zipper on his pants. She helped him shed his clothes and inhaled a sharp breath when she saw the purple bruise on his ribs. This was not how she imagined undressing him for the first time. His cold flesh startled her. She drew him close and tried to warm him, and when she couldn't, she turned on the shower and got him under the spray and he leaned against the tiled wall and slowly thawed in the hot steam. She shut the door behind her and made coffee while he dressed.

Now they sat on the hearth by the fire, which emitted uneven flames and a loud, airy hiss. Blackened, charred scraps of fabric littered the grates.

"I shouldn't have thrown the towels in there," Jake said. "Some of the jets clogged." His voice sounded dull, without inflection, but his body had finally stopped trembling.

"Are you warm?"

"Thank you." He stared at the fire and sipped his coffee. The clock on the mantle read 1:27 a.m. He said, "I should have listened to you. We should have taken our chances and called the police."

"You can't say that now. Not after what we decided." She took note of her use of the word *we*.

He told her about the canoe tipping over, sending both of them into the river, Adam sinking, Jake having to swim to save his own life. The mistakes. The stupidity.

It was no help hearing about everything that went wrong. "What about his car?" she said. "We have to move it."

He stared at the globe on the table. He looked as if he'd been awake for days. No doubt she looked just as bad. She reflexively brushed her hair back with her hand, tucked the loose strands behind her ear. She swallowed and felt the ache in her throat. She wanted to cry. She wanted to quit. But it was her turn to step up and help him.

"I could drive his car back to his parents' house and leave it there," she suggested.

He looked at her long enough to reject the idea. "His parents might see you. Or they would see that his car was home but Adam wasn't. They'd immediately wonder."

"Adam used to take these trips to Turning Stone—the casino," Celeste said. "I thought he was traveling on business to see clients, but I found out he was gambling. Sometimes he'd stay two or three days at a time. Sometimes more."

"The one near Utica?"

She nodded. Childish, but the simple act of nodding in the affirmative made her feel more in control.

"What about Mohegan Sun, or Foxwoods?" Jake said. "Those are closer."

"He had a favorite dealer or something at Turning Stone. It was his lucky place." Some luck. "We could take his car there, it would be like he took a gambling trip and never came back."

No response. She leaned into him and whispered. "I know what you did for me—I owe you my life and my son's," she said. She believed her words but they didn't soothe him as she'd hoped. Or her. "Adam was going to take Spencer, he might have killed us all. It could have happened, you did what you had to."

"Whatever I did, he's gone. And you're not involved, Celeste. You haven't seen Adam. You haven't seen him since the court hearing. If you're ever asked, that's all you need to say—you last saw him in court." Some light returned to his eyes, confidence to his voice.

"Did you tell anyone you were coming here tonight?"

"No, no one. Only Spencer and I know."

"I'll deal with the car," he said. "I'll take it to Turning Stone, that's a good idea. I'll leave now, I won't be back until tomorrow sometime."

Tomorrow. And the next day. Her future—a disaster. That doorway to a better life Jake had been holding open for her? Now a passage to darkness. The promise of shared intimacy and pleasure from a few hours ago? Shattered.

"We won't be here," she said. "When Spencer wakes up, we're going home."

"Yes, I'll call you."

She began to shake her head. "No, don't call me. I can't talk to you now. I can't—not after this, Jake. It's too awful." She couldn't look at him while she said the words, yet he had saved her; she didn't know how to accept this contradiction.

"Trust me," he said. He took her hand and she tried to meet his eyes. "I know what happened is terrible, but I love you. I do. We should stay together through this. It will be easier, things will get better. We'll have each other."

She wished it could be that way, she wished his declaration of love could be a beginning and not an end. "No, Jake, don't say that."

"If Adam's body ever turns up, within the first hour of the investigation our phone records will be examined. We can't stop being in touch the last day anyone hears from Adam. Not when even the judge in Family Court thinks we're together."

"You said he sank in the river. He's gone forever."

"I told you—I had to cut the rope. There's no rock holding him down."

"I'll say I broke up with you after what happened in court. I was angry. I had to step back. You weren't my new boyfriend, I wasn't colluding with you. This will prove it."

She looked to him for approval, didn't get it.

"We shouldn't change how we act," he said. "Nothing should be different."

Except everything was different. "No, Jake, I'm sorry. I can never see you again."

34

Light filtered through the window shade. Mom lay next to him, on top of the blankets, still in her clothes, hair over her face. He leaned close to see if she was asleep. Yep. He smelled her breath and pulled back. Bet she forgot to brush her teeth last night.

He got up and stood at the door for a few minutes. It was no longer closed all the way and he could see the wall opposite in the hallway and a slice of the big outer room where the noise had come from last night. Where he'd seen . . . what had he seen? He thought he heard Dad but that couldn't be.

Mom said he had a bad dream and that was the answer. He'd been having a lot of bad dreams lately, mostly the same dream, the one where he's walking home from school and senses someone sneaking up behind him and every time he turns around he glimpses a person disappearing behind a tree or into a house or a car parked along the street, but no one's there and he keeps walking, except the feeling returns and the next time he turns around the person is a little closer than last time and he recognizes his father.

But that wasn't the dream from last night. He couldn't remember last night's.

His neck felt stiff, like he'd slept in the wrong position, and he didn't want to open the door farther but he had to pee and the bathroom was across the hall. He was at Mr. Atwood's house. Jake's house—Spencer was supposed to call him Jake. He wondered if school was closed today because of the storm. They hadn't had a snow day all year and last winter they didn't have any, although in May a pipe broke and the floors flooded and they got a day off for that. He wanted a snow day today. He wanted to go home and get in his own bed.

He grabbed his penis and squeezed—he had to pee bad—and he finally opened the door far enough to slip out and he tiptoed to the bathroom, not to be quiet, the floor was cold. He raised the seat and peed, watching the yellow bubbles foam up, then pulled a piece of toilet paper and wiped the drops off the rim the way Mom had taught him. He lowered the seat and flushed and washed his hands. He reached up and opened the medicine cabinet and looked inside. A razor and shaving cream. A stick of deodorant. A plastic bottle of medicine. One shelf empty. He closed the cabinet and went back and stood in the bedroom doorway again and watched his mother sleeping. The other bedroom door—Jake's room—was closed. He went into the kitchen and looked out the window. The ground and trees appeared covered with snowy glass. It wasn't raining or snowing but Spencer guessed no school because of the ice. He slid his hand along the cool, hard countertop he recognized was made from granite. He picked up each of his rocks, saving his favorite for last: the obsidian, smooth and black and shiny. He passed the rock back and forth between his hands, then put it back with the flat side facing up and the tip to the right the way he liked to display it.

He opened kitchen drawers and they slid out quietly and he touched the stuff in them. Cooking tools and pans and plates, nothing much interesting; then he went into the living room and spun the globe a few times and picked through a pile of magazines on the coffee table: *Law Enforcement Technology*—he saw Mom reading that one at home—*Geo* something . . . *Geospatial Solutions*, *The Economist*, *The New Yorker*. No *National Geographic Kids*, no *Sports Illustrated Kids*. Shelves of books but not one of them a kid's book, not one game or toy anywhere to be seen. He opened a door that led to the garage and Jake's car was parked on one side and on the other side was a kayak upside down on a rack and . . . where was the canoe? Last night when he and Mom came in through the garage, Spencer had seen a big silver canoe on a rack that was now empty. Jake said he'd take him for a ride in the canoe when spring came, they'd go way out on the river and see the Tappan Zee Bridge.

"What are you doing?"

He jumped at her voice. He hadn't heard Mom get up. "Nothing," he said.

"Come on, we have to go."

"Mommy, where's the canoe?"

"You shouldn't be snooping around."

"I wasn't." Although he was doing exactly that, but since he hadn't discovered anything of interest—except the canoe was missing—it didn't count.

"And don't tell me it was Kathy's idea."

"Mom, she's just make-believe." It couldn't have been Kathy's idea because he hadn't thought of her once this morning, even though every other morning when he woke up there she was waiting for him and he imagined her standing next to him sharing the sink and brushing her teeth, too. Sometimes she watched him pee. But she was gone this morning. His friend was gone. Maybe she'd taken the canoe. Funny.

"Where's Jake?"

"He's probably still in bed."

"How come you slept in your clothes?"

"I guess I was resting with you and fell asleep," she said. "I need to rinse my contacts, then we're going."

"I have to get dressed."

"Your clothes are in the bag on the bedroom floor."

He changed while his mother used the bathroom.

"Mom, where's my toothbrush?" he asked when she came back in the room.

"You can brush at home, we need to go."

"Why are we in a hurry?"

"Just move along, okay?"

What was she so mad about? She rushed to make him come over here last night and now she was rushing to make him leave. "You should brush your teeth," he said.

"I said we can brush at home." She picked up his pajamas and stuffed them in the bag. She got down on her knees and searched under the bed.

"What are you looking for?"

"I just want to make sure we don't forget anything."

"Is school closed today?"

"Probably, we'll listen in the car."

"Will our power be back on?"

"All the questions—come on, let's go."

"What if we don't have power yet?"

"We'll be fine." She finished packing the bag. They went out the front door and down the slushy porch steps. He splashed his way toward their car, getting a *hot foot,* as Dad called it, which didn't make sense because your feet got cold and wet, not hot, when you stepped in an icy puddle.

He looked toward the dock and the creek and realized what had happened. His mother and Jake had an argument, just like he'd seen her have with Dad, and now they weren't going to be friends anymore and Jake wasn't in his room sleeping—that was just a lie Mom told him. Jake went out in the canoe this morning alone to get away from them, and he wouldn't be taking Spencer for a ride on the river and he wouldn't be coming to Howe Caverns for Rock Day.

He looked again at the creek, flowing toward the river, its surface glistening in the morning sun. He wished they'd stayed home last night.

"Spencer." She had the car started. "Spencer. What are you waiting for?"

"I'm coming!" he snapped back.

35

On the car radio they heard that schools were closed due to yesterday's storm and power outages. Spencer gave a halfhearted cheer, not the full-throttle yippee an unexpected day off called for. When they got home, their house was silent and cold. Celeste called the utility company and after navigating a series of menus and inputting her address, she came to a recording that estimated their electricity would be restored in twenty-four to forty-eight hours. She phoned Chantal and asked if she and Spencer could visit for a long weekend, which if she had done yesterday or gone to a hotel instead of going to Jake's . . . If and if and if. But Celeste had known what she'd wanted—she wanted Jake.

She changed her clothes and tied a silk scarf to hide the new bruises stamping the sides of her neck where Adam's thumb and fingers had squeezed; her hair covered most of the evidence this time, although the scarf provided extra insurance. She called Emery because Celeste needed to chat with her about the inconsequential, and they did, and Celeste told Emery she was going up to her sister's for a few days and Emery said their power had stayed on, and so the Webers' home was another warm refuge Celeste could have chosen last night but didn't. When she got off the phone, she packed a suitcase and made sandwiches for the trip. She stopped on Delaware to put gas in the car and bought a coffee to help her stay awake. She let Spencer sit up front with her and he played with the radio and found the sports talk station. He sometimes had listened to sports talk with Adam, but that seemed forever ago.

Spencer kept the signal tuned to the host prattling about the March Madness tournament coming up.

"Wouldn't you rather hear some music?" she said.

He reached and shut the radio off.

"I didn't say you couldn't listen."

He'd been moody all morning. She was afraid of what he'd seen last night when he came out of the bedroom. How long had he stood there before finding his voice and calling to her? And then this morning, that comment about Kathy being make-believe, his tone implying his mother was stupid for mentioning her name. What was that about?

"You don't seem like your usual self today," she said. "Is something bothering you?"

"Not really."

"Have you thought any more about the bad dream you had at Jake's?"

He answered with a shrug, stared out the window.

"You know you can talk about anything with me, don't you?"

He did. But he wouldn't. He didn't say a word, and so Celeste filled the silence, chatting as idiotically as the sports-radio host. She told him stories about when she and Aunt Chantal were little kids. Most of them she'd told him before, but Spencer always enjoyed hearing them again. Like the time she and Aunt Chantal were in a park and a bird flew by and pooped on both their heads. That one always cracked him up. And the time when Chantal was thirteen and slipped on a tiny patch of ice, the only bit of ice left on the ground, and broke her arm. All the times they pretended to be twins because they looked so much alike and were about the same size, even though Chantal was older. About how she and Chantal had the same taste in fashion, which was like having twice as many clothes because they shared everything; if Spencer was a girl he'd understand how great that was. The story about when they each won $10 from their father because they could hula-hoop for an entire hour and it was easy, they could have kept going.

She looked over. Spencer had fallen asleep, his head against the window. She checked to make sure his door was locked. Now what? Now she was alone with her questions and they barreled at her like a train through a tunnel. Why had Adam come to Jake's last night? Was he going to steal Spencer? Kill them all? Should they have called the police? Why did Jake—

Don't know, and don't know, and don't know—many questions, one insufficient answer. She was a fugitive heading up the highway, that much she knew. Her husband, the man she had once loved and believed she'd grow old with, was now dead because Jake had killed him defending her. That she must accept. Yet the images she retained, the words forming her thoughts, the almost stoned and fuzzy feeling enveloping her—it was all so alien and unbelievable. Vertigo struck when she did anything as simple as turn her head to check for traffic in the passing lane; she breathed on the edge of a dizzying precipice. Yet she drove on, two hands on the wheel, speed steady, her son lightly snoring.

She noticed one of the mile markers on Interstate-91 and beyond that a green barn with two horses standing in a fenced, snowy field, and she thought about the time when she was twelve and in love with horses and her father had taken her riding for her birthday. They lagged behind the rest of the group and pretended they lived a century before on the prairie. Her horse was named Clover. He acted mopey and slow on the ride until they turned and started back toward the stable and then Clover perked up, knowing he was heading home to a bale of sweet hay; he even tried to pass the group leader and had to be restrained and Celeste had to hang on tight for the wild ride. The stable gave her a free pass to come back and ride because of the way her naughty horse had misbehaved.

Then she noticed another mile marker along the highway and realized she'd driven six miles since she'd thought about what happened last night. So this is how it would be: Not every minute would be usurped, although every minute would pass. Like when her father died and at first she was consumed and overcome with the loss, and every moment felt bleak and the future hopeless, but eventually she experienced moments of relief, and then hours, and hours became days, and over time the sadness weighed her down only occasionally and then only on the anniversary of her father's death or his birthday and eventually the reality became not just manageable but woven into the fabric of how she defined herself. *My father died when I was fifteen.* You can and will go on. You have a son, you have a life. She would manage the stain and strain of Adam's death, control the affliction, perhaps in the same way she managed her acid reflux. Even the discomfort affected the same area of her anatomy, perhaps a little lower left, closer to her heart. Maybe she'd find a medicine to alleviate the symptoms. *My first husband was killed by a man trying to protect me from harm.*

At Chantal's, with Spencer and his younger cousins playing in the backyard and Howard teaching a class that evening at the medical school, Celeste and Chantal cooked dinner together and opened a bottle of wine, even though it was not yet five o'clock.

"What's the point of staying in Brookfield, anyway?" Chantal said. "You'll be divorced soon and even though you didn't get the order of protection you'll still get custody of Spencer because Adam put you in the poorhouse. You can make moving here part of the divorce agreement. You'll hardly ever have to see him—a few times a year at most."

Not until that moment did Celeste understand she would never be able to tell Chantal what happened. She could never tell anyone. Not her sister. Not Emery. No one could offer comfort or sympathy. She would harbor this knowledge alone for the rest of her life. Except for Jake—he was the only other one who knew, and she'd told him she could never see him again.

"Adam said he wasn't going back to court, and if that's the case I probably will get full custody of Spencer," she said.

"Good. That makes things even easier. I was talking to Howard and you could live with us until you find your own place, or just live with us permanently. There's plenty of room."

"I have my business now, and my clients are in Brookfield."

"What—you're a graphic designer. You can work anywhere, can't you? Isn't all that stuff done over the Internet?"

"You're simplifying too much," Celeste said. "Sometimes I need to meet clients face-to-face. My life is still in Brookfield." What remained of it, anyway.

"You know, you can find single men here, too. You can meet someone new. Howard has this colleague who's a neurologist who got divorced last year and—"

Celeste cut her off. "You're sounding like Mom."

"You're right—sorry."

"I can't even think about that right now."

"No, I know, I'm just saying that when you're ready to think about the future, there's a future for you right here."

Once she got an idea in her head, Chantal could be relentless, and although Celeste was flattered her sister wanted her in Burlington, now was not the time to make that decision. "I'll have a better feeling for what I want to do once the school year ends," she said, thinking her statement would close the subject.

Chantal stirred the spaghetti sauce. "I won't keeping bugging you, but I'll say one more thing." She set down her spoon and folded her hands in prayer position and said, "Sister, sister. Please please please please. It would be great to live closer again."

Celeste laughed—she hadn't completely forgotten how. She looked out the back window. Spencer was showing his cousins how to balance a stick on end in the palm of your hand. The three of them wobbled around the yard, shouting and laughing, dropping and resetting their sticks.

When they returned to Brookfield on Sunday, their power was back on, and almost overnight the season had turned to spring. A row of crocuses had poked up from the hard-packed ground and formed a fragile line of yellow, white, and purple blooms along the cracked walkway leading to the porch steps. Celeste had no idea flowers would come up and never would have guessed it; when she moved into the house last fall, the front landscaping consisted of dying weeds and dirt.

The flowers infused her with unexpected cheer, which lasted until Adam's father called that evening. "Celeste, Joseph here. How are you and Spencer doing?"

"We're okay," she said. "We just got back from a weekend at my sister's."

"I was wondering if you've seen Adam."

"I saw him in court on Thursday," she said, feeling the slow drip of deception beginning to enter her, mixing with her blood, becoming part of her.

"What a shame, that business. I'm sure you wouldn't have gone to court unless you believed it was necessary, but I hope you two can work out a reasonable coexistence. You have Spencer's best interests to consider, and I'm sure you realize that. I'm not passing judgment, I'm just expressing my concern."

"I understand." She bit down on her lip. This man had no idea he'd lost his son.

"Adam hasn't been home this weekend and his mother and I are beginning to worry. His car is gone, and he hasn't answered his phone. We were hoping he might be with you."

With me? "No, I'm sorry, I haven't seen him."

"I figured that was unlikely." After a pause, he said, "Has

Adam mentioned anything to you about owing someone money? A lot of money—like $25,000?"

"How much? No. Adam and I don't talk about those things anymore."

"How about when he used to go on his gambling trips—do you know where he went?"

"He always told me he was on business trips." The effort of speaking to her father-in-law was withering.

"Did he go to Foxwoods or something? Out to Las Vegas?"

"Both. Everywhere. I'm not sure what he was doing. He hid everything from me for so long."

"Stupid boy," Joseph said, more to himself than Celeste. "If you hear from Adam, let us know, would you?"

"Yes. I will. I'll call you right away."

"And I'm going to file a missing persons report with the police—just in case. I'm hoping he didn't get mixed up in any trouble."

The police. She stared at her phone for a long time after the call ended, as if blaming the device for saying those words to her.

She met with Iris Mair again. Although Jake had promised he would find her a better lawyer, that was no longer necessary, unless the time came to hire a criminal defense attorney; if that happened, they'd both need good lawyers.

"Jasper is going after us again," Iris said. "He's emboldened now and going to fight for joint custody of Spencer. I'll certainly bring up Adam's history of gambling and violence and dismissals from employment, which will hurt their case, but his living in a stable environment at his parents' house could work in his favor."

Celeste should have been patient, but the woman annoyed her. Her phone wouldn't stop chiming, and Iris couldn't stop looking at it. "Well, what will work in our favor?" she said.

"That you're a good mother," Iris said. "That you've always been there for your son, you've taken care of him through this traumatic period."

That's right, she was a good a mother. Wasn't that why she agreed to Jake's plan? She remembered what he'd said: He didn't want to risk Spencer seeing his father like that. And from there, he didn't want to risk that they would be accused of a crime, in which case the court would take Spencer away from her. And being a good mother meant Spencer came first. And Spencer coming first meant she had to accept Jake's plan, despite all the other risks it entailed.

"I wouldn't worry too much," Iris said. "Regardless of Howard Jasper's best efforts, I believe you will be awarded sole custody of Spencer."

Right. Just like Iris believed the order of protection would definitely be continued.

Iris explained her recommended strategy for negotiating custody, but Celeste hardly listened. She was looking at the open folder on Iris's desk and in particular the copy of the photo Adam had taken of her and Jake kissing in the car. She recalled that moment as a torrent of almost unbearable desire—for Jake, but not just for Jake, for a fresh start. She would remember that kiss the rest of her life.

"Do you mind if I have that photo?" Celeste asked.

"This? Go ahead." Iris pushed the photograph across the desk toward Celeste, as if she were relieved to be rid of it.

"Did you hear me?" Iris said. "I believe you will be awarded sole custody. This is good news."

"Just do everything you can."

In the end, Iris Mair didn't have to do anything. When Adam couldn't be located, his attorney, Howard Jasper, motioned to delay the proceedings, and the judge granted Celeste full and sole custodial rights until Adam Vanek decided to petition the court for another hearing, and if he did, his decision to no-show at the scheduled time would be taken into account.

A month passed. Nothing happened. Or everything happened. Joseph Vanek filed the missing persons report and a detective from the Chappaqua police came by and asked Celeste when she had last seen Adam. At the court hearing, she said. Not since then. The detective took her statement, left, and she didn't hear back from him. Some nights she cried after Spencer went to bed. Other times she fell asleep with him and slept the entire night in his bed. Spencer asked why he hadn't heard from Dad and she said no one has heard from him—he must have taken a trip somewhere. A gambling trip? She didn't know. She took Spencer to visit his grandparents on a Sunday afternoon and they went to the Vaneks' country club for lunch and afterward Joseph taught Spencer how to putt on the practice green while Celeste sat with Eva on the deck overlooking the green. Eva broke down because she was afraid something terrible had happened to Adam. Celeste didn't know how to reassure her, but she hugged her mother-in-law and said everything would be okay.

Spencer decided to play soccer and Celeste registered him for the town recreation league and drove him to practice on Wednesday evenings and to his games on Saturday. Kristin came over to be with Spencer while Celeste went out for drinks with Emery and other friends. The one time Emery mentioned that Celeste didn't seem like herself, Celeste told her no one had seen or heard from Adam. "Everyone seems to think he went off on a gambling jaunt," she said.

"I was pulling for Adam, of course," Emery said. "But I can't say I'm surprised. He just didn't seem like he was going to get better. And attacking you—well, that's just unforgivable."

Emery asked if she was still seeing Jake. Celeste shrugged off the question, saying she wasn't ready to get too involved with anyone. They continued to run together three times a week. They got their kids together for playdates. They talked about signing up for a Caribbean cooking class at the CIA. The advertising agency GeoPol used saw her freelance work and offered her design projects on another account. Celeste bought a new and more powerful computer and updated her design software. She started sketching with charcoal and bribed Spencer with candy to sit as her model. He didn't mention Kathy's name anymore. She didn't hear from Jake or try to contact him. She was a widow, although the word sounded foreign to her.

36

Sara sat in the Tenth Precinct in the office of the CO, Paul Krewski. He was a squat, powerful man constructed from a series of rectangular shapes: a locker for his midsection, a shoebox for his head, flower boxes for arms and legs. Even his haircut had four sides.

The office smelled like scorched coffee, as if the same

scalded pot had sat on the burner since Sara last worked here two years ago. The pit of her belly stirred. Every smell in the world poked her now—magnolia blooms, steam from subway grates, peanut vendors, exhaust fumes. Bugs scaled her stomach from the time she woke up until midmorning, when she vomited and then could eat, usually starting with a box of crackers or a salted bagel, and continuing through the day with whatever edible item she could find and shove into her mouth.

Krewski was talking about this morning's double hit on Wall Street. Broad daylight, two victims, two headshots at close range with what appeared to be a nine-millimeter Glock.

"Wasn't one of them an executive at a pharmaceutical company?" Sara said.

"He rang the opening bell at the exchange," Krewski said. "And then he walked out and someone rang his bell, along with an investment banker who was underwriting the drug company's IPO. The early betting line is on some lunatic shut out of the initial stock offering. Or a disgruntled employee of one of the firms. Half the department is on the case, including your former partner Walsh, and I'm short-handed."

"What about Maney?"

"Broke his leg last week on a fire escape. He's sitting home watching TV and drinking beer."

"Give him another day and he'll be in here on crutches," she said.

"Hundreds of witnesses. You know what that means: hundreds of versions of the events, hundreds of descriptions of the shooter. You ready to lift your nose out of the cold files?"

She'd been content to bury herself in the unsolved cases, flipping through stained and tattered pages, clicking on links that hadn't been visited for months or years. She hadn't uncovered the overlooked gem that could illuminate a case again, and to be honest she didn't mind. If she did nothing but read forgotten reports until October rolled around, that would be fine. Although one particular case still bothered her—Vincent Canto and the murder of the jockey Roberto Peña—the investigation that had been hers four years ago. She'd dug around but hadn't discovered any new evidence or leads to open the case again.

"You want me on Wall Street, too?" she asked Krewski.

"Something else. We got one churned up by the ferry just south of Forty-second. Bit of turf war in reverse. We don't want it on our CompStat sheet and neither does Midtown North. But we'll probably get it because the ferry docks at Thirty-ninth." He turned up his left palm, as if showing something to Sara. The mannerism she knew well, and it meant: *You explain it.*

"I got a call from the ME," Krewski said. "Blunt-force trauma. The ferry propellers took a few whacks as well but that's unrelated."

"How long in the water?"

Krewski gave an indifferent shrug. "I haven't had a chance to read the report and have no one else available. That's why I could use you."

Sara nodded reluctantly. "You got a name?"

"Sure." He rearranged a disaster of papers strewn on his desk, shuffling, flipping. "Around here somewhere."

"Never mind," Sara said. "Is the body at the morgue?"

"Tagged and tabled."

She stood up to leave. Okay, so it was back to real work.

"That fuckhead Falcone make you turn in your service weapon?"

"We don't carry firearms in the crime center."

"That mean you still got yours?"

"And my shield."

"I've got a car for you, too, unless your driver's license has been taken away."

Twenty minutes later she was inching crosstown with the mob of delivery trucks and cabs on Twenty-third Street. Krewski had prodded her into action again, which meant she'd have to analyze information, conduct interviews, and make decisions. If only she could do the same for her own situation. She hadn't scheduled the abortion, hadn't told Connie, wondered should she tell Jake. At first she imagined scenarios in which she would have the baby. She'd tell Connie and pass the child off as his; with these multiracial babies you can never tell for sure who the father might be. Her marriage would stay intact and she'd fulfill her dream of motherhood. What they call the win-win. But the math didn't check; she was about thirteen weeks, and until last month, she and Connie hadn't had sex in half a calendar year. Connie was a numbers guy, he carried his CompStats analysis to the hundredths decimal place; he wouldn't mess up this simple addition problem. Then she daydreamed a fantasy where she told Jake and he insisted she leave her husband to start a family with him. After all, he told her she was lovely, he promised he hadn't slept with her only for professional gain. But a future with Jake was even less likely than Connie screwing up the math and believing in a miracle baby. Finally, Sara imagined going back home to her mother in San Diego and having her baby there, although her mother was sixty-five and within a few years Sara would have two people to care for.

None of those scenarios worked. Which left termination and its smothering finality as her only option.

She turned on First Avenue, passed the NYU Medical Center, and entered the underground garage for the morgue. The attendant swiped her credentials and she found a parking spot a level down.

She'd been out of the murder business for two years while working analytics in the crime center, but when she pushed through the door to the morgue the world of corpses welcomed her back with the familiar smells of formaldehyde and orange blossoms. The masking orange scent always annoyed her more than the chemicals, and especially now with her constant nausea. She swallowed a sickly taste in her mouth and introduced herself to the assistant coroner on duty. He could pass for a skinny teenager, complete with pimply face. He wasn't anyone she knew from back in the day.

He shook her hand. "I'm Dr. Joshua Barth."

"Sara Montez. I'm here for the one from the river."

Eight guttered tables lined one wall, three of them occupied. On one was a child, on another an elderly woman, which meant the big one at the end was hers.

"This the one the ferry wrestled?" she said, heading toward the last table. She peered into the gray face, the flesh like melted wax. The lips were gone, likely nibbled away by hungry fish. The eyes had sunk behind concave lids or else had been eaten, too. The body was still clothed, with one arm set in the soggy remains of a cast and a rope tied around the torso. The rope had been cut and its end frayed. Below the waist was a jumble of torn fabric and shredded limbs, the inadvertent work of the ferry's steel propellers.

Sara snapped on a pair of gloves from the box next to the table. She picked up the right arm with the cast. It cymbaled against the stainless steel when she let go. She fingered the rope.

"Someone must have been trying to weigh him down, but the weight is gone. Looks like the rope was cut."

Dr. Barth stood behind her, watching. "Someone changed their mind and wanted the body to float?"

"Sometimes the big ones don't float at all, especially if the water is cold. But usually it only takes a few days of warming and they start popping up like corks. You'll see, now that it's spring. This is just the first of the season. You've heard the term *Easter parade*?"

She turned the head to the side and studied the location of the trauma, a concave mass of colorless jelly, much of it eaten or washed away. "A month in the river?"

Dr. Barth scrunched his brow. "About, more or less. Long enough to dissolve physical evidence."

She traced her finger along the broken skull. "More than one blow to the head."

"At least two. The upper one occurred first; you can see bone fragments from the lower one compressed into the initial wound. We'll get it all in the report when we do the full autopsy."

"You got an ID?"

"Wallet was still in his pants. Name Adam Vanek, address on the license up in Brookfield."

Her thoughts halted for a few seconds, then began to slowly turn. The name meant something to her. Adam Vanek. Someone she met working in Brookfield? A name she'd heard. She waited for an image or memory to surface. Nothing did.

She walked around to the other side of the table. The shirt was unbuttoned. The chest had the same warship coloring, a smattering of flattened hair. Rope around the belly. She pulled the left arm out of its sleeve. There was a dark mark along the bicep, a word tattooed into the flesh. She twisted the arm to read the letters, still legible—*Celeste*—and the name Vanek clicked into place.

The mangled legs hadn't gotten to her. Or the caved-in skull or eaten lips or waxy flesh. But the tattoo punched her gut. She tasted vomit in the back of her throat and before she could turn away she spewed, the watery contents of her stomach showering Adam Vanek's corpse.

"Dammit!" she said.

Dr. Barth barely controlled the glee in his eyes. "You must be new to this."

Oh God, he thought she was a rookie. "I'm old," she said. "Old and pregnant."

His face got serious, almost alarmed. "Can I get you something—a glass of water?"

"Do you have any bagels?"

37

Celeste stood at the stove cooking macaroni with broccoli for dinner. Spencer played trumpet in the living room: Beethoven's *Ode to Joy.* He'd chosen the piece and his instructor helped simplify the measures and Spencer had worked to eliminate most of his mistakes. Celeste had heard the same four bars over and over, day after day, and couldn't get the tune out of her head.

He stopped halfway through. An abrupt silence replaced the music.

"Mommy, someone's on the porch."

The doorbell rang. Celeste went to the front and peered

out the window. A Hispanic woman wearing a black car coat belted around her waist stood outside. A door-to-door solicitor, Celeste thought. A quick *No thank you* would suffice. The woman noticed Celeste in the window and gave an apologetic smile that appeared and faded.

Celeste opened the door.

"Celeste Vanek?" the woman said. She reached into her coat pocket and presented police identification in a foldout wallet.

"Yes," her voice cracked. She glanced at the shield and the photograph, then her eyes sought out and found Spencer, who stood only paces from her, but seemed far away and shrinking, as if she were already losing him.

"I'm Detective Montez, with the New York City Police Department. May I come in?"

Should she ask what this was about? Refuse? She needed to act now and perform smoothly.

"Please." Celeste stepped back to let the detective enter, then closed the door behind her. The woman was several inches shorter than Celeste and more substantial in the midsection, with an angular face and a flat nose and dark eyes.

"*Ode to Joy*," the detective said. "I could hear from the porch. Such a lovely classic."

"It's even better after you've heard it two hundred times," Celeste said. A quick laugh escaped her and the pain in her chest dissipated. She could handle this.

Detective Montez glanced in Spencer's direction, then lowered her voice. "Could we speak in private for a moment?"

"Spencer, do you mind practicing in the kitchen so we can talk out here? And if the water's boiling, please turn it down."

Without once looking at the detective, Spencer blew a final, barking note, as if in protest to his mother's request, but dutifully got up and carried his trumpet and music stand through the swinging door into the kitchen.

Celeste noticed that the detective studied Spencer all the way, as if trying to place him, and although there was nothing sinister in her stare, Celeste took offense: *Do not look at my son.*

Detective Montez sat in the wing chair. Celeste centered herself on the edge of the love seat. "Is this about Adam?" she said. "No one knows where he is. I already spoke to the Chappaqua police—they were here a few weeks ago."

The detective leaned closer, peered into Celeste's eyes. "I'm afraid I have bad news. Your husband Adam is dead. His body was recovered yesterday from the Hudson River in Manhattan."

Celeste's hand shot up and covered her mouth. She squeezed her eyes shut and opened them again. This reaction—press her lips and grimace, as if she'd swallowed something bitter—she'd chosen and practiced ahead of time, daring to watch herself in the mirror, in case this moment ever came. She knew it would, and feared its eventual arrival as she feared her own death: inevitable, but hopefully painless and many years away.

"I'm sorry to have to tell you this," Detective Montez said.

"The river? He drowned?"

"He was the victim of a homicide."

"Somebody killed Adam?"

The detective nodded. "And then disposed of him in the river."

"He wasn't a good swimmer," Celeste said. "He was so dense he had a hard time staying afloat. We used to tease him because other than swimming he was such a good athlete—"

"Adam didn't drown, Ms. Vanek."

Detective Montez retrieved a pen and a palm-sized notebook from her coat. "I know this is a difficult time for you."

Her eyes welled with tears, a gesture she had not practiced. "Where is he now?"

"His body is in the morgue, in Manhattan, but we can release him to you—to a funeral home."

"Adam's been living with his parents, they'll want to decide what to do. We were separated, and getting divorced."

The corners of the detective's mouth turned up in a sympathetic expression, as if she supported Celeste having separated from her husband. "When was the last time you saw Adam?"

"In court, it was February 28," she said. "I already told the Chappaqua police." Just as Jake had advised: All you need to know is the date you last saw Adam. "I was seeking an order of protection because he had assaulted and threatened me, he'd taken my son without permission and I feared for our safety."

The detective held her notebook open to a blank page, the pen poised but still not put to use.

"You probably know that already," Celeste said.

"I've read the petition and the court transcript," Detective Montez said. "And you haven't seen or spoken to him since?"

"We had another court appearance scheduled for the divorce hearing, but Adam couldn't be located. Was he already dead then?"

"Most likely."

In the kitchen, Spencer finished with *Ode to Joy* and started on *Let's Get Lost*, the Chet Baker torch song. The piece was too advanced for Spencer, but he was improving. If only Celeste could get lost now, disappear into her lover's arms the way Chet Baker had. And whose arms would those be?

"Ms. Vanek, do you know if Adam had any enemies? Anyone who might do him harm?"

"We didn't speak to each other very often."

"Can you think of anyone?"

"Excuse me." She went into the bathroom and pulled two tissues from the box, looked in the mirror and saw the teary, red face of genuine grief. You're doing fine, she reminded herself. No, you're crumbling. *You're in control.* You're terrified. *You can get through this.* Only she couldn't. She needed to tell the detective everything that happened. She needed to tell the truth.

She blew her nose and returned to the living room.

The detective took up where she'd left off. "Can you think of anyone he had arguments with or contentious dealings?"

"No . . . I don't know."

"His arm was in a cast. Do you know how that happened?"

"He said he slipped on the ice." Then she remembered something useful. "I know Adam owed someone a lot of money. I think he lost it betting on college basketball games. He told me they had one of the players working with them, so it was supposed to be a sure thing. You know, a completely safe bet—as if that would make me more understanding about what he was doing."

"Fixing games? Like a point-shaving scheme?"

"When he tried to explain, I wasn't exactly in a receptive mood. He was making excuses for gambling again and I wouldn't hear it. That's when he choked me."

"Who is *they*? Do you know who he owed money to?"

She shook her head. "No. But it could be $25,000. His father said something about that amount."

"How about the player, or the team he was betting on?"

She thought for a minute. "It might have had to do with Taconic State—that's where Adam went to school. He told me he was doing consulting work there. One day he gave me money he said he earned advising players about keeping up with their schoolwork and planning for life after basketball."

"Taconic State," Detective Montez repeated. This time she used her notebook. "Anyone else? Any recent conflicts you know about?"

"Well . . . me. Every time I saw Adam it was a conflict. There were times I wished he would just go away. But not like this. I didn't want him dead." She chewed on her lip and felt a layer of skin starting to tear. She stopped.

"What about Jake Atwood?"

Why was she asking about Jake? If the detective had reviewed the order of protection case, then she already knew the official record. "I haven't seen him, either. Does he have something to do with this?"

"Were you dating him at the time you last saw Adam?"

"I'm not sure how to answer. I guess you could say we were almost dating."

"*Almost dating*? That's a new term to me. Did your husband know about this *almost dating*?"

Another question the detective already knew the answer to. "He knew," Celeste said. "But things didn't work out with Jake. What happened in court . . . well, I couldn't keep seeing him after that." Although she wished he was here now to help her through these questions.

"Yes, I understand."

At that moment, the trumpet stopped and the swinging door opened. Spencer stood there, leaning into the room, his head down but his eyes trained on Celeste. "I'm done practicing."

"Come here, sweetheart," Celeste said.

Spencer took tiny steps toward his mother. "Why are you crying?"

She took his arm and guided him onto the couch. "This is Detective Montez, she's a policewoman from New York City. She had some very upsetting news to tell us."

"Is Dad dead?"

Celeste nodded, barely. Detective Montez shifted to face him. "How did you know your father was dead?"

Spencer shrunk under her gaze. "It's okay, honey," Celeste said, but it wasn't. Was he about to reveal something terrible about that night?

"Sometimes you just know something is going to happen," Spencer said. "Dad told me he was that way, too." He paused, then said, "He stopped calling me."

He buried his face in his mother's chest and contracted into a fetal curl. Celeste absorbed him into her arms. Detective Montez's eyes lost their dark distance and became wide and transparent, like windows, brilliant with emotion. Again, she was studying Spencer, but this time instead of feeling protective of Spencer or annoyed, Celeste experienced a sudden, unexpected connection to the detective, as if they had just communicated soundlessly, perhaps something that could be shared only woman to woman.

The detective looked as if she might cry. But that made no sense. Detectives don't cry. They make arrests.

38

Sara phoned to say she was in Brookfield and asked if she could come by GeoPol after business hours to show Jake something with the system. A strange request, now that GeoPol was holding a worthless, canceled contract and Sara had been removed from the project on her end, but Jake agreed to meet with her. He owed her that much, anyway.

When he let her in the front door they came together in a clumsy hug. He stood back and looked at her. Her face appeared fuller, rounder than he remembered, her skin flush. Was he forgetting her already? Another ex for his crowded archives.

He escorted her down the hall to the computer lab, a room chilled from air-conditioning to prevent overheating of the electronics. An array of diode lights blinked on the server stacks. Jake flipped the light switch and the overhead fluorescents flickered on.

"The system has been meeting expectations since we went live—and the address matching is giving high hit rates," Sara said.

"Is that what you want to show me?"

"It's too bad Oracle is getting all the credit because, really, GeoPol did all the hard work." She sighed wistfully. "We messed up, Jake."

He gave an indifferent shrug. "The best thing we can do is put that behind us." Jake already had. He hadn't given Sara much thought recently or the voided contract—he had new business to worry about. After the Toronto deal fell through, Jake barely saved his job by working in a frenzy to get a contract from the city of Santa Cruz, California, and a letter of intent from Charleston, and he was close on another from Madison, Wisconsin, but he knew if he made one more misstep he'd be gone from GeoPol. He hated every minute spent inside a police facility now; he kept expecting to hear the iron clang of locking bars.

"By the way, I rotated back to homicide," Sara said. "I basically got kicked out of IT. I'm working out of the Tenth again, my old precinct."

"I thought you were burned out on major crimes."

"It was either back to homicide or lose my position, and

that would impact my retirement benefits. But I'm working on an interesting case. That's what I want to show you."

He motioned to the bank of computer stations. "Take your pick."

Sara planted herself in a chair in front of one of the screens and centered the keyboard. She entered the address of the log-in page. Jake wheeled a chair next to her.

Sara typed in her user name and password. "At least they didn't take away my system credentials." She clicked several menus, entered a date range. While studying the screen, she said, "You remember Celeste Vanek—the woman who was choked by her husband? The one you helped out?"

Jake felt a twitch inside that made him think of a lock tumbler turning. "Sure I do."

"How about her husband? You remember him?"

He shifted in his seat, feeling the first distant drumbeats of fear, knowing he'd just entered hostile territory. He said, "I saw him at a court hearing where Celeste requested an order of protection against him. I testified as a witness to his choking her."

"How did that turn out?"

He was about to answer that it hadn't turned out very well, but he said, "I get a sense you already know what happened."

"Oh, here we are," Sara said, her attention back on the screen. "Murders in Manhattan over the past month."

A map of Manhattan centered onscreen, displaying major roads, parks, and police precinct boundaries. On top of the map, triangles appeared with a legend in the corner. Jake scanned and counted twelve—eight green triangles for cleared cases, four red for the open ones.

"Twelve this past month," he said. "Is that a lot?"

"A little higher than usual for Manhattan—there was that

double murder on Wall Street. It's keeping homicide pretty busy. If that hadn't happened I'd still be reading cold cases."

"I heard about Wall Street. Anyone arrested yet?"

"It's a big investigation." Neither of them spoke for a few seconds, until Sara said, "Look at this." She clicked one of the red triangles located near the ferry pier on the West side. A window popped up with a form. The NAME field at the top was completed in bold lettering: Adam Joseph Vanek.

Immediately his heart rate doubled. The air-conditioned room became blazingly hot and he began to sweat beneath his shirt. Sara watched his reaction. He willed himself to remain calm, although inside a hurricane raged. His skin seemed to hum. He inhaled a slow, deep breath. Nothing audible. Another. But it was already over. Sara didn't need to say another word, she didn't need to present her theory or assemble the puzzle for him. Adam Vanek had been murdered and Sara held some piece of evidence tying Jake to the crime. Otherwise, why would she be here? He remembered Sara telling him that in homicide cases, 90 percent of the time you knew right away who committed the crime—someone who knew the victim: the spouse, the lover, the rival, the friend.

"Does Celeste know?" he asked.

"I just came from Celeste Vanek's. She seems like a nice person, and that son of hers is pretty cute."

He attempted conversation. "From what I saw, she's completely devoted to him—not that I know much about parenting."

"Neither do I. But she's going to need all her parenting skills now that her son doesn't have a father," Sara said. "Did you know Adam's parents had reported him missing to the Chappaqua police almost a month ago? He'd been living with his parents at the time."

Jake shrugged and shook his head. Why would he know that?

"I thought the police might have talked to you. According to Celeste Vanek, the two of you were *almost dating* at the time Adam was last seen. What does that mean, Jake—*almost dating*?"

It meant they were going to be together that night, it meant he'd finally found a woman he could love—until Adam ruined everything. "We were getting to know each other," he said.

"You do move quickly," Sara said, but her tone was factual, not critical. "Anyway, without the new data integrated from the outlying communities, I wouldn't have known the Chappaqua police were involved, at least not without some digging."

"Do you have any leads? Any idea what happened?" He had to play the game out.

"There are always suspects, but tying someone to the crime is a different matter. As for what happened, I can tell you he died from blunt-force trauma to the head, then was dumped in the river, probably somewhere around here, and the current took him down to the city. Someone likely messed up trying to weight the body—or else changed their mind. We're close enough here to New York that the body might have gotten washed forever out to sea if a crossing ferry hadn't churned him up."

Jake turned his attention back to the screen, which would not come into focus. He blinked twice, his own eyes betraying him. He squeezed one of his fists in his lap to steady his hand.

"Here's more of GeoPol's good work helping the police," Sara said. She selected the Link Map icon and the map zoomed out from the triangle representing Adam in Manhattan. Lines from the triangle extended to Brookfield, Chappaqua, and all the way to Verona, New York.

"I discovered in a few seconds what might have taken days to compile," Sara said. "Former address in Brookfield, still on his driver's license. Where he most recently lived in Chappaqua with his parents—that address taken from a database of New York State court documents. All of this data available now to the NYPD with a few mouse clicks."

The moisture evaporated from his mouth. He sucked his tongue to get something going so he could speak, but realized he had nothing to say.

"Hmm. Here's something interesting," Sara said. "When Adam's father reported his son missing, he gave the police in Chappaqua the idea to check casinos. Sure enough, Adam's car was found way up in Verona at Turning Stone Casino. That's a piece of information a New York City police detective might take a while to uncover, information only the local police would have on hand. But not anymore, because GeoPol did its job well."

Jake affected a casual stance in the chair, slumping a bit, one hand hanging over the arm, the other still clenched and hidden.

"How does his car end up at Turning Stone and he ends up in the river?" he said.

"Yes, that's one of those questions," Sara said. She rubbed her chin, as if contemplating an answer. Jake could give her one. He could tell her how he'd driven three and a half harrowing hours in the middle of the night to ditch Adam's car in the parking lot at Turning Stone. How he weighed the risk of getting into an accident in poor weather or being pulled over against the necessity of moving the car off his property. How he wore gloves and a hat and stopped in Verona at a twenty-four-hour drugstore after exiting the Thruway and bought a box of antiseptic wipes and scrubbed the seats and floor mats and pedals where a hair from his head or a flake from his skin might have landed. Left the steering wheel and controls and dashboard alone so he wouldn't wipe the car of Adam's own prints. How he parked in the huge, free lot where a car could go unnoticed for weeks or more. Took a taxi from the casino to Rome. Boarded the Amtrak back to Penn Station, the subway to Grand Central, Metro North to Brookfield, another cab to his house and arrived home the next afternoon. The sun was dazzling, the ice melted, but his heart beat cold and scared and dark.

His perfect plan. Except the canoe capsized, the rock wedged under the seat, he cut the rope, the body was discovered, the car located.

"Could he have gone to Turning Stone and met somebody who killed him?" Jake said. "Celeste told me he was a big gambler. That he had a lot of debt."

Sara's mouth opened to reveal a small gap and a line of straight, white teeth. The tip of her tongue peeked out. "And then transported the body all the way back and dumped him in the Hudson River? There are other waterways much closer to Verona—the Mohawk River, for instance."

He shrugged and frowned, as if admitting to her how amateur his idea was. "I'm no detective."

"Someone was trying to create a diversion," Sara said. "Someone who knew Adam Vanek gambled. Someone who thought—correctly—that casinos are crawling with loan sharks, con artists, mobsters, prostitutes, drug dealers. You get mixed up with the wrong person at a casino and it's not such a far-fetched possibility that something happens. Are you with me?"

Jake nodded.

"You could even disappear from a place like that," Sara said. "If the body hadn't floated up, there would be nothing but a missing persons case."

"Hard to believe he's dead," Jake said, speaking the truth.

"One thing, though," Sara said. "Adam was a big man. Six-foot-three. A man like that driving a car has to move the seat all the way back. But when his car was found, the seat was in a forward position. Which leads me to conclude that Adam did not drive his car to Turning Stone. Whoever did was quite a bit shorter than six-three. Whoever drove his car accounted for some variables, but not all of them. Whoever murdered Adam Vanek knew he was gambler."

Another mistake. He'd forgotten to move the seat back.

Then Sara asked, "About how tall is Celeste Vanek?"

He lurched in his chair, then tried to cover by adjusting his posture, making himself more comfortable. "Sara, there's no way Celeste could have done such a thing."

"Five-six, five-seven?"

"You just saw her a little while ago."

"She wants to divorce him—he won't divorce her. He chokes her, he takes their son. She wants an order of protection against him—the judge denies it. How can this happen to her? She's been wronged by him, he's wrecked her life. And no one is doing anything about it. One night he comes over, maybe he wants to see her, maybe he wants the kid. They have an argument."

Not that much different from how Jake had laid out the story for Celeste. He scanned his brain for counterpoints. "She's so much smaller than him. How could she overpower him?"

"By striking him suddenly and unexpectedly from behind with a heavy object," Sara said. "It doesn't take that much force to crush a skull. He was a one-armed man at the time."

"Come on. Are you saying she bludgeoned him with a rock, then got him down to the river and dumped his body and drove his car all the way to Turning Stone Casino? And then what? Took a bus back? The train? And where was her son in all this—along for the ride? If you're asking me, I'm telling you there was no way she could have done it."

"Jake, I didn't say anything about a rock."

His last trickle of hope evaporated. Could he be any more stupid? "Lead pipe, baseball bat—I was just . . . not Celeste. I'm just saying—"

"Maybe she had help. Maybe it was planned."

No comment.

"Jake, how tall are you?"

Before he could answer or protest the question, Sara said, "Don't say anything. Don't. Not yet." She pushed her chair away from the table and placed her palms on her stomach, then on the arms of the chair.

"There's something I need to tell you," she said, her voice almost soothing in tone.

Celeste must have already broken and admitted the whole story and this entire conversation was nothing but a trap for him. He waited, expecting Sara to arrest him, or at least tell him to get an attorney before opening his mouth again.

"Would you say that you and I were *almost dating*? Would that be accurate?"

Okay, she wanted to torture him. "Sara, we've been through this already."

"Yes, I know. But I'm thinking that in some ways our relationship might be the best thing that ever happened to me," she said. "I know what I did was unethical—exchanging inside information for affection. And I know I took risks."

"You didn't gain much. You got kicked out of your division."

She waved off his comment. "I got more than you realize. I learned about myself, I learned I'm not the person I thought I was. I'm capable of doing things I never thought I could do."

Yes, they had that in common. He saw her struggling, the inward turn of her gaze, the computations in her mind. He guessed then where she might be heading: Sara knew he killed Adam, but if he agreed to stay with her in a relationship, she wouldn't pursue his arrest. That would be the price of freedom—spending his life with Sara Montez.

She quickly erased his theory. "I never wanted to leave my husband for you," Sara said. "I don't think I could have loved you—and I know you couldn't love me. But I don't think you simply used me to get a deal for your company."

"No, I didn't."

"Under different circumstances—a different place, a different time—we might have done well together. We might have done more than *almost date*. I believe you're a good person, Jake. I believe that deep down you want to do the right thing."

Yes, yes. He nodded his agreement.

"But Adam Vanek—the more I learn about him, the more I realize he was not a good person. Maybe at one time he was a good husband and father, but he changed. He attacked his wife, he destroyed his family. I don't know if that means he deserved to die—although people die for a lot less than that. Still, he left behind people who loved him. Ask his parents if their son deserved to die. Ask Adam's own son. What do you think, Jake? Did Adam Vanek deserve to die?"

"I can't answer that question," Jake said, his voice quiet, at the edge of crumbling. "We don't know the whole story."

"You're saying he might have deserved to die? You're not ruling it out?"

"It's not for me to judge his life." Except he had.

"Ahhh," Sara said, as if Jake had made a good point, one she should have considered herself but hadn't. Then she asked: "Why did you stop seeing Celeste Vanek?"

He could give any number of answers. Like he didn't want to get involved in yet another unsustainable relationship, although he didn't believe that was the case with Celeste. Or he'd learned from Sara about the pitfalls of dating married women, although that was no longer an issue. Or Celeste had told him she never could see him again. Yes, that's the one.

"I didn't want to stop," Jake said. "She broke it off after the court hearing."

She looked surprised, then started to smile. "Really? Knowing you, I would have expected it the other way."

39

He knocked on her door and waited. The curtain in the front window parted and a moment later she let him in. He hadn't seen or spoken to Celeste since the night he struck and killed Adam. He had accepted and respected her decision about never seeing him again and didn't fault her for shutting him out, although for this reason alone he regretted what he'd done to Adam.

He stepped inside and despair struck him. He was overwhelmed to be in her presence and resisted the urge to take hold of her, to touch her face, feel her in his arms. He'd survived the past month on handshakes in business meetings in order to have physical contact with others and feel somewhat human. And he'd spent torturous hours chasing the reasons for striking Adam that second time. Because he panicked in the moment when Adam stirred, still a formidable threat. Because Celeste had endured too much and he acted to free her. Because he wanted to transform himself and demonstrate his commitment to her and, having no experience in the matter, chose a demented way. Well, then, here was his opportunity to discover the meaning of commitment, to prove he really could save her from trouble or harm.

"I knew you'd come," Celeste said.

"I wanted to make sure Spencer was asleep."

"It wasn't easy for him. Even if your father is a brute, when you're ten years old you still cry when he dies. Your heart still breaks."

"What about you?"

"I thought I was fine, but once the detective came here I wanted to tell her. I didn't, but I'm afraid, Jake. What are the police going to do?"

"I thought I would take care of everything—I wanted to take care of you."

"I know you tried. I know you wanted to."

"I still can. I'll tell them what I did," Jake said. "I hit him the one time I had to—and then again when I didn't. I'll tell them I convinced you how the police would see it. You only went along because of Spencer."

"I did go along for Spencer."

"You'll be safe, you and Spencer. It's what you deserve, and I can make it happen this time."

"You can't tell the police, Jake. Anyone would advise you not to do that. You don't know what evidence they have—they might not have anything. You'd be giving yourself up for nothing."

For you. I'd be giving myself up for you. "If I wait, then I put you at risk," he said. "I can't let them come after you. I made a terrible mistake—and I'll take responsibility."

"You saved me, Jake. That wasn't a mistake, was it?"

No, that part wasn't a mistake.

"Wouldn't they already have arrested you if there was evidence? They would have. Which means they don't have the answer. The detective left here thinking Adam was in trouble over some kind of gambling debt. She wasn't suspecting you or me."

He could contradict her, because he knew what Sara was thinking: that he and Celeste had murdered Adam together. But Celeste was right that he shouldn't turn himself in. If it came to his arrest, he could still protect her. He could make a convincing case that he'd acted on his own.

"I went along with your plan for you, too," Celeste said. "Because you were right. It was the only way, we had no other choice. Promise me you won't talk to the police. Not yet."

"Not yet," he said. "But I will when the time comes." He turned to leave. He waited for her to call him back, to reach for him. She didn't. He kept moving, out the door, forcing each step.

40

Sara entered the park and scanned the benches surrounding the fountain, but didn't see her husband. Lunch hour throngs crowded the space, waves of pedestrians flowed along the walkways. She found a seat and waited and tumbled over in her mind her interview yesterday with Celeste Vanek. She didn't think Celeste was capable of murdering her husband, but if Jake had been stupid enough to do it for her, then Celeste was at least aware of what happened, and likely an accomplice. The woman was hiding something, she had a secret—but what? Had she gotten Jake to do the dirty work? It happened all the time, the femme fatale casting her wicked spell on a smitten man. Had Jake Atwood fallen prey to an evil woman's charm? But Celeste Vanek didn't seem the type. Neither did Jake, for that matter. But if not them, then who? Who else could have murdered Adam Vanek?

Equally mystifying was that throughout her interview with Celeste Vanek, the crime and investigation and Celeste's role, if any, hadn't been the key question nudging Sara. The question had been: *What does she have that I don't?* A selfish, petty, envious question—but Sara was not jealous of Celeste Vanek, not bitter that Jake was drawn to her. Sara was simply in the dark and craved illumination. She did not want to be with or possess Jake, but she wanted to know what about Celeste was so alluring to him. What was so special? Physically, Sara and Celeste were contrasts. Celeste taller and thinner. Deep green eyes. Thick auburn hair, but come on, it was just hair. Fair rather than dark. White skin to Sara's walnut tone. So what. Could an alternative palette of physical features make that much of a difference—incite a man to murder for you?

And Sara could see how they would score differently on personality indicator tests: Sara analytical, Celeste intuitive; Sara thinking, Celeste feeling. But paper scores, what do they really mean?

What does she have that I don't?

And then Celeste's son came out from the kitchen and

upon hearing the news of his father's death he fell like a broken bird from the sky into his mother's arms. Sara witnessed an immediate and powerful change in Celeste Vanek. From wary and dispirited and anxious about having this cop questioning her, to complete disregard for Sara's presence, as if this suspicious homicide detective were no longer there; and what transpired next was intimate and primal, Celeste Vanek transforming into a protective and nurturing presence for her son. She became a mother. And that's when Sara understood what Celeste had that she herself didn't.

She got up from the bench and walked once around the fountain, the veils of spray making rainbows in the sun, the passersby hustling about their business. There—she spotted Connie on a bench, his posture angled forward and his legs spread apart, a sandwich in his hand.

Had he been there all along without her noticing? Some detective.

He set his sandwich on the bench next to him and stood to greet her, taking her hand and sliding over to make room. "We've been coming to this park for how many years?" Connie said. "Remember we stopped here after getting our marriage license?"

"It was growing dark and the lights on the trees came on as we were walking. I thought they turned on just for us."

The sun peered in and out of clouds. The fountain sprayed and drained.

"You hungry?" He picked up his sandwich and offered it to her. She was hungry, but shook her head.

"I have a class at one, I have to eat and get back," he said.

"I wish you had more time." She'd planned to share the

news gently, with backstory—how she'd met someone, was drawn in, made a mistake. How she'd been afraid Connie didn't love her anymore, that he would die and leave her alone; and in her distress she turned to the arms of another man. But the words that flew out of her now were not gentle or prepared, but direct and targeted as a missile.

She said, "I'm pregnant."

Connie stiffened against the back of the bench, as if she'd just given him a command to sit up straighter. He looked to see if she were kidding. He shook his head. "No, you can't be," he said, dismissing her statement.

"About thirteen weeks." She held her breath and waited.

"Already? But how could you—" He blinked in rapid succession, then reason took over and he examined the facts and did the math and nothing added up. He kept getting the wrong answer, just as Sara knew he would.

A chuckle rumbled from him. It wasn't the polite laugh elicited by an amusing joke, but the nervous, it-can't-be-true response some people have when you deliver bad news. She'd witnessed the reaction many times. A desperate chortle of disbelief and dismissal, replaced almost immediately by a crushing few seconds of silence, the electric interval between lightning and the ensuing thunder, the devastating strike of awareness.

It was wrong to tell Connie this way, in this most public of places with the sun shining, flowers blooming, people passing back and forth just inches from where they sat. But someone please show her the right way; there was no right way.

"You're having an . . . an *affair*?" Connie said. As if trying out the meaning of the word. Not a real word, a silly one a kid would make up, although right now Connie looked like an old man, wrinkled and worn.

She hesitated with her answer because the verb tense confused her. *Having . . . had . . . an affair.*

"Is it someone I know?"

"From this company GeoPol. I met him at a conference."

"The company that messed up your project?" Two weeks ago she had finally told him the story that resulted in her transfer back to homicide, while leaving out the most pertinent details.

"It was a mistake," she said. "I'm sorry, Connie. I never meant to hurt you."

He dropped his sandwich and clutched his chest and bent over, his breathing rapid and shallow. She reached for him as he straightened and recovered, the sudden wave of pain that had crashed on him now retreating. He squinted his eyes at her and slowly shook his head back and forth, a gesture he used in the classroom setting to let students know they'd made an inane comment or answered a question in a senseless, foolish fashion.

The ruins of his lunch lay on the ground. "Are you leaving me?" he said.

"I don't want to, I love you." The lack of breath, the searing in his chest—he wasn't faking, but he wasn't dying, either; he was soaking up her betrayal.

"What are you going to do?" he said.

She tried to formulate an answer that wouldn't inflict further harm on him, which was like stabbing him eleven times and then agonizing over whether to make it an even dozen. "The timing is terrible, I know," she said. "Just when we were . . . just when—Connie, you never paid attention to me, I was so lonely for—"

"—What are you going to do?" he demanded a second time, his voice angry and insistent.

"I was afraid you were going to die and I'd be alone. I didn't want to be left alone."

"So you had an affair and got pregnant? What the hell!"

"All these years, I was so sure it couldn't happen."

"I'll ask you one more time: *What are you going to do?*"

There was only one answer now. "I'm going to have a baby."

He set his gaze on the fountain. "Are you out of your mind?"

She may be, but at the same time she'd never been more in control of her feelings or sure of her decision. "Connie, I don't want to lose you. I know this is a lot to take in . . ."

"Shut up!" He stood to face her. "What the hell is wrong with you?" He kicked at the remains of his lunch and merged into the crowd, leaving her to clean up the mess on the ground.

41

The funeral was held on Monday in Chappaqua at St. Thomas the Apostle, the Vaneks' parish, the church where Celeste had married Adam eleven years earlier, the same priest presiding, although heavier and grayer now. Two days later, on Wednesday, Detective Sara Montez of the NYPD came to Celeste's house again. Spencer had gone back to school after taking Monday and Tuesday off. Chantal and Howard returned to Burlington. Joseph and Eva Vanek retreated to their home, and Emery and Stephen back to Cider Mill. Celeste's mother hadn't come up for the service; she couldn't fly due to a blood clot in her leg, but Celeste had spoken with her on the phone more in the past few days than she had in the past few months. She reminded Celeste that she was still young and pretty, she could find someone else, someone better. Thanks, Mom.

Detective Montez showed up within minutes of Spencer leaving for school, and Celeste wondered if she had been watching the house, waiting for the right moment to find her alone.

To be polite and instill a sense of normalcy, Celeste offered the detective coffee. "It's still fresh," she said.

"I had to give up coffee. I have a terrible reaction to it now—plus I'm avoiding caffeine."

"That happened to me when I was pregnant with Spencer," Celeste said. "I had a difficult pregnancy, but giving up coffee felt like one of the hardest parts. I was totally addicted to caffeine back then."

"I'll be grateful if it's the hardest part of mine."

"Oh . . . congratulations. You're pregnant. When are you due?"

"September 19—although I don't know how anyone can put an exact date on it."

"It's really just a guideline. I remember Adam called the two weeks leading up to my due date the red zone. Some reference to football."

"It's when the team on offense is in scoring position inside the opponent's twenty-yard line."

"You know football?"

"A few years ago I investigated the murder of Donald Zak—he played for the Jets. I learned a lot of football terms then."

"Adam watched a ton of games, but I didn't pay attention," Celeste said. "I couldn't be in the room with him when a game was on."

What was she doing having a conversation about football and pregnancy with a homicide detective? Then, as if the detective were thinking the same thing as Celeste, they both became quiet. The strain of anticipation was like a tug at her hair, Celeste thought, or a hand on her throat: forceful, insistent, foreboding.

Finally, Detective Montez said, "I came here to let you know we've made an arrest in your husband's case."

Jake.

Her heart drowned, a sudden, painful thrashing followed by slow, deep descent. Jake. Jake. Please don't say his name out loud.

She remembered when he had given her the photograph of the road sign that said *Heaven Ahead.* The frame was not expensive, the photograph poorly lit. She didn't love the wordplay on her name, another reminder that she wished her mother had chosen a different name for her. She didn't believe in heaven. Or in God. It was all fantasy—like an imaginary friend—to help us face the dark and endure terrible things. But at that moment when Jake gave her the gift, she believed in resurrections, in second chances; she believed she would somehow be able to make a clean break from Adam and start over. She and Jake had not known each other long, but in Jake's gift she saw a better life—it was possible, it was going to begin that night, at that moment, with him.

The next morning she'd forgotten the photo, hadn't thought of it in her rush to get out and must have left it on the couch or coffee table.

Now she must come forward with her story, how Adam had attacked Jake and then started for the bedroom where Spencer slept, and she blocked his path and he pushed her and choked her again and Jake . . . She must speak up now, she must do her part for him. But what about her son? Spencer needed her—she needed him.

Detective Montez watched her. They hadn't exchanged a word since the detective said an arrest had been made. It was Celeste's turn to speak. She had to ask, it was expected of her: Who was arrested? She opened her mouth, but before she could say anything, the detective said, "Let me explain."

Sara began assembling the pieces the day she drove up to Taconic State to interview the athletic director and ask him if he had ever hired Adam Vanek as a consultant to the players. The director said, "Who?"

"Adam Vanek, former student and basketball player. Graduated in 1994. Supposedly performed consulting work to help the players plan for a productive life after basketball."

"A lot of these kids could use the advice, but we don't have the budget for that."

She asked if he had a video of a basketball game between Taconic and Siena from the night of January 6. It was the night Celeste Vanek claimed her husband had lost a lot of money on a basketball game and later assaulted her.

The athletic director made a call and an assistant located a disk.

Sara didn't know as much about basketball as she did football, but she took the disk back to the Tenth and her commander, Paul Krewski—who dabbled in gambling, paid into betting pools, and played fantasy leagues—watched the game with her. He set up a screen in an interview room. They watched the game into the second half. By then, a small crowd had gathered, other detectives and desk cops. So what if the game had been played months ago, the outcome on record, the season over. It was sports, on TV, at work.

Krewski picked out Elevet. "He's the one. He's the most athletic kid on the court and he's making bonehead plays. See how he keeps looking up after each basket? He's watching the scoreboard, he knows where to keep the spread."

Sara took a second trip up to Taconic State and visited Kevin Elevet in the dorm where he lived with other basketball players. There wasn't a person around who wasn't at least a foot taller than her. She craned her neck and introduced herself to Kevin and told him he could either tell her about his participation in a game-fixing scheme and she would be on her way or he could come with her to police headquarters in Manhattan to be questioned about a murder.

She showed him a photograph of Adam Vanek. Kevin folded right away, didn't even spout the *I want to speak to my lawyer* protest. "That dude," he said.

He gave up Adam Vanek, who had approached him about the scheme. Gave up Vincent Canto, who had arranged the details for each game, paying Kevin his share after each success.

Vincent Canto—oh, sweetness. Oh, serendipity. That was the name she wanted, had wanted for years, ever since he slipped through her hands for murdering Roberto Peña. Back in her car, she logged into the crime center databases from her laptop, pulled the report on Vincent Canto, then paid Mr. Canto a visit at a gentleman's club called Mario's in Brookfield to ask him some questions. When was the last time you saw Adam Vanek? Did Adam Vanek owe you a large amount of money? Did you know that a witness identified your picture in a photo book as directing an attack on Adam Vanek outside a sports bar called Checkers on February 26?

She arrested him for aggravated assault over the incident at Checkers and sat him overnight in the communal pen with the street thugs and derelicts. The next day Mr. Canto didn't look so good when he entered the interview room to face a couple of Sara's mates for another round of questioning. They let Canto know his fingerprints were found on the glove compartment door of Adam's car abandoned at Turning Stone Casino. He played dumb, naturally; he lawyered up, he was no newborn. Nonetheless, the district attorney reviewed the case and charged Vince Canto with murder and whether he'd done it or not wasn't relevant to Sara; she knew he'd killed that jockey at Belmont Stakes four years ago and justice had not been served. One thing she wasn't going to do was arrest the father of her child or the woman he loved. She could have pursued the case in that direction and blown up a few more lives, but when Sara told Celeste Vanek she'd made an arrest in the murder of her husband, in the stunned silence that ensued Sara studied her tiny facial movements, saw the woman dying inside, and as Celeste was about to speak—say something Sara did not want to hear—Sara cut her off.

"His name is Vincent Canto," she told Celeste.

"What. Who?" The shock transformed her face, as if the doctor just said your disease is not terminal after all.

"Vincent Canto. Your husband owed him a gambling debt—you were right, $25,000. We believe he murdered Adam because he couldn't pay his debt."

"But why would he kill Adam? Now he'll never get his money."

"The man ran an illegal gambling operation," Sara said. "For the serious ones, it comes down to reputation. They can't let people owe them, or they'll lose control over their business."

"How do you know it was him?"

"The DA is building the case, but he has a motive and we know he fired a warning shot, so to speak. He's the one who broke Adam's arm. A witness identified Vincent Canto in a group of men who attacked Adam and the witness overheard Canto telling Adam next time he'd be dead."

"And he killed Adam."

"He's been on NYPD's list for years. Four years ago he was arrested in another murder case, but that one never went to trial. Now we've got him."

"Oh my God, he killed Adam." She even put a hand to her heart. This Celeste Vanek was a decent actress, not that Sara couldn't break her. Maybe another time, another life.

Okay, she'd delivered her news, it was time to leave, but she made no move to get up. She sat and fidgeted and didn't say a word.

"Is there something else you wanted to tell me?" Celeste asked.

Sara folded her hands in her lap. "I know this is unrelated, and personal, if you don't mind my asking . . . but when you were pregnant, did you find out if you were having a boy or girl? I can't decide what to do."

Sara let herself into the apartment. The air inside smelled stale. She ran hot now and was constantly overdressed and sweaty. She opened the living room window facing the courtyard. A breeze ruffled the sheer curtain. She stuck her head out and breathed. Ah, better. In the kitchen she struggled with the sticky sash. She wedged a knife between the sill and sash and forced the window open, bending the knife. She poured herself a glass of cranberry juice, added ice from the freezer, and drank. The ice struck her teeth when she tipped the glass. She chewed the cubes.

She walked into the second bedroom that had served as Connie's home office, her footsteps echoing off the hardwood floor. Connie's desk was gone, his lamp, both file cabinets. The bookshelves were empty. Only the stuffed leather chair remained. Sara collapsed into it, kicked off her shoes, closed her eyes. She was forty-two years old and would be a month from retirement and all alone when she gave birth. She rested her hands over her belly and pictured the life growing inside her, the tiny beating heart, the toothpick limbs—and the complicated world that awaited her child.

When she opened her eyes she noticed the drab and dingy beige walls, the marginally brighter square where Connie had taken down the photo of the two of them riding the Maid of the Mist in Niagara Falls. Her marriage of eighteen years was about to end—it was still hard to believe. Yet she didn't have any regrets about her life with Connie and only a few regrets that she was moving forward without him.

What color should she repaint the room? Not pink or blue, since she didn't know if she was having a boy or girl and had decided not to find out. Celeste Vanek told her the mystery of not knowing kept her excited throughout the long months of a difficult pregnancy; the discovery was part of the miracle of birth. Maybe a gender-neutral shade would work here—moss green with a hint of lime. Maybe the color of clouds. Although she wouldn't have the room painted yet, not too soon. She didn't want to jinx anything. For the first few months, or maybe first few years, her baby would sleep in her room, perhaps even in her bed. She didn't know what the experts currently had to say about the practice of co-sleeping, a silly term she'd recently discovered. So much to learn.

Dust bunnies circulated in the corner where Connie's desk had been. She got up and swept them up with her stocking feet. A soft, diffused light came in the window. No direct sunlight, no harsh glare.

42

Spencer insisted on saving the cave tour for last to let the excitement build up, or, in Celeste's case, the anxiety. When she discovered you rode an elevator down the equivalent of thirteen stories to reach the caves, she asked Spencer if he'd be okay with only visiting the Museum of Mining & Geology.

"You're kidding, right, Mom?"

All that way underground, beneath tons of rock—the world hiccups and you're buried alive.

Celeste yawned in the museum as she read the captions fronting a scale model of the caverns, yet still wished the clock would stop moving and their tour time never arrive. When they finished in the museum, Celeste purchased a bag of mining rough for $8. Spencer emptied the flaky, clay dough into a strainer and held the pan in a water sluice, shaking back and forth like a real gold prospector and watching as the running water rinsed away the rough to reveal his gems. Then they viewed Spencer's obsidian under a microscope. One of the workers used a high-speed saw blade to shave a thin slice of the rock and place it under magnification. Celeste was reluctant to put her eye to the microscope, but Spencer said, "You have to see this," and when she hesitantly looked into the lens, she could almost see the beginnings of crystals in a haphazard, feathery pattern that never quite materialized.

Put down another $10 and you could fill a small bag from a bin of colored stones. She didn't mind splurging on all the money traps to invest in Spencer's interests. Besides, she had a real job now. The advertising agency GeoPol used had offered her a position. Two half-days in the office per week and two days at home, working on a new healthcare account the agency had landed, but not on GeoPol, whose account the agency lost when the company reported weak earnings and scaled back its advertising budget. Celeste had flexible hours, basic health benefits, and a savings plan. It wasn't going to make her rich, but she and Spencer would be secure, plus Spencer had the trust fund that Joseph and Eva Vanek had established, to transfer over to him at age eighteen. Joseph had told Celeste about the fund after Adam's funeral, and when he mentioned its current value she stifled a gasp.

Her sister continued to nudge her about moving to Burlington that summer, once the school year ended. "What's keeping you in Brookfield?" she wanted to know. But Celeste put her off. She wasn't ready to leave.

After the mining sluice and microscope, Celeste retrieved their lunch from the car and set out a blanket on the lawn in front of the lodge. They ate sandwiches and clusters of grapes and vanilla yogurt under a pleasant sun. There was enough of a breeze for Celeste to keep her sweater on. A long open meadow in front of them offered a view of the low, rounded mountaintops in the distance. Other families had put down their blankets.

All the picnic tables were occupied. Celeste noticed a man with two young girls at one of the picnic tables and their eyes met and held for a second. He acknowledged Celeste with a brief smile and a peace sign, of all things, keeping his hand level with his waist and raising two fingers. He turned away to pour drinks for his girls, then looked again in Celeste's direction. She felt a flutter inside, and wondered if he was going to approach her. Then Spencer said, "Mommy, look, there's Jake."

He pointed behind her.

Before Celeste could react, Jake was upon them. The world around her drew back, people and sounds blurring and shrinking into the distance, leaving only Jake in her field of vision. She suddenly remembered a middle school dance when she watched a boy she liked cross the room toward Celeste and a group of her friends, and she didn't know if he was going to ask her or someone else to dance and then he asked her.

"You came!" Spencer said.

"May 21, right?" Jake said. "It's been on my calendar. How are you?" He shifted a paper bag to his other hand and shared a handshake with Spencer and then turned to Celeste, a cautious smile tugging the corners of his mouth. She caught her breath, as if she'd been running, steadied herself against that feeling of vertigo.

"Have you toured the caverns yet?" Jake said.

"We're going after we eat," Spencer answered. "Mom's afraid. Do you want some of my sandwich?" He held up the other half of his sandwich, the egg salad falling out the back of his bread and onto the blanket.

"You're spilling," Celeste said. She reached and scooped up the egg salad, set it on Spencer's wax paper wrapping. She hadn't completely ruled out seeing Jake again, and she'd thought about him and what might have been for them, but she wouldn't seek him out in order to be less alone with the secret they shared. Although if she was going to live with what happened—and she was, she had so far—it would help to have someone who understood why some hours had to be so dark, and why that dark had to be confronted and overcome.

"This belongs to you," Jake said. "You left it at my house." He handed her the bag and she slid out the framed photo of the sign *Heaven Ahead.*

"Thank you. I hadn't forgotten about it," she said.

"What is it, Mommy?" Spencer looked at the picture. "Oh, that's weird. What does it mean?"

"Are you going to join us on the tour?" Celeste asked.

"Mom needs someone to hold her hand."

"Isn't that your job?" Jake said.

"You need a ticket."

"Already got one." Jake pulled a ticket from his back pocket. He'd purchased it as soon as he arrived, figuring that as long as he'd made the trip he'd take the tour whether he found Celeste and Spencer or not.

He'd been hanging around waiting for this day. After Sara had informed him that a man named Vincent Canto had been arrested for Adam Vanek's murder, and this man Canto had been on Sara's list for several years after escaping prosecution for another murder, Jake experienced an incredible sense of relief and lightness, followed by the devastating loneliness that accompanies absolute freedom, and bewilderment over what to do next. He resigned from GeoPol, exhausted from chasing revenue and drained from his constant interactions with police, and knowing he could find a new position when ready, although he might not be ready for a long time. Financially, he could fritter away several years, but the owner of the house he rented was returning to the States and Jake had to be out by the end of May, so he had embarked on a tour of the region to help him decide if he wanted to remain in the area or move to another part of the country or even Europe or Asia. He drove to the Berkshires and the Catskills for hikes, Long Island for a fishing trip, to the Finger Lakes to visit wineries, into the Adirondacks for a white-water kayak trip. The activities helped fill the time until May 21 when he planned to take a day trip to Cobleskill and keep his promise to Spencer that he would go to Rock Day at Howe Caverns, and his promise to himself that he would not abandon Celeste without a final attempt to connect with her. Sometimes he thought of what he did to Adam, but not every hour or even every day, which made him realize his capacity for cruelty and also his ability to sequester that cruelty, leaving other parts of him open for compassion and love.

They rode an elevator with a dozen other people in their group. Celeste wondered if her barely contained trembling was due to Jake's presence or the chill in the air or her claustrophobic fear. Most likely all three. They descended 150 feet and were herded on a walking tour of dimly lit, clammy tunnels with handrails along their path and an underground river by their side. Their tour guide was named Amber, probably a local girl, about twenty years old and lumpy, with a cute face, blond hair, and a nasally voice. She spoke as if she had memorized verbatim the script for the tour, including inflection points. Celeste and Jake hung toward the back of the group, while Spencer elbowed his way up front, where he could hear Amber recite facts about the geological features and how the caves were formed eons ago by the stream.

At one point the cave opened into a massive underground room with cathedral-height ceilings and tiny lights strung up the walls. Spencer ran back to them. "You want to know something?" he said, addressing Jake.

"What's that?"

"Those are stalagmites growing from the floor and stalactites from the ceiling."

Celeste had heard this fun fact often enough.

"I never could keep those two straight," Jake said.

"It's easy," Spencer explained. "There's a *g* in stalagmites, so think of *ground*, and a *c* in stalactites so you remember that means *ceiling*."

"Hey, that's a good memory device."

"Isn't this the best place you've ever been?"

"Zip up your jacket," Celeste told him. "It's chilly down here."

"I'm not cold." But he zipped up and went back to the front of the group.

"I really like that kid," Jake said. He took Celeste's hand and she let him because his warmth calmed her and she'd had a dream a few weeks ago about holding hands with Jake, but after a moment she separated and walked next to him and they didn't touch again.

For the grand finale they got to ride in a boat. The cavern floor came level with the river and the tour group piled into a long narrow gondola with bench seats across the keel. Spencer wanted to skip the ride, saying he didn't like boats, but Celeste said, "Since when," and promised this would be the best part, and if she was willing to take the elevator down thirteen stories for him, then he could take a short boat ride for her. Spencer finally agreed and sat in the middle of a bench with Celeste and Jake on either side of him. They left the dock and the boat slid along the smooth current with Amber standing in the stern and using a long pole against the river bottom to steer. The sound of distant rushing water grew louder as they cut forward through the water and the cavern walls narrowed around them near enough to touch.

Amber shouted above the roar, "That sound is a waterfall up ahead. This underground river formed the entire cave we walked through today and it continues on for miles beyond our reach."

The air was damp and a shiver passed through Celeste. Jake stretched his arm behind Spencer and found Celeste's shoulder and drew her closer.

"Getting closer!" Amber shouted.

The falls were right ahead of them in the blackness beyond where the lights ended. Spencer tensed in his seat.

"Oh, no!" Amber cried. "I hope we don't go over the falls! The edge is right here!"

Everyone knew it was a joke. Everyone except Spencer. He jumped as if he'd been struck with an electric wire. He would have fallen over the side if Jake hadn't held him back.

Celeste said, "It's okay, she was only kidding." She hugged him to her chest and felt his rapid heartbeat and she understood how young and vulnerable her son was, how much he needed his mother to love and protect him, and how much she needed to fulfill that role.

The boat bumped to a gentle rest at a gate along the precipice. A spotlight flicked on and illuminated the falls and they gazed at the thundering water spilling into a black pool below.

READING GROUP GUIDE

Warning: Some plot points are revealed in the questions below.

1. Celeste believes with her marriage ending that "she was a different person now, with a new life ahead of her, a prospect that was both exhilarating and terrifying" (99). In what ways does she experience both of these emotions throughout the novel?

2. Celeste admits that she may have turned a blind eye to her husband's addiction, "avoiding stepping into the cracks in their life" (21). How does her denial mirror that of an addict?

3. Professionally, both Sara and Jake behave unethically. Jake begins a relationship with a potential client, and Sara gives Jake confidential business information. Why do they act this way? Is one of them more at fault than the other? Is their relationship mutually beneficial?

4. Throughout the novel, Celeste tries to make decisions that are in the best interest of her son, Spencer. How successful is she in doing this? What kind of mother is she? Is she justified in her decision to prevent Adam from seeing Spencer after he attacks her?

5. After Jake witnesses the altercation between Celeste and Adam in the GeoPol parking lot, Sara criticizes him for not contacting the police: "Keep your distance. Show you care,

but not too much. That's you, Jake" (66). Is this a fair characterization of Jake? How does Jake open himself to intimacy and vulnerability later in the novel? Why does he choose to change his pattern of behavior for Celeste?

6. What is the basis for the attraction between Celeste and Jake? Why do they become close? What do they see in each other? How do their feelings evolve over time?

7. Adam is a compulsive gambler, has acted violently toward his family, and threatens Jake when Jake befriends Celeste. Is there any way to consider him as a sympathetic character? How so?

8. Adam tells his son that his gambling problem is like a disease, comparing it to his own mother's cancer. Celeste tells Spencer exactly the opposite: "Your father doesn't have a disease. He didn't contract or catch anything that made him sick. He made a *decision* to gamble. No one makes a decision to get cancer" (206). Whose point of view do you agree with more? Why?

9. In Family Court, Howard Jasper manipulates the facts in order to satisfy his client's demands, leading to a ruling that feels less than fair to Celeste. How does this impact the decisions Celeste makes involving Spencer and Adam for the rest of the book? How are we supposed to respond when the systems designed to protect us are turned against us?

10. At one point Sara tells Jake, "I'm capable of doing things I never thought I could do" (351). What things is she referring to? How could this statement apply to other characters in the book?

11. When Sara sees an opportunity to tie up an old loose end by implicating Vincent Canto in the murder of Adam Vanek, she exclaims, "Oh, serendipity." Is this form of "justice," which comes via the manipulation of information, any different than Jasper's manipulation of the court system? Is one more "justified" than the other? Is justice served in the novel?

12. When faced with moral dilemmas, Klein's characters often make choices that risk *everything*—their jobs, their spouses, and their integrity. Why do they take such risks? Which characters truly learn from their mistakes?

13. Is *Clean Break* an appropriate title for the novel? Celeste seeks to make a break from Adam, but can the phrase be applied to other characters in the book? Is it ever possible to make a clean break from your past and start a new life?

14. Each of the main characters is dishonest in some way: to spouses, jobs, lovers, and children. What are the different degrees of deception and which ones feel more justified than others? How does the reader think these lies will affect the characters' long-term relationships with one another?

15. The novel ends on a positive note. Do Jake and Celeste deserve a hopeful future? Are they better off than they were at the beginning of the book?